GUIDE ON HOW TO FAIL AT ONLINE DATING

Published originally under the title of《网恋翻车指南》
Author © 酱子贝 (Jiang Zi Bei)
English publishing rights authorised by 北京晋江原创网络科技有限公司
(Beijing Jinjiang Original Network Technology Co., Ltd.)
English edition copyright © 2025 HT Books, LLC
Website: haitangbooks.org
Follow us on Twitter: @haitangbooks
All Rights Reserved.

No portion of this book may be reproduced or transmitted in any form or by any electronic or mechanical means without written permission from the publisher. This is a work of fiction. Names, characters, places, and incidents are the products of the author's imagination or are used fictitiously. Any resemblance to actual events, locales, or persons, living or dead, is entirely coincidental and not intended by the author.

——

Translation: Juurensha
Translation Editor: Divetus
Translation Checker: Shukun Xue
Rewriter: Nineteen
Proofreader: Nineteen, Alicia Zhou
In-House Editor: In

Art Director: Zhong Dian
Designer: Zhong Dian
Cover Art: Fueki
Interior Illustration: Jessie L.
Photographer: Zhao

——

ISBN: 978-1-966870-00-5
First Printing: Apr 2025
Printed and Bound in China

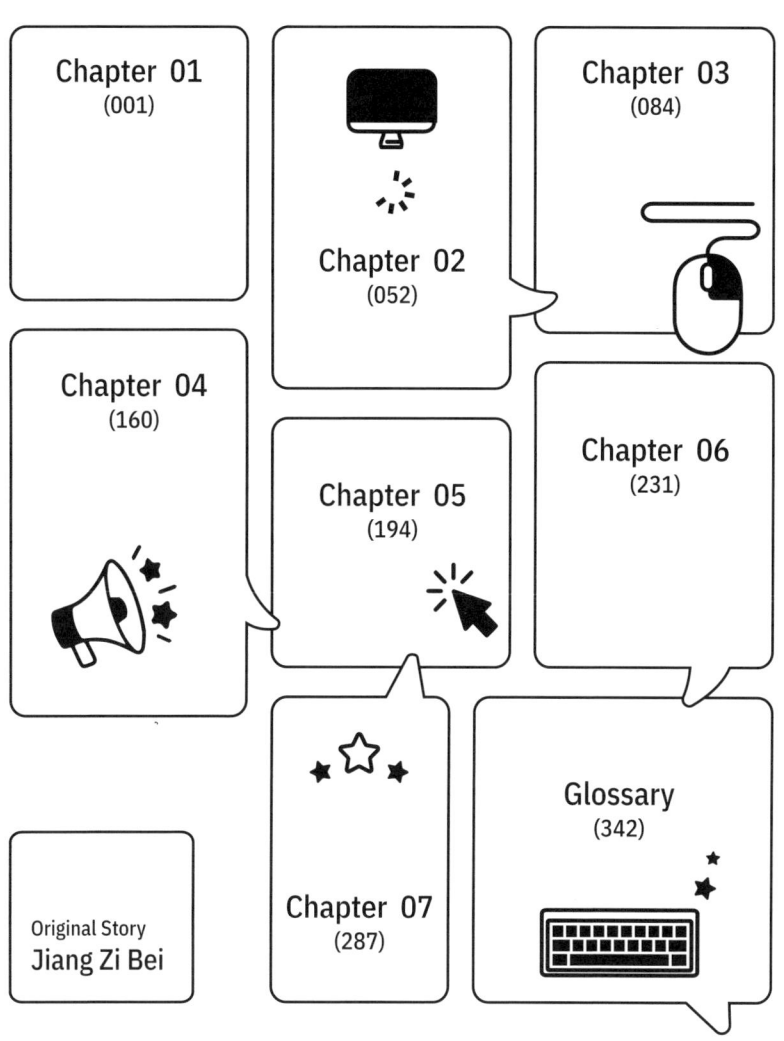

Guide on How to Fail at

ONLINE 1
DATING

Original Story
Jiang Zi Bei

Chapter 01 (001)
Chapter 02 (052)
Chapter 03 (084)
Chapter 04 (160)
Chapter 05 (194)
Chapter 06 (231)
Chapter 07 (287)
Glossary (342)

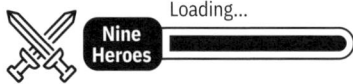

Guide on How to Fail at Online Dating

Chapter 01

Jing Huan came out of the airport just as a sudden gust of wind swept directly into his face.

He looked up at the overcast sky. The weather forecast released this morning stated that a typhoon would make landfall tonight, and the wind was already starting to pick up across Mancheng. Airplanes basically couldn't take off in this kind of weather.

However, his cousin insisted on booking a flight to the United States, saying that she couldn't stay here a minute longer. If flying today had been an option then she would've taken it, and if it wasn't, then she'd stay at a hotel arranged by the airport.

Jing Huan had just gotten into the car when his phone rang.

"Huanhuan, is your jie gone now?" It was his roommate, Gao Zixiang.

Everything sounded irritating to Jing Huan right now. "*Your* jie is gone."

"Don't be so sensitive, okay?" Gao Zixiang said. "All I'm asking is if your jie is really headed to the United States?"

It started to drizzle outside. Jing Huan watched the raindrops fall on the car window and let out a muffled "mm."

Gao Zixiang sighed and said, "Ah, your jie is truly pitiful, but in my opinion, it wasn't that serious. No one really gives a fig about who you are the moment you pull the plug with anything online. Is it even worth it going all the way abroad for anything so trivial?

The moment Jing Huan remembered why his cousin left, his belly filled with anger. "Do you seriously have to bring up those fucking idiots from the game right now?"

"No, no." Sis-cons could not be provoked. Knowing that he was in a bad mood, Gao Zixiang quickly changed the topic. "All right, hurry back to the dorm once you're done seeing her off. There's a heartbroken person today, and I can't handle him by myself."

Jing Huan frowned. "Who's heartbroken?"

"There are only three of us in the dorm, so who do you think it is?"

No sooner had Gao Zixiang finished speaking that Jing Huan heard a choking sob, reminiscent of a pig's squeal, coming from beside him. "Hey, Hao'er, don't cry. Wipe your tears first."

Upon hearing the voice of his other roommate Lu Wenhao, Jing Huan started the car. "What's up with Hao'er?"

"It's a long story, you should come back first," Gao Zixiang said.

Lu Wenhao sniffled. "Get a pack of beer before you come back, Jing Huan."

After parking his car, Jing Huan slipped into the nearby corner store. He knew how much the two of them could drink, so he only bought three bottles of beer and hid them underneath his clothes before returning to the dormitory.

He'd barely opened the dormitory door when he heard Lu Wenhao mournfully wailing from inside, *"Why did they have to do this to me?"*

"What did she do to you?" Jing Huan asked as he pushed the door and came inside.

Lu Wenhao sat in the center of the dormitory room with a tissue box propped on his thigh, actually crying.

Gao Zixiang was in a tough spot, so when he saw Jing Huan, it was like he'd just seen his savior. He quickly jumped up from his chair and exclaimed, "You're finally back."

Jing Huan closed the door and handed him the plastic bag. "What exactly is going on?"

Gao Zixiang looked at Lu Wenhao. "Are you going to say it, or should I say it?"

Lu Wenhao's somewhat chubby face was flushed from crying. "I won't say it! I won't!"

"Okay, okay, okay, I'll say it, I'll say it, don't cry anymore!" Gao Zixiang sighed. "Do you still remember Hao'er's online girlfriend?"

"They're in voice chat 24/7. I can hear them flirting in my dreams sometimes. You really think I've forgotten?" Jing Huan paused. "What, did they break up?"

Gao Zixiang nodded solemnly.

"And I thought this was going to be something big…" Jing Huan breathed out, relieved, and began to take off his coat. "Stop crying, Hao'er. So you got dumped; a man shouldn't shed tears so easily."

"That's not the main issue," Gao Zixiang continued awkwardly. "You're aware of how much money Hao'er spent on his online girlfriend in the game, right?"

Lu Wenhao played a game called *Nine Heroes*, a legendary game that had been popular for ten years and was famous for its cost in both

money and time. Having played the game a few years ago, Jing Huan knew that one outfit in that crappy game cost thousands of yuan.

That girl would call every day, asking Lu Wenhao for outfits. Lu Wenhao was generous, so his partner could get what she wanted almost every single time.

"It's just buying some outfits, how much could it cost?" In an effort to comfort his roommate, Jing Huan tried to downplay the situation.

Lu Wenhao let out a choked sob. "I've helped increase her cultivation points for the past six months."

"That's still okay," Jing Huan said after briefly hesitating. "It's only a few tens of thousands of yuan."

Lu Wenhao's crying intensified. "I bought six of her eight purple outfits. I even socketed a level fifteen gem in one of them."

Jing Huan was at a momentary loss for words. He patted his shoulder. "Hao'er, we need to act like men. We can't do something as petty as settling scores with an ex after breaking up."

Lu Wenhao had just calmed down, but at this mention, his anger surged again. "Of course I wouldn't! Why would I cry over that bit of money? No, I'm crying because I was deceived! I'm crying because I gave her six months' worth of genuine feelings and affection!"

Jing Huan asked, "How did she deceive you?"

Unable to bear it any longer, Gao Zixiang blurted out, "That person is a man."

"Hey, what's the big deal, isn't it just a man..." Jing Huan froze mid-consolement.

Lu Wenhao wailed, *"Waaaaaaah—"*

Jing Huan was stunned. "A man?!"

Guide on How to Fail at Online Dating

Gao Zixiang cautioned, "Don't say it again! Haven't you noticed that our dorm building is about to be flooded with his tears?"

"*No.*" Jing Huan was shocked. "How can that voice be a man's?!" He had heard Lu Wenhao's voice calls with his online girlfriend. The girl's voice was saccharine sweet, lilting higher at the end of every sentence as if it was dipped in sugar. Whenever she acted flirty, his entire body broke out in goosebumps.

"It was a voice changer," Gao Zixiang said. "This morning, his 'girlfriend' must have forgotten to turn that thing on and asked for a new outfit in a male voice. Hearing him act flirty nearly made me pass away on the spot…That voice was even rougher than Old Yan's; he sounded like he was over thirty."

Old Yan was their counselor.

Lu Wenhao bawled his eyes out.

Jing Huan didn't know what to say for a moment. "You guys never had a video call?"

"No, just some photos," Lu Wenhao said. "He admitted they were fake."

Jing Huan held his tongue.

Well, at this point, what do you think the scammer's going to do?! Deny it?

"You never even video called and yet you just gave so much money?"

"It's pretty typical." Gao Zixiang cracked open a beer and handed it to Lu Wenhao. "Isn't seeking online romance all about the setting up of expectations and fantasies before meeting in real life? Hao'er just had really terrible luck to run into such a ruthless one. I thought the most toxic ones would just send fake photos…"

Lu Wenhao sniffled and said, "It's not like I'm distressed over the money, I'm just feeling terrible and disgusted! I even deleted my character!"

Gao Zixiang was surprised when he heard this. "Deleted your character?! Have you lost your mind, Hao'er?!"

"It was just the character, I still have my equipment and pets." Lu Wenhao wiped away his tears. "I've never told you this but our characters had matching names, and we even bound them to be Eternal Lovers."

Gao Zixiang's jaw dropped.

Eternal Lovers was *Nine Heroes'* marriage system, where married couples could go to the matchmaker god, Yuelao, and apply for a marriage pact. Once the pact was signed, the marriage status between the two game characters was permanent unless they were put up for sale or a deletion request was made.

"Forget it, Hao'er. Consider this a lesson learned," said Gao Zixiang. "Don't jump into the same pit twice, and in the future, no online dating even if it kills you. That way, you definitely won't be deceived a second time!"

Lu Wenhao tearfully asked him, "What's the point of gaming if I can't do online dating?"

"Can't you game without online dating?" Gao Zixiang retorted. "I've been playing *Nine Heroes* for years and haven't gotten married once."

Lu Wenhao snapped back, "That's because your girlfriend is your childhood sweetheart!"

Gao Zixiang choked and turned his gaze to the person beside him. "Then what about Huanhuan? He also used to play *Nine Heroes* for several years, but he didn't do any online dating, did he?"

"If I were as hot as Jing Huan, and had girls lined up outside my door to date me, why would I bother with online dating? And, when he gamed in high school, he barely had enough time for his studies. Besides, what's wrong with online dating? Look at Jing Huan's cousin: she's beautiful, has so many good qualities, and yet she's also in an online relationship..." Lu Wenhao's chatter trailed off.

Gao Zixiang braced his throbbing head in his hand.

It's over, he stepped on a landmine.

Jing Huan listened silently without reacting or making a sound at all.

Lu Wenhao stammered, "Don't, Huanhuan. I was just rambling. I've had a terrible day, cut me some slack."

Jing Huan snapped back to reality and suddenly pulled up a chair beside Lu Wenhao. "Hao'er, are you feeling absolutely miserable right now?"

Lu Wenhao was taken aback. "Wh-what?"

After pondering briefly, Jing Huan asked, "If I gave you two choices, one to be catfished online by a man, and the other to have your account permanently banned due to a bug, which one would you choose?"

"The second one, of course!" Lu Wenhao's face was full of confusion. "Why are you asking this?"

Does being deceived in an online relationship really hurt that much? Could it be worse than having your account permanently banned?

Jing Huan hugged the backrest of the chair, lost in thought.

Gao Zixiang vaguely felt something was wrong. "Huanhuan, what are you planning?"

Chapter 01

The phone on the table suddenly rang. Lu Wenhao picked it up, and almost stopped breathing when he saw what was on the screen. He had to pinch himself. The other two quickly stepped forward to steady him with Jing Huan grabbing his phone to take a look.

Little Baby: Hubby, I've been thinking about it all afternoon, but I still feel very sad. I really do like you, but unfortunately, fate has decided our relationship must end here. [Bunny Weeping]

Little Baby: Let me send you a photo of the real me. I hope that you will remember that this silly boy will always be tenderly watching you from somewhere on this Earth.

Little Baby: [Image]

The middle-aged man in the photo appeared slightly overweight. A small patch of his hair had already gone white, and his eyes were filled with tears as he gazed affectionately at the camera.

Jing Huan stared, nonplussed.

Gao Zixiang exclaimed, "Fuck! This is fucking inhumane! Psychological torture! Hang in there, Hao'er, be strong!"

This photo attack scared Lu Wenhao half to death. He sat frozen in shock as if he was on his deathbed. "I'm going to delete him off my friend list! I'm going to abandon this QQ[1] account! This QQ account is tainted now!"

Jing Huan, mind abuzz with ideas, quickly intervened when he heard him. "Wait, Hao'er, I have something to say to him."

Lu Wenhao was touched. "What, Huanhuan? Are you going to help me flame him?"

---

1 QQ is an instant messaging platform created by Tencent, and often used by younger gamers in China, similar to WhatsApp or Discord, for group chats, casual voice and video chats.

"Why flame him? It's pointless to waste time on someone like this." Jing Huan took the phone and lowered his head, typing rapidly.

Gao Zixiang leaned in. "Then, what are you doing with Hao'er's phone?"

Little Baby: Haohao, darling, why aren't you replying to me...

LWH: Are you still there?

Little Baby: OvO Darling! I'm here!

LWH: Send me the link to the voice changer.

Gao Zixiang opened and closed his mouth, baffled.

Naturally, Jing Huan couldn't get the link to the voice changer. Instead, the other party threw out the sentence, "We were once in love, so how could you humiliate me like this?" and then blocked Lu Wenhao's QQ.

After learning what had happened, Lu Wenhao froze for a few seconds before breaking down. "What the hell? He blocked me? He still has the balls to block me first?! I'm going to doxx[2] him! I'm going to go all out against him!"

"Doxxing is illegal, don't go too far, Hao'er!" Gao Zixiang's head hurt. "Enough, everything is already deleted, so don't think about it anymore. What's life without some setbacks, right?"

Lu Wenhao spat out, "You call this a setback?"

"It's a heavenly tribulation. After getting through this, your life will be smooth." Jing Huan continued, "Hao'er, which server was your character on?"

---

2 The act of publicly revealing someone's private or personal information (such as their real name, address, phone number, or other identifiable data) online without their consent. Originates from the term, dropping documents.

"Match Made in Heaven," Lu Wenhao reported before picking up a tissue to blow his nose with. "What about it?"

Jing Huan shook his head and replied, "Nothing."

He opened his half-packed suitcase and stuffed all the miscellaneous items on the table into it.

Lu Wenhao moved his chair and sat next to him. "Huanhuan, are you moving out today? I'm in such a wretched state, why don't you stay a few more days to keep me company?"

The school had strict rules and treated their university students like high school students, having restricted entry and exit alongside nighttime power cuts. If it wasn't for the rule that freshmen weren't allowed to live off-campus, Jing Huan would've moved out long ago.

So, as soon as sophomore year arrived, he rented out a place in a small residential neighborhood near the school.

"I'm not staying. I'm afraid you'll be upset if you see any more men these days."

Just as Jing Huan finished packing his luggage, Gao Zixiang had also just finished eating his self-heating hot pot meal. He stood up and said, "Huanhuan, I'll help you move your things."

Jing Huan locked the suitcase. "No need, I've called for a small auto rickshaw. It's waiting downstairs."

Gao Zixiang insisted, "Then, I'll help carry your stuff downstairs."

School had just begun and Jing Huan was planning to replace things like bedding after he moved, so he didn't have much in the way of luggage. One person was more than enough to move everything.

In the stairwell, Gao Zixiang held Jing Huan's computer and tentatively asked, "Are you okay, Huanhuan?"

Jing Huan raised his eyebrows. "Why wouldn't I be?"

Gao Zixiang and Jing Huan's relationship was rock-solid. Having been classmates since junior high, Gao Zixiang was relatively familiar with Jing Huan's circumstances.

Jing Huan came from a well-off family, was handsome, and was easy to get along with—truly a favored son of heaven. The only weird thing about him was the sis-con aspect of his personality.

Jing Huan's jiejie was named Liang Ran. He got into fights for her in junior high, bought her milk tea and delivered meals to her in high school, and helped reserve library study spaces for her in university. If he had not been privy to the inside story, Gao Zixiang definitely would've had certain thoughts about this.

They said that when Jing Huan was a child, he was almost kidnapped. It was Liang Ran who desperately clung to him, choosing to dislocate her hand rather than let him go. She managed to drag him back, saving his life. Since then, Jing Huan had only one rule: you could mess with him, but do not mess with his jie.

So, when Gao Zixiang found out that Liang Ran had been romantically deceived by a scumbag in the game, and was being chased across the server by the scumbag's original partner, being cussed out as a mistress, he was constantly worried that Jing Huan would hire a hitman.

Unexpectedly, the person he was worried about didn't react at all and even peacefully sent Liang Ran off to the airport.

"Huanhuan, your jie's matters are all in-game. It's just a bunch of data, don't take it too seriously," said Gao Zixiang. "She'll surely come back after some time has passed."

Chapter 01

Jing Huan loaded his suitcase onto the auto rickshaw and turned around. "Let me ask you something."

"What?"

"How did you know that something had happened to my jie?"

Gao Zixiang paused, his expression shifty. "J-just from hearsay."

Jing Huan frowned. "The truth. Now."

Gao Zixiang sort of regretted following him down.

He first wanted to muddle through this subject, but seeing Jing Huan's serious expression, he didn't dare to bullshit and answered honestly, "That woman sent out many all-server megaphones, spamming about your jie for several days and I just…happened to see it."

Jing Huan took a deep breath. "All-server megaphones?"

Gao Zixiang hurriedly said, "Yes, but she hasn't sent any for the past two days, so I guess it calmed down."

Jing Huan stood there, and it was a while before he spoke. "I see. Go back up now. I'll invite you guys over for dinner after I finish tidying up my place."

Gao Zixiang nodded, but he still felt uneasy. He repeated his advice today to Lu Wenhao, "Um, so, Jing Huan, you know that doxxing is illegal, right?"

Jing Huan got into the vehicle. "I know, it's just all in-game matters. I won't make it a real life problem."

Gao Zixiang breathed a slight sigh of relief but still felt that something was off. Before he could ponder it further, the auto rickshaw had already set off and was heading out of the school gate.

The apartment Jing Huan rented was just over 100 square meters, new, and never lived in before. By the time he arrived, it had been cleaned.

He unpacked and put away everything from his suitcase, then turned on his computer and adeptly added *Nine Heroes* to the downloads list. It finished downloading just as he came out from his shower.

He looked at the *Nine Heroes* icon on the desktop and felt dazed for a moment.

Jing Huan wasn't a stranger to *Nine Heroes*; he had been one of its earliest beta testers. The game had been out for ten years with him playing for six of them.

If it hadn't been for his parents' warnings due to academic issues in his freshman year of high school, he wouldn't have quit the game.

It had been four years since his departure from *Nine Heroes* but Jing Huan's return this time was not for the sake of the game itself.

Liang Ran had recently met a man in *Nine Heroes*, and like other gamers, they had encountered each other, gotten to know one another, and then started an online relationship. Liang Ran deeply cherished her online boyfriend and even planned to meet him in person on on Valentine's Day.

Unbeknownst to her, the day before Valentine's Day, a woman claiming to be the guy's real girlfriend appeared, chased, and spammed Liang Ran on the World Channel for several days. She even posted the chat logs between Liang Ran and the scumbag on the forum, inciting countless *Nine Heroes* players to all flame Liang Ran together. The whole thing could almost be described as small-scale cyberbullying.

Not only was Liang Ran labeled as "the mistress," she was also thrust into the spotlight and vilified by thousands of people. That

Chapter 01

scumbag, however, never appeared even once and just allowed the situation to escalate.

Liang Ran, who grew up cradled in the palm of Jing Huan and their elders' hands, had never felt this wronged before. Within days of the incident, she had a breakdown, decisively deleting her game character, and going abroad for a break.

After learning about this, Jing Huan almost went to Shanghai to burn down the *Nine Heroes* headquarters.

The more Jing Huan thought about it, the angrier he got, especially since he had just found out that the other party had spammed the messages with all-server megaphones. These were different from server megaphones; everyone from any of the servers could see things sent by an all-server megaphone.

Liang Ran had never mentioned this to him, probably because she didn't want him to freak out.

Fuck! No wonder my jie deleted her account!

Jing Huan opened up *Nine Heroes* expressionlessly, entered his alt account credentials, and logged into a server called Mirage—his jie's former server. When Jing Huan found out what happened, he immediately decided game matters would be resolved in-game. He was going to kill that scumbag a thousand times over in the game until he apologized and left the server.

But things were not as simple as he thought.

The fundamental reason behind *Nine Heroes'* enduring popularity was because of their many gameplays options. You could become a Player Kill (PK) master, a dungeon expert, a skillful crafter, a guild leader, a famous underworld merchant, etc. Each gameplay style had its appeal, and players could choose as they wished.

And every player's dream was nothing more than to climb their server's power rankings.

The power rankings were divided into various categories: Mastery[3], Wealth, Popularity, Reputation, Guild leaders, etc.

On other servers, these rankings were almost always dominated by different players. After all, it wasn't easy to top the rankings, and even rarer for someone to keep up with two or more categories.

The Mirage server was the only exception.

Jing Huan had checked the official website earlier and found that, besides the Guild leader rankings, the top spot of each ranking list was occupied by the same player: someone named Yearning For.

As soon as Jing Huan logged in, he saw two players next to him chatting while they were AFK vending.

[Current] Maybe One Day: I've only been offline for just a few days, and the situation with Yearning For is already over?

[Current] Mistbb: Yeah, that mistress even deleted her character and quit the game. What did you expect?

[Current] Maybe One Day: Tsk, tsk, tsk, and I was hoping for a reversal.

[Current] Mistbb: How would a reversal happen?

[Current] Maybe One Day: Actually, that Yearning For is especially flirtatious and hits on everyone. His account is unmarried, so it's hard to say who the mistress really was.

[Current] Mistbb: ...How do you know that?

[Current] Maybe One Day: Because he hit on me once, duh.

---

3   The most prestigious, skill-based power ranking based on the number of Player vs. Player (specifically Player Killing) wins. The higher the wins, the higher the mastery ranking.

Unfortunately, I had a booster using my account at the time lolol. He also hit on my friend. She always has a couple title displayed, but Yearning For still dared to flirt with her, almost pissed her husband a heart attack...

[Current] Mistbb: So, that happened...Did her husband say anything?

[Current] Maybe One Day: Who'd dare to? After all, it's not like he can fight against him. Even if all the *Nine Heroes* players came together, I don't think they'd be able to touch even a strand of hair on his head.

Jing Huan pressed the skill hotkey, cast a spell for a few seconds, and teleported back to his sect.

Early last year, the official website had posted a screenshot of Yearning For's character attributes, along with several videos of him PKing in the arena. Those two players were right; looking at all the *Nine Heroes* players, he feared that there wasn't a single one who could beat him.

Jing Huan wasn't actually concerned about skill proficiency; he had topped the Mastery ranking list on another server four years ago and was very confident in his skills.

But...to develop a character that could surpass Yearning For's would take at least three years, not to mention the other party's strength would also be continuously growing during that time.

Therefore, Jing Huan's original revenge plan had to be temporarily shelved.

But that was fine.

He suddenly thought of a plan that was even more toxic than just killing the other party and forcing them to rage quit the game.

Jing Huan opened *Nine Heroes'* official marketplace, clicked on the character filter, and started selecting the keywords for the game character he wanted to buy.

Server: Mirage.

Required level: 150, the max level.

Maxed-out cultivation and support skills.

Gender of the character: Female.

Looking at the filtered female characters on the screen, the corner of Jing Huan's mouth drew up, and he let out a cold laugh.

Yearning For, your daddy is coming.

To avoid disrupting the market, *Nine Heroes* did not allow character server transfers. A character was bound to the server they were created in. Once a server's population became too large, the game moderators would close character creation for that server. This rule was an anomaly among similar games, but miraculously, *Nine Heroes* didn't have a single dead server among its major servers even after ten years of operation.

Apart from this, there were not too many restrictions; you could change your sect, appearance, or even redo your character's facial features.

As long as you had the money.

Since there was a lot of flexibility in the game, Jing Huan focused more on the character's cultivation points and core skills as these weren't just expensive in terms of money, but also time.

Jing Huan didn't have trouble choosing. After ten minutes of comparing characters, he selected one. It cost 35,000 yuan, wasn't linked to a phone number, and had no equipment or pets.

Chapter 01

This suited his preferences; he enjoyed the feeling of gradually getting stronger one step at a time.

While it took him a quick thirty seconds to pay, the system, on the other hand, needed time to transfer the character information with an average thirty-minute wait time before he could log into the character. As he waited, Jing Huan opened the StarfieldTV live stream site and saw that the only streamer he followed was live. He found him on his friend list and sent a message.

Happy Every Day: Xiao Yan, are you free?

yanxyan: What's up?

After graduating from high school, Jing Huan would play *PlayerUnknown's Battlegrounds (PUBG)* with Gao Zixiang and the others when he had nothing else to do. He occasionally watched live streams, and his most-watched streamer was yanxyan, to whom he generously threw many stream gifts.

Money had brought the two together as friends.

yanxyan: Wanna play? I have three people here; we can form a squad.

Happy Every Day: Nah. I want to buy a voice changer, but the ones on Taobao have poor reviews. Do you have any recommendations?

yanxyan: Voice changer? What kind do you want?

Happy Every Day: The kind that will make me sound like a loli, so flirty that people will run miles away when I speak.

yanxyan: ...

yanxyan: ...That might be a bit difficult. You might also need a sound card. I have a few friends, I'll ask around for you.

Happy Every Day: Okay, I'll wait to hear from you. Thanks.

yanxyan: No problem.

Not too long after, the other party sent over a store link. Jing Huan clicked on it and, without even bothering to read the product description, promptly bought the most expensive model.

The store's customer service, having seen it all, listened to his request, remotely controlled his computer without any questions, and quickly adjusted his sound card settings.

Jing Huan connected his thousand-yuan microphone and tried it out. Satisfied, he gave it a five-star rating.

Now, only the final step remained—the face.

Nine Heroes, like other online games, had a face customization system. Although Jing Huan hadn't seen what his newly acquired character looked like, a new character required a fresh start, and naturally, everything had to be changed for an enjoyable gameplay experience.

He opened the search bar, entered "*Nine Heroes* face customization settings," selected the store with the highest rating, and immediately contacted their customer service.

Happy Every Day: Are you there?

Customer Service Escort: I'm here dear~ [Blows a kiss], Customer Service Escort at your service.

Happy Every Day: Well, your display name isn't very civilized.

Customer Service Escort: ...You're overthinking it~ How may I assist you?

Happy Every Day: Customize a character's face for me.

Customer Service Escort: Okay, dear, any specific requirements or references?

Jing Huan didn't have any specific requirements. He thought for a moment and started typing.

Happy Every Day: I want a face that would make a man want to marry me at first sight.

Customer Service Escort: ...

If I had that ability, would I still be running this damn Taobao store?

Customer Service Escort: Dear, can you be more specific?

Happy Every Day: All right. I want it to be cute and lively, yet sexy and charming. Not too young nor too old. Maybe add a dash of dreamy mystery. The rest is up to you.

The customer service representative on the other end of the line drew in a deep breath and turned around to vigorously pummel the stress-relief toy next to the mouse a few times.

Customer Service Escort: I'm sorry, dear, but I'm afraid we can't complete your request. But it's okay! There are many other talented sellers on Taobao, so we suggest you check this store instead.

The customer service representative quickly sent over the link to a rival store.

Four customer service representatives later, Jing Huan finally found a store willing to take his order.

Jing Huan spent 999 yuan on the face and contentedly opened the game.

Once he entered the character selection screen, he scrutinized the character's facial features.

He had to admit, the character was really pretty. You could tell the original owner had some aesthetic sense, and even the character name was very lyrical—Don't Frown.

Jing Huan looked away and entered the game.

The slender and beautiful character appeared on the Riverside of Bianliang.

Guide on How to Fail at Online Dating

The Riverside of Bianliang was a low-level wilderness map. Hardly anyone touched the monsters here, so the place was abound with small beasts. Jing Huan took only a few steps before triggering a battle.

The character he bought belonged to the Putuo Mountain sect and was a Celestial race healer. Because the female Celestial characters were pretty and the sect only had a singular skill set that wasn't too hard to use, many female players naturally preferred the Putuo Mountain sect.

However, the Putuo Mountain sect was slow at monster farming, and there was very little skill-based play during PK, so Jing Huan didn't like it.

He softly clicked his tongue, cast a skill to kill two monsters, and prepared to use another to teleport back to his sect.

【Regardless of Lovesickness has initiated a forced PK against you.】

A talisman paper fell from the sky; that was a human sect skill, Sealing Talisman.

Jing Huan was startled, but his hands reacted very quickly and he managed to avoid the talisman paper. But as soon as he shifted positions, out of nowhere, he found himself surrounded by a large net. Jing Huan couldn't dodge in time and was thoroughly ensnared.

Several people appeared in front of him. Judging by their luminous weapons, they had some decent equipment. Two of the crowd-control members were still charging up their sealing skills.

[Current] Don't Frown: ?

[Current] Regardless of Lovesickness: Bitch, did you come back to die again?

Since the other party immediately hurled insults as soon as they

Chapter 01

met, Jing Huan quickly realized that they must carry an old grudge against the previous owner of his character.

[Current] Don't Frown: This character has changed owners.

[Current] Regardless of Lovesickness: Here we go again. Do you think we're idiots? Always falling for your lies?

[Current] Don't Frown: ...

If it weren't for this character having a special purpose and needing to maintain a certain image, he would've cussed them out already.

[Current] Don't Frown: I just bought it for 35k over half an hour ago. I even have the receipt.

[Current] Regardless of Lovesickness: When have you not had a receipt? I'm telling you, as long as I, Lovesickness, am in this server, don't even think about ever leaving the safe zone!

Jing Huan was about to say something more, but the other person had already lashed out with their whip.

He was facing off against five people, and because the character he bought was empty-handed, he was in no way shape or form capable of taking a few hits.

Fuck.

Jing Huan sat up straight and expertly used the common actions that was in every character's arsenal—rolling, jumping, and levitating to dodge their skills one by one.

[Current] Don't Frown: You fu...

[Current] Don't Frown: Be reasonable~!!

[Current] Regardless of Lovesickness: There's no being reasonable with a female scammer like you.

[Current] Don't Frown: No, really, this character has changed hands...What can I say to make you believe it?!

Guide on How to Fail at Online Dating

No sooner had he finished typing this, Jing Huan accidentally pressed the wrong key.

I'm finished.

On the game interface, he watched his weak body take a harsh axe blow, leaving only a sliver of health.

[Current] Regardless of Lovesickness: Either repay the money or die and lose levels, your choice.

The other party immediately went to finish him off. Jing Huan didn't struggle anymore and was quickly killed, returning to the respawn point.

He hadn't yet recovered from this inexplicable death when a large server megaphone popped up in the lower left corner.

【[Megaphone] Regardless of Lovesickness: Idle Pavilion will be hunting Don't Frown for 24 hours. As usual, if you choose to be in a party with her to clear dungeons, we won't be held responsible for collateral damage.】

What's with this situation?!

Jing Huan stood at the respawn point, pondering for a moment, then got on his mount and rushed toward the forum NPC.

Where there were people, there were communities, and the game world of *Nine Heroes* counted as a small community. Similarly, where there was community, there was conflict, and the forums were the best place to learn about fights and gossip.

Jing Huan scrolled down a page and found a post about himself—no, wait, about this character.

【Idle Pavilion's server-wide hunt for the female scammer Don't Frown.】

After a quick skim, Jing Huan finally understood why this

Chapter 01

character had so many enemies coming for it as soon as it logged in.

The previous owner was a scammer. She first deceived the leader of a small guild two years ago, cleaning out the account and transferring all the guild's money. After the scam was exposed, she listed the character on the marketplace and left without a trace.

Who would've imagined that wasn't the end of it? In less than half a month, the character was bought. The buyer claimed to be a "Ms. Perfect"—a beautiful rich girl who returned from abroad and was looking to join a powerful guild to team up for dungeons and PK. It didn't take long for her to infiltrate the server's top guild, Idle Pavilion, and successfully hook up with one of the guild officers. The two got married and were lovey-dovey for more than half a year. However, when that guild officer returned from a business trip, he found that his account had been cleaned out and that his little wife had also used his name to borrow a significant amount of money and equipment from the guild's brothers and sisters before vanishing once again.

It wasn't until someone noticed that the card number she used to borrow money was identical to the original owner's card number that everyone realized—the character had never changed hands!

Seeing this, even Jing Huan couldn't help but admire her. *With these abilities, why not use them for good?*

Having scammed both money and affection, this matter enraged the high-ranking members of Idle Pavilion. The entire guild of 200 members began a 24-hour watch on Don't Frown's account. After being killed twice, Don't Frown once again put her account back on the marketplace.

Idle Pavilion couldn't swallow this insult and sent out countless server-wide megaphones and official website forum posts, declaring that anyone who dared to buy this character would be slaughtered, regardless of whether there was a different owner behind it. This incident caused the character to remain on the market for a while, with the price dropping repeatedly until it was finally purchased by a clueless and unlucky person—unfortunately, none other than himself.

So that was why the character's price was so low.

Jing Huan expressionlessly scrolled to the bottom of the post, only to see the latest reply, which read:

1932L: The two biggest female scumbags of this server are Don't Frown and Ranxin. These two could team up to debut as a bitch duo.

Jing Huan memorized the original poster's ID.

The person, who didn't even frown while getting killed, now wished they could go through the screen and beat up that person.

Regardless of Lovesickness's megaphone was spammed a whole thirty times, making the World Channel very lively.

[World] Blinded by Beauty: What's going on? Don't Frown has risen from the grave? Have you already spent all the money you scammed before?

[World] Peach Cheese Stan: Let me see which guild will suffer this time!

[World] Youth Chasing the Wind: Lovesickness is powerful!

[World] The Wind is Freer Than Me: No, Frown-dajie, why go through all this trouble? Can't you just start over with a new character? Why do you insist on sticking to this one?

Chapter 01

[World] Peach Cheese Stan: Dammit! Shut up, the person above! Don't make suggestions! What if she actually listens?

The World Channel went wild, the chat moving so fast that people couldn't read the sentences properly, so much so that it took players a long time to react to the yellow system announcement that appeared in the chat.

【System Announcement: The player Don't Frown has used a renaming stone and changed their name to Sweet Little Jing. From now on, the player Don't Frown will officially be known as Sweet Little Jing.】

[World] Peach Cheese Stan: ???

[World] Blinded by Beauty: ???

[World] The Wind is Freer Than Me: ???

【[Megaphone] Sweet Little Jing: I'll say this one last time: this character has changed hands. Feel free to hunt me down if you want. I'm willing to play along.】

As soon as this megaphone went out, Jing Huan regretted it.

Did that sound too much like a catfisher?

So, while everyone was still in shock, he quickly sent out another megaphone.

【[Megaphone] Sweet Little Jing: QAQ, of course, it'd be best if I didn't have to fight~ May harmony prevail!】

With these two megaphones, the World Channel grew even livelier, with some watching the show while munching on popcorn as others cursed Don't Frown for being so shameless.

【[Megaphone] Regardless of Lovesickness: Starting today, there will be a server-wide bounty for Don't Frown. Kill her once for 100 gold, ten times for 1,200 gold. Bring screenshots to me to claim your gold.】

Guide on How to Fail at Online Dating

Wow.

Jing Huan marveled at this while doing his dailies in the safe zone, thinking, *Such a big spender.*

Nine Heroes divided its maps into three types of areas: the arena, battlegrounds, and safe zones.

In the arena, you could initiate PK against any individual or party without any loss upon death; it was a space to spar.

The battlegrounds consisted of all wilderness maps and some small cities where you could initiate a forced PK against any person or party. Dying would result in a loss of money and experience points.

The safe zones, as the name suggested, ensured that you couldn't be attacked as long as you stayed within its designated maps.

Nine Heroes had a total of nine major cities, among which only three were safe zones. Dungeons, high-experience quests, and event NPCs were almost all found in the wilderness maps.

If he wanted to avoid fighting, he wouldn't be able to even grind for experience points.

Killing him once would net someone 100 gold, which was equivalent to 100 yuan. For many players, this was like money raining from the sky. Jing Huan didn't even have to check the World Channel to guess how lively it must be right now.

If it were anyone else, they might have chosen to put this character back on the marketplace and bought another one. After all, the entire server was hunting down this character and, probably for at least the next week, no peaceful existence could be had.

But Jing Huan refused to do that.

He bought this account with real money and hadn't done any-

thing wrong. Why should he be bothered to go through the process of acquiring another character just because of these stupid grudges?

Besides, he had been killed and sent back to the respawn point as soon as he logged in. He hadn't forgotten this score and would make that group of people pay.

Jing Huan casually AFKed at the entrance of a general store and set up a stall to clear up some of the cheap junk items the account already had. Then, he minimized the game interface and opened up the marketplace again.

He initially hadn't been in a huge hurry to buy equipment, but given the current situation, improving his attributes was necessary.

Jing Huan came from a well-off family and was given a total monthly allowance of over 30,000 yuan. In addition, Liang Ran bought almost all his clothes and shoes, so he usually didn't spend much. After two to three years of saving money, he had accumulated quite a considerable amount.

So, when it came to buying equipment, he was quite confident.

After browsing the marketplace, he re-opened the game interface and was startled by the scene within.

His stall was crowded with players. There were so many people that his game interface was lagging.

[Current] Youth Chasing the Wind: What do you think she's doing now?

[Current] Peach Cheese Stan: Probably checking out the guild info to pick out her next target. I suggest that everyone keep an eye on their guild leaders for the near future, to avoid them being scammed to their underwear by her.

[Current] Is Gege Big: I'm in line, holding a number to kill Don't Frown.

[Current] The Wind is Freer Than Me: I've been short on cash to roll gems lately. Can you guys not compete with me?

The players were chatting energetically on the Current Channel and the chat bubbles covered the game interface. Jing Huan leisurely watched for a while.

[Current] Peach Cheese Stan: Speaking of which, I really want to hear Don't Frown's voice. I heard that it was particularly flirty, like a loli's voice.

[Current] Youth Chasing the Wind: Is that true? But that makes sense; if she didn't sound good, she wouldn't be able to trick men.

[Current] BrbOrNot: Come, come, I'll start a pot and we'll bet on whether Don't Frown will sell her character within a week. The payouts are yes: 0.3, no: 3.6.

[Current] Is Gege Big: What the hell is a 0.3 payout? Isn't that too small?! I'll bet she will, 500 gold.

[Current] Sweet Little Jing: I bet I won't, 1,000 gold.

Suddenly, all the chat bubbles disappeared. A few seconds later:

[Current] Youth Chasing the Wind: ?

[Current] BrbOrNot: ???

[Current] Peach Cheese Stan: Oh my god, you really don't buckle under pressure. One look and I can tell that she's a capable person who can do great things. I suggest you join a professional League of Legends team as a top laner.

[Current] Sweet Little Jing: Flattering, but no thanks. I'm not leaving the safe zone for now, so stop crowding around me. You're disturbing my business.

Chapter 01

[Current] Won't Abandon: ...What business?

[Current] Sweet Little Jing: Click open my stall and see for yourself. I have enhancement stones, morphing cards, dispel charms, etc. I have it all.

[Current] BrbOrNot: Wait, aren't these things too overpriced? Compared to the NPC merchants, you're totally ripping us off!

[Current] Sweet Little Jing: Buy it if you want, otherwise, scram.

[Current] BrbOrNot: ...

Jing Huan sneered and was about to type more when a sentence popped out of the crowd.

[Current] Peach Cheese Stan: Brothers and sisters, quickly make your way to another battlefield! Fae Bae has made a call-out post on the forum about Yearning For!!

One stone stirred up a thousand ripples.

Jing Huan barely had time to react when the people around him began disappearing one by one at lightning speed, leaving him alone at the general store entrance.

His line of sight shifted and lingered on the name Fae Bae, his gaze icy cold.

Just a while ago, this Fae Bae had incessantly spammed megaphones, flooding the World Channel, and forcing Liang Ran to quit the game and go abroad.

He closed his stall and flew to the NPC forum.

Jing Huan actually wasn't someone who loved gossip. A few years ago, he couldn't have imagined himself visiting the holy land of call-out posts twice in one day.

The title of Fae Bae's post was "Yearning For, I misjudged you."

Upon clicking on it, the dense and sentimental text took up the

entire screen. It was at least 3,000 words, but the actual content was quite scanty.

In her Yearning For relationship discourse, she claimed that Yearning For's real age didn't match his stated in-game age, that she had paid for the plane tickets and hotel expenses, and even when they were together, Yearning For used the excuse of credit card limits to make her cover their food and entertainment expenses.

The most crucial point was that right after their offline meeting, Yearning For ignored her in-game and even blocked her WeChat and phone number.

A typical case of being abandoned after putting out!

There were varying opinions below the post.

1L: Why do I feel like this isn't completely credible? Yearning For wouldn't be so stingy to not even pay for the hotel and airfare, right?

3L: I also feel that it's quite fake...

5L: Previous posters, if you don't know the situation, don't talk nonsense, okay? Patting Faefae.

6L: Are Faefae supporters mentally ill? If she doesn't want people to talk about it, why did she post it on the forums?

32L: I actually think what the original poster said is true. Yearning For is indeed really scummy; he's flirted with all of my female friends, even those who were married in-game.

39L: Didn't Yearning For recently have an affair? His mistress was that Ranxin.

76L: Must be great to be rich. I also want to be a scumbag.

88L: Isn't this just the typical fuckboi?!

Of course, Yearning For was a scumbag, otherwise, he wouldn't have doggedly pursued Liang Ran even though he had a girlfriend.

Halfway through scrolling the post, Jing Huan grew bored and closed the forum. He decided to take advantage of everyone's busy gossiping to visit the wilderness map NPC and pick up a quest.

Increasing character attributes required not only money but also a lot of experience points to increase equipment attribute limits. Relying solely on the few daily quests done in the safe zone was simply not enough.

As soon as he walked up to the quest giver, he noticed something shiny in the top right corner of the game interface.

This was the grandiose special effect of a divine artifact. After seeing it clearly, Jing Huan couldn't help but feel shocked—after all, a few years ago in his server, divine artifacts were only something you could see on the official website. Despite *Nine Heroes* being operational for over five years, not a single player managed to craft one because to be able to do so, you have to be able to defeat the God of War, afford the crafting materials, and have that one-shot luck.

Many people couldn't get past the first hurdle. Jing Huan had killed the God of War before, but only once; he spent eight hours in front of the computer without eating or drinking, and only defeated him after nearly exhausting all his potions. Ultimately, he only managed to craft complete and utter trash, which made him so angry that he couldn't eat for a whole week.

He immediately closed the NPC's chat interface and headed straight for the gleaming black light. Since the other party was also doing the wilderness map quests and currently helping the NPC weed their garden, Jing Huan only needed to take two steps to see their game character from behind.

The male character was dressed in the latest black ancient-style

robes, with red hair that signified him as part of the Demon race. In his hand, he held a pitch-black and murky long sword. In any given situation, he would be the most eye-catching person there.

Below his character was a title that consisted of only three words: God of War. And below that was his character's name.

Yearning For.

Yearning For?!

Jing Huan immediately sat up straight. He saw Yearning For standing in place for a while, then suddenly crouch down and start weeding.

Jing Huan exclaimed in his head, *No way, the forum has already hung you out to dry, but you're still in the mood to help people weed gardens?*

Yup. This is scumbag demeanor, ironclad composure. You have to give it to him.

However, this was exactly the opportunity that Jing Huan had been waiting for. In fact, the first step in his plan after buying a character was to add Yearning For as a friend.

It wasn't too late to do that now. He clicked on Yearning For's character to open the options menu and pressed the "Add Friend" option.

【The other party has temporarily disabled the "Add Friend" feature. Request rejected.】

Jing Huan laughed. He had played *Nine Heroes* for more than six years, and this was the first time he found out there was such a dumb setting in the game.

He opened the Current Channel and was about to talk when a line of yellow text suddenly popped up on the interface.

【OFF! has initiated a forced PK against you.】

Jing Huan reacted extremely fast, immediately jumping up and dodging the attack skill flying in from behind. With a slip of his hand, the words he hadn't finished typing were also sent out.

[Current] Sweet Little Jing: Gege, let's?

The man who had attacked him paused and stopped moving.

[Current] OFF!: Gege is here. Meimei, quickly accept your death!

Where did this idiot come from?

Jing Huan frowned, preparing to counterattack with his charged skill, but suddenly, he remembered something. His mouse followed his thoughts and slid to the right, canceling the skill cast.

[Current] Sweet Little Jing: Are you also here to kill me TVT?

[Current] OFF!: Isn't it obvious, who doesn't want to kill you right now?

After saying that, OFF! threw another skill at him, and Jing Huan dodged again.

[Current] Sweet Little Jing: *WAAAAH*, I just bought a character and didn't do anything wrong. Why do you have to kill me?

OFF! watched as she dodged all his skills while simultaneously *waaaahing*, and was speechless.

[Current] OFF!: Meimei, don't run anymore. If not me, the others are gonna kill you. We can't let them reap our rewards.

[Current] Sweet Little Jing: I just topped up 200 gold coins, it's my weekly pocket money. If I die, then it's all gone QAQ. Can't you just spare me just this once?

[Current] OFF!: No way.

Jing Huan was dodging and searching the area for someone all at the same time. In the time spent entangling with this idiot, Yearning

For had disappeared into some unknown corner, probably continuing to weed somewhere else.

He remembered that this quest would only be completed after weeding three times. Could the one he just saw have been the third time?

After using twelve jumps, he finally found the man holding the divine artifact in the corner. Yearning For was no longer weeding, but doing another quest and clearing out monsters.

Feeling like he had acted pitifully enough about now, Jing Huan started typing.

[Current] Sweet Little Jing: God of War-gege, save me TVT!

Yearning For continued casting spells to kill monsters, not even turning his head.

[Current] Sweet Little Jing: God of War-gege, are you there?

OFF! rushed to the scene in a flurry, feeling a bit anxious at the sight—Yearning For wouldn't want to compete with him over 100 gold, right?

Although 100 gold was just a drop in the bucket for Yearning For, if he wanted to kill Sweet Little Jing, it would be as easy as lifting his finger. It was basically free money!

Thinking of this, OFF! accelerated the pace of his casting skills. Jing Huan jumped around Yearning For, completely unharmed, even managing to type in the meantime.

[Current] Sweet Little Jing: God of War-gege, please help me. I'll give you all the gold I have on me, all 200! [Cry][Cry]

[Current] OFF!: Damn, even if I kill you, you'll only lose half of your gold! Aren't you running at a bit of a loss there?!

[Current] Sweet Little Jing: But I would also lose experience.

 Chapter 01

Experience is more valuable than money. [Tapping fingers together]

[Current] OFF!: Then, just give me 200 gold, and I won't kill you, okay?

[Current] Sweet Little Jing: I don't want that, you big villain!

[Current] OFF!: ...

Jing Huan was getting tired of dodging, but Yearning For hadn't moved at all.

Did he not see him? That couldn't be right; logically speaking, he chose the perfect position, and Yearning For should be able to see their conversation.

He hesitated for a moment and turned his gaze to the group of wild monsters.

OFF!'s skill cooldown had just ended. Just as he was about to type out some insults, he caught sight of the delicate and slender female character rolling on the ground and finally unleashing her first attack skill in the past few minutes.

But the skill's target wasn't him.

To his surprise, he saw a fine net flying straight to the right, beautifully hitting the wild monster that Yearning For had been battling for two minutes, causing seventy-nine damage. The wild monster fell over.

【[Nameless City] Player Sweet Little Jing has successfully killed the Roadblock Bandit and found the rare loot treasure map on him!】

Jing Huan pressed his lips together.

This wild monster had a special restriction; no matter how high a player's attack attributes were, they could only inflict minimal damage on it. This was also why Yearning For had spent two whole minutes here.

 Chapter 01

Yet, Jing Huan's Sky Snare had killed it with only seventy-nine damage. It even dropped the extremely rare treasure map; most of the players who came to do this quest were all farming for this loot. Moreover, this item was bound and untradeable, and could only be obtained from looting.

Yearning For finally reacted, taking a step forward and then stopping.

[Current] OFF!: ...

[Current] OFF!: To be honest, I think you're more over-the-top than I am.

Jing Huan regretted not sending this chatterbox back to the respawn point.

[Current] Sweet Little Jing: Aaaaah...

[Current] Sweet Little Jing: Oh my god TVT!

[Current] Sweet Little Jing: Gege, I didn't mean to do that. I didn't aim my skill right. TVT

No response.

Jing Huan clicked his tongue. *What's with this guy, I've TVTed so much, but he still hasn't said a word?*

Seeing OFF! cast another skill at him, Jing Huan was about to dodge when a line of text popped up in the interface.

【Player Yearning For has used the Celestial Binding Rope on you.】

Utterly baffled, Jing Huan watched helplessly as he was immobilized by the Celestial Binding Rope and took OFF!'s powerful skill head-on, losing twenty percent of his health.

[Current] Sweet Little Jing: ?

[Current] Sweet Little Jing: Ge?

Yearning For turned his head, his long sword swaying lightly in his hand, looking extremely indifferent.

[Current] Yearning For: Don't be a scammer in your next life.

After saying that, the man cast a spell in place for three seconds and left the wilderness map.

Jing Huan froze for a few seconds, his confusion steadily growing before his delayed anger creeped in—*Shit?!*

How did a scumbag like you have the nerve to say that to me?!

Neither of them had expected Yearning For to make a move, so they were momentarily stunned.

Jing Huan thoroughly cursed Yearning For's entire family in his head, then silently recited fuck in eight different languages through gritted teeth.

The Celestial Binding Rope was a high-level wilderness map item drop that could immobilize a target for six seconds which was enough time for him to eat a full set of OFF!'s skills. Who would've thought that even after OFF! threw out his ultimate skill, he continued to stay frozen.

[Current] OFF!: ...Why are you a Spirit Fox Den? Did you switch sects?

The Sky Snare that Jing Huan used was a skill exclusive to Spirit Fox Dens. OFF! clicked open the character's profile and glanced at it. Sure enough, the three words "Spirit Fox Den" were brightly listed as the sect.

Spirit Fox Dens were different from Putuo Mountains. Although they were both healers, Spirit Fox Dens placed more emphasis on crowd control and support, with very little healing. The sect's skills were complex, with small casting ranges, to the point that the players

 Chapter 01

of this sect were split into two extremes—either very skilled and capable of fighting in all-server PKs, or so noob that they couldn't even seal a quest monster and were completely useless.

OFF! hesitated for a moment and was about to continue typing when all of a sudden, the yellow rope on Sweet Little Jing disappeared, and the female character jumped up from the ground, shooting a pink fireball skill straight at him!

OFF! was startled and immediately jumped to dodge it. It wasn't until he landed that he realized—he had actually jumped in the direction of the fireball's path.

No, to be more precise, Sweet Little Jing had anticipated his movements in advance.

[Current] OFF!: ???

[Current] OFF!: Wait...

Sweet Little Jing didn't pay any attention to him and summoned a beast. Spirit Fox Den's attack skills were only good for clearing monsters, and they relied on beast summons in actual PK.

She summoned a small white fox with a plum blossom mark on its brow and nine tails unfurling behind it: the Nine-tailed Spirit Fox, a ninth-rank divine beast. The cheapest on the marketplace was for tens of thousands of yuan.

The Nine-tailed Spirit Fox shook its tails and hurled a few fireballs at OFF!, immediately cutting his health bar in half..

[Current] OFF!: Wait!!

[Current] OFF!: Wait...Jie! I was wrong, jie!

Without a word, Sweet Little Jing cast another sealing spell at him, leaving him completely immobilized and forced to stand there dumbly and take damage from the Nine-tailed Spirit Fox.

In front of the computer, Jing Huan was carefully studying the skills of Spirit Fox Den.

The Spirit Fox Den sect was niche, and he had never played it before. There were about twenty skills in total, and just the skill descriptions were complicated enough.

[Current] OFF!: Jie!! I just sold a beast summon and have over 2,000 gold on me…Begging you to let me go!!

[Current] Sweet Little Jing: Who the fuck is your jie?

[Current] OFF!: …

Was this the same person who had just been so coquettishly begging for mercy?

[Current] OFF!: Then, meimei. Meimei, don't kill me, I'll give you 500 gold, okay?

[Current] Sweet Little Jing: Who needs your 500 gold?

[Current] OFF!: Yes, yes, yes, I could tell at a glance that you're not short of money.

[Current] Sweet Little Jing: I want 1,500.

[Current] OFF!: …

[Current] OFF!: You're going too far, meimei!

[Current] Sweet Little Jing: Didn't you want my 200 gold before? [Cute]

[Current] OFF!: Of course I was joking, how could I really want your money? [Kneeling for mercy]

[Current] Sweet Little Jing: Cut the crap, just tell me whether you'll give it or not.

OFF! gritted his teeth.

This game had a shitty setting, which was that if you initiated a forced PK but got killed instead, not only would you lose more

money and experience, but there was also a small chance of dropping your equipped gear.

He opened his inventory and looked at the glowing equipment. He felt a piercing pang—who would dare gamble on this gear?!

【OFF! gave you 1,500 gold.】

The money was transferred and Jing Huan moved his fingers to recall the fox back to him.

These people were ready to kill others at the drop of a hat; they needed a taste of their own medicine.

After taking the money, he didn't waste any time talking and flew back to the main city, leaving OFF! alone there.

Who would have thought that not long after, the friend icon at the bottom right of his screen would suddenly flash?

[Friend] OFF!: [Wronged] Guess this account really did change owners.

Taken aback, it was only then that Jing Huan remembered to click open his friend list. Since logging in, he was so preoccupied with other things that he had no time to check it.

And there OFF! was on his friend list.

[Friend] Sweet Little Jing: ...Why did you have this person as a friend?

[Friend] OFF!: I've completed quests with the original owner before.

[Friend] OFF!: Based on your gameplay just now, she definitely couldn't play like that.

[Friend] Sweet Little Jing: ...

Despite being friends with the original owner of this character, he still launched a forced PK against it and even asked him for money?!

He should've just taken away all 2,000 gold earlier.

[Friend] OFF!: Are you a guy?

Jing Huan's fury instantly dissipated.

[Friend] Sweet Little Jing: Ah 0.0! How could I seem like a guy? [Beating your chest]

[Friend] OFF!: Hmm. Because it's rare to see a girl play this well.

[Friend] Sweet Little Jing: You're mistaken~ Your gameplay isn't that great, and many girls can beat you up like you're their little brother. [Cute]

[Friend] OFF!: ...

[Friend] OFF!: Sigh, actually I didn't want to kill you at first, but I saw an elite party from Idle Pavilion was nearby doing a quest. You would've been discovered sooner or later, so why shouldn't I be the one to get the money? Plus, think about it: Idle Pavilion has a party of five. Doesn't matter how good you are, you can't kill them all. So, if you think about it, I saved you!

[Friend] Sweet Little Jing: All right, since this misunderstanding has been cleared up, let's peacefully delete each other from our friend list. Thankful for the time we spent together, but this is the end, I guess.

[Friend] OFF!: Don't, don't, don't, I have something else to tell you.

Jing Huan took a sip of water.

[Friend] Sweet Little Jing: Talk.

[Friend] OFF!: Look, now that Idle Pavilion has put a bounty on you, your character is basically useless. Why not make a big profit off them before you sell your character?

[Friend] Sweet Little Jing: ?

[Friend] OFF!: Take off your equipment and let me kill you. I'll split the bounty with you 50/50, how's that?

[Friend] Sweet Little Jing: ?

[Friend] OFF!: ...Then 30/70?

[Friend] Sweet Little Jing: [Smile]

[Friend] OFF!: 20/80, leave me at least something please, meimei.

[Friend] Sweet Little Jing: Alrighty, but if I accidentally kill you and make you lose your equipment, you can't blame me. [Tapping fingers together]

[Friend] OFF!: ...Okay, just pretend I didn't say anything. [Waving handkerchief]

A few days after moving into his new place, Jing Huan finally found the time to go to the supermarket.

It wasn't good for his home to stay empty, so after picking out some household essentials, he strolled to the food section.

As his mother was a chef, Jing Huan had been exposed to the kitchen since childhood, so making some small home-cooked dishes was not a problem for him. Moreover, he had promised Gao Zixiang and Lu Wenhao that after settling down, he would invite them over for dinner.

Gao Zixiang called him on his phone. "Where are you, Huanhuan?"

Jing Huan actually didn't like people calling him Huanhuan; it sounded like a girl's name. But it didn't matter how hard he threatened or bribed them, he couldn't make them drop the name, so he just went along with it.

"I'm in the food section. Go ahead and wait for me at the checkout counter."

After paying, Gao Zixiang and Lu Wenhao grabbed the bags.

"Huanhuan, did you buy or rent your place? It doesn't look like anyone has lived here before?" Gao Zixiang remarked as he examined every inch of Jing Huan's home.

"Rented, but it's newly built, so no one has lived here before." Jing Huan casually put on an apron. "You guys can wait outside and watch TV."

Jing Huan breezily whipped up a few home-cooked dishes, and after taking a bite, Lu Wenhao hollered, "Holy shit! Huanhuan, you should've told us how good you were! Why do I need to find a girlfriend when I can just marry you!"

Gao Zixiang said, "If you want to marry him, you need to ask for permission from our department's head beauty. She has been pining after Huanhuan for a long time."

Jing Huan didn't join in their banter. Mid-meal, he suddenly stopped eating and turned to Lu Wenhao. "Hao'er, I have something to ask you."

Lu Wenhao wiped his mouth. "Speak."

"What type of girl do you like?"

Lu Wenhao paused. His expression grew strange, and he immediately clarified, "No…Huanhuan, I was just kidding earlier. I…I'm a pure straight man!"

"Don't worry, even if I were gay, I wouldn't seek you out as my partner," Jing Huan said. "What I mean is…haven't you been in an online relationship a few times now? What kind of girl do you like to pursue in-game?"

"Ah." Lu Wenhao thought for a moment. "A girl with a sweet voice, who loves to be all flirty, and can sing, I guess."

Gao Zixiang commented, "Tacky!"

"*Tch*, what do you know? You're going to die with your childhood friend in this lifetime," Lu Wenhao countered.

Jing Huan ate silently. Didn't he fulfill all three of these requirements?

With the voice changer, having a sweet voice was no problem; he could learn how to act flirty; and as for singing, he loved standing out back in middle school, even winning third place at the school's Top Ten Singers competition that he participated in.

After chatting for a while, Gao Zixiang suddenly changed the topic and said, "By the way, Huanhuan, I won't be able to help you wash the dishes after we finish eating. I have to rush back to the dorm; I made plans with some of my guildmates to kill the God of War at seven."

Jing Huan raised his eyebrows. "Kill the God of War? You want to craft a divine artifact?"

"Yes, the all-server PK is about to start, so I'm giving it another shot. If I manage to get the divine artifact, the championship could be mine." Gao Zixiang sighed. "And I'm still missing a lot of crafting materials. There are three teams from our server competing this year, and all of them want to upgrade their equipment, so we have to fight over the materials...My life is so hard."

Jing Huan nodded thoughtfully and said, "Okay, that's fine. I bought a dishwasher."

After seeing the two of them off, Jing Huan returned to his computer to see his friend icon constantly flashing.

[Friend] OFF!: Jing-meimei, what are you doing?

Jing Huan had planned to unfriend him after their chat that day, but OFF! said that he had an alternate character in Idle Pavilion and could help him gather information on them anytime. Several moments of consideration later, Jing Huan decided to keep him as a friend.

[Friend] Sweet Little Jing: I just finished eating. Let me ask you something.

[Friend] OFF!: What's up?

[Friend] Sweet Little Jing: Who represents this server for the server battles every year? Yearning For?

To put it simply, server battles were an all-server PK battle, an annual PK feast, with the championship rewards being a trophy, game title, and money.

Each server could only send one team to compete. If multiple teams registered from the same server, they must first have a civil war amongst themselves with whoever emerged as victor acting as the server representative in battle.

[Friend] OFF!: Ah? No, he doesn't. Yearning For doesn't do server battles.

Jing Huan jerked back.

With that top-tier equipment and those high-level summoning beasts, he actually didn't participate in server battles?

[Friend] OFF!: Yearning For participated once a few years ago and won the championship, but he hasn't registered since. It's always been Regardless of Lovesickness's team who represented our server in the battles for the past couple years.

[Friend] Sweet Little Jing: So, it's like that~ Then that's a pity. I

think if he went, our server would definitely take the championship.

[Friend] OFF!: Not necessarily. Being powerful on his own isn't enough. These PK battles are a five-person affair. You see, he isn't even part of a guild, and based on my investigations, the party members he usually grinds experience points with are quest bots. If he wants to compete, the only choice he has is to do it with Idle Pavilion.

[Friend] OFF!: Hey! Don't tell me he got involved last time because he wanted to join Idle Pavilion? If that's really the case, then you're doomed. Have you heard of his nickname?

[Friend] Sweet Little Jing: ...What nickname?

[Friend] OFF!: Spirit Fox Slayer! He once went to the all-server arena to play 1V1 and matched against the top Spirit Fox Den player. Wow...Yearning For completely demolished him. He was unable to fight back at all and couldn't gain a single advantage.

Jing Huan sneered. *That's because that Spirit Fox Den was too noob.*

[Friend] Sweet Little Jing: That's really impressive 0.0! No wonder the pro is a pro!

[Friend] OFF!: He he, exactly.

[Friend] OFF!: Right, meimei, have you thought it over these past few days? Are we going to make some money together or not?

[Friend] Sweet Little Jing: I don't want to. It's such a small amount, so I turn my nose up at it. [Turning head]

Jing Huan closed the chat window, readying himself to do his dailies.

【[Megaphone] Yearning For: Buying golden finch feathers for 100

gold each. Trade directly at the Sunken Moon City's lord, will pay more for larger quantities. DM me. 】

As soon as this megaphone went out, the World Channel imploded.

[World] Peach Cheese Stan: Holy Shit! Yearning For showed up!

[World] Fae Bae: Heh :)

[World] Blinded by Beauty: Wait, aren't golden finch feathers used for crafting divine artifacts? God Xiang[4] already has a divine artifact, so why is he still collecting them?

[World] Is Gege Big: God Xiang your ass, he's just a scumbag.

Meanwhile, Jing Huan's gaze was locked onto the last two words of this megaphone.

DM me.

If people could DM him, didn't that mean Yearning For had opened up his friend chat?!

He promptly gave it a try, and sure enough, he could add him to his friend list.

It was a one-sided friending, but as long as the other party was on his friend list, he could send them messages.

[Friend] Sweet Little Jing: Gege! [Excited]

Three minutes later, there was still no response.

[Friend] Sweet Little Jing: Gege, pay attention to me~ Aren't you collecting golden finch feathers? [Wronged]

[Friend] Yearning For: Trade directly at the city lord.

---

4   Refers to Yearning For. The Chinese characters for Yearning For is 心 向 往 之 - xīn xiàng wǎng zhī and the players here are addressing him as 向神 - xiàng shén (God Xiang) out of respect for him being an extremely skilled player.

 Chapter 01

[Friend] Sweet Little Jing: Gege, I don't have any golden finch feathers, but I do have a way that can help you earn thousands of gold daily! >.< Feathers are so expensive, but luckily, I can help save your wallet!

On the other end of the computer, Xiang Huaizhi frowned slightly after reading this line of text.

What was the difference between this manner of speaking and the QQ account-stealing scammer's from a few years ago?

Oh, she was indeed a habitual scammer.

He had almost collected enough feathers and was about to turn off the friending functionality when another message came in.

[Friend] Sweet Little Jing: Idle Pavilion put a bounty on me after all. You get 100 gold coins if you kill me once. Let me strip down for you to kill me, how about it, gege~ [Blows a kiss]

[Friend] Yearning For: ...

[Friend] Yearning For: No.

[Friend] Sweet Little Jing: Why not? I'm really easy to kill! I won't even fight back!

[Friend] Yearning For: Not short on money.

Xiang Huaizhi hesitated for a moment and typed.

[Friend] Yearning For: Why are you looking for someone to kill you?

[Friend] Sweet Little Jing: Ah. I'm not looking for anyone else, I'm only looking for gege OvO. Nobody else can kill me, I'm very good at escaping!

[Friend] Yearning For: ...Why did you come to me. Is it because you kill stole my monster?

[Friend] Sweet Little Jing: No, it's not that.

[Friend] Yearning For: ?

[Friend] Sweet Little Jing: Ahhhh~ It's because I am your fangirl...

[Friend] Sweet Little Jing: QAQ, suddenly so shy.

[Friend] Yearning For: ...

[Friend] Sweet Little Jing: I've been secretly watching a lot of your arena videos, your gameplay is so cool~ I started playing this game because of you. [Blushing]

Okay! Model answer! One hundred points!!

Jing Huan! You're the best!

Jing Huan read and reread the messages he sent, becoming increasingly satisfied with each perusal.

There was no reply from the other side.

Jing Huan couldn't help but laugh. *Heh, he must be so nervous that he doesn't know how to reply.*

He could practically smell victory; now he just had to go for the kill.

"Even though I bought a character with...a not-so-great reputation, and it cost me most of my pocket money so I can only live on instant noodles these days, seeing you in the game makes it allll worth it."

Oh my goodness, what a heartwarming speech.

Jing Huan himself felt moved.

He thought for a moment and added a cute game emoji at the end of the sentence.

Perfect! Send!

As he pressed the key, a line of yellow text popped out—

【Player Yearning For has refused to receive the message. Sending failed.】

Jing Huan stared silently at the screen, baffled.

After the friend functionality was disabled, the entire game interface finally quieted down.

Xiang Huaizhi flew to the storage NPC and stuffed all the newly obtained golden finch feathers into the storage box.

Suddenly, a head poked out of a bunk bed across from him. "Scumbag, how many feathers have you collected?"

Xiang Huaizhi didn't even turn his head at this address. "What, you want to take a stroll around the respawn point?"

Lu Hang immediately stopped. "Tch, what the hell, dude. Can't you take a joke? Anyway, back to the topic at hand, how many feathers have you collected?"

"Enough," Xiang Huaizhi said. "In the future, you can collect your own things yourself."

"This is only because the system temporarily banned me from trading since I logged in from a different location...I go through this every time I come back from a long vacation, you know that." Lu Hang logged in while speaking, only realizing something was wrong mid-sentence. "Wait a minute, I only asked you to help me collect the feathers ten minutes ago. How

did you collect enough so quickly? How much did you pay for them?"

Xiang Huaizhi said, "One hundred gold each."

Lu Hang was furious to the point of spitting blood, exclaiming, "It's seventy gold apiece everywhere in the Merchant Union! And you paid a hundred gold for each?!"

"Everywhere? Go digging through the Merchant Union. If you can find one hundred of them, I'll give you my character."

"Creating one divine artifact only requires a hundred feathers!"

Xiang Huaizhi raised his eyebrows. "*One* divine artifact? Do you think your family runs the game? You might not get a decent one even if you try ten times."

Lu Hang's right eyelid twitched. "So how many did you actually collect?"

"Didn't count them."

If he didn't count them, then there was probably enough to fill a whole storage box.

Lu Hang drew in a cold breath and calmly picked up his cellphone, scrolling through his bank account balance.

"Don't worry, I'll count this as collecting them for myself. I'll sell them to you for seventy-one gold a feather," Xiang Huaizhi said indifferently.

Lu Hang clenched his fist and said, "Damn, I will never call you a scumbag anymore! You're my ge, my forever ge."

Xiang Huaizhi laughed. "Get lost."

"Right, I almost forgot to interview you," Lu Hang said. "How does it feel to be a scumbag?"

"Pretty good."

Chapter 02

Lu Hang stared, incredulous, but Xiang Huaizhi didn't bother explaining.

He wasn't lying; it did feel pretty good. During this time, no one contacted him to party up to PK, no guilds tried to recruit him, and even the number of girls sending him friend requests had gone down.

【Your friend Long Road Ahead is online.】

"Hey! The login restriction has been lifted now! I can create a party!" After logging in, Lu Hang shouted over to the opposite bed, "Come on, I'll take you to do quests. There happens to be an event going on right now."

Experience points would be doubled during the event. Xiang Huaizhi let out an "mm," and accepted Lu Hang's party invite.

In *Nine Heroes*, apart from special events and high-level dungeons that required more players, most regular activities and PKs were done in a party of five. Xiang Huaizhi opened the party menu and saw that, the two of them aside, the other three in the party were all girls.

【Yearning For has entered the party.】

[Party] Baby Luoluo: ...

[Party] Love is Sharing Noms: [Fainting]

[Party] Ji Xiaonian: Uh.

[Party] Long Road Ahead: What's wrong?

[Party] Love is Sharing Noms: Nothing, Roro. Is this your friend?

[Party] Long Road Ahead: Yup, that's my bro, Yearning For. None of you know him? His name is on the rankings list though.

[Party] Ji Xiaonian: ...Even if we didn't know him before, we've

gotten to know him these past two days. [Shut up]

Lu Hang burst into laughter beside him. "Ha ha ha, Old Xiang, why do I feel like this fuss has made you even more popular in the server than before?"

Xiang Huaizhi couldn't be bothered to deign him a response. He just opened his inventory and checked which potions he had on him.

Lu Hang connected his headset, coughed lightly twice, and then deliberately lowered his voice to ask, "Can you hear me?"

To make communication more convenient, *Nine Heroes* had a built-in voice chat.

Goosebumps erupted all over Xiang Huaizhi's skin at the sudden bass voice. He frowned slightly and slid off one side of his headset.

"Ah…I can hear you."

"Are we going to tackle the new event? Is it hard?"

"What if we can't beat the boss?"

Invigoration shot through Lu Hang as soon as he heard the girls' voices. "It's okay, I'm here, I won't let you die. You're free to kill the small monsters in front of us. When we get to the boss, just hide behind me."

Before the girls could answer, Xiang Huaizhi said, "Lu Hang, mute your mic first."

"Relax," Lu Hang said. "I'm using push-to-talk, they can't hear you."

"What kind of people did you call over?" Xiang Huaizhi opened their character profiles and noted that the two of them hadn't reached the level cap yet. Most importantly, he added,

Chapter 02

"Three healers? What, you didn't drink enough milk[1] as a child?"

"Hey, I've looked into this event, and it's not that difficult," Lu Hang said. "Anyway, what choice do I have? I have to carry my wife. Help a bro out."

Xiang Huaizhi asked dryly, "Which one is your wife?"

Lu Hang replied calmly, "I can't say for sure yet."

Xiang Huaizhi stared expressionlessly at him.

During the holidays, *Nine Heroes* would run corresponding festive events with different gameplay experiences; the only commonality between them was the abundant amounts of experience and rewards offered.

While the other players were busy grinding the event, a little spirit fox who had been AFKing in the main city for quite some time suddenly sprang into action.

The little spirit fox quickly packed up her stall, *whooshed* onto her mount, and hurried to the safety of the wilderness outpost before setting off for the wilderness maps.

Jing Huan was practically bursting with impatience. It wasn't like he was raring to farm experience; after all this time playing *Nine Heroes*, he was never one to enjoy AFK grinding quests.

He wanted to go dig up the loot from the treasure map that he had "stolen" that day.

The Roadblock Bandit's Treasure Map was a special item with a very low drop rate; someone with bad luck like him wouldn't

---

1   Chinese gamers often refer to "healing" as 奶 - nǎi which literally means milk. This term comes from the metaphor of providing nourishment or sustenance, which is what healing is.

manage to get a single map despite grinding for over half a month.

According to the official description, you could dig up lots of unexpected loot with the Roadblock Bandit's Treasure Map. Jing Huan had seen people dig up worthless health recovery steamed buns, as well as precious hard-to-come-by materials. It was this uncertainty that made it both nerve-wracking and exciting.

At the same time, in Idle Pavilion's guild chat—

[Guild] Scarlet_Shadow: Reporting! My alt character spotted Sweet Little Jing at the Western Liang riverside!

[Guild] Silent Affection: Damn, this female scammer deliberately chose the time when we were busy to leave the city.

[Guild] Echoes of Spring: I'm in combat and can't leave now. Can someone in the guild go there?

[Guild] Fae Bae: I can go, but is there anyone willing to come with me? I'm a bit scared to go by myself. [Tapping fingers together]

[Guild] Silent Affection: It's okay, Faefae. That character is empty, so she'll be easy for you to kill.

[Guild] Fae Bae: I know...It's just that it's my first time killing someone, so I'm naturally a bit scared. [Pitiful] If it weren't for my hatred toward these romance scammers, I wouldn't even want to get involved.

[Guild] Silent Affection: Ha ha, then go on ahead. Just think of it as a bit of venting.

Fae Bae quickly formed a five-man party and flew to the Western Liang riverside.

Upon their rushed arrival, they saw Sweet Little Jing's character holding a shovel...and jabbing it into the ground.

"She's digging for treasure!" a party member said. "Stop her! Hurry! After we kill her, maybe we can get the treasure map as a drop!"

 Chapter 02

Just as Jing Huan was halfway through digging up the treasure map, he was brutally interrupted by an attack skill.

Scowling and without clearly seeing who was approaching, he threw out his decoy skill to escape.

He had switched sects not only because the Spirit Fox Den had an interesting playstyle, but also because this sect excelled in evading attackers. With their incredible speed and various smokescreen skills, their escaping skills were top-tier, so betraying party members to save themselves in the arena was a common tactic for Spirit Fox Den players.

The people behind him reacted a bit too late; he was nearly out of the map before they remembered to give chase.

Just as Jing Huan was about to enter the safe zone, he suddenly heard from behind him, "It's okay, Faefae. We didn't kill her this time, but I'll accompany you again next time to block her path. Kill to your heart's content."

It seemed like they had forgotten to change the voice chat settings to be party-only.

Jing Huan's female character, with her swaying fox tail full of villainous intentions, stopped running. His character turned around and sure enough, saw the loli in the party chasing him. It was her with the in-game name Fae Bae.

"Ha ha, she actually turned around. Is her game lagging?"

"Damn, how can she run like that..."

"Who cares? It's better if she disconnects, because if she does, she can't manually return to the respawn point. We can camp there for her and then kill her as many times as we want." The Beastmaster in the party immediately summoned a beast. "Quick, Warlock, seal her first."

The Warlock immediately threw out a sealing talisman, but while it was still in flight, the other party unexpectedly jumped first and summoned a Nine-tailed Spirit Fox.

The Mage in the party laughed and said, "What's she doing? Is she going to fight back?"

"Who'd you scam to get that Nine-tailed Spirit Fox?"

Fae Bae suddenly turned on her mic. "Sweet Little Jing, just stand still and let us kill you once; I won't even camp your corpse. Just don't scam people in the future, it really disgraces us women."

Her party member laughed. "Ha ha, Faefae, you sweet summer child."

"Don't laugh," Fae Bae said shyly. "I'm seriously trying to persuade her."

As soon as she said that, Sweet Little Jing took action again.

They saw her charge a spell for half a second and then a sealing web jumped from the palm of her hand, heading straight toward them.

The web wove between them and shot toward the back, hitting the Monk healer in the party.

It took the Monk by surprise but before he could react, Sweet Little Jing disappeared in a flash. The Warlock in the party realized what happened and shouted, "It's a stealth teleport! Move quickly!"

Yet it was too late.

Just moments before, Fae Bae was leisurely casting buffs on her party members, but now, in the blink of an eye, she found herself entangled in webs.

She was taken aback. "What is this?!"

"Oh crap, you need to break yourself outta there. Quickly

spammed the left-click! The web is a debuff that seals you and reduces your character's attributes," the Warlock exclaimed in shock.

This person actually cast a teleport-web combo, wrapping her in several layers of webs in just a few seconds?!

Panicking, Fae Bae squawked, "I can't break free!"

At that moment, the Nine-tailed Spirit Fox, obeying its master's command, spewed flames right toward where Fae Bae was standing. Fae Bae was already poorly equipped, and with so many layers of debuffs on her, the flames burned her alive.

【System Announcement: During a forced PK, Player Fae Bae was inadvertently killed by her target instead and lost a Jade Ribbon.】

Sweet Little Jing took the chance to escape again, and that was when the others finally realized: this person had no intention of fighting back right from the start! Instead, her goal had been to take out one of their party members!

Snapping out of their shock, they spat out a string of curses before giving chase again.

"Holy fuck." On the other side of the map, Lu Hang's eyes widened in amazement as he exclaimed, "Old Xiang, did you see that combo just now?!"

Xiang Huaizhi remained silent.

They had completed the quest a long time ago and were now just rotating around the wilderness map, waiting for the next monsters to respawn in each area.

That Spirit Fox Den really could play well.

But could anyone tell him why this Spirit Fox Den's name was Sweet Little Jing?

Lu Hang continued speaking, "Tsk tsk tsk, with so many layers

of webs, even the top Spirit Fox Den in the Aqua server might not be able to compete, right?"

"As long as the opponent isn't me, he'd be able to manage." Xiang Huaizhi looked away. "Are we still doing the quest or not?"

"Still farming. Hey, don't you want to watch a bit more?"

"No."

All right then.

With a light click of his mouse, Lu Hang was about to leave the wilderness map when he caught sight of the little spirit fox in front of him suddenly spin to dodge the Warlock's skill and charge straight toward them.

"Hey! She's coming over!" Lu Hang squinted and leaned toward the screen. "Wait, Sweet Little Jing…Why does that name sound kind of familiar?"

A girl in the party reminded him, "She's the female scammer Idle Pavilion is hunting down."

Lu Hang suddenly realized, "Oh, right! It's her! What the…Are female scammers these days this skilled?"

Xiang Huaizhi watched the little spirit fox fly toward them and suddenly remembered the monster that she kill stole from him the other day. Feeling slightly uneasy, he asked, "Are we leaving or not?"

"We're going, we're going now, what's the rush…"

"*Ah,*" an unfamiliar female voice suddenly wormed into their headsets.

The voice wasn't too sweet; it was clear and crisp, inexplicably giving people a sense of comfort. And right at this moment, that voice was filled with surprise and excitement.

"Gege—"

Chapter 02

Taken aback, it took Lu Hang a long time to figure out that the voice was coming from Sweet Little Jing.

Lu Hang asked, "Who is she calling for?"

Xiang Huaizhi said, "I don't know."

As soon as they said that, Sweet Little Jing suddenly back-tracked in midair, and, with her little white fox, pounced right on Yearning For. "God of War-gege! Help me, aaaah—"

Xiang Huaizhi, the only one in the server with a "God of War" title, stilled.

When the other four arrived at the scene, they saw Sweet Little Jing careening right for Yearning For.

This call of "gege" almost numbed Lu Hang's heart. "Are you sure you don't know her?"

In the game, there were two options after joining a party: one was to follow the party leader automatically without requiring any input; the other was to control your character yourself, but movements were limited to an area.

Xiang Huaizhi pressed the hotkey to have the party unfollow him, then shifted back, avoiding the person falling from the sky. "I don't."

Jing Huan never thought that Yearning For would catch him, so in the last few seconds before he hit the ground, he used his jump to step on a nearby cliff, landing safely in front of Yearning For.

He gave a brief once-over of Yearning For's team. *Ah yes, three whole healers.*

He didn't even care about building an effective party formation that he could kill monsters with; all he was concerned about was picking up girls. Truly, a scumbag's style.

While Jing Huan internally ridiculed him, he maneuvered his game character to hide behind Yearning For. In a very aggrieved tone, he said, "God of War-gege…people are hunting me."

The Idle Pavilion members happened to hear this and had a quick exchange within their party.

"Yearning For? Why is he in this wilderness map?"

"Didn't you see the three girls in his party? Guess he's picking up girls. Tch, Faefae is truly pitiful." The Warlock paused. "But…this Sweet Little Jing has quite a nice voice."

"Obviously! How else do you think our guild officer got into such trouble?! But what's her relationship with Yearning For?"

"Don't know. So, what should we do now? If Yearning For takes action, we're probably no match for him…"

Because there were penalties for being counter-killed during your initiated forced PK, everyone in the party hesitated, standing frozen and doing nothing.

"Let's not rush into things yet. I'll ask." The Warlock switched his voice channel to the Current Channel.

"God…Yearning For." He swallowed that "God Xiang" down. "Do you know her? She just destroyed Faefae's equipment."

Xiang Huaizhi frowned.

[Current] Yearning For: Who is Faefae.

Everyone present except Lu Hang instantly froze. In the prolonged silence, they all seemed to be thinking the same word: "scumbag."

[Current] Sweet Little Jing: Fae Bae hunted me first. Am I wrong to defend myself and fight back? [Question]

 Chapter 02

[Current] Sweet Little Jing: God of War-gege QAQ, they just wanted to destroy the treasure map you gave me. They're so bad.

[Current] Sweet Little Jing: I definitely won't let them succeed!

The people present fell silent again.

Lu Hang couldn't hold back anymore, laughing so hard that he was convulsing. "You gave her a love token already and you're *still* saying you don't know her?!"

"I didn't give it to her," Xiang Huaizhi corrected with a dark expression. She had stolen it, using a skill to deal seventy-nine damage points to snatch it away from right under his nose.

The Idle Pavilion members spoke up again, "Yearning For, does this mean you want to get involved?"

[Current] Yearning For: No.

[Current] Sweet Little Jing: See that?! My gege is telling you all to get lost now! And then he'll maybe consider not killing you all! [Angry]

[Current] Yearning For: ?

[Current] Sweet Little Jing: Gege sent a question mark, so if you guys don't run now, say goodbye to your equipment! [Pounding the table]

The Warlock was the leader of this current hunting party. Already feeling a little off-kilter at Fae Bae losing her equipment, he was having some misgivings. Seeing the current situation now, he grew even more uncertain.

"All right...you guys better watch yourselves."

Having said that, he chanted a sect skill in place for half a second, quickly teleporting his party away from the scene.

Xiang Huaizhi, who had just been about to type, paused.

How do you have the audacity to hunt people down with so little courage?

In the game, the little spirit fox jumped and twirled around him, and blew him a kiss using the character's in-game action.

[Current] Sweet Little Jing: Thank you, gege, I was scared to death~ [Weeping]

Xiang Huaizhi had wanted to say something, but he stopped typing halfway through.

Forget it, what's the point of me getting tangled with a female scammer?

On the other hand, Lu Hang was interested.

[Current] Long Road Ahead: Why would you be scared? With your skills, they can't catch up to you.

[Current] Sweet Little Jing: I was so scared just now that I performed exceptionally QAQ. Fortunately, God of War-gege was here.

[Current] Long Road Ahead: Did Old Xiang really give you that treasure map? Isn't that a bound item?

Xiang Huaizhi frowned. "Why are you talking so much nonsense? Are we clearing dungeons or not?"

"Hey, I'm just asking a few questions," Lu Hang said. "Don't you think this woman is very interesting?"

"No."

[Current] Sweet Little Jing: Mhm. I originally wanted to dig up something good and send it to God of War-gege, but the Idle Pavilion members arrived when I was only halfway through digging QvQ.

Lu Hang slapped his thigh. "Pretty good, Old Xiang! That girl is dead-set on you!"

Chapter 02

Xiang Huaizhi let out a cold snort. "All right, how about you date her? You can have the kind of relationship where your character gets completely emptied."

Xiang Huaizhi didn't care about gossip and usually didn't even pay close attention to megaphones. It was Lu Hang who had told him about this female scammer.

At that time, Lu Hang had confidently said, *It's a trick, definitely a trick. This character still has the same owner!*

"No, look at what she said, she'll give you whatever she digs up from the map. Weren't you grinding quests for days because you wanted this treasure map?" Lu Hang said. "Even if she is a scammer, we're not gonna come out as the losers of this deal!"

Xiang Huaizhi indeed needed the treasure map.

More precisely, what he needed was a rare material that could only be unearthed with this treasure map: enchanted spirit orbs. Unfortunately, despite grinding countless quests, he had only gotten the treasure map drop once—only for it to be stolen by Sweet Little Jing.

[Current] Sweet Little Jing: Gege, you don't have enough enchanted spirit orbs, right? I can dig it out! [Clenching fist]

[Current] Yearning For: ...

[Current] Long Road Ahead: Wow, how did you know that?!

[Current] Sweet Little Jing: I've been reading the system announcements these past few days. Gege has been grinding the repeatable quests, probably because he wants to hatch a spirit beast?

Xiang Huaizhi remained silent.

He was indeed trying to hatch a spirit beast, and the final step of that required enchanted spirit orbs.

Enchanted spirit orbs were tradeable items, but could only be obtained through treasure maps, and the drop rate wasn't high—currently, at least, there wasn't a single orb up for sale on their server.

It turned out there were things even in this world that money couldn't buy.

Jing Huan formed a party next to them.

"Gege." Jing Huan pitched his voice up, the echo in the headset rattling his brain. "Shall we go dig up the treasure together? If you don't come with me, I'm afraid I'll be killed again soon…"

Xiang Huaizhi didn't necessarily want her to return the treasure map to him. But if, as she said, she was hunted down by Idle Pavilion, and the treasure map was destroyed, then his days and nights of grinding quests would have been in vain.

After hesitating for a while, he left his party and applied to join Sweet Little Jing's, saying, "I'll go with you once."

Digging up treasure maps was such an exciting activity; Lu Hang also wanted to join in on the fun, so he said, "Hey girl, take me with you too…"

Before he could finish speaking, Sweet Little Jing had already run out of sight with Xiang Huaizhi.

"Fuck, this grown-ass man is so difficult to sweet-talk. Would it kill him to just join me?" Jing Huan muttered to himself, staring at the person in his party.

[Party] Sweet Little Jing: God of War-gege, what quest were you just doing?

[Party] Yearning For: Wilderness map dungeon.

[Party] Sweet Little Jing: Oh, oh.

[Party] Sweet Little Jing: Wouldn't it be hard to clear the dungeon with three healers? 0.0

[Party] Yearning For: It won't be.

Heh, of course not. With three girls accompanying you to raid dungeons, you're probably grinning from ear to ear in front of your computer right now. Scumbag.

[Party] Sweet Little Jing: That's true, I nearly forgot! Gege is a super strong DPS! [Holding up a heart]

In order to watch them dig up the treasure, Lu Hang reluctantly gave up the three wives-to-be in his party and jumped out of bed to sit next to Xiang Huaizhi.

"Old Xiang, spit it out, when did you and Sweet Little Jing meet? What did you do to make her so devoted to you?"

"I really don't know her; do I get any money for lying to you?"

Lu Hang stared at him suspiciously.

Xiang Huaizhi relented. "We met once on a wilderness map. She kill stole my Roadblock Bandit."

Surprised, Lu Hang asked, "There's someone in this world who can steal your mobs?"

"I was on the phone at the time and wasn't paying attention." Xiang Huaizhi hesitated for a moment. "And I thought she was a guy."

Lu Hang was nonplussed.

Xiang Huaizhi looked at the little spirit fox who was constantly fangirling over him in the Party Channel and said, "Would any woman talk like that in this day and age?"

[Party] Sweet Little Jing: God of War-gege, your character's face is so beautifully crafted. It must take such deft and beautiful hands to create this kind of game character~! [Starry-eyed]

[Party] Sweet Little Jing: I'm so nervous, we're about to reach the coordinates on the treasure map.

[Party] Sweet Little Jing: [Is anyone there?]

[Party] Sweet Little Jing: Sigh, gege is very handsome even when he's not talking QvQ.

Lu Hang snorted. "I think…she's quite cute?"

Xiang Huaizhi didn't bother responding.

His friend chat suddenly lit up, and he casually opened it.

[Friend] Fae Bae: You're actually in the same party as that female scammer?

[Friend] Fae Bae: Heh heh, that desperate now?

[Friend] Fae Bae: Do you realize that she just destroyed my equipment?

After a quick glance, Xiang Huaizhi closed the chat box.

Lu Hang said, "Hey, you should at least say something."

"Not replying. Annoying."

Puzzled, Lu Hang inquired, "Does she even know that you weren't the one playing your character these past few months?"

"She knows."

He had told Fae Bae everything that needed to be said.

But Fae Bae simply didn't believe it and insisted that he was just trying to evade his responsibility by pushing blame onto an imaginary person. She had even added fuel to the fire by exaggerating the story.

Lu Hang still wanted to say something else when his phone suddenly rang. He answered it, exchanged a few words, and walked to the dormitory door.

"God of War-gege." A girl's voice came through the headset. Sweet Little Jing asked cautiously, "Are you still thereee? We've reached the coordinates displayed on the treasure map."

Chapter 02

[Party] Yearning For: Mm.

[Party] Sweet Little Jing: Then I'm going to dig now~

[Party] Yearning For: 1[2]

Since they were partied up when Jing Huan activated the treasure map, the two characters in the party started digging together.

Jing Huan picked up the glass of water by his hand and took a sip, pondering on how to make Yearning For add him as a friend.

Jing Huan never expected to dig up anything good; after all, he had his legendary unlucky hands that could even craft a divine artifact into utter trash.

Enchanted spirit orbs? Was he even worthy of them?

The treasure-digging progress bar disappeared. It wasn't until a line of eye-catching yellow text popped up on the game interface that Jing Huan realized what was happening.

【You accidentally dug into a monster's house with your shovel and angered the secluded Spirit King (Luojia Mountain 132, 72)! Please go to seal him immediately! [Required players: Sweet Little Jing, Yearning For. Time limit: 48 hours.]】

【System Announcement: Amazing news! Players Sweet Little Jing and Yearning For accidentally dug into a monster's house while digging for treasure at Luojia Mountain. The now-homeless Spirit King is causing trouble at Luojia Mountain 132, 72!】

【All-server System Announcement: Players Sweet Little Jing and Yearning For on the Mirage server have triggered the hidden quest [Wrath of the Spirit King] from the Roadblock Bandit's Treasure Map.】

Before the two people involved could react, the World Channel

---

2   A quick short-form for "Okay."

exploded first. The lines in the chat were scrolling at an incredible speed, making it impossible to read without locking the chat in place first.

[World] Is Gege Big: ?

[World] BrbOrNot: ???

[World] The Wind is Freer Than Me: Am I hallucinating from an all-nighter?

[World] Speck of Dust: Yearning For and Sweet Little Jing? Scumbag x Scammer? Clash of the masters? Strong vs. Strong? The decisive battle at the summit???

[World] Go to Bed Early: Wait? What's this hidden Wrath of the Spirit King questline?!

[World] Peach Cheese Stan: Does it matter? I just want to ask, what kind of strange combo are these two? I step out for just an hour to eat, and the gossip mill suddenly doesn't have any space for me anymore?

[World] Dumpling Devourer: Damn, that scamming character is so lucky. She actually got a treasure map drop and triggered a hidden quest. The rewards must be through the roof, huh?

[World] Shameless Luoluo: He he. As an insider, I'll reveal it to everyone. This treasure map was actually a gift from Yearning For to Sweet Little Jing.

[World] BrbOrNot: ???

[World] Go to Bed Early: [Doubtful]

[World] Goodnight World: [Completely confused] Isn't a treasure map a bound item? How can it be gifted?

[World] I Really Like Lulu: They must have partied up and got it together. Yearning For is truly something. How much did he need

to grind to get a treasure map to drop? He can be considered the benchmark for all scumbags.

[World] Dumpling Devourer: And his partner is even Sweet Little Jing. The sky is warm, the earth is warm, and even the scammer's heart is warm. I love this scumbag.

[World] Peach Cheese Stan: @Today's Confusion Awards.

And so on.

In shock, Jing Huan watched with his own eyes as players in the World Channel wrote out fanfiction of him and Yearning For in one breath, getting all the way to Chapter 42—*On the day of their lavish wedding, Yearning For elopes with his new love, while Sweet Little Jing runs away with the betrothal gifts.*

Shit, how did it get to this point?

He moved the cursor over to the taskbar, wanting to take a glance at the quest notification.

Hidden quests were a special feature in *Nine Heroes*. When the servers had just launched, players were triggering these left and right, but they later grew quite rare.

Jing Huan had played for so long, but he had never even seen a hidden quest before, let alone trigger one, so he knew next to nothing about this.

The quest notification simply read: "Please go to Luojia Mountain (132, 72) to seal the Spirit King."

Fine.

[Party] Sweet Little Jing: Gege...did I get us in trouble? [Crying]

Xiang Huaizhi didn't reply immediately, since Lu Hang's roar had almost rendered him deaf.

"What the fuck! A hidden quest!!" Lu Hang was so excited that

he almost dropped his phone. His voice was booming as he said, "So treasure maps also contain hidden quests? You really hit the jackpot here! The rewards were already awesome enough with the treasure map, but now that the hidden quest was triggered, who needs enchanted spirit orbs?! You might even get the divine artifact to drop without them!"

"That's impossible. Hidden quests never offer equipment rewards," Xiang Huaizhi interrupted his fantasies.

"Okay, fine, a divine artifact might be a little far-fetched…" Lu Hang leaned over. "Quick, ask Sweet Little Jing if what she said before still counts."

"What did she say before?"

"What else? Didn't she promise to give you whatever she dug up?"

Xiang Huaizhi didn't respond to him. Right now, he wasn't interested in anything other than the enchanted spirit orbs. He only followed Sweet Little Jing to dig up the treasure because he thought that if she really excavated some enchanted spirit orbs, he'd be able to buy them from her at market price immediately.

"God of War-gege?" Sweet Little Jing's voice came through the headset again. "I really caused trouble."

Xiang Huaizhi placed his hands on the keyboard, typed two words, and then deleted them.

He pressed his push-to-talk key and said, "No."

Jing Huan jolted.

This person's voice sounds strangely pleasant?

He didn't deliberately try to lower or deepen it; it was a very normal, but very soothing, tone to listen to.

That made sense; he couldn't be a scumbag without this attractive trait.

"But people on the World Channel are cussing me out," Jing Huan said, indignant.

Xiang Huaizhi hadn't opened the World Channel, so naturally, he didn't know it had already become a chaotic mess. "Just block it."

"Okaaay, I blocked it," Jing Huan said. "Then what should we do now? Should we do this quest?"

Xiang Huaizhi glanced at the taskbar. "Let's wait first."

"But this quest has a forty-eight hour time limit."

Xiang Huaizhi opened the official website and said, "The time limit for hidden quests is always forty-eight hours. Let me do some research first. Dying in hidden quests is the same as dying normally; if you go in rashly, you may die and drop levels."

"Is the boss monster really so scary?" Jing Huan paused and then exclaimed excitedly, "Gege, does this mean you'll help me kill the boss?"

Xiang Huaizhi threw out the facts: "My name is on the quest, so you can't initiate the fight without me."

Sneering on the inside, Jing Huan sweetly answered, "Thank you, gege!"

Xiang Huaizhi responded, "I'll do some research. Will you be online tomorrow afternoon?"

"I'll be on, gege," Jing Huan said, ever so docile. "I can log on anytime."

"Let's set it for tomorrow afternoon then, and give ourselves more time in case we can't kill the boss in one go." Xiang Huaizhi

moved his mouse over to the "Leave Party" option. "Then, that's it for now."

"Gege, wait!" Jing Huan hurriedly called out to him. "Should we add each other as friends? Otherwise, how can I contact you?"

Xiang Huaizhi's brow twitched. "Mm." He sounded very reluctant.

Jing Huan let out a cold chuckle.

Dislike me all you want now, but there will come a time when you'll be crazy in love with me but can't have me.

As soon as they added each other as friends, Yearning For flew away. Jing Huan returned to the main city, found Yearning For among his friends, and checked his profile.

Yearning For, male, level 150, Demon Race, Qiya Mountain Sect.

Personal signature: None.

Today's mood: None.

Friends' ratings: None.

Was this person putting up a cold and aloof front? These days, even his seventy-year-old grandmother had a personal signature.

Jing Huan propped his chin on his hand, clicked on the friends' ratings, found the word "gege" from the system tags, and frantically spammed it.

【Yearning For has not enabled friend comments. Rating failed!】

Jing Huan just closed the profile.

The next day, Jing Huan went to the university. He had a class in the morning and the old professor paid special attention to him, leaving him no choice but to attend.

Gao Zixiang had saved him a seat early on. When Jing Huan

arrived, he and Lu Wenhao had their heads huddled together, talking about who knows what.

"What, did my departure create an opportunity for you two?" Jing Huan sat in the empty seat and crossed his legs. "You guys got together just like that?"

"Bullshit!" Gao Zixiang's head snapped up. "We're looking at some big news."

Without paying it much mind, Jing Huan asked, "What news?"

"You wouldn't be interested even if I told you. It's about *Nine Heroes*."

Jing Huan cast them a sidelong glance. "Tell me."

"Actually, it's nothing big. Someone from another server dug up a treasure map and found a hidden quest. This game has been live for ten years, and there are still hidden quests that haven't been triggered, isn't that funny?" Gao Zixiang put his phone away. "Last night, an all-server announcement suddenly popped up in the game while our guild was in the middle of a dungeon, and we were all dumbstruck by the news."

Didn't this news spread a little too quickly?

Jing Huan looked away and said, "Isn't it just a hidden quest? What's so strange about that?"

"Ha! You're one to talk. Have you ever seen a hidden quest?" Gao Zixiang mocked him.

"I"—*How haven't I seen one before? The quest in the announcement screenshot you're looking at was triggered by me truly!*—"haven't seen one before."

Gao Zixiang patted his shoulder to console him and said, "Actually, the hidden quest isn't the most interesting point of this matter, but the people who triggered it—" Halfway through his sentence, he suddenly realized something and shut up.

"The people who triggered the quest? Who?"

"N-no one." Gao Zixiang paused for a moment. "Anyway, they're bad people. One's a scumbag, and the other is a female scammer. They're both pretty notorious and they seem to have gotten together."

A measure later, Jing Huan said, "When it comes to certain matters, don't just listen to one side of the story."

"But I'm not making things up, everyone on that server is saying that. One of the biggest guilds in that server is also hunting that female scammer so she's probably too scared to even log on now. The guy isn't great either. If his character weren't so strong, he would've been hunted down a long time ago as well." At the mention of the scumbag, Gao Zixiang felt dissatisfied on his friend's behalf for his jiejie and slammed his desk hard. "If you ask me though, these two deserved to be cussed out by their server. They have only themselves to blame."

Jing Huan hadn't expected to be scolded by his friend so early in the morning and felt his head ache. "Shut up, you."

Lu Wenhao was idle and bored, so he opened the *Nine Heroes* forums and refreshed it again. Unexpectedly, this refresh resulted in some amazing things appearing: a post written by a Mirage server player.

【OMG, I received a system alert first thing in the morning. All I can say is that the Idle Pavilion guild is truly pitiful!】

The original poster wasted no time in attaching a game screenshot below.

Chapter 02

【System Alert: Players Sweet Little Jing and Yearning For of this server have successfully triggered the [Wrath of the Spirit King] hidden quest, which is linked to server stability. If these two players successfully seal the Spirit King within 48 hours, the server's stability will increase by 200 points; if they fail, it will decrease by 100 points. Within these 48 hours, players in the server can enhance the equipment attributes of Sweet Little Jing and Yearning For by "donating materials" at the Forge King's workshop. Contribute to the strength of your server, and cheer on your warriors!】

Server stability was one of the most important attributes of a server, and it had a significant impact on all large guilds; reduced server stability greatly increased the likelihood of guilds being robbed by bandits. In the worst-case scenario, it could even destroy the guild's potion material farms.

This meant that all the large guilds in the server must contribute some materials within these forty-eight hours to…cheer on Sweet Little Jing and Yearning For.

At this moment, the usually lively and bustling Idle Pavilion guild chat was suddenly like a ghost town. The atmosphere was heavy.

In the ten minutes after the system alert was released, not a single member typed out anything. It was unclear how much time passed, but finally, a response appeared in the chat—

[Guild] Regardless of Lovesickness: So…are we still hunting Sweet Little Jing for these next two days?

Now that one person had brought the matter up, everyone else who hadn't dared to say anything broke the silence with follow-up questions.

[Guild] Deep Forest Deer Sighing: Yeah, are we still hunting her

or not? We haven't even avenged Faefae's equipment getting destroyed yet.

[Guild] Echoes of Spring: I still don't get it. Five of you went to corner Sweet Little Jing. Letting her escape is one thing, but how did she also manage to take one of you out?

[Guild] Silent Affection: Sigh, who knew that Sweet Little Jing was so cunning! That was something unavoidable though.

[Guild] Echoes of Spring: With a dedicated healer and a Monk healer, how was it unavoidable? Even if the Monk healer was sealed, the healer could have healed herself.

Echoes of Spring was the vice guild leader of Idle Pavilion. She was a woman and rumored to have a thing with their female guild leader, Regardless of Lovesickness. This matter wasn't a secret in the guild; when Regardless of Lovesickness wasn't around, the guild was mostly managed by Echoes of Spring.

[Guild] Silent Affection: No, Echo, Faefae only died because she was helping our guild hunt someone down, and even had her equipment destroyed...you shouldn't say that, right?

[Guild] Echoes of Spring: I'm just stating the facts.

[Guild] Fae Bae: ...

[Guild] Fae Bae: I'm sorry. [Weeping] I didn't expect it either. By the time I realized I needed to heal myself, that fox had already killed me...

[Guild] Echoes of Spring: Be more cautious when you go out to hunt someone next time or you might be the one to get killed. Not only do you lose your equipment and experience points, but the guild's reputation can also suffer.

After sending this message, Echoes of Spring immediately minimized the game interface and continued to discuss the hidden quest with the other large guilds on the server in a QQ chat.

The World's #1 Guild Leader: I just went to check with the NPC, and this damn quest requires high-tier materials! *Nine Heroes* is so lame. Isn't this just forcing us to spend our resources?!

South Side of the Painting Pavilion Guild Leader: That's unfortunate. Our guild just opened an experience dungeon not too long ago, so we don't have many high-tier materials left.

Shatter the Sky Guild Leader: Painting Pavilion, you're really something. There's clearly a bunch of high-tier materials in your guild's resource storage. Do you think we're all blind?

South Side of the Painting Pavilion Guild Leader: Fuck! Shatter the Sky, you bastard, you put a spy in our guild again!

Shatter the Sky Guild Leader: Stop talking shit, a friend sent me a screenshot! Who would spy on you? You wish!

Shatter the Sky Guild Leader: What? If you think you're so tough, let's set ourselves as enemy guilds right now!

Idle Pavilion Guild Leader: If you want to fight, wait until this matter is settled. Don't argue here and waste everyone's time.

Idle Pavilion Guild Leader: I'm just going to cut to the chase; I propose that each guild contributes a hundred Fairy Whiskers, twenty Fish Heart Pills, and five Fire Phoenix Eyes. Our Idle Pavilion guild will contribute 20% more materials than you guys. If anyone has objections, you can raise them now.

All of the rare materials she had mentioned would require two months of the entire guild's efforts to gather. However, upon hearing that Idle Pavilion was contributing twenty percent more materials than them, they immediately didn't feel as bad anymore.

Shatter the Sky Guild Leader: You guys are contributing 120%?

Idle Pavilion Guild Leader: Is there a problem?

Shatter the Sky Guild Leader: Oh, there's no problem, just a little surprised. I didn't think your guild would contribute at all.

South Side of the Painting Pavilion Guild Leader: Wait, are you Echoes of Spring or Regardless of Lovesickness?

Idle Pavilion Guild Leader: ?

South Side of the Painting Pavilion Guild Leader: It must be Echoes of Spring then. Will Regardless of Lovesickness go along with your plan?

Idle Pavilion Guild Leader: You don't need to worry about this. Then it's settled. Hand in the materials within half an hour.

After tossing out this sentence, Echoes of Spring closed the QQ group chat, opened her friend list, and found the name Yearning For. Tentatively, she sent out a "1."

Unexpectedly, the message went through.

[Friend] Yearning For: ?

[Friend] Echoes of Spring: When will you two start the Spirit King quest?

[Friend] Echoes of Spring: You saw the system alert by now, right? Give us a time, so we can contribute the materials.

[Friend] Yearning For: This afternoon.

[Friend] Echoes of Spring: Can you kill it?

[Friend] Yearning For: Don't know.

[Friend] Echoes of Spring: 1.

Xiang Huaizhi didn't reply again. He had only opened up friend DMs because he was worried that the little spirit fox wouldn't be able to find him.

"Old Xiang, do you really not need the number one Warlock of *Nine Heroes* to step up?" Lu Hang asked him while leaning over the bedside with his chin propped up with his hand.

Xiang Huaizhi didn't turn his head as he said, "She and I are the only ones who can participate in the battle."

"I know, I mean I can just play with her character," Lu Hang said. "You know how difficult hidden quests are. The last hidden quest was triggered by a God of War party on the other server, and they barely made it after three hours of fighting. If you just take Sweet Little Jing with you, isn't that a suicide mission?"

Xiang Huaizhi said, "The dungeon boss's difficulty scales according to the number of players."

"But if you take Sweet Little Jing, it'll be like fighting the Spirit King solo...Besides, what if she jumps on you while she's running for her life? Wouldn't that be the end?"

Xiang Huaizhi asked, "Do you really want to help?"

Lu Hang nodded frantically. This was a hidden quest, who wouldn't want to join in?

"Come over to the city lord."

Lu Hang immediately moved his character to walk over to Yearning For, asking, "What?"

Xiang Huaizhi emptied his inventory to make a lot of space. "Give me some high-tier potions."

Lu Hang's brow furrowed.

"And give me a Nine-tailed Spirit Fox transformation card as well."

"No way, that transformation card costs 700 gold, how dare you ask me for that?! High-tier potions are also extremely expensive, and I saved them specifically to do the God of War quest..."

Xiang Huaizhi raised an eyebrow. "Didn't you want to help?"

"You call this helping?! You're killing me!"

"Do you still want to witness the sealing of the Spirit King firsthand?"

The crease in Lu Hang's forehead deepened.

"Do you still want to kill the God of War?"

Lu Hang fell silent.

"Do you still want to bring three healers into the dungeons in the future?"

Teeth gritted, Lu Hang said, "How many high-tier potions do you want, you bastard?"

Chapter 03

After class, Jing Huan picked up a bowl of hot and sour potato noodle soup from a street stall to-go and rushed home. Once there, he turned on his computer and was about to log into *Nine Heroes* when...

【Hello, Mirage server is currently at max player capacity. Please be patient and wait in the queue. There are still 999+ players ahead of you, with an estimated wait time of 37 minutes.】

Huh?!

Jing Huan felt as if he had gone back ten years. Back when *Nine Heroes* had just launched with a few servers, every player had to queue for more than ten minutes before they coud log in.

But isn't it already 2019? Why is there still a queue?

Is the game bugging out?

He tried to log on to other servers, and all of those took seconds. Mirage was the only one with a queue.

Thirty minutes later, he finally managed to squeeze into the server. As soon as he logged on, he received countless friend messages and, upon closer inspection, all from the same person.

[Friend] OFF!: Meimei, when will you go kill the Spirit King?

[Friend] OFF!: This quest only lasts for 48 hours!

[Friend] OFF!: If you don't start it soon, it'll be too late, hurry, hurry, hurry!

After he had finished reading all of them, Jing Huan replied.

[Friend] Sweet Little Jing: What's up with *Nine Heroes'* servers today? The game's so laggy that I had to queue for half an hour to log in.

[Friend] OFF!: You're finally on! A bunch of new characters suddenly logged onto the server, so of course, it's laggy!

[Friend] Sweet Little Jing: ?

[Friend] OFF!: Everyone made alt characters to watch you kill the Spirit King.

[Friend] Sweet Little Jing: ?

[Friend] OFF!: Right now, all the *Nine Heroes* streamers are live streaming their tutorial quest grind.

[Friend] OFF!: Meimei! You're super famous on *Nine Heroes* right now!!

As Jing Huan finished reading this message, a megaphone popped up in the bottom left corner of his chat.

【[All-server Megaphone] Stop Raining: Sweet Little Jing, Yearning For, wait a little longer for me! I'm only two levels away from leaving the novice village! Don't rush to kill the boss! Prepare yourselves some more!】

【[All-server Megaphone] Fleeting Online Dating Bliss: Shit, I'm still queuing. Can some of the players in front of me go offline so I can sneak closer to the front?】

【[All-server Megaphone] Destined to You: Do any insiders know when these two are planning to start the quest? Viewers have been camping in the stream for a whole day now.】

Chapter 03

Jing Huan was a little stunned.

The friend message interface flashed again. Frowning, he opened it, already preparing to tell OFF! to shut up.

[Friend] Yearning For: 1.

[Friend] Sweet Little Jing: OvO! Gege!

[Friend] Sweet Little Jing: Sorry aaaaah, I'm late. I had to queue for half an hour before I could log in. [Biting a handkerchief]

[Friend] Yearning For: Come to the city lord.

Jing Huan immediately flew over, only to find that the city lord was completely surrounded by players. With such a bustling crowd, it was impossible for him to locate Yearning For.

[Current] Peach Cheese Stan: She's here, she's here!! Sweet Little Jing is here!

[Current] Awaiting Nightfall: Finally, it's time to kill the Spirit King! HURRY!

[Current] Bloodlust: Why is Sweet Little Jing a Spirit Fox Den? How can they kill the Spirit King? Can she understand the sect skills?

How exactly does this group see me?

【Yearning For has sent you a party invite.】

Jing Huan quickly accepted it.

[Party] Sweet Little Jing: God of War-gege, why are there so many people here~? QvQ

[Party] Sweet Little Jing: If we wipe, won't that be really embarrassing? [Frightened]

Suddenly, a man's voice came through the headset. "Clear your inventory."

Before Jing Huan could react, a bunch of yellow text prompts appeared on the game interface.

【Yearning For has thrown you a Nine-tailed Spirit Fox Transformation Card x1.】

【Yearning For has thrown you Soul Revival Pills x5.】

【Yearning For has thrown you Red Recovery Beads x10.】

Xiang Huaizhi then said, "Go and deposit any money that you have."

Jing Huan was surprised but quickly came to his senses. "I don't have much money on me…"

Xiang Huaizhi acknowledged the admission and said, "Check the effects of these potions first. When the fight starts, find a corner to hide in. As long as you don't touch the boss, he won't attack you. Be aware of his AoE attacks, remember to heal yourself, and don't die."

"Huh?"

"If I die, run." Xiang Huaizhi paused. "Do what you did the last time you were being hunted, got it?"

Jing Huan blinked and finally understood. *Does he want to solo the Spirit King?*

Jing Huan had made good use of his time last night. After turning off his computer, he spent some time digging around for videos of players from other servers completing hidden quests.

Hidden quests could be described in one word: difficult.

The five battleground players barely managed to defeat the boss even after exhausting all their potions. By the time it fell, the ground was littered with bodies, and the lone survivor had only a sliver of health remaining. The scene was gruesome.

Where does Yearning For get this confidence to think that he can solo the Spirit King? He even had the audacity to ask me to just AFK in a corner? Who does he think he's looking down on?

Chapter 03

Lip curling, he turned on his microphone. "Gege, wouldn't I be slacking off a bit too much…I can't let you go and fight the monster alooone."

Xiang Huaizhi was busily checking his inventory to see if he was missing any potions, and didn't catch the poorly hidden mockery in the girl's tone. "It's fine. Get that transformation card ready."

Transformation cards were an essential item for PK, allowing one to transform into a beast summon from the game for a limited time and temporarily enhance one's attributes.

Each transformation card had different effects; the Nine-tailed Spirit Fox transformation card was best suited for the Spirit Fox Den sect since it boosted a player's movement speed by fifteen percent.

Jing Huan had just used the card and finished transforming when suddenly his friend messages started flashing.

[Friend] OFF!: [*Nine Heroes* live stream link: Yearning For's ex-wife, live streaming Mirage server's Spirit King quest.]

[Friend] OFF!: Meimei…come and take a look.

As soon as Jing Huan entered the live stream, he heard an affectedly sweet, loli voice.

"I believe everyone already knows about the matter between me and Yearning For, so don't poke at my sore spot during my livestream, okay?"

This voice was particularly familiar, and Jing Huan checked the voice chat list in the live stream. The live streamer was, of course, Fae Bae.

He couldn't help but find it funny. She had used Yearning For's name on her live stream title for clout, and yet she wasn't allowing people to bring him up?

"What kind of person is Yearning For? How should I put it…

When we first got together, he was very considerate and extremely thoughtful. He would log into my account every day to help me complete dailies, and even took me sightseeing and set off fireworks for me..." Fae Bae leisurely answered the viewer's questions, "Let's not talk about the IRL meeting, all right? If we talk about it anymore, I'll cry...You guys are asking about Sweet Little Jing?"

Fae Bae laughed. The disdain in her voice was thick when she spoke, "She's a female scammer who conned our guild elites out of their equipment. She has questionable morals and has become a household name on the server. Everyone is out to killl her. Who knows? Maybe after they finish the Spirit King quest, someone will initiate a forced PK against her."

Jing Huan had only heard her once and hadn't thought much of her. But now, after listening a bit longer, he realized that Fae Bae's voice was genuinely sweet; it could even be called an otaku's waifu voice!

Jing Huan glared at his voice changer, resentful. Although it turned his voice into a feminine one, it wasn't overly cutesy at all! With this voice, Lu Wenhao probably wouldn't even fall for it, let alone allow him to seduce Yearning For.

In the game, Yearning For had already brought them to Luojia Mountain. A large, roiling crowd trailed behind their party, so tightly packed that even the game IDs became unreadable.

He closed the live stream and pinched his voice, saying, "Gege, there are so many people following behind us. I'm so nervous..."

Yearning For's character continued moving forward, ignoring her.

Xiang Huaizhi wasn't good at sweet-talking young girls, so he simply remained silent.

Chapter 03

Jing Huan propped his chin on his hand and asked, "Gege, did you gather all these potions for me? They're such high quality, it must've taken a long time, aren't you busy?

"Are you working or still in school, hmmm?

"Gege, how long have you been playing this game?

"Gege…"

"A few years," Xiang Huaizhi interrupted him with a vague response.

Jing Huan gnashed his teeth.

What the hell do you mean by this? You take other women sight-seeing and set off fireworks for them, and yet you remain tight-lipped when it comes to me?

What, people don't have human rights unless their voices are sweet?

Finally, they arrived in front of the Spirit King, and Yearning For commanded, "Leave the party, and click on the NPC to receive the attribute enhancements."

"Okay, gege."

The Spirit King was a spider-like creature, pitch-black and unsettling to look at.

Jing Huan left the party, clicked on the NPC, and couldn't help but laugh.

Idle Pavilion was the top contributor for materials; he could feel the guild's pain through the screen.

After receiving the attribute enhancements, he rejoined the party.

Just as Xiang Huaizhi was about to ask if she had gotten it or not, he saw his party member typing.

[Current] Sweet Little Jing: Wow, 50% attribute enhancements!

[Starry-eyed] Thank you for all the large guilds' support, especially

Idle Pavilion for contributing the most materials. Thank you Idle Pavilion for your generous contribution~ [Heart]

Xiang Huaizhi was at a loss for words. *Aren't you kind of asking for a beating?*

[Current] Peach Cheese Stan: ...

[Current] Deep Forest Deer Sighing: ???

[Current] Echoes of Spring: [Smile]

[Current] Regardless of Lovesickness: What's your problem?

Worried that she would be forced into PKing by Idle Pavilion, Xiang Huaizhi said, "We're starting," and immediately entered the battle.

Unlike PK, players would be forcibly pulled into a battle map when fighting a boss monster. This time, the map chosen by the system was a gloomy cave—very fitting for the spider-like character setup.

Jing Huan crossed his legs like a boss and said, "It's so dark in there, I can't see anything…Gege, what do we do now?"

Xiang Huaizhi remained composed and checked the boss's attributes first.

Indeed, it was as he had thought.

Since it was a two-person boss battle, the battle difficulty had scaled down. In the absence of multiple healers, Warlocks, debuffers, buffers, and DPS, the system would definitely give the boss a few weaknesses including its inability to heal, its vulnerability to physical attacks, and its lack of buff skills.

On the other hand, the spider could cause extremely high magic damage, resist seals, even use seals on enemies.

"Make sure you hide yourself well." As soon as Xiang Huaizhi

finished speaking, the spider suddenly lowered its head and spat out a web aimed right at Jing Huan.

Xiang Huaizhi frowned and was about to shout at her to dodge when the other party jumped high into the air, evading the web.

Xiang Huaizhi let out a breath and began to examine the nearby terrain.

They had incredibly bad luck to be assigned the gloomy cave map, which consisted of a long tunnel, completely empty except for scattered rocks.

This meant Sweet Little Jing had absolutely nowhere to hide.

Jing Huan also noticed this. The entangled spider web on the ground disappeared in six seconds. If one carelessly got themselves trapped a second time, there would basically be no way for them to escape alive.

He picked up the grape and took a bite, the sweetness spreading through his mouth. "*Waaah,* gege, what should I dooo? There's nowhere to hide here."

The boss had already started throwing out AoE attacks. Xiang Huaizhi jumped out of the fireball's path, then unsheathed his longsword and struck the boss's face, his first blow landing a critical hit. "It's all right, try your best to dodge. If we die, we'll restart."

In her live stream, Fae Bae tittered with schadenfreude.

"Do you see Yearning For dealing all the damage while Sweet Little Jing only knows how to run around in circles? They'll probably wipe in less than ten minutes.

"Sweet Little Jing's gameplay? Of course, it's terrible. It was our guild elders who helped to play her character in the past. When she was playing herself, she'd even die during dungeon runs."

"I only got killed that time because I wasn't paying attention. I missed my heal, otherwise, there's no way she could have taken me out.

"She might've been able to heal better if she played as a Putuo Mountain, but she switched to Spirit Fox Den, a sect that relies on player skill for something as simple as healing teammates...She's really stupid."

She then spotted Sweet Little Jing, who was weaving in and out to dodge the boss's skills, suddenly turn around and place a Healing Spring in the southwest direction.

The healing skills from the other healer sects were all player-targeted and couldn't miss. Only Spirit Fox Dens' skills required predicting their party members' positions, with a miss meaning a wasted skill, therefore this required a high degree of player awareness. After all, in PK situations, party members were constantly moving and wouldn't just stand in place waiting for a heal.

Fae Bae laughed. "Look..."

Before she could finish speaking, she saw Yearning For descend from the skies and land perfectly on the Healing Spring, restoring a small section of his health bar.

Fae Bae's smile stiffened for a moment before she said, "How lucky, Yearning For must've seen the Healing Spring and jumped over to reach it."

But soon, she had nothing left to say.

Ten minutes had passed, and every Healing Spring Sweet Little Jing tossed out had landed precisely at Yearning For's feet.

If it was just once or twice, you could say that Yearning For was good at catching her skills, but ten times...No one could afford to

be distracted to look for Healing Springs while fiercely battling a boss.

What surprised her the most was that the battle had been underway for so long, but Sweet Little Jing was still at full health!

[Current] Peach Cheese Stan: Holy shit? Those Healing Spring throws are awesome!

[Current] Inexplicable Feelings: …Is she using hacks?

[Current] Transforming Into Wind: So, is Yearning For really good at receiving, or is Sweet Little Jing great at pitching?

[Current] Melted Snow: Isn't Sweet Little Jing's positioning the most awesome thing?! She hasn't lost a single health point, isn't that too ridiculous?!

[Current] Silent Affection: What are you bragging about? Isn't this normal? Her movement speed was increased by 15% after all. If Yearning For wasn't the one DPSing, he also wouldn't lose any health.

[Current] OFF!: God Xiang's DPS is really fucking insane…

The people watching from outside couldn't figure things out, but those involved knew exactly what was happening.

Lu Hang's eyes were locked onto the game as he crowed in wonderment.

Xiang Huaizhi took another sip of the delicious Healing Spring and couldn't help but raise his eyebrows. "Thanks."

Jing Huan replied sweetly, "You're welcome, gege."

Throwing out Healing Springs was no challenge for Jing Huan; his prediction skills had always been very accurate, and most of his attention was focused on Yearning For.

Not to mention that despite being a scumbag, Yearning For was

highly skilled, avoiding most of the boss's skills while dealing maximum damage.

Had it been anyone else, they probably would've been beaten down by the boss by now. Not even a hundred Healing Springs would've been sufficient enough to heal them.

Half an hour later, the boss was finally enraged, meaning it only had five percent of its health points left.

"Watch out," Xiang Huaizhi said. "It's about to unleash its ultimate attack."

Just as he said that, they watched the spider demon spring into the air, releasing a densely packed swarm of baby spiders.

The crowd watching the battle outside instantly erupted in excitement.

[Current] I Really Like Lulu: The fuck?! This ultimate skill animation is too disgusting! Kill the *Nine Heroes'* concept designer!!

[Current] The Wind is Freer Than Me: What skill is this? I've never seen it before.

[Current] BrbOrNot: The official website just updated the boss information two minutes ago! This is the spider demon's ultimate attack: if a small spider hits a player, it'll seal them and deal triple the damage!

[Current] Silent Affection: Ha ha, then aren't they about to wipe?

"Damn it, isn't this a foul? They didn't even give the players any time to prepare!" Lu Hang slammed the table.

"It's fine." Xiang Huaizhi was unfazed. "Now that we know the pattern, it's fine if we wipe. We can just do it again."

A few seconds later, the spider army disappeared, and the players could finally see the situation on the map clearly.

 Chapter 03

Sweet Little Jing was hunched over, her claws firmly embedded in the soil and forming a magical shield just large enough to perfectly cover the two of them.

This skill was widely recognized by the players as the most useless shield skill in the Spirit Fox Den sect. Its drawbacks were plenty—it had a limited range, a long casting time, and could only be set right at the caster's feet. For most, dodging early was a far more effective strategy than wasting time casting this shield.

But now, Sweet Little Jing had used this mediocre skill to securely protect Yearning For.

Sweet Little Jing must have jumped behind Yearning For just before the boss's ultimate attack. Moreover, to accomplish such a maneuver like this, she must have cast this skill four seconds in advance.

The Current Channel instantly fell silent, and Lu Hang's mouth hung open, speechless for a long time.

Only Xiang Huaizhi quirked up a corner of his mouth and whispered, "Nice."

When Jing Huan pulled himself out of his daze, he felt his fingtertips tingle slightly.

It had been a long time since he had played such an exciting dungeon, and it was truly draining. Near the end of the fight, he had gone to block this enormous attack with only the thought of trying it out.

Fortunately, his gamble paid off.

Holy shit, I'm really awesome, Jing Huan thought to himself. *With skills like these, who needs Yearning For? I can solo the boss myself, right?*

"Ah." He felt his heart thump quickly, and even his tone was tinged with joy as he cheered insincerely, "Gege praised me!"

With a graceful leap, Yearning For raised his longsword with both hands and plunged it straight into the top of the spider's head. The spider struggled and howled twice before falling to the ground with a crash.

【System Announcement: Congratulations to Sweet Little Jing and Yearning For for successfully sealing the trouble-making Spirit King and earning the title "Spirit King Slayer."】

The moment the spider demon fell, a large treasure chest beside it popped open.

Ignoring the collective astonishment and questions from the onlookers, Xiang Huaizhi said, "Go pick it up."

Jing Huan startled. "Ah? You want me to pick it up?"

"Yes."

The most thrilling moment of killing a boss was opening up the reward afterward. Jing Huan quickly moved his character in front of the treasure chest and promptly sat down.

[Current] Sweet Little Jing: This faithful girl is willing to be a vegetarian all her life, all I wish for from the GMs is a divine artifact, a spiritual beast, enchanted spirit orbs, divine artifact crafting manuals, or dragon claw seals…[Beating a wooden fish while chanting a sutra]

[Current] Yearning For: …

[Current] Peach Cheese Stan: …

[Current] Echoes of Spring: …

[Current] I Really Like Lulu: …

Ritual completed, Jing Huan moved the mouse, bursting with anticipation and gently left-clicked.

Chapter 03

【Congratulations on successfully sealing the current Spirit King Spider Demon! After packing up and heading home, the Spider Demon left behind a delicious steamed bun (a low-level medicinal item that restores a hundred health points when used). Please accept it with a smile, young heroes!】

Jing Huan stared silently then shouted, "Huh?!" A string of expletives ran through his mind before he choked out, "GMs, you mother…"

Xiang Huaizhi lightly coughed.

Jing Huan forcefully swallowed all the colorful words bubbling to his mouth. Incensed and aggrieved, he changed his words last minute, "…your mother will definitely see an inflation in grocery prices!" He still didn't feel that was enough. "Everything will be ridiculously overpriced! Prices will double!"

Upon hearing these words, Xiang Huaizhi went slightly rigid at first but then couldn't help but chuckle softly.

"Steamed buns?! Damn, this is too much, not even a decent guaranteed reward? You can get ten for one copper coin at the general store…" Lu Hang noticed him laughing and cried out in horror, "What are you doing? Have you gone mad from anger?"

"No." The game was still playing the cutscene. Xiang Huaizhi hurried him out the door as he said, "You've already finished watching, so you should go now."

"Shit, you tricked me out of so many potions, and now you're kicking me out after using all of them up?" Lu Hang *tsked*. "You truly are a scumbag."

"I still remember the IDs of those three healers."

"Okay, okay, okay, I can't afford to mess with you, I'm leaving now. There's also a basketball game at 7 p.m., and I hate playing at night. I can't see anything without my contacts, and we have to compete with those square-dancing grandmothers for the court." Halfway through his speech, Lu Hang's gaze unconsciously shifted to Xiang Huaizhi's calf. "Does your leg still hurt?"

"It stopped hurting a long time ago," Xiang Huaizhi said. "Bring me back a bowl of cold skin noodles."

"Okay." Lu Hang quickly changed into a jersey and left with his phone.

As the dormitory door closed, the cutscene ended, and the game interface returned to Luojia Mountain. They were surrounded by people, and with chat bubbles overlapping everywhere, it was impossible to see what was being said.

His friend message icon was constantly flashing.

[Friend] Echoes of Spring: After you're done, disband your party.

[Friend] Yearning For: ?

[Friend] Echoes of Spring: Our guild has five parties waiting outside to kill Sweet Little Jing.

[Friend] Yearning For: .

Xiang Huaizhi opened the party menu and glanced at the little spirit fox in the party.

【Sweet Little Jing throws you Steamed Buns x99.】

"Gege, I'm sorry, *waaah*, I didn't find anything good for you." Sweet Little Jing's voice rang through his headset. "I promised to give you whatever I dug up. Don't shun them, they can heal you, at least a little."

Xiang Huaizhi had never been one to meddle in other people's business. He'd never even joined a guild despite being a long-time

Chapter 03

player of *Nine Heroes*. His EXP farming party was a pickup group, and even in the arena, he only played 1V1. Lu Hang had mocked him more than once, saying that he turned a large social MMORPG into a single-player game.

He closed the party menu and reopened the friend chat window.

[Friend] Yearning For: Are you guys sure that this character's owner hasn't changed?

[Friend] Echoes of Spring: We're sure.

[Friend] Echoes of Spring: It has changed.

[Friend] Yearning For: ?

[Friend] Echoes of Spring: While the previous owner of this character couldn't play that well, we can't rule out that she hired someone to play for her.

[Friend] Echoes of Spring: But regardless if the owner is the same person or not, we're still going to kill her.

[Friend] Yearning For: Griefing[1]?

[Friend] Echoes of Spring: I wouldn't call it that. She previously caused one of our guild members to lose their equipment. If we don't kill her, the guild members will not be pleased.

Xiang Huaizhi closed the chat window, grabbed the little spirit fox, and sprinted toward the teleportation NPC.

[Friend] Echoes of Spring: ?

[Friend] Echoes of Spring: What's your intention here? Do you want to get involved?

---

1   This is when a player in a multiplayer video game deliberately and intentionally irritates, harasses, annoys, or trolls other players so that the targeted player is not enjoying themselves.

[Friend] Yearning For: I have no reason to kick out my party member for you guys to kill.

[Friend] Yearning For: There are only two people in this party. If you want to initiate a forced PK, go ahead.

[Friend] Echoes of Spring: ...

Yes, there were, and this time, the core members of Idle Pavilion were waiting outside to ambush Sweet Little Jing. The odds of victory were high with five parties against two people.

But high odds were one thing; they were apprehensive of ending up with the same fate as Fae Bae where they were the ones being killed, consequently losing their equipment. And they were all wearing top-tier equipment; they didn't want to take this risk.

On the other end, Jing Huan grabbed the newly opened bag of spicy strips next to him and fiercely ripped out a big piece.

Stupid GMs, right now you're this spicy strip, being chewed up into shreds and swallowed up by me.

After gulping down the spicy strip, he was about to count the leftover potions on his character when his friend message icon flashed.

[Friend] OFF!: Meimei! Why are you still strolling around Luojia Mountain?! Do you know that five parties are hot on your heels right now, just waiting for the right moment to kill you?!

Jing Huan glanced back, and it was true.

However, he was a Spirit Fox Den, so why would he be afraid of being hunted? Besides, even if he died, he had nothing valuable to lose.

Using his mic, he called out, "God of War-gege, are you still there?"

"Mm," Xiang Huaizhi answered after bringing her to the safe zone.

"How much did the transformation card and potions cost? I'll pay you back." Jing Huan opened *Nine Heroes'* currency recharge menu.

Xiang Huaizhi refused, "No need."

"No way, you even helped me kill the Spirit King. It's unreasonable to have you also pay for the potions."

Not wanting to argue about this kind of thing any longer, Xiang Huaizhi said, "Pay whatever you want, I guess. I didn't spend anything." He paused for a moment then suddenly asked, "Have you played *Nine Heroes* before?"

"Nope." Jing Huan had fabricated a story a long time ago. "But I've played other games similar to *Nine Heroes*, so I found it very easy to get into. Did I play pretty well just now?"

Xiang Huaizhi tossed out a single syllable, "Mm."

"Mm"???

Who wouldn't be awestruck at bearing witness to my godly, earth-shattering play just now? Who wouldn't give me a thumbs up?!

And you're just giving me an "mm"?!

"Then, gege," the girl's voice was cautious, with a hint of humility, as she spoke, "can I...run dungeons with you in the future?"

Xiang Huaizhi didn't respond.

"I'm very accurate with my heals, you saw it just now! I can handle any dungeon, I definitely won't hold you back!" Jing Huan paused. "Ah...Gege, do you find me too troublesome because I'm being hunted?"

"You can open up party recruitment by the dungeon NPC,"

Xiang Huaizhi said. "You won't get killed if you stay in the dungeon area." His implication being that you wouldn't be hunted in dungeons, so you could find others to form a party with.

The polite refusal couldn't have been more obvious, and if it were anyone else, they would have given up a long time ago.

Jing Huan had a whining tinge to his voice. "But I just want to run dungeons with you, gege."

[Party] Sweet Little Jing: [Crying my eyes out]

[Party] Sweet Little Jing: [Rolling on the ground in a tantrum]

[Party] Sweet Little Jing: [*WAAAAAAAH*]

Xiang Huaizhi was getting a headache from these stickers, but he also inexplicably found them amusing.

[Party] Yearning For: ...

[Party] Sweet Little Jing: [Hugging thigh]

"Why does it have to be me?" Xiang Huaizhi asked.

A rustling sound came from the other end of the headset.

Not expecting that Yearning For would speak through the mic again, Jing Huan hastily put down his spicy strips and said softly in a nervous, shy, and somewhat girlish tone, "Because…I started playing *Nine Heroes* for you, gege."

After an interval of time, Xiang Huaizhi said, "We'll see."

Yearning For's in-game character disbanded the party and zoomed away from the crowd.

Jing Huan considered what he had just said, and shook his head while clicking his tongue.

Amazing.

He learned a lot thanks to Lu Wenhao's daily voice calls with his catfishing wife; acting flirty and cute now came naturally to him.

He was planning to teleport back to his sect to do dailies when a message suddenly popped up on the screen.

【Fae Bae has set you as a private chat recipient.】

[Private] Fae Bae: Are you there?

[Private] Sweet Little Jing: [Doubtful]

[Private] Fae Bae: What is your relationship with Yearning For?

[Private] Sweet Little Jing: Ah, this has nothing to do with you, right? [Shy]

[Private] Fae Bae: Heh, you want to pursue him romantically, don't you?

[Private] Sweet Little Jing: O-O! Ah!

[Private] Sweet Little Jing: ...Is it that obvious? [Covering face]

Fae Bae sneered at these two stickers. *Who are you trying to act cute to?*

[Private] Fae Bae: Save it, he'll never fall for you.

[Private] Sweet Little Jing: You don't get to decide that, right? Jiejie. [Tapping fingers together]

[Private] Fae Bae: ?

[Private] Fae Bae: Who are you calling jiejie? Are we that close?

[Private] Sweet Little Jing: I just wrecked your equipment two days ago. Of course, we're not close, but you're the one privately chatting with me. [Aggrieved]

[Private] Fae Bae: ...

[Private] Fae Bae: Forget it, I won't argue with you. I've come to give you some advice: open your eyes. Yearning For is a giant scumbag, and it's best you stay away from him.

[Private] Sweet Little Jing: Ah, jiejie, I thought you of all people would understand me.

[Private] Fae Bae: ?

[Private] Fae Bae: Understand what?

[Private] Sweet Little Jing: Women only fall for bad boys. [Shy]

[Private] Sweet Little Jing: Jiejie, don't try to dissuade me, I've made up my mind.

[Private] Sweet Little Jing: In my heart, I already belong to Xiang-gege. [Holding heart]

Jing Huan was so focused on trolling Fae Bae that he didn't realize that all his words had been live streamed to Fae Bae's 30,000 viewers.

Xiang Huaizhi had just finished some dailies when he received a system notification.

【Friend Sweet Little Jing has gifted you 1,200 gold, which has already been placed in the special vault for you. Please check it promptly.】

He went to the vault and immediately transferred this gold, along with the money he had spent himself, to Lu Hang.

After a moment's thought, he transferred 500 gold back to Sweet Little Jing.

Although killing the Spirit King didn't reward them with any items, it did have a very generous experience reward, plus they also got a double EXP boost for the next seven days along with a Spirit King buff. In addition, Sweet Little Jing did so well with her Healing Springs he hardly used his potions. This 500 gold could be considered a service fee.

After finishing all his dailies, he was about to log off when his private chat started flashing.

Fae Bae had sent a sixty-second voice message. Xiang Huaizhi frowned, his reluctance clear as he did not want to even click on it.

[Private] Yearning For: Just type if you have something to say.

[Private] Fae Bae: You don't even want to listen to my voice messages anymore.

[Private] Fae Bae: You used to insist on calling me before sleeping.

Xiang Huaizhi felt like he couldn't communicate with this person and decided not to reply.

[Private] Fae Bae: You got bored of me and you're ready to move on to that Sweet Little Jing now, right?

[Private] Yearning For: ?

[Private] Fae Bae: She's throwing herself at you like this, yet you're still interested?

[Private] Yearning For: I'm going to say this one last time: I wasn't the one playing this character for the past few months, and the person you were online dating and met IRL wasn't me. Don't drag me into this, and don't drag other people in either.

Having said his piece, Xiang Huaizhi logged off.

Just as he turned off the computer, his phone rang. He glanced at the caller ID and went to the balcony with his phone in hand.

It was the rainy season in the city now. Gazing at the downpour outside, Xiang Huaizhi picked up the call and greeted, "Mom."

"Mm." The clacking of mahjong tiles sounded from the other end. "Have you eaten yet?"

"Not yet, what about you?"

"Yes, I'm just chatting with a few of your aunties right now," Mrs. Xiang said. "I noticed it was raining outside, so I thought I'd call to check if your leg is hurting."

A few months ago, Xiang Huaizhi had accidentally fallen while playing basketball and bruised his bone. It wasn't especially serious; even the doctor said he'd be fine with a brace and after resting for half a month. However, his mother didn't feel that way. She ordered him to recuperate at home for more than two months, forcing him to drink so much bone broth soup that he grew sick of the taste, before she finally allowed him to return to school.

"It doesn't hurt. I just fell, it's not like it's arthritis." Xiang Huaizhi leaned against the windowsill. "You should worry more about Dad."

"And why would I need to do that?" A muffled sound came from the other end. "Oh sorry, I just won again…Xiangxiang, Mom's going to hang up now, take care at school."

Xiang Huaizhi smiled helplessly. "Understood."

The next day, Xiang Huaizhi had a whole day of classes.

Lu Hang was lethargic in the early hours of the morning and fell so soundly asleep beside him that he began to snore. Xiang Huaizhi jabbed him awake before the professor could notice and get mad.

Lu Hang rubbed his eyes and said, "What's going on? Is class over?"

Xiang Huaizhi said indifferently, "No, it's not, but if you keep sleeping, say goodbye to those course credits."

Lu Hang jolted awake and immediately straightened his back.

"Shit, it's because that movie was almost three hours long. It was close to four when I finished watching it." Lu Hang yawned. "Oh man, I'm still super tired. Whatever, I'll find something to do."

He pulled out his phone and started scrolling through the *Nine Heroes* forums.

 Chapter 03

"Hey, someone posted a spectator video of you and Sweet Little Jing killing the Spirit King. It got over 10,000 views overnight. Wow, so awesome, bro."

Xiang Huaizhi replied, "Only 10,000?"

"Hey, watch your tone. Other people's all-server PK videos don't get views as quickly as yours." Lu Hang scrolled down on his screen and paused when he spotted something. He yelped, "What the hell!"

The professor couldn't take it anymore. "Lu Hang, if you don't want to listen, leave, but do not disturb the other students in class!"

Lu Hang apologized, "My bad, Professor."

As soon as the professor looked away, Lu Hang quickly tugged Xiang Huaizhi's sleeve and handed over his phone, saying, "Look!"

Xiang Huaizhi lowered his head and glanced down. "What is it?"

"Sweet Little Jing's grand love confession!" Lu Hang said. "And you're the object of the said confession!"

It was an extremely long time before Xiang Huaizhi finally shifted his gaze to the phone.

This was a recording of Fae Bae's live stream, featuring the private chat between Fae Bae and Sweet Little Jing.

When he saw the words "women only fall for bad boys," the corners of his mouth twitched slightly, unsure of what expression to make.

Lu Hang held back his laughter until his face turned red and said, "Xiang-gege, you there?"

"At your mom's." Xiang Huaizhi threw his phone back at him.

"What, Sweet Little Jing can call you that, but I can't?" Lu Hang said. "Two years of sleeping with you, all in vain!"

"We shared a dorm room for two years," Xiang Huaizhi corrected him. "And she never called me that."

Lu Hang asked, "Then what does she usually call you?"

Gege. God of War-gege. Neither of which seems that much better than Xiang-gege.

Xiang Huaizhi pursed his lips and said, "Anyway, she doesn't call me that. Are you going to pay attention in class or not? If you don't want to listen, leave and don't disturb my studies."

Lu Hang nodded and saved a screenshot of the chat. "All right, you study. I'm just going to read these comments."

After a moment, Xiang Huaizhi put down his pen. "What are the comments saying?"

Lu Hang said, "Don't get distracted now. Why don't you focus on your studies, hm?"

At the look Xiang Huaizhi shot him, Lu Hang hurriedly said, "All right, all right, all right, they're not saying much, just that Sweet Little Jing is shamelessly throwing herself at you. Oh, and someone is making up stories about you and Fae Bae, which, I have to say, is written quite realistically. It's more moving than the TV dramas that my mom watches. They make Fae Bae look so pitiful. If I didn't know the truth, I'd also be sharpening my knives to stab the scumbag."

Xiang Huaizhi said, "Like you can kill me."

"Right," Lu Hang relented.

After class, the two had dinner and then headed back to the dormitory.

When Xiang Huaizhi came out of the shower, he heard Lu Hang shouting, "Are you done messing around? Hurry up and log in, the dungeon progress refreshes at midnight. We still have three dungeons left to clear!"

Xiang Huaizhi dried his hair and said coldly, "If we didn't

Chapter 03

have to drag three healers around, we could finish in two hours."

"Nope, not anymore. This time, I only called for two. I eliminated the other healer because her voice wasn't sweet enough." Lu Hang opened his friend list and scrolled through it. "I'll call for a DPS then...Haa, at this time, almost everyone on my list has already ran all their dungeons."

Xiang Huaizhi turned on the computer. Just as he logged into *Nine Heroes*, he received a message from Sweet Little Jing.

[Friend] Sweet Little Jing: 0.0 Gege, why did you refund me 500 gold?

[Friend] Yearning For: Spirit King service fee.

[Friend] Sweet Little Jing: No, no! You carried me, so if anyone has to pay, it should be me.

[Friend] Sweet Little Jing: After I finish gathering herbs, I'll transfer it back to you. [Patting head]

Xiang Huaizhi's cursor hovered over Sweet Little Jing's game profile picture. Her coordinates showed she was in Herb Valley.

He flew to Luoxia Mountain, planning to squeeze in two quests while Lu Hang was recruiting someone. He saw a five-person party approaching from the right, and what caught his attention was the title "Elites of Idle Pavilion" above their names.

He wasn't sure if it was his imagination, but it seemed like the party leader deliberately steered out of his line of sight and changed routes after seeing him.

In just a few seconds, Xiang Huaizhi understood why.

In the world of *Nine Heroes*, every map was interconnected. Some zones had a direct path of flight, while the other zones required a designated teleportation portal.

Herb Valley was one of those zones that couldn't be flown to directly, and could only be accessed through the teleportation portal at Luoxia Mountain.

Those five people were hunting Sweet Little Jing.

"Hurry up, let's go," someone in the party said softly, not realizing that their microphone was set to all. "Don't let Yearning For see us. If he intervenes, we won't be able to kill her."

"Who says he won't? Do you really think Sweet Little Jing's interest is one-sided? Didn't you see Yearning For help her kill the Spirit King yesterday?"

"Crap, my microphone was accidentally set to all…" The voice cut off abruptly.

Xiang Huaizhi controlled his character and began helping the NPC copy the painting scroll.

Idle Pavilion was aggressively hunting Sweet Little Jing. If she really wanted to hide, staying in the safe zone for a week would dampen the enthusiasm of those in pursuit.

But she was extremely stubborn, always wandering outside the safe zone. If she got killed, she only had herself to blame and was unworthy of pity.

Just as he was thinking about that, the said stubborn player sent him a message.

[Friend] Sweet Little Jing: [Restorative Spirit Herb]

[Friend] Sweet Little Jing: Gege, I dug this up!

[Friend] Sweet Little Jing: This material is needed to kill the God of War, right? I'll bring it to you when I'm done digging. [Blows a kiss]

Xiang Huaizhi could only wonder, *What exactly is going on in that person's head?*

 Chapter 03

He calculated that it would take about two minutes to walk from where he was to her coordinates. Those five people should be getting there soon.

Forget it. Getting killed once might teach her a lasting lesson. She didn't care about being killed, so why should he worry?

Ten seconds later.

[Friend] Yearning For: Have you cleared the three Water Demon dungeons before?

[Friend] Yearning For: Fly to the main city NPC. If you're not here in 10 seconds, I'm starting without you.

Jing Huan had been happily gathering herbs and was surprised by this message.

Ten seconds? Do you want me to kill myself?

After complaining, he quickly stopped the gathering herb action, chanted for three seconds, and whooshed back to the main city.

The five Idle Pavilion members who had just arrived in the zone stood there dumbly. They watched with their own eyes as Sweet Little Jing flew away, unable to react for a long time.

"Damn it! Didn't I tell you Yearning For would definitely tip Sweet Little Jing off? Look, she even stopped gathering herbs halfway!"

On the other end, Lu Hang scrolled through his friends but still couldn't find anyone to invite. "Forget it, I'll just grab a random player from the World Channel. Tsk, I hate taking randoms into the Water Demon dungeon, it's too easy for everything to go to shit."

"No need, I got someone," Xiang Huaizhi said. "Go gather at the main city."

"Coming!" Lu Hang soared over to the main city with two healers in tow. "We're here, just apply directly to join my party. Who did you call over? A Warlock? A Mage? Or a physical DPS?"

"Spirit Fox Den. Give me party lead."

Lu Hang passed over the party lead. "What?! Why did you call someone from that sect? Are they supposed to be there as cheerleaders? This is worse than calling another healer…Wait." He stilled. "Which Spirit Fox Den did you invite?"

As soon as he said that, an additional person suddenly popped up in the party menu. It was a very familiar character wearing a familiar outfit, and swishing a familiar fox tail.

[Party] Sweet Little Jing: [Surprise][Cheer][Tossing flowers everywhere]

[Party] Sweet Little Jing: Good evening, everyone. [Blows a kiss]

The two healers in the party knew each other. They were originally chatting happily, but when Sweet Little Jing joined, they immediately muted their mics and didn't say a word.

On the other hand, this sparked Lu Hang's interest. "Hey…how did you end up calling her over?"

Xiang Huaizhi succinctly replied, "Just asked her on a whim."

Lu Hang enthusiastically crossed his legs.

[Party] Long Road Ahead: Good evening. [Blows a kiss]

[Party] Long Road Ahead: Have you ever done the Water Demon dungeon before?

[Party] Sweet Little Jing: Nope. [Shut up]

Jing Huan was telling the truth; he really hadn't done it before. In the four years that he had been away from the game, *Nine Heroes* had added many new dungeons, one of which was Water Demon Wreaking Havoc.

[Party] Sweet Little Jing: Is this dungeon difficult?

[Party] Long Road Ahead: It's the hardest dungeon, but to be honest, it's actually not that bad. You can even auto the little mobs at the beginning, but the boss is difficult to kill, and squishy characters can be wiped out in one hit.

[Party] Sweet Little Jing: Got it! [Patting head]

After replying, Jing Huan casually opened a Water Demon dungeon guide and skimmed through it.

As Long Road Ahead said, the little mobs at the beginning were the Water Demon's "battle intent" and weren't much of a threat. However, after they died, they got absorbed into the Water Demon, bolstering its power. According to many players, it took only ten minutes to clear the little mobs but two hours to kill the boss.

Other guides only had double-digit comments, but the number of comments in the Water Demon dungeon guide reached into the thousands, most of them telling the game developers to eat shit.

However, difficulty aside, it was still just a dungeon. With five people working together, it could still be cleared, especially with Yearning For's stats. Having a character like that in the party, even carrying four healers would be a breeze.

During the few minutes Jing Huan was reading the dungeon guide, everyone in the team was AFKing, not making a sound.

Only the two healers were venting in a private chat.

[Friend] Love is Sharing Noms: Why is Sweet Little Jing here? I don't want to run dungeons with her at all.

[Friend] Ji Xiaonian: I don't know either. We already have two healers, what's she here for? Is she here to be a cheerleader? [Rolling eyes]

[Friend] Love is Sharing Noms: And she's a male catfisher, right? Look at how she talks, it's so fake...[Shut up]

[Friend] Ji Xiaonian: She shouldn't be. Someone heard her voice before; she's a girl. Maybe she's just a freak.

[Friend] Love is Sharing Noms: Those guys must've been blind, right? Have they never seen a woman before? They all got fooled.

[Friend] Ji Xiaonian: I heard from a friend that the character has a new owner. The previous owner couldn't play as well as her.

[Friend] Love is Sharing Noms: That's unlikely. Why would Idle Pavilion still be hunting her if she wasn't the scammer? Really though, her skills are pretty average. It was mostly luck + Yearning For's positioning skills with the Spirit King last time. Anyway, I don't like her!

[Friend] Ji Xiaonian: Me neither. I could beat up ten people who talk like that! Hey, wait a minute, I suddenly have an idea...

It was impossible to predict when girls were going to be kind or hostile; Jing Huan had no idea he had already made enemies of some of his party members. He bit off the rest of his popsicle and switched back to the game.

[Party] Sweet Little Jing: God of War-gege [Peeking out], have you had dinner yet?

Xiang Huaizhi glanced at these words, then lowered his head and continued to read WeChat.

"Hey, Sweet Little Jing is looking for you." Seeing this scene, Lu Hang couldn't help but comment, "You're so mean, pretending to be AFK in this day and age?"

"Mind your own business," Xiang Huaizhi replied without looking up.

Lu Hang *tsked* twice, then typed on the keyboard.

[Party] Long Road Ahead: He's AFKing to watch a movie. [Shh]

[Party] Sweet Little Jing: Oh, oh, how do you know. 0.0

[Party] Long Road Ahead: I'm in the same dorm as him.

[Party] Sweet Little Jing: Ah, the company dormitory?

[Party] Long Road Ahead: No, the student dormitory!

Student dormitory?

Jing Huan frowned in confusion. He remembered Fae Bae had said Yearning For was a thirty-year-old middle-aged man.

Was it possible he just looked old?

His friend message icon flashed, and Jing Huan shook his head, temporarily putting his perplexity aside.

[Friend] OFF!: Wow, meimei!

In the past few days, Jing Huan had cleared out his friend list, leaving only Yearning For and OFF!. The former went without saying and the latter...was rather interesting, so keeping him around didn't hurt.

[Friend] Sweet Little Jing: [Doubtful]

[Friend] OFF!: You're too wild, aren't you?

[Friend] OFF!: But it's very enthusiastic, gege supports you! Don't take it to heart! Never mind what others say!

[Friend] Sweet Little Jing: ...What are you talking about.

[Friend] OFF!: Your love confession to Yearning For! I watched it all!

Jing Huan was bewildered.

He had been planning to confess his love but that was all it was—a plan. With Yearning For's attitude toward him right now, he'd be crazy to say anything.

[Friend] Sweet Little Jing: I didn't confess to him~ [Surprised] What did you watch?

[Friend] OFF!: No way, you still don't know?

[Friend] OFF!: [Link share: Broadcasting Sweet Little Jing's Heartfelt Confession!]

Just seeing the title made Jing Huan feel uneasy.

He clicked on the video, and the moment he saw the chat, an indescribable embarrassment immediately surged from his feet and rushed straight to his head.

Shit!

How did my chat logs with Fae Bae appear here?!

Jing Huan was immediately dumbfounded, his scalp tingling with shock from his own bold remarks in the video. The worst part was that the video was edited to only show what he said with all of Fae Bae's replies cut out.

It took Jing Huan a while to regain his composure. He took a sip of water to settle his nerves.

Calm down, I have to calm down. The video has only a few hundred views, and most of those are probably just people hunting for drama. Most likely, very few people in-game know about it, let alone Yearning For.

He looked at the game, hoping for the best.

[Party] Long Road Ahead: What about you, Sweet Little Jing? How old are you? Are you also still in school?

[Party] Long Road Ahead: Hello?

[Party] Long Road Ahead: [Doubtful] Are you ignoring me because I'm not enough of a bad boy?

Jing Huan's brain froze.

Chapter 03

Ah fuck! I'm going to kill Fae Bae!!!

Xiang Huaizhi also saw what Lu Hang wrote. Frowning, he asked, "Are you that bored? Did you have to mention that?"

"Just teasing her," Lu Hang said. "Don't you think she's quite interesting? Nowadays, the girls in these games are all fierce, and when they start tearing into each other, it's like World War III. Someone so soft and cute as Jingjing is a rare species."

Noticing that the little spirit fox was staying quiet, Lu Hang mumbled, "Hey wait, did she AFK halfway through our conversation?"

Of course, Jing Huan hadn't just tabbed out of the game. He had outright left his computer desk and sprinted to the bathroom to wash his face.

That video was too embarrassing, and his cheeks were burning hot. Pretending to be a woman and acting cute in front of Yearning For was nothing to him. Having the chat history shoved in front of his face out of the blue though...

He was even wondering if he had been possessed back then.

Just as he finished wiping his face with a towel, his phone suddenly rang. It was a special notification tone from Weibo.

Jing Huan's Weibo was a wasteland, filled with stupid comments he made when he was younger. He couldn't be bothered to post anything new or delete his old posts. He had a few dozen followers, all friends, and the only person he specially followed was his jie, Liang Ran.

He instantly opened up Weibo.

【Liang Ran: Everything will be better. [Photo]】

The photo she had taken was of the sea, a vast expanse of blue without waves or ripples.

Jing Huan liked and commented on the picture immediately.

【Top Dog of Mancheng No. 1 High: [Hug][Hug]】

Liang Ran replied extremely quickly.

【Liang Ran: [Crying]】

Looking at the tears on the yellow emoji's face, Jing Huan recalled Liang Ran's haggard appearance when passing through the security check. The emotion that he had felt earlier was instantly stamped out, trampled on, and buried deep.

He sat back at the computer desk and threw his phone aside.

[Party] Sweet Little Jing: Aaah sorry, I just went to the restroom... Thankfully, we haven't started the boss fight yet. QAQ

[Party] Sweet Little Jing: Long Road Ahead, you're so annoying, why did you mention that!! [Angry] [Blushing]

[Party] Sweet Little Jing: ...Don't tell me that God of War-gege saw that video too? Ah, I don't want to live anymore~! [Screaming while covering face][Crying]

Jing Huan selected all the cute stickers in the game and sent them all at once.

Embarrassment? Shame? Bashfulness?

Nonexistent.

The passionate confession in the video came from Sweet Little Jing. What does that have to do with me, Jing Huan?

Xiang Huaizhi looked at those cutesy stickers and felt his head hurt more than when he was solving those advanced math problems. Not to mention, this person typed at lightning speed, sending out a flurry of stickers in seconds.

[Party] Yearning For: Didn't see it.

Once the message was sent, he warned, "If you tease her again, go clear the dungeons by yourself in the future."

Chapter 03

"Weren't you chatting on WeChat? When did you have eyes on your forehead?"

[Party] Sweet Little Jing: That's good then. [Nearly crying]

[Party] Yearning For: Get ready, we're about to reach the boss.

Jing Huan sat up straight and summoned his Nine-tailed Spirit Fox.

[Party] Sweet Little Jing: I'm ready now~ Gege. ^^

"Yo, she even has a Nine-tailed Spirit Fox," Lu Hang remarked. "Why didn't she summon it when you guys were fighting the Spirit King before?"

Xiang Huaizhi replied, "The Spirit King dealt AoE attacks the entire time. Since beast summons can't dodge, should she have summoned it to die?"

"That's true..." Lu Hang said. "I heard she bought this character for tens of thousands of yuan, so it seems like she's a little rich lady."

The scenery and characters in *Nine Heroes* were very beautiful, and the beast summons were no different. Players often summoned them just to show them off outside of battles. Lu Hang and the two healers had summoned their beasts a long time ago. Lu Hang's beast was a spotted deer, while the two healers led rabbits around.

Jing Huan put down his water glass and saw Yearning For slowly summon...a flower?

To be precise, it was a huge, tightly closed pink flower. He watched as the flower stood still for two seconds, then suddenly bloomed, revealing a slender and elegant flower fairy inside. The fairy was tiny and cute, sitting gracefully in the center of the flower, her head swaying slightly, glowing all around.

...What an extravagant and flamboyant beast summon.

[Party] Sweet Little Jing: Wow 0.0! What kind of beast summon is this? It's so cute!!!

[Party] Long Road Ahead: Ha ha, it's normal not to recognize it. This is a legendary beast summon called the Mystic Star Flower Fairy. Its damage attributes are very high, plus it's the only one in the entire server.

Damn.

Jing Huan instantly turned green with envy.

How lucky was this person? How could his luck be so good that he could even hatch a legendary beast summon?!

[Party] Sweet Little Jing: Gege is really amazing, *rubrub* >.<

Jing Huan promptly turned off his auto follow, made his game character prance over to Yearning For's side, and used the "rubbing for luck" action.

They watched Sweet Little Jing lean over and rub affectionately against Yearning For's shoulder several times.

At lightning speed, Xiang Huaizhi clicked the boss's chat option, entered the battle, forcibly ending her action.

As soon as they entered, the Water Demon unleashed a full-map AoE attack, cutting Jing Huan's health in half. His character wasn't properly geared yet, so he took the brunt of it. The other four in his party fared better, with more than half their health intact. Long Road Ahead, in particular, seemed to have only lost five percent of his health; he seemed to have some pretty decent gear.

"Road, give me a damage buff." With his attention occupied by the boss, Xiang Huaizhi didn't have time to type so he turned on his mic. "Everyone, watch your health. Healers, heal Sweet Little Jing. Sweet Little Jing..." after a pause, he said, "just defend."

Chapter 03

Most of the bosses in the game were resistant to sealing, rendering half of the Spirit Fox Den's skills useless. Healing Springs were also hard to land, so she was better off defending; this way, she could block half the damage.

"Ah…" Jing Huan paused, thinking he had heard wrong. "I'm defending?"

Jing Huan used to play a physical DPS sect, and his parties had previously relied on him to DPS in dungeons and PKs. In his mind, being told to defend felt like he was being looked down on.

"Defend." Xiang Huaizhi didn't say more.

"Okay…gege," Jing Huan answered and pressed the defend button in humiliation.

Lu Hang followed Xiang Huaizhi's order and buffed him, who then stabbed the boss, dealing 13,000 damage instantly.

Jing Huan's eyes were glued. He really wanted to see the attributes of the divine artifact Yearning For was holding.

However, the way the battle was progressing so far didn't give him much time to think.

They watched the Water Demon activate its skill again, directly targeting the player with the lowest health: Sweet Little Jing. The Flooding of the Jinshan Temple attack cut his health in half once more. Jing Huan immediately placed a Healing Spring at his feet to restore himself a bit.

Xiang Huaizhi glanced at his remaining health, and reiterated, "Healers, heal her."

The two healers in the party acted as if they hadn't heard him, standing motionless in the corner of the map. Even their beast summons stood dumbly alongside them.

"Hey, what gives…" Lu Hang quickly gave Sweet Little Jing a defense buff. "Healers, are you there?"

No one responded. Biting out a "shit," Lu Hang said, "Oh no, those two are probably AFKing. What do we do now? Run?"

Jing Huan said, "But if we run away, they'll be killed by the boss, right?"

"You still have the mind to worry about others even now, huh? And those two are really something. They obviously knew we were about to fight the boss, so why would they still AFK?" Lu Hang muttered under his breath before asking, "Old Xiang, what should we do now?"

There was a cooldown period for Spirit Fox Den's Healing Spring skill; it would take twenty seconds before it became available again. If they kept going like this, Sweet Little Jing's health wouldn't recover in time and she would die.

And with both healers AFKing, there would be no way to revive if someone died.

"It's fine, keep going." Xiang Huaizhi cast a calm gaze over to the healers. "Give my beast summon a defense buff."

Without questioning it, Lu Hang quickly gave the Mystic Star Flower Fairy a defense buff.

The most annoying thing about the Water Demon boss was that it would target the player with the lowest health on the map; it was completely unavoidable. Jing Huan glanced at his health and said without much thought, "It's fine, you guys can probably kill it. Don't worry about me; I don't have much money on me, so I won't lose much gold when I dieeee!"

Right as he finished saying that, the boss's skill was shooting

toward him again. At the same time, the Mystic Star Flower Fairy beside Yearning For rushed in front of Sweet Little Jing, blocking most of the damage for him.

"Holy shit, you're actually using the Flower Fairy to block damage. What a total waste!" Lu Hang couldn't resist lamenting. "Have the Flower Fairy deal damage, I'll use my deer to help shield her."

"How many hits can your deer take?" Xiang Huaizhi retorted.

Lu Hang's deer, like Jing Huan's Nine-tailed Spirit Fox, had high damage but low health, so it couldn't compare at all with the Mystic Star Flower Fairy. It would fall to the ground dead after taking one hit.

"...Fine."

Jing Huan didn't expect Yearning For would use his beast summon to shield him. Dazed, it took a while for him to remember to speak. "Thank you, gege. *Waaah*, it's all my fault for being too noob."

"Mm."

Jing Huan stilled.

I was just acting humble, did you have to agree with me?!

Itching for flattery, Lu Hang urged, "Little Jingjing, please praise me too. Look, I've given you so many buffs."

In an utterly formal and rigid voice, Jing Huan said, "Thank you."

Yearning For once again landed a critical hit on the boss. Seeing the large, bright red damage numbers, Jing Huan smashed the keyboard, typing, "Gege is so awesome! Go, gege! Charge, gege~! Gege, hit his head!"

Lu Hang was flabbergasted. Shit, he hadn't expected Xiang Huaizhi to really bring Sweet Little Jing just to cheer him on.

Five minutes later, the boss's health dropped sharply and it was about to enrage. Once enraged, it would unleash a full-map AoE attack again and then target specific players to kill, with any damage dealt being augmented.

Jing Huan shot a glance at his health bar and thought, *It's over.* He might not survive this.

Right before the boss was enraged, Yearning For suddenly stopped attacking.

【Yearning For used a Red Recovery Bead on Sweet Little Jing.】

The Red Recovery Bead was a high-tier potion, and Jing Huan watched his health bar fill up instantaneously.

Voice full of bewilderment, Lu Hang said, "Hey, you didn't… Did you just casually throw a potion that costs a few tens of yuan? It's just a dungeon…Was that really necessary? Plus, she might not even die."

Xiang Huaizhi replied, "Just in case."

The Water Demon used the full-map AoE attack again. As soon as Jing Huan recovered from the shock, he watched the Water Demon, which had been facing him, whip around and change attack targets. After consuming this Red Recovery Bead, his health was no longer the lowest in the party.

The boss's target for this attack was one of the healers in the party—Love is Sharing Noms.

Startled, Love is Sharing Noms instinctively wanted to dodge, but realized, with dawning horror, that because she had been AFKing for the majority of the time, it would look too obvious if she suddenly came back now.

So, she could only stand there dumbly and let the boss attack her.

Chapter 03

Just as she thought she was doomed to die, the Nine-tailed Spirit Fox suddenly jumped in front of her and helped block some of the damage. Immediately after, Sweet Little Jing bounded up and placed a Healing Spring at her feet.

Two minutes later, Yearning For slashed the Water Demon into pieces with one strike, ending the battle with everyone still alive.

[Party] Sweet Little Jing: [Sigh] Scared me to death, I thought we were going to wipe.

[Party] Sweet Little Jing: Thank you, God of War-gege, for carrying me through the dungeons~ [Blows a kiss]

[Party] Yearning For: It was on the way.

[Party] Love is Sharing Noms: ...

[Party] Love is Sharing Noms: I had an emergency just now and couldn't come back in time, sorry...

[Party] Long Road Ahead: It's okay. As long as we killed the boss, it's fine.

[Party] Sweet Little Jing: God of War-gege, can we do dungeons together again in the future? [Wiping away tears]

[Party] Sweet Little Jing: I'll buy better gear, I won't be this noob again!!

[Party] Sweet Little Jing: [Begging you]

Xiang Huaizhi didn't even get a chance to type.

[Party] Long Road Ahead: Okay, we'll call you over next time!

After sending this message, Lu Hang immediately said, "These two healers are really too unreliable, dropping the ball at such a critical moment. We're better off bringing Sweet Little Jing; she can chat with us when we're bored."

Xiang Huaizhi clicked his mouse. "Whatever you want."

[Party] Sweet Little Jing: Does God of War-gege also agree? [About to cry]

[Party] Long Road Ahead: Of course, he's very easygoing. But since we don't have a set time to clear dungeons, how can we contact you when the time comes?

[Party] Long Road Ahead: How about adding each other on WeChat?

WeChat?

Jing Huan froze and finally remembered something that he had overlooked. He panicked and opened WeChat to take a look—

His WeChat ID was "What are you looking at Jing-ge for."

His WeChat profile picture was Kobe Bryant.

The background of his Moments was a basketball court.

Damn it, none of this looks like a cute loli girl's WeChat!

[Party] Long Road Ahead: ?

[Party] Long Road Ahead: Did you AFK again?

[Party] Sweet Little Jing: No, no!

[Party] Sweet Little Jing: My phone isn't with me. How about you send me your WeChat ID and I'll add you later. [Patting head]

[Party] Long Road Ahead: Okay, it's luhang123.

Jing Huan noted down Lu Hang's WeChat ID and was thinking about what to do when a message suddenly popped up on the screen.

【Love is Sharing Noms has added you as a friend.】

[Friend] Love is Sharing Noms: ...Are you there?

[Friend] Sweet Little Jing: [Noding] I'm here.

[Friend] Love is Sharing Noms: Sorry for not healing you earlier.

[Friend] Sweet Little Jing: Ah, it's okay, there's no need to apologize specifically to me.

 Chapter 03

[Friend] Love is Sharing Noms: ...Anyway, I'm sorry. [Shedding tears]

[Friend] Love is Sharing Noms: If you need any help in the future, you can call me.

Jing Huan was puzzled. This girl had been disdainful toward him before, why was she suddenly so friendly?

But that wasn't important.

[Friend] Sweet Little Jing: Ah, really?

[Friend] Sweet Little Jing: I need your help with something right now!

[Friend] Love is Sharing Noms: Go ahead.

[Friend] Sweet Little Jing: Can we add each other on WeChat?

A few minutes later, Jing Huan picked up his phone and searched for Love is Sharing Noms's WeChat.

He had thought it over, and before adding Long Road Ahead's WeChat, he needed to modify his profile to look like a girl's. But with so few female friends on WeChat—those being family members and teachers—he had no reference point at all.

Fortunately, there was one ready to go, right here.

Soon, the search result rolled out.

WeChat Name: Die If You Curse Out My Idol [Horse head]

Her profile picture was of famous scumbag Hong Shixian from the 2011 drama *Home Temptation* which also had a caption below: You're such a slut.

Did he type it wrong?

Jing Huan searched the WeChat ID again and still came up with the same result: Die If You Curse Out My Idol [Horse head].

He hesitated for a moment and clicked on her Moments. Fortu-

nately, her settings allowed strangers to view ten photos without friending her.

The personal bio below the profile picture read: Here to stalk your ancestor again?

Jing Huan silently swiped through the photos.

The first Moments post was: These idiots are so interesting. They tell me not to boast about my idol, so should I boast about you? [Horse head] [Doubtful]

The second post: What kind of crappy outfit did *Nine Heroes* just release? I fucking look like I gained twenty pounds after putting it on! If your designers can't do their job, fuck off and let me do it [Okay?]

The third post: It's already 2019, how am I still meeting such shitty men on blind dates who want me to quit my job to become a housewife? And he asks for a 500,000 yuan dowry? Keys are three yuan each, ten yuan for three. Do you think a discount store padlock like you is worthy of me?

He remained speechless for a while, closed her WeChat, and then went back to look at his own profile and Moments.

I'm such a wuss.

Jing Huan was spiraling in self-doubt when his friend message icon flashed again.

[Friend] Love is Sharing Noms: Shit, wait, I sent you the wrong WeChat ID.

[Friend] Love is Sharing Noms: ...Did you already search for that ID?

[Friend] Sweet Little Jing: ...

[Friend] Sweet Little Jing: Not yet...

Apparently, the previous ID was a side account for other purposes.

Love is Sharing Noms quickly sent another WeChat ID over, and the two exchanged cute stickers, very tactfully avoiding any mentions of the other WeChat ID.

Jing Huan searched for the new WeChat ID, and sure enough, the profile picture was of a cute anime character wearing an orange hoodie. The WeChat name was Nomnom, and her Moments weren't visible to strangers.

Now, this was more like it.

So, he didn't misconceive anything.

The other healer named Ji Xiaonian was still AFK, so after leaving the dungeon, Yearning For kicked her out and picked up a random healer from the World Channel.

With these healers not being AFK, Jing Huan could essentially do nothing while running the remaining two dungeons. They were highly efficient and finished everything in half an hour.

The party disbanded on the spot, and Jing Huan tossed the previously gathered Restorative Spirit Herb and 500 gold coins to Yearning For before returning to the safe zone.

[Friend] Yearning For: Come back.

[Friend] Yearning For: Tossing you some money.

Restorative Spirit Herbs could be sold for a handful of coppers at the Merchant Union.

[Friend] Sweet Little Jing: No need to pay, gege. Consider it a protection fee for carrying me through the dungeons. [Patting head]

Xiang Huaizhi raised an eyebrow. Protection fee? It wasn't like he was part of The Triads.

Forget it, he'd toss her some money the next time they ran dungeons.

After a moment, he moved his mouse over Sweet Little Jing's profile picture and checked her coordinates. Once again, she wasn't in the safe zone.

This person really is something...

[Friend] Yearning For: Try not to leave the safe zone for now.

[Friend] Yearning For: Getting killed and losing levels isn't good for running dungeons.

[Friend] Sweet Little Jing: All right, gege. QAQ

[Friend] Sweet Little Jing: But gege, how did you know I'm not in the safe zone?

[Friend] Sweet Little Jing: You're looking at my profile!!!

[Friend] Sweet Little Jing: [Twirling in circles][Excited]

Xiang Huaizhi closed the chat window in silence.

"That healer who was AFKing came back and said she lost her connection," Lu Hang said. "Oh by the way, Old Xiang, how many dungeon points do you have left?"

Every time a dungeon was completed, the system rewarded the players with the corresponding number of dungeon points. Once the points reached a certain amount, they could be exchanged for item rewards at an NPC.

Xiang Huaizhi glanced at it. "Eighty."

"Eighty?!" Lu Hang shouted in shock. "So that idiot spent all the points you saved up before?! Fuck! Was he that desperate that he resorted to stealing dungeon points?"

"He didn't spare anything that could be taken." Xiang Huaizhi closed the page.

Chapter 03

"Good thing you locked all your equipment, or else I would've definitely doxxed him and fucked him over." Lu Hang couldn't hold back anymore. "You're so unlucky; the one time you hired a professional grinder, and you ran into such a piece of work. And on top of that, he ruined your character's reputation."

Xiang Huaizhi didn't respond. After finishing his dailies, he closed the game and randomly clicked open an NBA game replay.

"Hey, I've seen this game before." Lu Hang walked up to him with a toothbrush hanging from his mouth. "The end score is 113 to..."

Xiang Huaizhi picked up the basketball at his feet and flung it at Lu Hang's face. "Shut up."

Lu Hang caught the ball steadfastly, scolding him, "Shit, I'm in my pajamas right now. If you got them dirty, just you watch, I'll rub up against your bedsheets."

After he was done watching the game, Xiang Huaizhi got into bed. He picked up his phone and was about to set an alarm when a WeChat message popped up on the screen.

【Little Jing~ has sent you a friend request with a message: God of War-gege, I'm Sweet Little Jing! >.<】

"...Lu Hang," Xiang Huaizhi said.

Lu Hang said, "Hey, that little miss has been begging me for so long, and I don't have the heart to say no. Besides, she'll be our party for dungeons, adding her on WeChat makes it easier for us to contact her!"

Xiang Huaizhi frowned and clicked the Ignore button.

But the other party refused to give up that easily.

【Little Jing~ has sent you a friend request with a message: Why is gege *i*gnoring poor little me...】

【Little Jing~ has sent you a friend request with a message: QAQ Gege, *waaaaah*, I'll just lurk in your friend list, I definitely won't bother you!】

【Little Jing~ has sent you a friend request with a message: Gege, can you add me when you're in a good mood? T.T】

Jing Huan lay on his side on the sofa, his feet dangling relaxedly as he considered what else to write while tossing grapes into his mouth.

His phone suddenly vibrated. Joy rocketing through him, he quickly closed the Friend Requests page—

Lu Wenhao: [Kitty wink]

Lu Wenhao: My apologies, but I didn't leave any notes here. Can I ask who you are? Meimei~

Little Jing~: ?

Little Jing~: Guess.

Lu Wenhao: A meimei from the neighboring class?

Little Jing~: No.

Lu Wenhao: Someone I met at the bar?

Little Jing~: Also no.

Lu Wenhao: You can't be from the Werewolf game club?

Jing Huan remained silent. Suddenly, he felt like it wasn't that suprising that this idiot had gotten deceived online.

Lu Wenhao: Why aren't you saying anything?

Lu Wenhao: Meimei.

Jing Huan lifted his phone up, pressed the voice message button, and in an incredibly deep voice, he intoned each word, "I'm your daddy."

A few seconds later, Lu Wenhao's voice call popped up.

"Fuck!" Lu Wenhao was still shell-shocked. "You sicko! What's with this profile picture?! Why is it fucking pinker than my ex-girlfriend's profile picture? And what's with your Moments? Why are there so many pictures of plushies?"

"You're the sicko." Jing Huan spat out a grape seed. "Don't you know how to read the chat history? Also, ex-boyfriend, not ex-girlfriend."

"I clear my chat history every day, so there's nothing to read."

"Scumbag behavior," Jing Huan noted.

"Shit, it's just my habit from before when that liar used to check all my social media apps...*Ptui ptui ptui,* let's not fucking talk about him anymore," Lu Wenhao said. "Why'd your WeChat become this gross?"

Jing Huan was calm. "I lost a bet."

"You really bet big, huh." Lu Wenhao didn't doubt him. "By the way, Xiangxiang[2] and I are having hot pot in the dorm this weekend. Join us and bring some alcohol too."

"Okay, noon or evening?"

"Of course in the evening, noon isn't as fun. Oh yeah, and come over early with your computer so we can game together."

His phone vibrated again, but after what had happened with Lu Wenhao, Jing Huan's excitement had all but vanished. It was probably someone else coming to mock his profile picture.

【Xiang: I've accepted your friend request. Now let's chat!】

Lu Wenhao said, "You didn't know, but just two days after you left, the brats from the dorm next door kept provoking me and

---

2 Gao Zixiang in this case.

A-Xiang every day. They really need to be taught a lesson. We have to teach them to behave by completely dominating them in-game..."

"Hanging up now," Jing Huan interrupted him.

"...Have them cry and beg for daddy...What? You're hanging up? Wait, I have more to say..."

Before he could finish talking, Jing Huan had already hung up.

He opened up the stickers, wanting to greet Yearning For. But he forgot that WeChat wasn't *Nine Heroes,* and did not have as many cute built-in stickers for him to use. Most of the ones he saved on WeChat were goofy images.

So, he forwarded the cat sticker that Lu Wenhao had sent.

Little Jing~: [Kitty wink]

Naturally, there was no response from the other side, not even so much as a "typing..." indicator.

Jing Huan clicked on Yearning For's Moments. The profile was largely empty, but the few posts that were there were all photos of basketball courts.

Although he hadn't received a reply, Jing Huan didn't mind. It was late at night, and sleep was crucial.

They had a long way to go; they could take it slow.

The next day, as soon as Xiang Huaizhi returned to his dormitory after class, he saw Lu Hang coming out with a bag on his back.

"Old Xiang!" Seeing him, Lu Hang hastened over. "Perfect, I needed to tell you that today is my mom's birthday, and I have to hurry home. I can't join you for the arena tonight...It's my bad, I only found out about it today, and I was scolded by my dad just now."

Chapter 03

To ensure that his character stayed at the top of the rankings, Xiang Huaizhi had to participate in the weekly arena matches. He had solely played 1V1, but two weeks ago, *Nine Heroes* had an update and changed the arena mechanics, providing a point bonus for playing 2V2 and above.

In the past few months, that "professional grinder" had messed up his character, and his points had dropped significantly. If he didn't climb the ranks this week, his Mastery rank would drop. So, he had made plans with Lu Hang to play 2V2 from now on.

"It's fine, go home. It's the same if I play 1V1."

"Don't do it. I've read up on the new system, and winning a 1V1 match only adds three points, whereas winning in other brackets adds seven points. If you only play 1V1, you'll definitely be overtaken by the people below you on the Mastery ranks," Lu Hang said then suggested, "How about you find someone to partner with for now? Oh yeah, I've added several top players from the Mastery rankings on WeChat. Want me to ask around? What sect do you need?"

"No need." Xiang Huaizhi shook his head. "It's okay, you can head back. I'll take care of it myself."

Returning to the dormitory, Xiang Huaizhi opened *Nine Heroes* and browsed the game bulletin board. Sure enough, as Lu Hang had said, the 1V1 points had been significantly reduced.

He opened his friend list and took a quick look through it.

Having played *Nine Heroes* for many years, he did have some friends, but he didn't communicate with them much. He hadn't talked to most of them after he added them, so they weren't that much different from strangers.

He scanned the list back and forth twice and decided to stick with

1V1 in the end. It didn't matter if he got fewer points; he'd just have to win more matches.

Because he didn't need to find a teammate, he still had plenty of time to do a few dailies.

He controlled his character to walk outside of the city. As soon as he reached the teleportation portal, he saw a familiar little spirit fox sitting at the city gate, her fox tail swaying back and forth, creating a picturesque scene.

She's AFKing here?

Xiang Huaizhi's fingers paused, and for some odd reason, his gaze couldn't help trailing back to her a few more times.

[Current] Sweet Little Jing: [Surprise] God of War-gege!

So, she isn't just AFKing.

[Current] Sweet Little Jing: Are you going to do dailies? [Question]

[Current] Yearning For: Mm.

[Current] Sweet Little Jing: Alrighty, take care *^0^*.

[Current] Yearning For: ...

[Current] Yearning For: What are you doing sitting here?

[Current] Sweet Little Jing: Ah, I also want to go do dailies, but there are a few Idle Pavilion members lurking outside, so I'm afraid to leave.

[Current] Sweet Little Jing: I figure that the arena will start soon, so I'll wait for them to go and then I'll do my dailies.

[Current] Sweet Little Jing: I'm so smart, right? [Pushing glasses up]

Xiang Huaizhi didn't say anything.

He couldn't understand how, despite being a miserable victim

of a hunt, this little spirit fox could still be so cheerful. Anyone else would've switched characters and left long ago.

[Current] Yearning For: Smart.

[Current] Sweet Little Jing: [Shy]

[Current] Sweet Little Jing: Gege, go ahead and do your dailies.

[Current] Yearning For: What's so fun about getting hunted to the point where you can't even do your dailies?

[Current] Yearning For: Never thought about selling your character?

[Current] Sweet Little Jing: Ah? No, I haven't~ 0.0

[Current] Sweet Little Jing: I finally managed to run dungeons with you now! I'm definitely not selling my character.

[Current] Yearning For: …

[Current] Yearning For: Leaving now.

Yearning For walked straight into the teleportation portal and went outside the city.

Jing Huan typed halfway, then stopped.

Damn it, his "gege, bye-bye" message hadn't been sent yet!

Jing Huan was about to change his position and continue to keep watching over the city gate when he saw the teleportation portal light up and a man in a black robe reappear in front of him.

Jing Huan did a double take. Why did he come back?

He was about to type and ask when a line of text appeared above the man's head.

[Current] Yearning For: Want to fight in the arena?

Jing Huan was stunned for a while again, and it took him a long time to remember to type.

[Current] Sweet Little Jing: Gege...are you talking to me?

[Current] Yearning For: Who else is here?

The passerby on the side quietly looked away.

[Current] Sweet Little Jing: But I haven't bought all my equipment yet...

[Current] Yearning For: It'll be fine as long as you know how to run away.

[Current] Sweet Little Jing: ?

What did he mean? Does this person intend to make me run for my life around the arena all night?

Just as Jing Huan wanted to make a few sarcastic quips, the teleportation portal light up. The elite member of Idle Pavilion skulking outside had noticed something was off and was coming in to check on the enemy situation.

Xiang Huaizhi glanced at that person and clicked to form a party.

[Current] Yearning For: Join.

The little spirit fox immediately stood up, and the game character even dusted off her butt before turning around and joining Yearning For's party. Then, the two of them flew away together.

Astounded by what they had just witnessed, the elite member of Idle Pavilion immediately reported to the guild.

[Guild] Deep Forest Deer Sighting: Report: Sweet Little Jing has joined Yearning For's party!

[Guild] Deep Forest Deer Sighing: Be careful, everyone, don't initiate a force PK against Sweet Little Jing!

[Guild] Silent Affection: ???

[Guild] The Girl in My Heart: Why is she in Yearning For's party? [Surprise]

 Chapter 03

[Guild] BrbOrNot: My friend told me Sweet Little Jing and Yearning For were even clearing dungeons together yesterday.

[Guild] Carpe Diem: ...No way, are they really having an affair? Was Yearning For moved by Sweet Little Jing's confession?

[Guild] Fae Bae: Impossible.

[Guild] Fae Bae: Yearning For has very high standards~ Sweet Little Jing probably begged him to take her to run dungeons. It's fine, in ten minutes, Yearning For will play in the arena, and then we can rest easy and go kill Sweet Little Jing.

[Guild] Star in the Sky: ...Um, about that...

[Guild] Star in the Sky: I saw Yearning For take Sweet Little Jing into the 2V2 arena zone.

[Guild] BrbOrNot: ...

[Guild] The Girl in My Heart: ...

The screen was filled with shock.

[Guild] Silent Affection: ...It's okay. Worst case scenario, tonight's plan to snipe Sweet Little Jing gets postponed. Look on the bright side: Yearning For will definitely lose if he has to carry Sweet Little Jing, and then our vice guild leader can top the Mastery rankings!

[Guild] Star in the Sky: Yeah lol, I noticed that Yearning For's points have been dropping continuously these past few months. If our vice guild leader wins a few more matches, she'll surpass him.

[Guild] Fae Bae: Star in the Sky, what do you mean by that?

[Guild] Star in the Sky: ?

[Guild] Star in the Sky: What did I do...

[Guild] Fae Bae: You're implying that his points dropped in the past few months because he was carrying me in the arena, right?

[Guild] Star in the Sky: [Dazed] No, how would I even know he took you along back then?

[Guild] Fae Bae: We were together every single day. You didn't know?

[Guild] Star in the Sky: So what if you were together? Did you get married? Now that Sweet Little Jing and Yearning For are doing arena battles together, are they also together?

【Guild: Azure Dragon Officer Fae Bae has asked Star in the Sky to leave Idle Pavilion due to "."】

[Guild] BrbOrNot: Oh man, damn…Was that really necessary?

【Guild: BrbOrNot has enabled a guild-wide mute.】

[Guild] BrbOrNot: Don't quarrel, Faefae, calm down a bit.

[Guild] BrbOrNot: Let's split for tonight, go do whatever you need to do. I'll unmute the chat tomorrow.

Jing Huan had no idea that their partying up had caused such a stir in Idle Pavilion. He didn't even have time to refuse before being dragged into the arena.

To be honest, although he was eager to interact with Yearning For, he didn't really want to come to the arena with him to lose points.

With the equipment he currently had, he wouldn't be able to put up a fight at all; he'd be a mere sitting duck. Moreover, he hadn't fully mastered the Spirit Fox Den's skills yet. This dumb sect had an exhausting number of skills and it was overwhelming. It would take at least half a month to truly be proficient at playing the sect.

"Gege." He hesitated for a moment and pretended to be afraid. "Why don't you call someone else over? I-I've never fought in the arena before."

"That's fine, you're just a body count," Xiang Huaizhi replied. *If it weren't for the fact that I can't kill you, I would've fucking come to blows with you ages ago.*

Seeing her quiet, Xiang Huaizhi thought for a moment then added, "I won't let you lose points."

Each person started with an initial score of 1,000 points.

Jing Huan actually didn't care too much about points; even if he lost everything, once he bought all his equipment, he'd just come back and earn his points back.

He simply didn't like to lose.

Games were meant to entertain. What was the point if he was constantly getting chased around and beaten up in the game?

"Okay then," Jing Huan said. "I'll leave the party to buy some potions."

No sooner had the words left his mouth, many small pop-ups appeared, informing him that Yearning For was tossing him potions.

"I called you here, so I'll provide the potions," Xiang Huaizhi said shortly.

"Thank you, gege." Jing Huan sat up straight. He hadn't fought in the arena for a long time, so suddenly being here did pique his excitement.

He instinctively scanned his surroundings and instantly fell speechless.

Most of the people standing around them were actually from Idle Pavilion.

In fact, what Xiang Huaizhi had just said made sense. Tonight's scene in the arena was just going to be of him running for this life.

Fortunately, arena matches were randomly assigned. If players could initiate battles independently, he feared that they wouldn't even get a chance to catch their breath tonight.

At 7:30 p.m., the arena officially opened. As soon as Xiang Huaizhi clicked the match button, they welcomed their first opponents of the night.

They were two male players: one healer and one physical DPS, which was similar to Jing Huan's party composition.

Their opponents hadn't expected to be matched up against Yearning For and were visibly stunned. Before they could react, they saw Yearning For draw his sword and charge straight toward the healer.

Startled, the healer instinctively moved to the right. He never expected that this move would put him right into the path of Yearning For's sword. Yearning For didn't hold back and immediately unleashed a two-hit combo.

9113.

The bright red numbers burst out, and the healer fell to the ground.

Jing Huan's jaw dropped.

Fuck. What kind of insane damage is this?

Even if the players they matched against weren't strong, he shouldn't be able to...one-shot the healer, right...

This was the very definition of getting completely annihilated by good equipment. These pay-to-win players were inhumane!

Jing Huan, who had spent tens of thousands of yuan to buy an empty character, cursed inwardly.

[Current] You're Trash: [Horrified]

[Current] You're Trash: Great God, I only have 2,200 points, why did I get matched against you...

 Chapter 03

In the arena, the system averaged the points of both players in the party and then used that average to match them against opponents of similar strength. Due to Jing Huan's character having very low points and Xiang Huaizhi's character having suffered consistent losses, they were matched with low-point opponents.

Yearning For didn't respond and turned around to kill the DPS. Knowing he couldn't win, the DPS gave up on fighting and stood there, letting himself be killed.

[Current] You're Trash: Great God, can you wait ten seconds before matching again? [Shedding tears] I don't want to run into you guys again.

A final sword strike sent You're Trash flying out of the PK zone, giving him no further chance to speak.

It wasn't until they returned to the waiting area that Jing Huan remembered to say something. "Wow, gege, you're so amazing."

Naturally, there was no response from the other end of the headset. Yearning For stood there, completely motionless.

Jing Huan was about to ask something when the matchmaking interface popped up, indicating that they had already entered the next match.

Ah...so Yearning For had been waiting out those ten seconds.

The next few matches were almost identical to the first match. Yearning For's equipment was so strong that even a noob playing his character could probably win.

The opponents they matched with were either decimated by Yearning For, or they immediately forfeited as soon as the match began. Three matches down, and Jing Huan had done nothing but throw Healing Springs.

After this match ended, the arena channel had its first system announcement.

【Congratulations to Yearning For, Sweet Little Jing for defeating Listen to the Rain, Accompanying Winds, and achieving three consecutive victories!】

Echoes of Spring glanced at the time. "The arena opened just seven minutes ago, and they've already won three straight matches?"

"Sweet Little Jing's points are low, and they keep getting matched against noobs, so of course those are easy wins." The female voice coming from the headset was delicate, carrying a hint of displeasure. "Why are you paying attention to Sweet Little Jing again?"

Echoes of Spring helplessly said, "I just happened to see it."

"Then what about last time when they went to kill the Spirit King? Did you also just 'happen' to contribute the guild's materials?" The voice belonged to Regardless of Lovesickness. Every explanation from Echoes of Spring seemed to stoke her anger rather than abate it.

Echoes of Spring replied, "If we didn't contribute materials, bandits would've raided the guild."

"Then let them in! At most, we'll just lose a plot of our potion farm!"

Echoes of Spring frowned. The match ended. As she tied up her long hair, she said, ever so patiently, "It wasn't easy for us to expand our potion farm, so if we can avoid some trouble, why not? Be good now, you haven't been able to go online much lately, and I don't want to argue with you."

Regardless of Lovesickness wilted as soon as she heard her words. "But I'm just not happy with this. Who does she think she is? Scam-

 Chapter 03

ming one of our guild elders is one thing, but she even tried to seduce you. Isn't she afraid of choking with her eating up both men and women?"

"That was the previous owner's matter. This time, it seems like the character really does have a new owner."

"Didn't they say the same thing last time? And in the end, it was still that scammer. Anyway, I won't believe her." Regardless of Lovesickness pouted. "You're not allowed to look at her anymore!"

Echoes of Spring chuckled and said, "Okay, okay, okay, I'm not looking…"

The game interface suddenly changed, and they were matched with their next opponents. The first things Echoes of Spring noticed were that black robe and sparkling divine artifact.

[Current] Regardless of Lovesickness: ?

[Current] Regardless of Lovesickness: Little Green Tea[3], seducing a new man to boost your points again?

[Current] Sweet Little Jing: …

[Current] Sweet Little Jing: Green tea is really too high of a status.

Before Jing Huan could finish typing, he saw Regardless of Lovesickness wave her wand and shoot a Thunderbolt Strikes Fury spell at him.

Jing Huan was in the midst of typing when he noticed several dark clouds materialize above his head. He instinctively tried to dodge but ended up typing the hotkey letters into the chat box.

---

3   A reference to the term "green tea bitch," which describes a woman who pretends to be innocent but is secretly scheming inside. Also, someone who is very good at seducing people.

[Current] Sweet Little Jing: hhhhhhh

[Current] Regardless of Lovesickness: You can still laugh right now?

The wand in her hand morphed into a claw weapon, and she charged right at Jing Huan.

"But I'm innocent. I just wanted to dodge her skill…" Given no time to type, he could only mutter softly in the voice chat.

Lifting his sword, Xiang Huaizhi took one step forward and shielded Sweet Little Jing. "Mm, stop talking and focus on dodging."

After Jing Huan bought the character, the character's arena points were reset. Because they had won three in a row, the system deemed her hidden power to be very high. Coupled with Yearning For's presence in the party, it wasn't surprising that they would be matched against Echoes of Spring.

Xiang Huaizhi's eyebrows slightly furrowed. Both of their opponents were all-server PK players. During the years he didn't register for the all-server PK, the two of them were the ones who always represented Mirage server to fight in the all-server battle. They were undeniably good.

He and Sweet Little Jing might not win this match.

"Gege, I recall that Regardless of Lovesickness was also a Spirit Fox Den not too long ago?" Jing Huan leaped backward, dodging. "Why is she a Mage now?"

"Mages got buffed this year, and she probably changed sects for the upcoming all-server battle," Xiang Huaizhi replied.

The two of them collided in the center of the map, each landing their attack skills on the other. Thanks to his good equipment, Xiang Huaizhi managed to evade several of Regardless of Lovesickness's skill

shots. After about ten seconds, Regardless of Lovesickness lost half her health, while Xiang Huaizhi only lost about thirty percent of his health.

"Gege is so awesome!" Jing Huan immediately showered him with praise and threw out a Healing Spring. "Hurry up and drink my essence, gege!"

Xiang Huaizhi choked. "Speak properly."

Shaking off his momentary surprise, Jing Huan scoffed. People with filthy minds sure do have their minds in the gutter!

He said innocently, "I am speaking properly."

The Healing Spring was delivered precisely to Xiang Huaizhi's feet, and his health immediately recovered by a small amount.

Jing Huan exclaimed, "Gege, my heal landed!"

As soon as he said that, Echoes of Spring, who hadn't moved this entire time, raised her hand slightly. A lotus flower appeared under Regardless of Lovesickness's feet, and with a swish, her health bar was instantly fully replenished.

Fully. Replenished.

Jing Huan sagged.

Seeing her silence, for some reason, Xiang Huaizhi couldn't stop a laugh from escaping. He then said in a low voice, "Echoes of Spring is a Mount Putuo, and all her equipment attributes enhance healing effectiveness. It's a sect difference, it's not your fault."

In the arena, there were always wins and losses—a fact that Xiang Huaizhi had long ago accepted. He glanced at the map, wondering if he should focus on killing Echoes of Spring. After all, with her standing behind Regardless of Lovesickness, it would be hard to deal with the latter.

Suddenly, Sweet Little Jing darted past them. She hopped onto a big rock and swiftly threw out a light-colored spider—the Spirit Fox Den's sealing skill—straight at Echoes of Spring.

Upon seeing this, Echoes of Spring's first reaction was to jump to the right. Unexpectedly, as soon as she landed, the spider landed on her toes and quickly spat out a web, sealing her spell casts.

This Sweet Little Jing had actually predicted her movement.

That's right—the Spirit Fox Den sect wasn't just a healer sect. Its main characteristics were agility and sealing, with a wide range of sealing skills. The only downsides were its limited casting range and low skill hit rate, which were even worse than the sect's Healing Springs.

"Gege! I've sealed her! She can't use spells right now!" Jing Huan cheered. "Am I amazing or what—"

"Amazing," Xiang Huaizhi said hurriedly. "Now, run fast."

Jing Huan was momentarily stunned, but before he could understand what Yearning For meant, he watched in shock as the ribbons Echoes of Spring was holding suddenly transformed into two long swords. With a burst of speed, she charged directly at him.

He dove, and Echoes of Spring's sword struck the rock, shattering it on impact.

"She's an offensive-type healer," Xiang Huaizhi finished, cadence slow.

Jing Huan, who had already delivered himself right to Echoes of Spring's feet, glowered.

Shit, why didn't you say that earlier?!

Watching the little spirit fox hopping around the field, Xiang Huaizhi felt indescribably bemused. However, as time went on, he noticed something was off.

Chapter 03

Echoes of Spring chose to play as an offensive-type healer for one reason: her good prediction skills. She could hit enemies without relying on her skills' range but after a few minutes had passed, Sweet Little Jing had only been hit once.

"*Waaah*, she's still chasing me!" Jing Huan said. "Gege, how are you doing over there? Can you beat her?"

If you can't win, then forfeit. If you can, help me out by hurrying up and killing her!!!

This Echoes of Spring struck terror in his heart. He had only barely avoided several of her attacks, and it was quite strenuous since he hadn't played PK in a long time.

No sound came from his party member, but the game character was still moving. Jing Huan urged again, "Gege?"

Some time passed before Xiang Huaizhi's voice broke through. "Take a look at your skill list."

"I am, what about it…"

"There is a pink skill called Charming Threads."

"Hm?"

"Throw it at Echoes of Spring's face."

Jing Huan looked at the casting range of Charming Threads, dismayed. "Gege, this skill's casting range is smaller than my fingernail…"

"I can't get to you right now," Xiang Huaizhi cut him off abruptly. "If you seal her, you live. If you miss, you die."

Jing Huan gritted his teeth, jumped over two rocks, and spun around to throw out the Charming Threads.

Unsurprisingly…he missed.

Voice soft, he implored, "Gege…"

"Keep going," Xiang Huaizhi said. "Just think of her as me."

Jing Huan made a noise of confusion.

"Like you're throwing a Healing Spring at me. Toss it slowly, don't rush."

Jing Huan automatically ignored the latter sentence.

Think of Echoes of Spring as Yearning For?

Now that he said it, although Echoes of Spring had a mature-looking female character, she was dressed in all-black and held long swords—just like Yearning For.

Xiang Huaizhi stole a glance over. The little spirit fox was still being chased around and slashed at, her tail swaying in the air.

He suddenly felt a bit foolish. How could he place his hopes on Sweet Little Jing?

He was about to abandon his fight with Regardless of Lovesickness to go rescue the little spirit fox when he saw the sprinting figure suddenly turn on her heel and obediently throw out Charming Threads.

This time, the Charming Threads skill hit Echoes of Spring, immediately immobilizing her in place.

He raised his eyebrows and just as he was about to call out "nice," something weird occurred.

Instead of rushing back to a safe position after sealing Echoes of Spring, Sweet Little Jing pulled out a whip and started viciously lashing at Echoes of Spring.

A bright red "1" appeared on Echoes of Spring.

Charming Threads would only seal someone for seven seconds. Seven seconds later, Echoes of Spring once again struck the rock next to Sweet Little Jing, who took the opportunity to throw out another Charming Threads, which landed again.

 Chapter 03

Then she pulled out the whip and flicked it at Echoes of Spring once more, dealing two points of damage.

A bit at a loss for words, Xiang Huaizhi asked, "What are you doing?"

[Current] Echoes of Spring: ?

[Current] Echoes of Spring: You're really something.

Jing Huan jolted awake as if from a dream.

I fucked up.

"...Didn't you tell me to think of her as you?" he stammered. "I just...I just couldn't help it. I wanted to touch you more!"

Jing Huan stole the precious few seconds of Xiang Huaizhi's silence to gather himself enough to speak in a smoother voice, "I want to flirt...and joke with gege..."

Xiang Huaizhi felt that he might be getting immune to her talk now. "Oh?"

"But she seems to have misunderstood, what should I dooo..."

"It's fine." Xiang Huaizhi finished off Regardless of Lovesickness and rushed over to them. "Run far away."

As an offensive-type healer, Echoes of Spring's weakness was her low resistance. After chasing each other around for a while, Xiang Huaizhi almost depleted her health.

Seeing this, Jing Huan hurriedly said, "Wooow, gege, are we about to win?"

Just as Xiang Huaizhi was about to respond to him, he saw the little spider under Echoes of Spring's feet vanish—the spell's sealing duration had ended.

It was Jing Huan's first time participating in a PK as a Spirit Fox Den player, and he hadn't yet adjusted. Unable to quickly reapply the seal, he had no choice but to watch as Echoes of Spring switched back to her ribbons, lightly waving them. Instead of healing, she opted to cast a resurrection spell.

Xiang Huaizhi thought, *Not good.*

The once-fallen-now-revived Regardless of Lovesickness used her sect's ultimate skill on Jing Huan straightaway.

This ultimate skill was a guaranteed hit, a three-hit spell combo. Jing Huan didn't have a complete set of equipment, and the three hits instantly wiped out his health bar. The little spirit fox crumpled to the ground, her large tail concealing the entire character.

[Party] Sweet Little Jing: ...

[Party] Sweet Little Jing: QAQ *Waaaaah*!!!

Yearning For was a DPS sect and didn't have a resurrection skill. Fortunately, Echoes of Spring's skill cooldown was long. He said, "Don't worry, we can still win. Wait while I kill Regardless of Lovesickness and then I'll use an item to revive you. Otherwise, they'll turn your corpse into a puppet. After you get up, seal Echoes of Spring first."

Before he could finish speaking, a line of notices flashed on the screen before his eyes.

【Due to Echoes of Spring and Regardless of Lovesickness forfeiting, you have won this match.】

【Congratulations to Yearning For for defeating Echoes of Spring, Regardless of Lovesickness, and achieving four consecutive victories!】

However, since Jing Huan was dead when the battle ended, he not only didn't gain points, he lost three of them.

It was very obvious that their opponents forfeited and ran to prevent him from gaining points.

This tactic had been around for a long time, but few people used

Chapter 03

it because it was too underhanded. If you lost, you lost; there was really no need to pull this sort of stunt. There would be a throwdown pretty much every year in the *Nine Heroes* community due to someone using this tactic.

Jing Huan sighed; he had been truly wronged here.

"Sorry," Xiang Huaizhi said.

Surprised, Jing Huan said, "Hm? What's wrong?"

"I didn't manage to revive you," Xiang Huaizhi said. "How many points did you lose?"

"It's okaaay, I was the one who forgot to reseal her. And I only lost three points."

Xiang Huaizhi let out an "mm," before saying, "I'll help you get them back."

Jing Huan didn't understand what he meant until Yearning For talked in-game.

[Current] Yearning For: Let's play another match.

Because the other parties were still in battle, their and Echoes of Spring's parties were the only ones in the rest zone. It was clear that this was directed at them.

[Current] Echoes of Spring: All right.

[Current] Regardless of Lovesickness: Bring it on!

[Current] Sweet Little Jing: [Surprised]!!!

[Current] Sweet Little Jing: Wait! Harmony brings wealth, harmony brings wealth…How about we take this opportunity to clear the air? Fighting and killing all the time is so bad. QAQ

Damn it! He didn't want to play PK against these two with his shitty gear! Winning would depend on luck, but if he lost, it'd be too embarrassing!

Guide on How to Fail at Online Dating

[Current] Regardless of Lovesickness: What do you and I have to talk about?

[Current] Regardless of Lovesickness: It's bad enough that you scammed my guild elder, but you dared to try and seduce my wife. I'm already being very polite by not doxxing you!

"Who's her wife?" Confused, Jing Huan asked, his voice lifting up at the end. "Isn't she a woman?"

Xiang Huaizhi paused and said, "I heard that she and Echoes of Spring are a couple."

Jing Huan suddenly realized what was going on.

No way, the original owner of this character was too indecent. It was one thing to go after both men and women, but she even tried to seduce a married woman?

[Current] Sweet Little Jing: That bad thing was done by the original owner of this character. It has nothing to do with me, sis. QAQ

[Current] Regardless of Lovesickness: I don't believe you.

[Current] Sweet Little Jing: If you don't believe me, come listen to my voice, it's nothing like the original owner's!

[Current] Regardless of Lovesickness: You're using a voice changer, aren't you?

Fuck, I've been seen through.

Jing Huan decided to change his approach.

[Current] Sweet Little Jing: ...I'm not! [Enraged]

[Current] Sweet Little Jing: Your guild bullies me, tries to kill me, and insults me all the time, and I've put up with it all!

[Current] Sweet Little Jing: But you can't lie about my sexual orientation in front of my crush!!

[Current] Sweet Little Jing: This is my bottom line! My heart,

my soul, my body all belong to God of War-gege! I didn't try to seduce your wife!!! [Pounding on the table][Enraged]

The message left Regardless of Lovesickness and Echoes of Spring standing there dumbfounded. Jing Huan's screen changed and suddenly, they were thrown into the match.

Xiang Huaizhi couldn't stand watching anymore and just clicked to start the match.

Eyebrows twitching, he felt like he had gone crazy just now, thinking that he would help this little spirit fox win back her points.

The arena matches ran from 7:30 p.m. to 9:30 p.m. When Lu Hang returned to the dormitory, he saw Xiang Huaizhi with one side of his headset on, controlling his game character to send his opponent out of the PK zone with a single sword strike.

"Awesome, awesome." Lu Hang dumped his backpack on the bed and complained, "What's wrong with older adults nowadays? It's just a birthday, but they called the entire family over to gather around a big table to eat like it's a New Year's Eve dinner. They just asked one question after another, first asking about my studies, then about my relationships; it was so frustrating that I couldn't even enjoy my meal. I ran away as fast as I could when my dad went to the bathroom…Who did you play with in the arena tonight? Without me here, you must have lost a lot of points…The fuck?"

Lu Hang swallowed down his yapping when he caught a clear view of the other member of Xiang Huaizhi's party.

The arena matches ended promptly at 9:30 p.m. All the parties that were waiting or fighting were instantly sent to the arena teleporter by the system, and immediately, the city was filled with people.

Xiang Huaizhi spoke to his party member, "Leaving now."

He didn't give his party member a chance to react before disbanding the party.

[Current] Sweet Little Jing: Thank you, gege, for taking me to play in the arena! Bye-bye gege! *^o^*

This chat bubble stunned all the players around. For quite some time, no one flew away, still crowding the city.

Without looking back, Xiang Huaizhi was the first to leave the area.

Lu Hang coughed twice then proceeded to act flirtatious. "Thank you, gege, for taking me to play in the arenaaa."

Xiang Huaizhi said, "Are you a parrot?"

Plus, his tone wasn't similar at all; if it was Sweet Little Jing, she would've definitely dragged the last syllable for a lot longer. And after listening to it for the past two hours, he was about to have a nervous breakdown.

"I'm just imitating her, don't attack me." Lu Hang moved a chair over and sat next to him. "Old Xiang, you've got a situation here! You actually took Sweet Little Jing to fight in the arena?! Does she have all her gear now? You gave up points just to carry a girl?!"

"Spirit Fox Dens don't rely on equipment," Xiang Huaizhi replied. "No points were lost."

"No points were lost?" Lu Hang thought for a moment. "Oh, her character's points were reset, so you were just matched against noobs, right? Was it any fun?"

Calling all of them noobs wasn't entirely accurate. The first three pairs of opponents were indeed not that strong, but after encountering Echoes of Spring's party, they kept getting matched against opponents who had over 2,500 points.

However, since Sweet Little Jing had become much more well-

 Chapter 03

versed in the Spirit Fox Den's PK skills, they never lost a single match. The flip side was that she was nearly assassinated by Idle Pavilion members several times. Fortunately, she had learned from her past experiences; every time a match was coming to a close, Sweet Little Jing would start sprinting all over the arena, determined to not appear within the enemy's casting range.

He had to admit it: this little spirit fox's skills were much better than he expected.

"It's no different from 1V1," Xiang Huaizhi said.

Lu Hang never turned off his computer. In *Nine Heroes*, there was a zone called Penglai. You could earn experience every three minutes just by AFKing in Penglai. Although it wasn't much, it was better than nothing. He sat in front of his computer and glanced at the friend messages he received while he was AFK.

"How could there be no difference? Jingjing-meimei is so talkative..." Lu Hang frowned as he looked at the message he just received. "Why did Regardless of Lovesickness DM me...Oh, Old Xiang, she's asking me what your relationship with Sweet Little Jing is? How should I answer that?"

Xiang Huaizhi raised an eyebrow. "You even added Regardless of Lovesickness as a friend?"

"Yeah, she tried to recruit me to join Idle Pavilion before, but I thought that guild had too much drama, so I didn't join. Good thing I didn't, otherwise, things would be really awkward between me and Little Jingjing right now." Lu Hang looked up. "So, tell me how I should answer."

Xiang Huaizhi left his character in Penglai and, as he went to the bathroom, tossed out, "Friends."

[Friend] Long Road Ahead: They're friends, what about it?

[Friend] Regardless of Lovesickness: Impossible.

[Friend] Regardless of Lovesickness: Sweet Little Jing just confessed to Yearning For during an arena match.

Fuck, that happened?!

Lu Hang turned his head to look at Xiang Huaizhi, who was washing up, and shook his head.

Young man, you're not honest.

[Friend] Long Road Ahead: Haven't you heard of a certain saying?

[Friend] Regardless of Lovesickness: What?

[Friend] Long Road Ahead: First a friend, then a meimei, and finally, she's your baby.

[Friend] Regardless of Lovesickness: ...

[Friend] Long Road Ahead: Anyway, just letting you know in advance that Sweet Little Jing has been running a lot of dungeons with us recently. If anyone from your guild tries to initiate a forced PK on my bro…

[Friend] Long Road Ahead: You know, scumbags have bad tempers. Who knows what he might do in his efforts to impress a girl? [Shut up]

Xiang Huaizhi, who was rinsing his mouth, suddenly sneezed and thought to himself, *Winter is coming.*

During the weekend, Jing Huan returned to the school dormitory, a bag of food and booze in hand.

As soon as he walked into the dorm room, he heard Gao Zixiang shouting, "Hurry, hurry, hurry! Heal me up! Or else, I'm going to get aggroed[1] by the boss! Fuck, you missed again...Do you even know how to play a Spirit Fox Den?!"

"Fuck, if you can do it, then you heal!" Lu Wenhao said. "This stupid sect's skill range is so small—if you can get even one out of three Healing Springs, you should kneel and thank Buddha! Besides, don't skills have cooldowns? Do you think I have 36D's that can be squeezed for heals all the time?"

Gao Zixiang said coolly, "I feel like those two lumps on your chest are indeed no smaller than a 36D."

"Bullshit, have you felt them before?"

Jing Huan froze.

The fuck is this NSFW conversation.

---

1 Aggro refers to the level of hostility a player generates toward an enemy (boss or mob). The player with the highest aggro will typically be targeted.

He put down the bag and glanced at the empty makeshift dining table, asking, "Where's the pot?"

Lu Wenhao barely spared him a glance. "Huanhuan, you're here so early. Wait a bit, we're in the middle of a twenty-five-man dungeon."

"Why are you playing *Nine Heroes* again?" Jing Huan asked. "Didn't you delete your character?"

"Well, I don't have many classes this semester and I'm dying of boredom every day. So I bought a character to accompany this dummy to clear dungeons. His party is about to participate in the all-server battle and they need a lot of materials." Lu Wenhao snorted twice. "And yet, instead of thanking me, he complains about my playstyle every day!"

Gao Zixiang replied, "But do you know what sect he bought a character for? Spirit Fox Den! Isn't he fucking with me on purpose? I asked him to switch sects but he didn't want to."

Jing Huan paused and asked, "What's wrong with Spirit Fox Dens? Aren't they pretty strong?"

"Other players are strong. He, on the other hand, can't even place a Healing Spring..." Another missed Healing Spring, and Gao Zixiang couldn't bear it anymore. "After this dungeon, you're switching sects for me!"

Jing Huan had no patience left for their quarrelling. "So, I brought all our food and drinks, and I still have to wait for you two young masters to finish playing before we can eat?"

"No, no, no, it's almost done, just ten more minutes...No, make that five," Gao Zixiang said. "Room 102 borrowed our pot, so we'll need to get it back from them."

 Chapter 04

Jing Huan was filled with regret. He should've bought a pot and seasoning himself, then cooked and eaten everything at home.

He picked up the bag again and turned around to leave.

"Hey Huanhuan, where are you going?" Gao Zixiang hurriedly called out to him.

"Going home to have hot pot."

"Don't!" Gao Zixiang cried out. "We're almost done, ge! Just sit down for a bit. Five minutes, I promise!"

Jing Huan raised his arm and glanced at his watch. "If you're not done in five minutes, I'll unplug your ethernet cable."

He threw the bag onto the bathroom counter and opened the dormitory door.

"Didn't you say five minutes?" Lu Wenhao pleaded. "Why are you still leaving..."

"Getting the pot," Jing Huan said, without turning his head.

Jing Huan knocked on the door of 102. It took a while before someone stirred inside, and when the door opened, an odor wafted out.

Jing Huan couldn't help but frown slightly, suppressing the urge to cover his nose.

"Yo, a rare visitor. Jing Huan, what brings you here?" The person who opened the door was a classmate from their major. They had played basketball together but weren't close.

"Yeah, I just came to get our room's pot."

"Oh right, I'll get it for you right away. Wait just a moment." The other person headed back into the room.

Jing Huan peeked through the crack of the door and beheld the situation inside. Forget everything else; just the mountain of smelly socks thrown outside the bathroom door was enough to make him lose most of his appetite.

That person was back at the door pretty quickly and handed the pot to Jing Huan, saying, "Sorry about that, we meant to return it earlier but got caught up in gaming."

"It's okay." Jing Huan took the pot and prepared to leave.

"Wait a minute, Jing Huan, I have something I wanted to talk to you about," the guy said. "My birthday's next weekend, and we're celebrating at the bar across the street. It's nothing big. Would you like to come?"

Their relationship wasn't close enough to warrant an invitation to each other's birthday parties. However, as long as Jing Huan came, he'd be like a walking advertisement with his good looks, and the birthday boy could invite all the girls in their major over.

Jing Huan smiled and, in a polite and distant tone, answered, "I have plans, so I can't make it."

He turned and left at once, giving the guy no chance of inviting him again.

Jing Huan went upstairs and inspected the pot in his hands.

If he wasn't mistaken, the orange stain on the lid...could it be from the spicy hot pot oil when Room 102 had hot pot? They had borrowed this pot before he moved out two weeks ago. Could this stain even be fucking washed off now?

He should just buy another one.

He thought for a moment and decided to check the inside of the pot before making any plans. He walked to the window in the stairwell, placed the pot on the windowsill, and casually opened the pot's lid.

Inside, he saw a black creature with an orange sheen lying quietly in the center of the pot. It was very eye-catching. Upon sensing movement, it quickly scuttled around the pot, demonstrating that it was still very much alive.

Facing this head-on without any mental preparation, Jing Huan froze for a few seconds, and then suddenly his legs went weak, nearly folding underneath him.

He opened his mouth to scream, only to find that he was so scared that he couldn't even make a sound.

Using his last bit of strength, he flung the pot into the air!

Jing Huan's greatest fear in life was bugs. Even seeing spider models in games made him uncomfortable, let alone having a live one right at his fingertips.

For a moment, he even felt like he was about to pass out.

The pot hit the ground with a loud, clanging sound. The cockroach crawled out of the pot, scurrying aimlessly. Jing Huan had quickly retreated from fright and missed a step. His heart nearly skipped a beat—

He bumped into a fleshy wall.

Jing Huan breathed a sigh of relief. At least he didn't fall to his death.

The person behind him was also startled, but he reacted extremely quickly. To prevent Jing Huan from falling further, he swiftly wrapped his arm around Jing Huan's waist, holding him steady.

"Are you all right?" the person behind him asked.

This voice was very familiar. Jing Huan instinctively blurted out, "I'm fine, thank you, ge—"

Both of them froze.

 Chapter 04

Jing Huan immediately realized what was happening and unleashed a silent storm of curses in his head.

That son of a bitch Yearning For, babbling in his ear every day, cursing him to think that everyone fucking sounded like him.

He turned and sincerely said to the guy behind him, "Thanks, bro."

Because of their positioning, when Jing Huan turned his head, all he could see was the other person's ear. They were so close that he could even smell the faint scent of soap lingering on the other guy's skin.

"No problem," said the person behind him. "Can you get up now?"

Jing Huan froze, and only after ascertaining that the cockroach had already run off did he stand up straight.

"Sorry about that." He swiveled around and finally looked at the unfortunate classmate he had collided with.

Single eyelids, a high nose bridge, and even when standing on a lower step, the guy, who was wearing a black T-shirt, could look him straight in the eye.

Jing Huan stared at the guy's face for a few seconds before remembering to ask, "Um, I didn't hurt you when I bumped into you, did I?"

"No." Xiang Huaizhi was also studying him.

This guy's eyelashes are unusually long.

"That's good. I just lost my balance." Jing Huan felt too embarrassed to admit that he had been terrified by a bug.

Xiang Huaizhi had actually seen everything, starting from when Jing Huan had thrown the pot. "Oh." He nodded. "Can you shift over a bit?"

Guide on How to Fail at Online Dating

Jing Huan currently had the entire stairwell essentially blocked with him on one side and his pot taking up the other.

"Oh, right." Jing Huan immediately made way. Anyway, he wasn't touching that pot ever again.

Xiang Huaizhi was about to go upstairs when he felt a tug on his sleeve.

"Hey, wait a minute," Jing Huan said. "I bumped into you pretty hard just now. If you feel unwell later, come to Room 312 and ask for me."

Xiang Huaizhi nodded. "Got it."

After watching his savior leave, Jing Huan stared at the pot on the ground. He was worrying about what to do with it when he raised his head and made eye contact with his two friends.

Gao Zixiang and Lu Wenhao were standing on the third-floor balcony, peering through the stairwell window at him. No one knew how long they had been watching, but when Jing Huan noticed them, they instinctively tried to hide.

Jing Huan sneered and raised his hand, pointing first at Gao Zixiang and then at Lu Wenhao.

You, and you. Then he sliced a finger across his throat. *You're both dead.*

The two on death row were frozen for some time. Then they started banging their heads against the railing.

The commotion brought the dormitory supervisor running over, who subsequently confiscated the pot. She also gave Jing Huan a few warnings, saying that the school strictly prohibited students from cooking in the dormitories.

He had already bought all the ingredients, and if they weren't

cooked tonight, they would spoil. Jing Huan stood atop the stairs, consoling himself before turning his steps toward the small shop outside the school gates where he bought a pot.

When he came back, he opened the dormitory room door to the sight of the makeshift dining table packed with washed vegetables and plated sliced meat. The beer had been poured into glasses, with his glass even decorated with a cherry on the rim.

"Big bro, you're back." Gao Zixiang scurried over to the door and made a welcoming gesture. "Your little brothers have been respectfully waiting for you!"

Lu Wenhao stood at the dining table and said, "Welcome, big bro! Sit in the seat of honor!"

Jing Huan's anger had already dissipated on the way here. "Idiots."

The three had already established on WeChat that Jing Huan would buy the food and booze while the other two would be responsible for washing the vegetables and dishes as they were the ones at fault here. Gao Zixiang stood up righteously and said, "Yes, yes, yes, we are idiots. Sit down. Don't get so angry that you harm yourself because Hao'er and I really can't afford that."

Jing Huan's irritation came out as a laugh. "All right, get up and sit in your seats."

The three sat down.

Still jumpy from what he had witnessed, Lu Wenhao said, "Fuck, these crappy dorm stairs are so high, if you really fell and got hurt, I'd have no choice but to pay you back with my body."

"Don't bother, just pay up with cash," said Jing Huan. "I have no interest in 36D's."

"That's perfect, I don't want you to rub them either." Lu Wenhao poured the hot pot base into the pot. "But Xiang Huaizhi is really awesome. You bumped into him really hard, but he barely budged. Didn't they say he had a leg injury?"

Gao Zixiang said, "That was so long ago, he's probably recovered by now."

Jing Huan asked, "Xiang Huaizhi? Who?"

"Your savior, the guy standing behind you." Gao Zixiang handed him the chili peppers. "You don't know him?"

Jing Huan thought for a moment and asked, "Is he from our department?"

"No, he's a senior from the neighboring department. He moved into our dorm this semester and lives upstairs in Room 522," Gao Zixiang said. "Oh, right, you don't go to the basketball court near the west gate that often, so you probably haven't met him before. He's really fucking good at basketball."

"They say he's a top student, and most importantly…" Lu Wenhao drawled, "he's very handsome. He's a prominent figure in our school, I thought you knew about him."

"Sorry, but the only prominent figure I know in our school is myself." The spicy broth in the pot was already at a rolling boil. Jing Huan had deliberately bought a pot that looked different from the old one, and finally regained some of his appetite. As he spoke, he picked up a piece of pork tripe and swished it through the broth.

"So arrogant." Gao Zixiang laughed but didn't refute him. "Then, Mr. Prominent Figure, when exactly are you coming back to play *Nine Heroes* with us?"

Jing Huan paused. "Why are you suddenly bringing this up?"

Chapter 04

"How is it sudden? We agreed before that the three of us were going to fight in the all-server PK, but it's been an entire year, and we still haven't done it!" Something occurred to Gao Zixiang. "And I heard that there will be some particularly impressive rewards for the all-server PK this year."

"Where did you hear that?" asked Jing Huan.

"My guild leader knows someone who works for the game."

This kind of news was fake eighty percent of the time, and Jing Huan brushed it off. "Oh," he said. "We'll see, I'm busy right now."

Nodding, Gao Zixiang said, "If I hadn't seen your class schedule, I might've believed you."

"I really don't have time."

"So tell us, what are you so busy with?"

Busy picking up scumbags.

Jing Huan took a sip of beer and said, "Anyway, I'm just busy. Let's talk when I'm done."

After eating and drinking his fill, Jing Huan repeatedly warned his two friends not to lend out the pot before leaving the dormitory.

He had just taken two steps out when, by a strange coincidence, he looked up at Room 522.

A colorful pair of underwear was hanging on the clothes rack outside of the room. Jing Huan squinted and realized the underwear had various Pikachus in different poses printed on it.

Who would've thought? My savior might not have big anime eyes, but he's quite extravagant.

Jing Huan returned home and as soon as he logged into the game, his friend message icon started flashing non-stop.

[Friend] OFF!: Meimei, good news!

[Friend] Sweet Little Jing: Ah?

[Friend] OFF!: Idle Pavilion is no longer hunting you!

Jing Huan was taken aback. He scanned around and realized something: the familiar faces who usually camped him as soon as he logged on were nowhere to be found today.

[Friend] Sweet Little Jing: Why?

[Friend] OFF!: Hmm...I'm not really sure. The guild leader just posted a guild announcement saying we should work together to gather materials and not waste time on you.

Jing Huan's mouth twitched. *Who exactly is wasting whose time?!*

But this was good; he still had some serious business to take care of, and being hunted was really quite troublesome.

He left the city and did two daily quests. Everything was going very smoothly, and he wasn't used to it.

[Friend] Long Road Ahead: Are you there?

[Friend] Sweet Little Jing: Yes, what's up~?

[Friend] Long Road Ahead: Wanna clear dungeons? It's a twenty-man dungeon, and your crush is also here.

[Friend] Sweet Little Jing: Coming!!!

[Friend] Sweet Little Jing: [Cheer] Where are we gathering?

"Everyone is already here," Lu Hang said. "We're gathering in front of Yue Lao."

As soon as Xiang Huaizhi flew to Yue Lao, he saw Sweet Little Jing standing next to Yue Lao.

Without a word, he requested to join the dungeon party.

【Yearning For has joined the Second Young Master's Wedding dungeon party.】

【Sweet Little Jing has joined the Second Young Master's Wedding dungeon party.】

[Party] Long Road Ahead: Is everyone ready? If we're all okay, then I'll start the dungeon.

[Party] Love is Sharing Noms: 1.

[Party] Peach Cheese Stan: ...1.

[Party] Echoes of Spring: .

[Party] Regardless of Lovesickness: ...

[Party] Sweet Little Jing: ...0x0

All the other people in the party couldn't help but exclaim internally, *What kind of goddamn death train is this!!*

...These guys won't start fighting mid-dungeon, will they?!

[Party] Long Road Ahead: Just to be clear, any high-tier materials will be split among the party members. If a rare item drops, we'll roll dice for it. Anyone who objects to this can leave the party now.

This was the standard rule for large dungeons. After half a minute of silence with no protests, Lu Hang started the dungeon.

The Second Young Master's Wedding dungeon required a Mystery Invitation item to trigger it. Obtaining this item was purely based on RNG; the chances of getting it as a drop after clearing a dungeon were very slim. Since Lu Hang had just obtained the item this afternoon, he immediately rushed to run the dungeon.

Although the dungeon wasn't very difficult, the process was very tedious. Worried about unreliable random players, Lu Hang only invited people from his friend list.

The party's voice channel was eerily silent; no one was talking. The first phase of the dungeon was a solo search quest, and the

twenty players completed it quickly, moving directly to the next phase of quests.

As soon as he entered the portal, Jing Huan's game interface suddenly changed. He was pulled into a special scenario outside of the Second Young Master's mansion.

【Gate Guard: Lady Sweet Little Jing, we have never seen you before! Since you claim to be the Second Young Master's teacher, let me test you.】

Jing Huan had always found this dungeon annoying and had never done it before. Completely unprepared, he clicked the "Yes!" option.

【Gate Guard: May I ask, what category of trash do wet wipes belong to?】

It took Jing Huan several seconds to register what the question was asking.

This stupid game is too progressive.

All was quiet in his headset. Perhaps everyone was lazy, or maybe they knew some people in the party were at odds with Sweet Little Jing and didn't dare to break the awkward atmosphere. No one spoke up or gave him any hints in the party voice channel.

Jing Huan glanced at the answer choices and breathed a sigh of relief. Fortunately, the answer was very obvious.

He didn't hesitate to choose "Wet Garbage."

【Gate Guard: Guards! Drive out this imposter!】

Jing Huan's mind went blank with bafflement.

[Party] Love is Sharing Noms: Wet wipes are dry garbage...

[Party] Sweet Little Jing: ??

[Party] Sweet Little Jing: How do you know what I chose? [Shocked]

[Party] Long Road Ahead: This is a randomized phase, a player is chosen arbitrarily to complete the challenge while the rest of the party waits.

[Party] Sweet Little Jing: ...

[Party] Sweet Little Jing: So that means...?

[Party] Long Road Ahead: Yes, we're all watching you. But don't worry, you can answer as many times as you need. Fighting [Cheer]

[Party] Sweet Little Jing: ...Great! [Smile]

【Gate Guard: May I ask, in total, how many items did your party search for in the first phase of this dungeon?

a. 71

b. 99

c. 69

d. Video Playback】

Who would remember that? Jing Huan clicked on the "Video Playback" option.

【Gate Guard: There's no playback! Guards! Drive out this imposter!】

Jing Huan took a deep breath.

【Gate Guard: May I ask what the name of the young lady who is painstakingly waiting for her lover to return at Liuxi River is?】

This, Jing Huan knew; it was a wilderness map in *Nine Heroes* where there was indeed a young lady NPC.

What's her name?

To be safe, Jing Huan searched on Baidu and caught the name "Auntie Liu." Not wanting to waste everyone's time, he speedily switched back to the game and clicked on that option.

【Gate Guard: Guards! Drive out this imposter!】

Jing Huan was aghast.

[Party] Regardless of Lovesickness: You actually answered Auntie Liu here?! Did you not see the word "young lady"? Are you doing this on purpose? Are you trying to burn through our game time? [Suspicious]

What's going on? Is shitty Baidu misleading people?

Jing Huan switched back to the webpage and took another look.

【Netizen's answer: First of all, we can cross out the "Auntie Liu" option since the ages don't match up.】

Jing Huan had never felt as bewildered as he did in this moment.

You want to analyze a question that can be answered by just glancing at the wilderness map?!

[Party] Regardless of Lovesickness: I actually want to see how many questions it takes before you answer one right.

Why don't you answer them if you're so smart?!

Fuming, Jing Huan clicked on the gate guard again.

【Gate Guard: What is the next line in this poem, "water flies down three thousand chi[2]"?】

Finally—something he knew.

As Jing Huan recalled the poem, he couldn't help but murmur, " 'Water flies down three thousand chi…' "

" 'But nothing can compare to Wang Lun's feelings for me[3],' " a

---

2   A line from the poem Gazing at the Waterfall on Mount Lu by Li Bai. The next line should be "as if a silver stream is falling down from the heavens." Li Bai is the most famous Tang dynasty poet and is widely taught and quoted.

3   A line from A Gift to Wang Lun, another Li Bai poem. The line before it is actually "Peach Blossom Pool is a thousand chi deep." The rhythm is also "chi."

Chapter 04

familiar voice came through his headset. There was a teasing note threaded through the voice.

Right, right, that's the one.

Jing Huan instinctively clicked on the corresponding option on the screen.

【Gate Guard: Guards! Drive out this imposter!】

[Party] Love is Sharing Noms: ...

[Party] Echoes of Spring: ...

[Party] Regardless of Lovesickness: ...

[Party] Peach Cheese Stan: ...

Xiang Huaizhi huffed out a laugh. "You really believed me?"

Jing Huan stilled.

What type of trash are you?

Lu Hang sat on the bed, laughing hysterically as he rocked back and forth, causing the whole bed to shake with his movements.

"Old Xiang, you're too inhumane."

"Since you're so humane, why didn't you remind her?" Xiang Huaizhi asked.

"I wanted to, but I really didn't know the answers to the previous questions. Don't you remember the housekeeping auntie fined me for throwing trash into the wrong bin? Anyhow, who'd remember how many quests they just did or what the NPCs in low-level wilderness maps are called?"

Xiang Huaizhi didn't respond. He watched Sweet Little Jing standing in front of the guard at the door, her back looking even more desperate than when she had seen the previous question.

Just a moment ago, he had found the sight of the figure's

back amusing, so he couldn't help but blurt out that sentence.

[Party] Yearning For: My bad.

No shit, if it wasn't your bad, then was it my bad?!

You made me embarrass myself in front of Regardless of Lovesickness! I'm going to murder you!!

Jing Huan gritted his teeth while typing on his keyboard, letting out a flurry of clacks.

[Party] Sweet Little Jing: *Waaaaaah* T.T! Gege, you big meanie!

[Party] Yearning For: ...

Eventually, Jing Huan managed to pass this stage and he breathed a sigh of relief. He would never run this shitty dungeon again. It was so tedious and didn't give much experience. He wouldn't do it, even with a hundred thousand crushes.

This dungeon's main quest was to rescue the bride who was forcibly taken back to the mansion by the Second Young Master, so they spent most of their time searching for people and objects, with battles rarely triggering. After half an hour of questioning, they finally obtained a clue.

They saw a message appear on the quest log:

【Congratulations on obtaining Miss Liu's Bridal Sedan Chair Route. Quickly disguise yourselves and head to Chang'an City at (121, 47) to disrupt this wedding! (Two-person party required, 20-minute time limit.)】

Before Jing Huan could take a closer look, a quest item appeared in his inventory.

He dragged his mouse over it and saw it was a bright red wedding dress.

"Who got the wedding dress?" Lu Hang asked.

[Party] Sweet Little Jing: ...Me.

"You again, huh..." Lu Hang couldn't help but snigger. "All right, get changed."

Get changed? Why?

Upon seeing her motionless figure, Lu Hang understood and said, "You haven't done this dungeon before, have you? I'll explain: You need to choose a party member, form a 'wedding party,' and crash into Miss Liu's bridal sedan chair. We'll take advantage of the ensuing chaos to snatch the bride. You just need to sit in the bridal sedan chair and AFK, it's very easy."

[Party] Sweet Little Jing: Can't we just go snatch her? 0.0

Lu Hang replied, "Nope, the dumbass game designers insisted on this process."

[Party] Sweet Little Jing: Oh, oh, and I choose a party member? Can I pick anyone?

"Yes," Lu Hang answered.

As if sensing something, Xiang Huaizhi typed: I'm going to go AFK—

Before he could send the message, the little spirit fox jumped in front of him, and a prompt popped up in the game.

【Sweet Little Jing invites you to join her party: Yes, No.】

Xiang Huaizhi froze.

Her invitation couldn't have been more obvious; if he rejected her, he would humiliate the girl.

Xiang Huaizhi sighed and clicked "Yes."

Then he raised his hand and deleted the words in the chat box.

As soon as Xiang Huaizhi joined the party, a wedding robe

appeared in his inventory. He didn't think twice before he right-clicked on the robe to change into it.

The moment they both had the wedding gear on, the bridal sedan chair appeared. Xiang Huaizhi was aggressively placed on the horse by the system, and Sweet Little Jing was stuffed into the bridal sedan chair. The procession slowly advanced toward the city center.

The rest of the party followed alongside the bridal sedan chair, waiting for their chance.

"Gege." Jing Huan turned his voice chat to Party, and now, only Yearning For could hear him. "Are you going to fight in the arena later?"

"Mm."

He thought she would ask him to take her along, but unexpectedly, Sweet Little Jing merely chirped, "Mhm, mhm, good luck, gege."

A beat, then Xiang Huaizhi asked, "Do you want to go?"

Jing Huan lazily replied, "I waaant to, but my gear is still garbage. If I go, I'll just be giving away free points…"

"If you want to go, I'll take you."

Jing Huan jerked back.

When did this person become so nice?

"No…I don't want you to lose points because of me."

Xiang Huaizhi actually had no ulterior motives. He realized that Sweet Little Jing was playing the game because of him, and although he wasn't obligated to be responsible for her, he wouldn't be stingy about helping her when he could.

However, since the other person refused, he wouldn't insist. "Mm, up to you."

Jing Huan sat in the bridal sedan chair, unable to even see the scenery, bored out of his mind. He continued to chat with Yearning For, "God of War-gege, why don't you join a guild?"

"Too much trouble, don't want to join." Xiang Huaizhi paused. "Don't call me that anymore."

"Then what should I call youuu?" Jing Huan singsonged. "God of War? Yearning-gege? Yearning For-gege?"

Xiang Huaizhi's head was pounding listening to this, making it impossible for him to think of a suitable name on the spot. Reluctantly, he chose the most normal one: "Just call me gege."

Sitting behind him, Lu Hang couldn't believe his ears.

He'd said it offhandedly the other day, but Xiang Huaizhi really had accepted a meimei?!

Jing Huan replied, "Okaaay, gege."

"Don't use that tone of voice."

"Then how should I say it?"

"Don't act flirty," Xiang Huaizhi said flatly. "Speak in your natural voice."

Lu Hang thought, *That's hurtful, Old Xiang. Dense straight guy[4].*

If a girl heard this, she probably would've been offended, but Jing Huan wasn't. He didn't pitch his voice up anymore, and like a dedicated Taobao customer service representative who perfectly matched the customer's requirements, he asked, "Okay, gege, what about this?"

The girl's voice was a bit hoarse, not as coquettish as before, but

---

4 The Chinese social media slang 恶臭直男 - è chòu zhí nán which sarcastically describes men perceived as having stereotypical toxic traits, like toxic masculinity or sexism.

with more of a onee-san[5] vibe; it was much more pleasing to the ear.

Xiang Huaizhi said, "Mm. Let me take a look at your gear."

Jing Huan obediently linked all his equipment in the party chat.

After casually scanning the first two items, Xiang Huaizhi didn't inspect any further. Sweet Little Jing wasn't downplaying herself; her gear consisted of common items with her best weapon being just a blue item with no socketed gems. No wonder it had only taken three hits for Regardless of Lovesickness to kill her in the arena that day.

"Run more dungeons when you have time; you'll get equipment as loot. Even a random drop will be better than what you're wearing," Xiang Huaizhi said. "You're a Spirit Fox Den, so you should focus on seal accuracy rate, movement speed, and healing attributes."

Jing Huan listened for a long time before the realization struck him: *Is Yearning For trying to teach me how to play this game?*

It was strange to say, but Jing Huan realized that since they finished playing in the arena together, Yearning For's attitude toward him seemed much kinder. He even responded to his greetings, albeit briefly. Still, it was better than being completely ignored.

Jing Huan said, "Mhm, thank you, gege. I'll work hard and run more dungeons soon."

In that short time, the bridal sedan chair had already rushed to the center of the street and crashed fiercely into Miss Liu's bridal sedan chair, immediately stirring up chaos and uproar. Their party members acted decisively and swiftly, snatching the bride away in less than thirty seconds.

---

5   The Japanese term for "older sister" but is popular among otaku.

"Okay, secured," Lu Hang said. "Now, let's finish this and take down the boss. It's not hard, so everyone just go do your thing."

Three minutes later, the Second Young Master boss fell to the ground with a loud thud, and simultaneously, the dice-rolling interface appeared in the game.

This was *Nine Heroes'* dungeon reward system: the twenty participants would roll dice, and whoever got the highest number would get the item reward.

They called it rolling the dice, but it was really just clicking a button. Jing Huan clicked on the "roll" button and rolled three ones.

"Triple aces, amazing," Lu Hang said.

Jing Huan didn't say anything; he was used to it.

In the end, Yearning For won with his roll of seventeen. The moment the dice roll interface disappeared, a system message popped up.

【[Party] Player Yearning For acted heroically and drew his sword against injustice, successfully rescuing Miss Liu from the clutches of the Second Young Master. To express her gratitude, Miss Liu gifted the precious Nine Brahma's Lotus to Yearning For.】

Jealousy surged through Jing Huan. How was Yearning For's character so lucky? He just casually cleared a dungeon and managed to get a purple ring drop?

He checked the ring's attributes and couldn't help but curse, "Fuck."

Healing +18, stamina +17, and since good things came in pairs, it even had an added effect—players had the chance to double the healing output during battle. Although it wasn't very likely to happen, if it activated even once during a PK match, that would be more than enough.

It was the perfect ring for a Putuo Mountain player.

[Party] Love is Sharing Noms: ...[Lemon[6]]

[Party] Sweet Little Jing: [Lemon][Lemon]

[Party] Peach Cheese Stan: The rich just get richer.

[Party] Long Road Ahead: Boss, split the loot, hurry up.

[Party] Yearning For: Mm.

As per the rules, Xiang Huaizhi gave each party member seven gold as their share of the loot.

[Party] Echoes of Spring: Yearning For, name a price for that healing ring.

Echoes of Spring happened to be a Putuo Mountain player, and as soon as she laid her eyes on that ring, she wanted it.

[Party] Yearning For: Not selling.

[Party] Echoes of Spring: Why? It's not like you can use it.

[Party] Yearning For: I can.

[Party] Echoes of Spring: ...Okay then, but if you ever want to sell it, contact me.

Jing Huan had originally wanted to ask Yearning For to sell him the ring because even though the ring was better suited for Putuo Mountains, Spirit Fox Dens could also use it. But after he saw this conversation, that thought quickly disappeared.

The dungeon party disbanded on the spot. Jing Huan set his character to AFK vend in the main city and then slowly browsed the marketplace for equipment listings.

He actually enjoyed competing in the arena, but everything was

---

6   The lemon emoji represents the "sour feeling" someone gets when they're jealous. In Chinese, being sour/eating vinegar means they are envious.

Chapter 04

made infinitely harder without a decent set of gear. Unfortunately, the high-tier gear in the marketplace was too expensive at this time, and the cheap gear was just trash. Despite browsing for a long time, he didn't manage to find anything worthwhile.

Just then, the chat window in *Nine Heroes* lit up.

[Friend] Yearning For: Where are you?

[Friend] Sweet Little Jing: Selling items in the main city. 0.0

[Friend] Yearning For: Coordinates.

[Friend] Sweet Little Jing: (10, 11) What's up, gege?

Xiang Huaizhi ran to the main city at those coordinates, and sure enough, saw the little spirit fox sitting on the ground with a big sign above her head that read:

【Clearance, clearance, can't afford food.】

Gaze turned elsewhere, he moved his fingers and threw the Nine Brahma's Lotus to her; he had just gone to his storage to pick up some dungeon loot and had socketed a level 5 gem into it, making it barely usable.

Jing Huan was momentarily stunned when he saw the item that Yearning For tossed over, and then he remembered to type.

[Friend] Sweet Little Jing: [Shocked][Blinking]

[Friend] Sweet Little Jing: ...Did you throw the wrong thing?

[Friend] Yearning For: No.

[Friend] Sweet Little Jing: Oh, oh, how much is it? I'll transfer it to you.

[Friend] Yearning For: No need, you can use it for quest grinding, and also when you fight in the arena.

[Friend] Sweet Little Jing: ?

[Friend] Sweet Little Jing: [Screaming] GEGE!

[Friend] Sweet Little Jing: IS THIS A GIFT FOR ME?

Xiang Huaizhi quickly typed up a reply.

[Friend] Sweet Little Jing: A LOVE TOKEN?!

[Friend] Yearning For: Mm.

The two messages appeared in the chat window one after another, in the same second.

Xiang Huaizhi froze.

What's with this bad habit of splitting one sentence into three messages?

[Friend] Sweet Little Jing: !!!

[Friend] Sweet Little Jing: THANK YOU GEGE!!!

[Friend] Sweet Little Jing: I'll definitely cherish it! I'll put a level 15 gem in it! I won't let its durability drop below 300 points! I'll even hug it to sleep at night!! QAQ

[Friend] Sweet Little Jing: [Twirling][Kowtowing][Kissing][Blows a kiss]

Xiang Huaizhi was overwhelmed by all these stickers.

[Friend] Yearning For: Not a love token, it comes with conditions.

[Friend] Sweet Little Jing: Tell me, gege!

[Friend] Yearning For: When you send me stickers, you can't use more than three at a time from now on.

[Friend] Sweet Little Jing: Okayyy~ [Kiss kiss]

[Friend] Yearning For: [Kiss kiss] You're also not allowed to send this sticker.

[Friend] Sweet Little Jing: ...

[Friend] Sweet Little Jing: Oh. QAQ

Jing Huan glanced at his newly obtained ring several more

Chapter 04

times. The ring had great attributes and could easily be sold for a good price whenever, so it was considered a grand gift.

He didn't like taking things from other people for free. He had originally planned to pay for it, but then he thought to himself—— what was his purpose in playing *Nine Heroes* in the first place?

Wasn't it to screw over Yearning For?

It wasn't enough to simply deceive him; he also needed to pay up! Jing Huan wanted this scumbag to lose both his heart and money! He would make Yearning For regret it so much that he'd never dare to mess around with young girls online for the rest of his life!

If he thought about it that way, he didn't feel so guilty anymore.

He locked the ring and equipped it. A light blue lotus ring appeared on his character's finger instantaneously, dazzling in its bright glow, and looking quite beautiful.

This was also one of *Nine Heroes'* key features, in that all equipment worn would appear on the characters as well, to let the elite players flaunt to their heart's content.

Jing Huan stared at his character for a long time before suddenly recalling that this character had a lot of different cash shop outfits.

It was one of its biggest highlights. This character had every one of *Nine Heroes'* limited-edition outfits, all of which were bound to the character and discontinued, unlike cultivation skills that could be trained at any time. With this, the character would retain its value when he sold it in the future. This was also the main reason why he had chosen to buy this specific character back then.

He opened the wardrobe and picked out a discontinued blue dress to change into.

As he gazed at his character, he clicked his tongue, shaking his head. *Who wouldn't want to develop a passionate online relationship with such a lovely, mature onee-san?*

He nonchalantly took screenshots of her, erased the game ID, and sent them to his dormitory group chat.

Little Jing~: [Image]

Lu Wenhao: ...I double-checked the group chat name several times after seeing this. Why did you send this?

Little Jing~: Oh, I found it while scrolling through Moments, doesn't she look nice?

Lu Wenhao opened the photo and peeked at it a few times before muttering, "That outfit is so tacky though. It's the ugliest limited-edition dress..."

Lu Wenhao: Who is this?

Little Jing~: Why are you asking so many questions?

Little Jing~: It's a goddess I met while playing *Nine Heroes*, isn't she pretty?

Lu Wenhao: Graceful and elegant, a fairy who descended to Earth, devastatingly beautiful.

Satisfied, Jing Huan sent a thumbs-up.

With his attention and game screen occupied by WeChat, he was completely unaware that several familiar faces were standing next to his character.

Fae Bae and her group had passed by while doing a quest. When she saw Sweet Little Jing, she immediately stopped in her tracks. The girls in her party also quickly reacted.

[Party] Ji Xiaonian: What bad luck, why do we see her everywhere! And her outfit is sooo ugly! [Vomiting]

[Party] Ji Xiaonian: Wait a moment, look at what's on her hand. Is that the Nine Brahma's Lotus? Don't tell me that...

In *Nine Heroes*, when players obtained high-value items during quests or dungeons, the system sent an announcement to the World Channel. Therefore, all the players who had been online earlier knew that Yearning For had won a purple ring during a dungeon event.

[Party] Love is Sharing Noms: Meh, it's okay. Although it's not very pretty, at least it's a limited-edition dress.

[Party] Love is Sharing Noms: Let's go do the quest, or we'll run out of time.

[Party] Ji Xiaonian: What, you don't like hearing us talking about your friend?

[Party] Love is Sharing Noms: ...What does *that* mean?

[Party] Fae Bae: Didn't you just clear a dungeon with her?

[Party] Ji Xiaonian: Yeah, and you did the same thing before. We agreed that we'd screw her over together, but in the end, you wussed out, and let me look like the bad guy.

The two other male party members wanted no part in the matter, so they quickly went AFK, pretending they were not there.

Love is Sharing Noms now understood. No wonder these two had been purposefully ignoring her, their group chat dead.

[Party] Love is Sharing Noms: I just feel like we shouldn't go out of our way to ruin someone's gaming experience without clearly understanding the situation.

[Party] Ji Xiaonian: Weren't you the one who said you hated her before?

[Party] Love is Sharing Noms: Yes, I hate her playing cute, but

she hasn't done anything to hurt me, didn't do anything outrageous. She even saved me in the dungeon. I also felt that I was in the wrong there, so I apologized to her. Is there a problem with any of that?

[Party] Ji Xiaonian: So you're saying I have a problem?

[Party] Love is Sharing Noms: ...That's not what I meant.

[Party] Ji Xiaonian: So, you think it's okay for her to flirt with Faefae's husband? She's being a homewrecker by trying to seduce him!

[Party] Love is Sharing Noms: I think, at most, Yearning For would be considered Faefae's ex-boyfriend.

[Party] Fae Bae: All right, are you finished?

[Party] Fae Bae: So you're saying that you're siding with Sweet Little Jing and not me, right?

[Party] Love is Sharing Noms: When have I ever sided with Sweet Little Jing? Haven't I always been supporting you? Back when you posted about Yearning For on the forum, I even used my main account to help you curse him out with dozens of comments.

[Party] Fae Bae: Well, thank you for helping me back then.

[Party] Fae Bae: But I need to make something very clear to you: I never broke up with Yearning For. We had a fight, and he didn't want to make up. I impulsively wanted to use the public's opinion to pressure him, but we're not really over. So, Sweet Little Jing is a husband-seducing homewrecker, understood?

Jing Huan chatted for a while in the group chat, asking Gao Zixiang to help him save a seat in class tomorrow before closing WeChat.

He glanced at the items he had put in the stall for sale. Not a single one had been sold. He muttered, "Business is slow…"

 Chapter 04

He didn't really need the money but when he bought this character, it came with a plethora of useless junk. Value-wise, they weren't worth much but it'd be a pity to just toss them, so he usually put them up for sale when he had nothing else to do.

Just as he was about to pack up his stall and leave, he saw a very familiar little loli character in a pink dress standing next to him.

The loli neither set up a stall nor moved, and after a moment's thought, Jing Huan typed a message.

[Current] Sweet Little Jing: 0.0 Huh.

[Current] Love is Sharing Noms: ...Oh, you're here.

[Current] Sweet Little Jing: Just came back, were you waiting for me? [Doubtful]

[Current] Love is Sharing Noms: Sigh, no, I had an argument with a friend and was just standing here and spacing out.

[Current] Sweet Little Jing: It's not good to argue. [Shaking head]

Who did I do all that for?

Love is Sharing Noms couldn't even get mad looking at the sticker in the chat.

[Current] Love is Sharing Noms: By the way, where did you get the ring on your finger?

[Current] Sweet Little Jing: Ah!

[Current] Sweet Little Jing: [Shy][Blinking] So annoooying. Don't you know?

[Current] Love is Sharing Noms: ...How much did you pay for it?

[Current] Sweet Little Jing: [Shut up] Gege gave it to me, I didn't buy it.

Love is Sharing Noms frowned. She typed, wanting to ask if Sweet Little Jing knew about the situation between Yearning For and Fae Bae, but halfway through, she deleted her message.

Forget it, it wasn't appropriate to talk about these things in the Current Channel. Besides, she wasn't in a good mood right now and didn't want to meddle in other people's business.

[Current] Love is Sharing Noms: Oh, oh, I'm going to do quests now. Let's chat next time.

[Current] Sweet Little Jing: Okay, I hope you and your friend make up soon. [Waving]

With a new week came the latest "Rule Violater List" on the men's dormitory building's bulletin board, with Room 312 proudly emblazoned at the top. The reason listed said: "Brought a pot into the dorm to cook hot pot, repeatedly warned with no change in behavior, truly despicable!"

The word "despicable" was enlarged and bolded, an indication of the scale of the dormitory supervisor's rage.

When Lu Hang told Xiang Huaizhi about this matter, Xiang Huaizhi's thoughts immediately flashed to the boy he had met in the stairwell that day.

If he remembered correctly, didn't that guy mention he was from Room 312?

"Are you listening, Xiang-gege?" Lu Hang asked again when he didn't respond.

"Get lost," Xiang Huaizhi said. "Who are you calling gege?"

"Oh, so Sweet Little Jing can call you that, but I can't, I get it." Lu Hang said. "Xiangxiang, how about we buy a pot to cook hot pot in our dorm too?"

Xiang Huaizhi asked, "What, you want to compete with Room 312 for the dorm supervisor auntie's attention?"

"So you were listening." Lu Hang laughed. "Those two juniors are quite pitiful. I heard they were fined, had their pot confiscated, and even got the hot pot soup base taken away."

It was confiscated again?

Xiang Huaizhi asked, "Do you know them?"

"Yeah, but not that well. Everyone in their dorm plays *Nine Heroes*. I saw them at the last in-person game meetup. They're pretty strong, but unfortunately, they're not in our server."

Xiang Huaizhi logged into the game while listening to Lu Hang natter away. As soon as he logged in, a friend message notification popped up in the bottom right corner.

It wasn't an old message, the sender had been waiting for him to log on.

[Friend] Fae Bae: Xiang-ge, did you give Sweet Little Jing that ring?

[Friend] Yearning For: Mm.

"No way, why is she still looking for you and even calling you 'ge…'" Lu Hang paused mid-sentence. "Wait, you gave that purple ring to Sweet Little Jing? Damn, you're so generous, Xiangxiang! Are you interested in her?"

"No."

"I definitely don't believe that," Lu Hang said. "Who would give money to someone for no reason?"

"It's useless for me to hold onto it."

"But you could've just sold it. Just put it up on the marketplace, it would've been sold in minutes."

The words came out of Xiang Huaizhi's mouth very naturally. "It's just spare change. I'm too lazy to put it up for sale and withdrawing the money is too troublesome."

"Yes, moving your fingers to input your bank card number and withdrawal password will completely drain the rest of your elderly life," Lu Hang said. "Quick, she replied, see what she said."

[Friend] Fae Bae: We haven't cleared things up between us, and you're messing around with someone else. Isn't that inappropriate? [Aggrieved]

[Friend] Yearning For: Everything has been cleared up.

[Friend] Fae Bae: …Fine, you said it wasn't you who was playing the character for the past few months, I'll believe that. But you also said that you would compensate me, right?

"What? Compensate her for what? What does this situation have to do with you?" Lu Hang was puzzled.

"This all started with my character, after all," Xiang Huaizhi said calmly.

[Friend] Yearning For: Okay, name it.

The reply came without a moment's hesitation, as if she had already planned it.

[Friend] Fae Bae: Let's get married.

Xiang Huaizhi slowly typed out a question mark.

[Friend] Yearning For: Are you dreaming?

Fae Bae was very unhappy about the entire situation.

She had been in this server for five years and had followed Yearning For for just as long. Ever since the game launched, he had always been at the top with his name constantly ranking high on the lists, and was wholly unattainable.

What girl hadn't fantasized about being with such a shining beacon of a man?

So when Yearning For showed a bit of tenderness toward her, she couldn't resist and rushed forward with her eyes closed.

When she met Yearning For in person, he looked nothing like what she expected. She even felt a bit disgusted. However, she still willingly spent money on him, and just before leaving, as she lay in his arms, she insisted that he promise to marry her in-game when they got back.

Sometimes, Fae Bae couldn't even tell if she liked the real person behind Yearning For, or if she just liked the virtual game character itself.

What she didn't expect was that as soon as the two parted ways, before she even got off her plane, he would block her on WeChat.

When she confronted Yearning For in the game, he coldly told her that he had hired someone to play the character for the past few months; it had not been him.

All those inseparable months together had now become a joke. Yearning For refused to marry her, and to add insult to injury, he now refused to be in the same party with her.

What she couldn't stand the most was that Yearning For now had other women around him. First, it was Ranxin, and then it was Sweet Little Jing. That little spirit fox stuck to Yearning For like a shadow most days; they fought in the arena together, cleared dungeons together, and now Yearning For had given her a piece of purple equipment.

She took a deep breath and typed.

[Friend] Fae Bae: Of course I'm awake, let me finish.

[Friend] Fae Bae: It's just an in-game marriage, we're not actually gonna be together. I just want the couple's title.

"I find this woman really weird. Anyone else would've tried to find the scammer as soon as they realized they were being duped, but why does she keep pestering you like a leech?" Lu Hang was speechless. "And for the past few months, your character clearly didn't act like your usual self, right? If you just sent out a megaphone to clarify everything, I guarantee that everyone in this server will believe you."

That was true. Xiang Huaizhi had been playing in this server for so long that the other players' impression of him was that he was powerful, low-key, and rich. Apart from gathering materials, Yearning For rarely appeared on the World Channel chat or megaphones.

When this incident first happened, many of his friends had flocked to him, asking if his character had been hacked.

Xiang Huaizhi had remained noncommittal and silent, which had instead cemented his scumbag status.

Xiang Huaizhi replied, "It's not necessary." It wouldn't be appropriate to let the entire server know that she and another girl had both been tricked by the hired player.

Besides, this incident hadn't negatively impacted him at all, at least for now. He even got to avoid a lot of trouble because of it. He couldn't complain.

[Friend] Yearning For: The compensation I mentioned refers to reimbursing you for the airfare and hotel expenses that you previously paid.

[Friend] Fae Bae: I just want the title, is that too much to ask for?

[Friend] Fae Bae: Which city are you in? Let's meet and talk, okay?

Lu Hang jumped. "Is this woman crazy? You've barely chatted and she's already asking to meet in person?"

[Friend] Yearning For: If you don't need to be compensated for those things, then there's no need to talk anymore.

[Friend] Fae Bae: Fine, then I want another type of compensation: in-game items, okay?

[Friend] Yearning For: Name it.

[Friend] Fae Bae: I want the Nine Brahma's Lotus, the one you gave to Sweet Little Jing.

Xiang Huaizhi just glanced at that message and then closed the chat window.

"*Interesting,*" Lu Hang said. "She really wants to break you and Sweet Little Jing up, huh? Well, I, Long Road Ahead, will be the first to object! Xiangxiang, I don't think you should even compensate her for the hotel fees or airfare. Just delete her and wash your hands of this."

Xiang Huaizhi gave him a sideways glance. "You seem to really like Sweet Little Jing?"

"Not really, I just think she's quite fun. Watching her talk every day cracks me up," Lu Hang replied.

Xiang Huaizhi nodded. "Then go pursue her and she'll talk to you every day."

"Sure, when she logs in, you tell her to come and pursue me. She'll definitely listen to you, and when the time comes, I guarantee that I'll take care of her like a good gege."

"Get lost. Be serious for once." Xiang Huaizhi shot him a sharp look. "How much longer are you going to stand behind me? Are you addicted to peeking at screens now?"

"Tch...all right, all right, all right, I'm going now."

Xiang Huaizhi got on his mount and went to a wilderness map to gather materials. As he casually glanced at his interface, he saw a system notification.

【Your friend Sweet Little Jing has logged on.】

A few seconds later, his friend message icon lit up.

[Friend] Sweet Little Jing: [Scattering flowers]

[Friend] Yearning For: ?

[Friend] Sweet Little Jing: Gege, are we running dungeons today?

[Friend] Yearning For: Mm, after the dailies are finished.

[Friend] Sweet Little Jing: Okay gege, call me when you're done. I'll be here whenever you need me. #^0^#

The dailies were quickly completed, and Lu Hang created a party for the daily dungeon.

Chapter 05

When Lu Hang saw Little Jingjing's outfit, he couldn't resist turning on his microphone to roast her, "Change out of that outfit."

Jing Huan asked, "Why?"

"It's too ugly."

Jing Huan frowned; it didn't look ugly to him. "It's not uglyyy? It matches perfectly with the ring gege gave me!"

Lu Hang tutted. "Speaking of that ring...Just now..."

Xiang Huaizhi interrupted him, leaving the party to form his own. "I'll go get the magic relic in a bit."

"Okay." Lu Hang smartly shut up. "Little Jingjing, are you going with him?"

This dungeon had a part where two people needed to fetch the magic relic; it wasn't difficult and didn't require combat.

Before Lu Hang could finish speaking, Jing Huan had already left the party to join Xiang Huaizhi's party. The two of them walked out of the zone one after another.

"Gege." As if he were showing off a treasure, Jing Huan linked the ring to the party chat. "Look, I upgraded the gem on the ring to level seven!"

Xiang Huaizhi clicked on it, and sure enough, she had.

A level seven gem cost several hundred gold, so he hesitated for a moment before saying, "You don't play PVP, there's no need to upgrade the gem that high."

"It's not thaaat much. I promised you before that I would upgrade it all the way to level fifteen."

The price of a level fifteen gem was even more exorbitant. Xiang Huaizhi responded, "I didn't ask you to upgrade the gem that much.

It's your item, you can upgrade the gem to whatever level you want. Do you even have money to eat after the upgrade?"

Just as Jing Huan was about to answer, he suddenly froze—*Wait, why would I not have money for food?*

He had lied so many times that he couldn't react immediately. After deliberating for a while, he cautiously said, "Huh?"

"You're a student, right?" Xiang Huaizhi said. "Didn't you say you only get a 200 yuan allowance every week?"

Jing Huan reflexively bit his thumb.

When exactly did I make up that story?

Afraid that Yearning For was growing suspicious, he lightly coughed and said, "Y-yes, that's right...How did you know, gege?"

"You mentioned it before when you were being hunted," Xiang Huaizhi said. "Are you a high school student?"

It took a long time for Jing Huan to remember this had happened when OFF! had been hunting him. Back then, he had made it up on the spot to try to get Yearning For's attention.

What's with this guy's brain? How could he manage to remember one sentence from all the way back then?

"No, I'm a university student."

With the amount of time he spent gaming, it was hard to pretend that he was younger. The cogs in Jing Huan's brain spun rapidly, and in ten seconds, he came up with a perfect story.

He sniffled and sounded like he was on the verge of tears. "So it's like this, gege: my parents divorced a long time ago, and now they each have their own families and other kids. I'm just excess baggage to them. After fighting with them last week, I haven't asked for any money. Plus, all my savings were used to buy this character, so I can

only rely on part-time work to get by, and because I'm a student, my wages are low. After deducting the costs of food, clothing, housing, and transportation, I can only squeeze out 200 yuan per week..." Jing Huan couldn't bear to continue.

Good lord, I'm too pitiful, right?! Anyone who hears this would feel terrible, anyone who sees this would shed tears. Such a pitiful and helpless girl...What man could resist caring for her!!

Sure enough, the other end fell silent after listening to this.

Jing Huan forced a laugh. "It's okay, gege, you don't have to worry about me. I'll definitely work hard and create a better life for myself with my own two hands. Moreover, the owner of the shop I work at is very kind to me and often gives me instant noodles..."

"You're not doing the right thing."

"Sometimes, he even gives me a ham and sausage—huh?" Jing Huan did a double take.

"Even though you're clearly financially strapped, you still spend tens of thousands of yuan on gaming. Your internet addiction is too severe," Xiang Huaizhi said coldly.

Jing Huan was speechless. "I..."

"If you really want to succeed, you should spend more time hitting the books instead of games." Xiang Huaizhi thought for a moment. "Three hours a day for gaming is enough."

"I just..."

"Three hours is enough for you to do all your daily quests and dungeons."

Jing Huan clamped his mouth shut.

"From 7 p.m. to 10 p.m.?"

Heartless scumbag.

"I...don't necessarily need to create a better life for myself." Jing Huan's smile was strained as he emphasized each word, "Being able to live happily is already enough."

After delivering the magic relic, they returned to the main party and quickly pushed forward to the boss. As soon as they entered the boss fight, a megaphone popped up.

【[Megaphone] Fae Bae: Looking for a guild. I'm a Putuo Mountain, my cultivation skills are maxed, and I can play decently well. Guilds that can give me an officer position, DM me.】

Jing Huan was momentarily stunned. If his memory was correct, Fae Bae was part of Idle Pavilion, wasn't she?

He right-clicked her name to open her profile and found that her guild section was now empty.

[Party] Long Road Ahead: Nomnom, how come your sis left her guild?

[Party] Love is Sharing Noms: Don't know, maybe Lovesickness demoted her from the guild officer position.

[Party] Long Road Ahead: Amazing. I've always wondered; Regardless of Lovesickness is rather capricious, but Echoes of Spring is quite rational, so why did she let Fae Bae become a guild officer?

Because at that time, Fae Bae had told Regardless of Lovesickness that she would recruit Yearning For into the guild, she needed a position that had the power to recruit members.

Given Yearning For's strength and reputation, what guild wouldn't want him? Even Idle Pavilion, before the scumbag incident happened, would've rolled out the red carpet to invite him in.

Although this wasn't a secret, Love is Sharing Noms didn't want to say it outright with the person involved being present.

[Party] Love is Sharing Noms: I don't really know why. [Shut up]

Fae Bae was a female streamer with tens of thousands of viewers in her stream every day. Although many of these viewers were paid-for bots, she was somewhat internet-famous. As such, as soon as she sent out this megaphone, the World Channel immediately erupted.

[World] Crayfish Connoisseur: Why did Faefae leave the guild? Isn't Idle Pavilion pretty good?

[World] Whirling Blossom: I heard Faefae's guild officer position was revoked. [Surprised]

[World] Ten-mile Dowry Parade: Faefae, join my guild. I'll let you be the vice guild leader, +++.

【[Megaphone] Fae Bae: Don't ask why—I don't want to talk about it anymore, it'll just make me look stupid. All I can say is that we had our differences and parted ways amicably. I'm only calling the top fifteen guilds in the server—anyone else, don't DM me, thanks.】

It hadn't seemed like that big of a deal before, but Fae Bae's words seemed to imply that she had been bullied.

Jing Huan gazed at her megaphones, and his eyes slightly dimmed.

Back then, Fae Bae had used this popularity to cyberbully his jie into quitting the game. He may have destroyed one of her equipment before but it did little to assuage his rage.

He looked away from the megaphone and was about to toss Yearning For a Healing Spring when a notification popped up on the screen.

【Bishop Wood added you as a friend.】

[Friend] Bishop Wood: Are you there?

[Friend] Sweet Little Jing: ?

[Friend] Bishop Wood: I know about everything, so I'm here to apologize to you.

[Friend] Sweet Little Jing: ...Huh?

[Friend] Bishop Wood: I'm really sorry you were being hunted because of me. I happened to be caught up with things these past few days and couldn't get online, otherwise I would have stopped this farce.

Jing Huan had a peculiar feeling and opened the other person's profile.

Bishop Wood, Warlock, and his title read "White Tiger Officer of Idle Pavilion."

[Friend] Sweet Little Jing: You're...

[Friend] Bishop Wood: Oh right, I forgot to introduce myself. Hello, I'm your character's ex-husband, the unlucky dude who got scammed and had his character wiped.

[Friend] Sweet Little Jing: ...Hello, I'm the unlucky girl who got cussed out and hunted for buying your ex-wife's character.

Seeing her reply, Bishop Wood burst out laughing.

It seemed that Echoes of Spring was right. This character did have a new owner; even the way she talked was completely different.

[Friend] Bishop Wood: I'm really sorry, my friends were just standing up for me, and things got out of hand.

[Friend] Bishop Wood: How many times did you die and how much money did you lose? I'll compensate you.

[Friend] Sweet Little Jing: It's fineee. I didn't die that many times, and I even helped them save a lot on the bounty payouts.

[Friend] Bishop Wood: Ha ha, you're an interesting person. Even after dying such an unfair death, you can still joke around with me.

 Chapter 05

[Friend] Sweet Little Jing: You're also very interesting. You got completely cleaned out by the scammer, and yet you still have the guts to talk to the character.

[Friend] Bishop Wood: ...Touché. Indeed, I was scammed out of a lot of money, and I was the one who paid for all the limited-edition cash shop outfits and game time cards for this character these past few years.

Jing Huan saw the shadow of Lu Wenhao in Bishop Wood and couldn't help but feel some sympathy for him.

[Friend] Sweet Little Jing: [Patting shoulder] It's okay. Fall into a pit to gain some wit, just think of it as paying tuition to the scammer.

Bishop Wood was surprised; he hadn't expected this person to comfort him.

[Friend] Bishop Wood: Yeah, I've already gotten over it.

[Friend] Sweet Little Jing: By the way, since you spent so much money on this character, how about I repay some of it on her behalf?

[Friend] Bishop Wood: What do you mean?

[Friend] Sweet Little Jing: She left a lot of things on this character, and my storage can't hold it all. It'd be a pity to just toss them, so it's perfect if you take them.

Though, the items won't be anything valuable.

[Friend] Bishop Wood: Sure, come over to Fengming Valley.

Having just finished fighting a boss and with his party disbanded, Jing Huan was about to fly over there when something occurred to him.

[Friend] Sweet Little Jing: No, how about you come to the main city. That valley isn't a safe zone, and I'm afraid you might ambush me.

[Friend] Bishop Wood: Ha ha ha, okay.

Elegantly attired in white and holding a folding fan, Bishop Wood's character looked like a scholar. When he saw Sweet Little Jing's outfit, he felt like guffawing. With all the cash shop outfits on that character, how did she manage to pick the most hideous one?

Before he could type anything, countless yellow messages popped up on the screen.

【Sweet Little Jing gave you High-tier Teleport Scroll x3.】

【Sweet Little Jing gave you Moonstone x1.】

【Sweet Little Jing gave you Unknown Key x4.】

And so on.

They were all a bunch of trinkets that were hard to sell.

Bishop Wood couldn't help but laugh. It seemed this character's new owner was quite sincere, valuing these useless items so much and insisting on giving them to "comfort" him.

A flashy special effect appeared in the bottom right corner of the game interface, and when Bishop Wood examined it closely, he saw it was the radiance of a divine artifact. The long, pitch-black sword glowed grandiosely, and was being gripped lightly in someone's hand.

It was Yearning For.

He was about to look away when the yellow messages suddenly stopped.

[Current] Sweet Little Jing: Gege! [Blows a kiss]

Xiang Huaizhi paused and thought back for a moment. Didn't he prohibit this sticker last time?

[Current] Yearning For: Mm.

[Current] Sweet Little Jing: Where are you going? [Blinking]

[Current] Yearning For: Getting potions to fight in the arena.

 Chapter 05

[Current] Sweet Little Jing: Oh, okay, go ahead. Good luck, gege. [Cheer][Fist pump]

Xiang Huaizhi was about to leave when he caught a glimpse of Bishop Wood standing next to Sweet Little Jing. If he remembered correctly, that Bishop Wood had been Don't Frown's husband.

[Current] Yearning For: What are you doing?

[Current] Sweet Little Jing: Ah, I'm throwing out trash. [Cute]

[Current] Bishop Wood: …

[Current] Yearning For: ?

[Current] Sweet Little Jing: This guy in front of me was scammed by this character's previous owner. He's quite pitiful, so I thought I'd give him the stuff that was left behind as a warning to him not to get scammed again.

[Current] Bishop Wood: …Thank you…?

Xiang Huaizhi raised an eyebrow and let out a light chuckle.

This girl is quite good at throwing jabs at people.

[Current] Sweet Little Jing: Gege, take it easy. Gege, bye-bye! [Waving]

Bishop Wood found this girl extremely intriguing. After she was done tossing him stuff, he typed away, intending to say something, but he didn't even get to finish before Sweet Little Jing dusted herself off and flew away.

No "take it easy" or "bye-bye"; not even a sticker was given to him. She was so real for this.

He stuffed everything on him into his storage and then sent a message to Echoes of Spring.

[Friend] Bishop Wood: Echoes of Spring, what's going on between Sweet Little Jing and Yearning For?

[Friend] Echoes of Spring: ...What? Have you also been completely dazzled by Sweet Little Jing?

[Friend] Bishop Wood: Ha ha, what does that mean?

[Friend] Echoes of Spring: Nothing, Sweet Little Jing seems to be pursuing Yearning For.

[Friend] Bishop Wood: I can see that, but is she crazy? Why Yearning For of all people? Didn't everyone say that he's a scumbag?

[Friend] Echoes of Spring: Mm, but coincidentally, it fits Sweet Little Jing's taste exactly. The more of a bad boy he is, the more she likes him.

[Friend] Bishop Wood: ...

Jing Huan didn't know that his "special taste" had already become common knowledge. He got up early in the morning, and Gao Zixiang and Lu Wenhao sat on either side of him, chattering incessantly in his ears, even more talkative than the old professor on stage.

"She confiscated our pot and fined us!" Lu Wenhao said angrily. "Fining us is one thing, but she reported our dorm number to the school and said she would scold us in the class group chat. Come on, we're already adults, but she's still doing this to us."

"This is all your fault!" Gao Zixiang said. "I told you to eat faster, but you just kept going at a snail's pace, allowing the dorm supervisor the opportunity to catch us red-handed with just the hot pot broth left. Who else would they punish besides you?"

"You're talking like I was the only one eating. You just ate a bit faster, so how could you pin all the blame on me?"

Chapter 05

Jing Huan yawned. "I'm exhausted, can you guys stop nagging in my ear? Let me have some peace and quiet. Consider this as me begging you two bros."

"Who's bros with him? You wouldn't know, but we fought 300 rounds in the dorm yesterday!" Lu Wenhao threw his hands up. "Wait, what were you doing last night? How are you still tired in a 9 a.m. class?"

Last night, Jing Huan grinded a crafting material quest until midnight. He buried himself in it for two hours but had gotten fuck all.

In *Nine Heroes*, if you wanted to craft weapons and equipment, you needed to have the corresponding crafting materials. You could buy crafting recipes from players, but some small scrap materials could only be obtained by grinding quests. This shitty setup was really just tormenting his terrible RNG luck.

He leaned back and closed his eyes. "Nothing really, just stayed up late watching a movie."

Lu Wenhao dragged out a long "oh," and then asked, "How was it? Any porn you want to share with your bros?"

"Stop being gross, I watched a proper movie."

"Hey, Huanhuan." Lu Wenhao scrolled through his WeChat group chats. "313 invited us to play basketball again. How about it, are you going or not?"

Jing Huan opened his eyes. "When?"

"Today at 4 p.m., right after our class, at the basketball court downstairs."

Jing Huan thought about it for a moment. It had been a while since he exercised, and he'd been getting more easily fatigued these days since he was perpetually sitting in front of the computer.

"Okay, I'll play. I'll head back at noon and get my jersey."

In the afternoon, Xiang Huaizhi finished class and just as he left the classroom, he saw three boys rushing out of the restroom nearby, all wearing newly changed jerseys.

The boy standing in the middle had been hastily pulled out before he could put on his clothes properly. The upper half of his clothes were stuck above his waist, revealing a fair and slender midriff, and Xiang Huaizhi could clearly make out the defined grooves of his back.

"Xiangxiang, what are you doing?" Lu Hang asked as he came out of the classroom.

Xiang Huaizhi looked away and said, "Nothing, just getting ready to go back."

"Don't go yet, it's not even four o'clock, why are you heading back so early?" Basketball in hand, Lu Hang asked, "I'm going to the basketball court, want to tag along? I know you can't play right now, but you can at least soak up the atmosphere."

Xiang Huaizhi glanced at the time. It was indeed early, and it had been ages since he had stepped onto a basketball court.

"Okay."

The two of them strolled over to the east basketball court, which was the closest to the school building. They rarely came here, but today was an exception because Lu Hang had scheduled a match with the underclassmen.

Lu Hang ran on to the basketball court as soon as they arrived. Meanwhile, Xiang Huaizhi picked a seat at random and sat down.

His phone chimed. Picking it up, he glanced briefly at it.

Little Jing~: Gege >.< I have a yoga class today, so I'll be back

 Chapter 05

later. If you guys are going to run dungeons today, don't wait for meee.

Xiang: Mm, I also have something today.

After sending that, Xiang Huaizhi's gaze swept over a familiar yellow number 8 jersey.

It was the boy he had just seen at the classroom door. In the sunlight, the boy's skin seemed even paler, not at all the complexion of someone who played basketball year-round.

The boy turned around, and Xiang Huaizhi tensed slightly.

It was the underclassman who had thrown the pot in the stairwell.

He had only seen him up close before; the boy had standard double eyelids, a high nose bridge, and raven hair. At this moment, the corners of his mouth were slightly quirked up, and he was saying something to the person beside him.

Xiang Huaizhi's gaze unconsciously followed him. When he returned to his senses, the underclassman had already scored over twenty points in the small ball game between him and his friends.

His forehead was already beaded with a fine coating of sweat, soaking his eyebrows. He grabbed the hem of his clothes and casually drew it up to wipe his forehead.

Xiang Huaizhi's gaze fell on his waist, and the skin there was even paler than the skin exposed outside. He was quite fit. His abs were sculpted but not exaggerated; they were just right.

After evaluating him in his mind, Xiang Huaizhi turned around and focused on watching Lu Hang's game.

Jing Huan hadn't played basketball for almost a week and was so exhausted his breaths were coming out in heavy pants. After playing for a while, he went off the court and downed a bottle of water.

"Huanhuan!" Lu Wenhao wasn't playing and lowered his voice. "Don't you think there are so many more girls at the basketball court today?"

Jing Huan looked around and said, "There really are quite a few. What, have I gotten even more popular?"

"Look at you, bragging again." Lu Wenhao sneered at him and pointed to the sidelines. "Didn't you see the Adonis sitting there?"

Jing Huan glanced sideways and saw the face of his savior.

"Who knows what wind blew Xiang Huaizhi to our basketball court. It's such a rare sight...Hey? Huanhuan, where are you going?"

"Going to say hello," Jing Huan said without looking back.

Hearing the footsteps approach closer, Xiang Huaizhi was about to turn his head when the newcomer plopped down next to him, maintaining just the right distance between them.

"Senior," Jing Huan said with a smile, "we meet again."

"Mm." Xiang Huaizhi was a bit surprised that he had come over. "What's up?"

"Nothing, I just saw you and wanted to say hello." Jing Huan peeked at his leg out of the corner of his eye. "Um, I heard you injured your leg. I'm sorry for crashing into you so hard last time. Are you feeling any pain?"

Ever since he heard about Xiang Huaizhi's leg injury, Jing Huan had been fretting over it. After all, he was a grown man who weighed over a hundred and fifty pounds, and crashing into him could really hurt.

Xiang Huaizhi smiled. "It's okay, it's almost fully healed. You don't have to keep apologizing."

 Chapter 05

"That's good then." Jing Huan breathed a sigh of relief. "Are you here to play basketball?"

"No, I'm watching my friend play." Xiang Huaizhi pointed his chin toward the court. "Over there."

Jing Huan's gaze followed where he watched a tall guy, whose basketball skills were obviously better than those around him, play for a while. He didn't seem familiar, one look and you could tell he usually didn't come to this court.

Halfway through, Jing Huan remembered something. He unlocked his phone, glanced at it, then typed and sent a message.

At the same time, Xiang Huaizhi's phone chimed. Jing Huan paused and instinctively looked toward the source of the sound.

Eyes locked onto the game, Xiang Huaizhi held his phone lightly in his hands. He seemed to have no intention of checking his messages.

"Huanhuan!" Gao Zixiang called out from a distance. "It looks like it's going to rain. Should we go back early?"

Jing Huan looked up at the sky and saw a gloomy expanse. Rain looked imminent. He stood up and said, "Then, Senior, I'm leaving now. It's going to rain soon, so you should head back."

"Okay."

After the boy walked away, Xiang Huaizhi leisurely unlocked his phone to check the message.

Little Jing~: Gege, I didn't look at my phone during yoga class just now ^0^. That's great~ We can still run dungeons together today.

Little Jing~: I'm heading back now, so I'll wait for you in the game~ [Cupid][Heart]

Lu Hang was fully immersed in the game, so leaving was definitely not an option. It wasn't until the rain really started to come down that he decided it was time to go.

When they returned to the dormitory, both of them were thoroughly drenched. Lu Hang knew he was at fault, so he didn't dare to fight with Xiang Huaizhi for the bathroom. He obediently waited outside for him to come out.

After his shower, Xiang Huaizhi dried his hair with a towel before turning on the computer.

It was already 8 p.m., and he had missed the arena opening. However, he had already won back a lot of points in the past few days, so missing one arena run wasn't a big deal.

He glanced at his friend message icon, but it was quiet.

A few minutes later, he opened his friend list and confirmed that Sweet Little Jing was online.

Why was the person who usually messaged him the second he came online suddenly so quiet today?

Just as he was thinking that, his friend message icon started flashing.

[Friend] Love is Sharing Noms: Are you there? It's super urgent!!

[Friend] Yearning For: Mm.

[Friend] Love is Sharing Noms: Faefae gathered a party to force PK against Sweet Little Jing.

[Friend] Yearning For: ?

[Friend] Love is Sharing Noms: I'm serious! They're in Blackwood Forest, can you come over?

Fae Bae had indeed launched a forced PK against Jing Huan. In fact, as soon as he entered the Blackwood Forest map, he spotted

Chapter 05

the party following him very closely. He first thought they were just there to do quests, since after all...

[Current] Sweet Little Jing: I destroyed your equipment just a little while ago, haven't you learned your lesson yet~? [Doubtful]

[Current] Fae Bae: Stop talking crap, I was AFK at that time.

Jing Huan was halfway through typing when he had to stop to dodge a skill.

Fae Bae had come prepared this time, bringing two Warlocks and two Assassins—a very standard murder squad.

Soon, more and more people gathered around. Jing Huan found this a bit strange; *Blackwood Forest isn't a big map, why are so many people suddenly showing up?*

[Current] Peach Cheese Stan: So, they're actually still fighting...

[Current] Miss Watermelon: I rushed to the scene!

[Current] Ji Xiaonian: Today, we are relentlessly hunting down the homewrecker, Sweet Little Jing. Interested players are welcome to watch it at *Nine Heroes* livestream room 8121xx. [Scattering flowers]

Jing Huan immediately understood; so, Fae Bae was livestreaming right now.

Fae Bae was standing at the very back of the party, and after applying the defense and health regeneration buffs, she spoke slowly.

[Current] Fae Bae: Let's see how you escape this time. No matter how fast your Spirit Fox Den is, can it beat an assassin's speed?

He couldn't. This was Blackwood Forest, and the assassins' movement speed on this map was insanely fast.

Jing Huan cursed inwardly.

Yearning For, what kind of bullshit taste do you have?!

The Warlocks kept hurling charms at Jing Huan, and while he

Guide on How to Fail at Online Dating

managed to dodge them, every time he did so, an assassin would viciously stab him from behind. His Healing Springs couldn't do much in the way of healing, so his health bar was in dire straits.

[Current] Peach Cheese Stan: Hmmm, I feel like Sweet Little Jing's positioning is really good…If it were me, I'd be sealed and immobilized by the Warlocks by now.

[Current] Youth Chasing the Wind: You're not the only one who feels that way; she's really good. I've played against her and Yearning For in the arena, and my DPS couldn't even touch her.

[Current] Cloud Puffs: Nah, why do I feel like this is so sus? Fae Bae made a big deal about killing Sweet Little Jing, but why has she just been hiding in the back since the fight started? And, she cast so many defense buffs on herself? No matter how you look at it, her gear is also way better than the little spirit fox's. Hmmm…She shouldn't be this much of a wuss, right?

[Current] Ji Xiaonian: STFU if you don't understand the situation. Watch it if you like, or leave if you don't. Keep talking shit and you might be next.

[Current] Cloud Puffs: Why do you care? Are you Fae Bae's secretary?

[Current] Ji Xiaonian: I'm her friend, so watch your damn mouth.

When Jing Huan glanced at the money he had on him, his mood plummeted. To get some new equipment, he had bought 400 yuan worth of the game currency from the marketplace, which meant if he died, he'd lose a whole 200 yuan.

Jing Huan had to constantly remind himself of his fake persona; this was his budget for a whole week! He definitely had to use this situation to gain some sympathy from Yearning For later.

 Chapter 05

[Current] Sweet Little Jing: Do you have the guts to duel me 1V1?

[Current] Fae Bae: Why would I 1V1 you when money can solve my problem?

More and more onlookers gathered, and the players' opinions began to diverge. Some said that Jing Huan had it coming, while others retorted that Fae Bae was going too far. The chat bubbles popping up above the players' heads blotted out this corner of the forest.

[Current] Sweet Little Jing: Oh.

Jing Huan skidded to a halt and plopped down where he was. Immediately, he was hit by a Warlock's immobilizing charm.

[Current] Sweet Little Jing: Come on, if you're going to kill me, do it quickly. Hurry up.

[Current] Sweet Little Jing: Gege is still waiting for me to go run dungeons with him. [Patting head]

[Current] Fae Bae: ...

This undoubtedly hit Fae Bae's sore spot.

[Current] Fae Bae: Do you think I'll let you go after just killing you once?

[Current] Sweet Little Jing: You should count yourself lucky if you can even kill me once, sis.

After provoking her, Jing Huan sighed inwardly.

What little peaceful days he had were about to end again. He was even wondering if this character had cursed him; he had played *Nine Heroes* for so many years before, and he had never been hunted once.

Fae Bae said nothing more. Who knew what she said in their party voice chat, but the two Assassins suddenly charged. It seemed like they wanted to take him out in one fell swoop.

Jing Huan was just feeling the pain of losing 200 gold when suddenly a system prompt popped up on the game interface.

【Yearning For invites you to join his party: Yes, No.】

Jing Huan was stunned and instinctively clicked "Yes."

When did this person arrive?

Players engaged in open wilderness PKs wouldn't be pulled into specific PK maps, so they could join parties or invite party members at any time. In large-scale fights, it was common for party members to die, run back from the respawn point, join the party again, and continue PKing.

And now that he had joined Yearning For's party, this meant that Fae Bae's initiated forced PK against him was now also against Yearning For.

The onlookers watched, stupefied, as Yearning Fear leaped out from the crowd and landed in front of Sweet Little Jing. The weapon in his hand instantly transformed into a giant broadsword that blocked the two of them. All the concealed weapons that the Assassins had thrown clanged against the blade and clattered to the ground.

[Current] Rainy: When did Yearning For get here…I didn't see him at all?!

[Current] Peach Cheese Stan: It seems that our chat bubbles were so powerful, they could even overshadow the glow of a divine artifact.

[Current] Everyone Charge!: Holy shit, isn't this so exciting? Isn't Yearning For blatantly slapping Fae Bae in the face?! Such a ruthless man.

[Current] Fate's Fool: Well, what choice is there? When a new and old love clash, he has to give up one of them.

Chapter 05

Jing Huan slowly regained his senses. "Gege..."

"Can you seal one of the Warlocks?" Xiang Huaizhi asked.

Jing Huan instantly understood what he wanted to do. "Yes."

"I'll break through on the right and seal the Warlock there. Watch out for the Assassins, don't get taken down."

Almost at the exact moment Yearning For finished talking, the two of them moved simultaneously, barreling ferociously over to the right, startling the Warlock who thought he was about to be killed.

But that didn't happen. Sweet Little Jing rushed in front of him and suddenly cast a web, catching him off guard and immediately sealing his spells.

Yearning For switched the broadsword back to a long sword, and with a swoosh, swept past the Warlock. He was making his way straight for Fae Bae who was standing in the back.

Before anyone watching could react, they saw the long sword slash through Fae Bae's golden armor, striking at her body. After four consecutive hits, the wings on her back seemed to wilt, gently trembling twice before they collapsed heavily to the ground along with her character.

【System Announcement: During a forced PK, Player Fae Bae was inadvertently killed by her target instead and lost a Peacock Feather Spirit.】

Fae Bae's hairpin had been destroyed.

The tables had turned too quickly, and Fae Bae had died too fast. Even though the battle was now over, none of the spectators left. Even Fae Bae's hired murder squad stood there speechless for a while.

They specialized in solo player assassination requests, and in all

their years of business, this was the first time they encountered a situation where they failed to kill their target and had their client be fucking killed instead.

Just when everyone finally got a grip of themselves and was about to type to express their exhiliration, the two people standing in the middle of the map suddenly whooshed away to who knows where. Also, with Yearning For present, the murder squad didn't dare to chase after them.

Xiang Huaizhi's party member finally started to move only after he had brought her back to the main city. She spun around, her fox tail swaying with her movements.

[Party] Sweet Little Jing: !!!!!

Xiang Huaizhi's eyebrow twitched as if he had suddenly realized something.

[Party] Yearning For: I'm leaving.

[Party] Sweet Little Jing: AAAAH GEGE YOU'RE SO AWESOME QAQ. I love you so much. This girl has no way to repay you! I can pay you back with my body!! I'll work as a beast of burden for you! I'll cook and clean for you!

[Party] Sweet Little Jing: Of course! I can also be your wife! That's completely okay!

[Party] Yearning For: ...

[Party] Sweet Little Jing: I'll be obsessed with gege! Crazy for gege! I'll bang my head against walls for gege[1]! FOR THE REST OF MY LIFE!

---

1   Lyrics from the 2012 song "White-eyed-wolf" - 白眼狼 - Bái Yǎn Láng by 杨梓 - Yang Zi.

 Chapter 05

Xiang Huaizhi paused and decided to nip Sweet Little Jing's wild thoughts in the bud before he left.

[Party] Yearning For: She wanted to kill you because of me.

[Party] Sweet Little Jing: Huh?

[Party] Yearning For: You should know I'm the reason you were dragged into this mess. I got you in trouble.

Xiang Huaizhi thought for a bit before continuing.

[Party] Yearning For: I'm a scumbag.

Sweet Little Jing instantly froze, looking as if she was in a daze.

Is she dumbfounded?

Xiang Huaizhi's fingers rested on the keyboard as he waited for a while before typing: *So, in the future—*

[Party] Sweet Little Jing: What's wrong with being a scumbag?

[Party] Yearning For: ?

[Party] Sweet Little Jing: Scumbags are so great?!

[Party] Sweet Little Jing: A scumbag can write me poetry! Can *papapa* for three days straight! Warm up some green tea bitches and then immediately warm up some lolis! Available online 24/7! Warm-hearted for up to 72 hours! Never check their texts while dating! Never clings after breakups! Will make you brown sugar tea during your period! Says goodnight before going to sleep!

[Party] Yearning For: ...

[Party] Sweet Little Jing: Oh my god! Scumbags are treasures of the world! I will always love scumbags!!!

After sending that message, Jing Huan quickly opened Taobao, searched for, ordered, and confirmed his address for an effective stress-relief toy—all in under a minute.

How could someone actually say that shit?

Motherfucker.

Life forced me here.

Yearning For forced me here.

I have no conscience. In order to get revenge on Yearning For, I can do anything.

These are not my true feelings.

All scumbags deserve to die.

Jing Huan silently recited these words in his mind several times to calm down before he continued his onslaught of outrageous flattery.

[Party] Sweet Little Jing: So gege, don't sell yourself short~ [Holding small hands]

Yearning For stood there in place for a long time, motionless and silent.

Xiang Huaizhi almost burst out laughing. This woman's ability to bullshit without blinking had already reached the point where it could be called a superpower. And according to her words, the person she should be pursuing was Lu Hang.

After a moment of silent laughter, he typed out: *I'm not a scumbag—*

Just as he was about to hit send, he stopped. A few seconds later, he pressed the backspace key and deleted everything.

[Party] Yearning For: Okay.

Okay my ass!!!

Jing Huan got up to make himself a cup of tea. His mother had insisted that he bring these tea leaves to school, saying they were especially anti-inflammatory and calming. He hadn't been that happy to take them at first, but who knew they would really come in handy now.

Chapter 05

When he returned, he was a little surprised to see he was still in Yearning For's party. The two of them had been standing dumbly in the main city for a long time, their poses still the same as before.

They also happened to be standing in the busiest part of the main city where most players set up their stalls. The vending players had surprisingly cleared a small area around them, moving their stalls elsewhere. The two of them standing there looked especially conspicuous, like exhibits on display.

For a moment, Jing Huan had a sneaking suspicion that they might be the next "male and female protagonists" featured in the forum's gossip section—oh wait, at most he would just be considered a supporting female character.

Meanwhile, Xiang Huaizhi hadn't left because Love is Sharing Noms was DMing him.

[Friend] Love is Sharing Noms: Faefae actually wasn't like this before…I've known her for many years now, and even though her personality is a bit showy, she has a good heart. It's just that after getting acquainted with you…

[Friend] Love is Sharing Noms: She's logged off now and won't answer our phone calls. If it's okay with you, could you help us contact her?

[Friend] Love is Sharing Noms: I know she's in the wrong here. I'm not asking you to comfort her, I just want to make sure she's okay…

[Friend] Yearning For: I'm busy.

Xiang Huaizhi closed the chat afterward. Then, he saw that the little fox beside him had stopped the following action and was now twirling around him.

[Party] Yearning For: Are you angry?

Jing Huan was taken aback for a moment. He had just sent several stickers, but when Yearning For didn't reply, he thought the other person was AFK.

[Party] Sweet Little Jing: Eh, what?

[Party] Yearning For: The thing with Fae Bae.

It would've been better if he didn't mentioned it because as soon as it was brought up, Jing Huan's anger flared up again.

If Yearning For hadn't rushed in just now, Fae Bae would've really killed him in front of a crowd of players in this server as well as the livestream audience.

Losing money wasn't a big deal, but being humiliated was a different story altogether.

Jing Huan usually indulged girls, but he wasn't about to be a punching bag. If he didn't have other things to do right now, he would've helped her quit her internet addiction.

But he wasn't going to say any of that in front of Yearning For.

[Party] Sweet Little Jing: How could I quibble with a woman? [Cute]

[Party] Yearning For: Aren't you also a girl?

[Party] Sweet Little Jing: ...What I mean is, we're all sisters, why make things hard for each other? Besides, I'm not the type of person to hold grudges. [Patting head]

[Party] Sweet Little Jing: Love&peace~

A fully grown man like him, forced to act like a two-faced delicate doll.

Life isn't easy, Jingjing sighed, quite weary.

[Party] Yearning For: [Bunny nodding]

 Chapter 05

[Party] Sweet Little Jing: [Surprised] Gege!

[Party] Yearning For: ?

[Party] Sweet Little Jing: You sent me a sticker! This is the first time you've sent me a sticker!!!

[Party] Yearning For: [Wiping off sweat]

[Party] Yearning For: You haven't been to the arena lately?

[Party] Sweet Little Jing: Nope, I have too many points now, so I'm matched against all the top players. [Tragedy]

Jing Huan thought that Yearning For wanted to take him to fight in the arena again, but his next sentence was—

[Party] Yearning For: Mm, then good luck.

[Party] Sweet Little Jing: ...Okay.

[Party] Yearning For: I'm going to go do dailies now. If she initiates a forced PK on you again, just message me on WeChat.

[Party] Sweet Little Jing: All right, will gege still come to save me? [Shy]

[Party] Yearning For: Yes.

Jing Huan was a little dazed. He had merely wanted to flirt a bit but little did he expect Yearning For to say yes.

Xiang Huaizhi disbanded the party after sending his message and flew away from the main city, preparing to finish up the dailies he hadn't completed earlier.

"Holy fuck!" a piercing curse came from behind him. Lu Hang asked, "Xiangxiang, your ex-girlfriend initiated a forced PK on Sweet Little Jing?!"

Xiang Huaizhi didn't even look back. "I don't have an ex-girlfriend."

"And you even went to save her..." It was a mystery as to who Lu

Hang had been chatting with earlier, but his eyes were now the size of saucers. "You actually killed Fae Bae instead?! And a piece of her equipment was destroyed too, how unlucky…Man, how could you not call me over for something like this?"

"I'm enough on my own," Xiang Huaizhi said. "What would I call you over for? To be a cheerleader?"

"Fuck, man, that's not what you said when you took the Spirit Fox Den to the arena," Lu Hang said. "After all, I'm the number one Warlock in the server, and if I were there, the three of us could've wiped out their entire party! Especially those two Assassins; they're specialized for killing, so all their gear stats are focused on damage dealing, making them very squishy. If I crowd-controlled their Warlocks, you could probably take down those two Assassins with a couple of slashes, and they'd be all down on the ground."

Xiang Huaizhi said, "Cherish your number one Warlock status while you can."

Lu Hang was caught up in his daydream, but hearing that, he asked, "What does that mean?"

"Bishop Wood is back, and I think his cultivation points are only about 20,000 less than yours," Xiang Huaizhi spoke slowly. "And his arena points are just a bit behind yours as well…"

Upon hearing this, Lu Hang immediately opened the rankings list to check. "Oh no. No, no, no. Didn't he take a vacation to relax? How have his cultivation points been increasing this entire time?!"

"Their guild has a designated team of hired power-levelers, like a studio, with their office right next to Regardless of Lovesickness's neighborhood." Idle Pavilion had mentioned these things when they tried to recruit him a few years ago. "They may not be

 Chapter 05

great at PK, but they can grind cultivation points very quickly."

"Their office is right next to their guild leader's house? That's pretty neat. If you had joined Idle Pavilion back then, things would've been fine. At least you wouldn't be in this situation where you can't even find the person to settle scores with…"

Xiang Huaizhi frowned. "Are you done?"

"Okay, I'll shut up." Lu Hang mimed zipping his lips.

After finishing his arena run, Xiang Huaizhi left his character to AFK in Penglai and prepared to go to sleep as he had an early class tomorrow.

His phone suddenly chimed. He picked it up to see that Lu Hang had created a WeChat group chat with just three people.

Glancing at the group chat members, he asked, "Don't you have anything better to do?"

"Eh, won't this make it easier for us to do dungeon runs later?"

The group chat was empty for now since no one had sent a message yet. Xiang Huaizhi clicked on Sweet Little Jing's profile from the members list to look at her Moments. It was his first time seeing her Moments.

Sweet Little Jing's WeChat account, from her profile picture to the background of her Moments, was all pink, to the point that his eyes watered a bit. Her Moments only showed the past month, and there were only two recent updates.

【The rain is so heavy, glad I came back early~[Picture]】

The photo showed a window wet with rainwater. The angle was perfect, and it was very artistic.

The second post merely had pictures: a nine-grid picture post, filled with pink plush dolls. There was no caption.

For some reason, he felt that this color palette didn't suit Sweet Little Jing. However, Sweet Little Jing really was an affectedly sweet girl who loved to flirt.

Was it just my misconception?

With this thought in mind, he left Sweet Little Jing's Moments. He was about to watch a basketball game when Sweet Little Jing's WeChat ID caught his attention from the corner of his eye.

Kobe824.

Kobe, number eight, and number twenty-four jerseys?

For some reason, the figure of that underclassman appeared in his mind. Pale, slim, always smiling, wearing a yellow number 8 jersey.

A girl like Sweet Little Jing actually likes basketball and Kobe Bryant too?

This idea only survived in his mind for three seconds before he quickly squashed it.

Even the thought of it was laughable. It was probably just a coincidence.

That day after class, Jing Huan, Lu Wenhao, and Gao Zixiang went out to eat at a northeastern cuisine restaurant; Lu Wenhao was from the northeast and loved eating stews.

Sighing, Gao Zixiang tucked his chin on his hand. "If only we still had our hot pot. I'm really in the mood for coconut chicken soup. When I graduate, I'm going to open a coconut chicken restaurant near the school. It'll be super popular, for sure!"

"You're the only one with a taste for that," Lu Wenhao said.

"Bull, Huanhuan also likes it," Gao Zixiang retorted.

Chapter 05

That reminded Lu Wenhao of something. "Oh yeah, Huanhuan, what's the deal with you? Why did you steal my picture?"

He had snapped a photo of the window when it had rained a few days ago and posted it on his Moments. While happily waiting to see how many likes it would get, he refreshed and was shocked to see that Jing Huan had not only stolen his picture, he had even added a caption to it.

"And you used a tilde too. That's too girly, man."

Jing Huan said, "I couldn't take a photo as nice as yours."

Don't be fooled by Lu Wenhao's appearance as a big and burly northeastern man. He was really particular when taking photos, and often knelt down on both knees to find the perfect angle.

"And what's wrong with using a tilde? Didn't you often use it when chatting with your ex-boyfriend?"

"It's one thing to steal my photo, but did you have to attack me too?" Lu Wenhao said in a hurt voice.

"Just borrowing it, I'll delete it when I'm done." Jing Huan gestured toward the dish with his chin, saying, "Aren't I treating you to a meal as a thank you?"

Lu Wenhao's chubby hand shot into the air. "Ma'am, the menu! We'd like to order more food here!"

Jing Huan laughed and looked at Gao Zixiang. "What are you doing? You've been on your phone the entire time we've been eating dinner."

With a sigh, Gao Zixiang lamented, "The guild is trying to form parties to farm the guild dungeons. But there are so many people in the guild, and quite a few have personal grudges, so it's been hard

figuring out how to split the parties up. They've been arguing for most of the day."

Jing Huan took a sip of water and asked, "Guild dungeons?"

"Yup." Gao Zixiang didn't even look up. "Oh yeah, you wouldn't know. The *Nine Heroes'* official website released next week's content update today. They're launching several new guild dungeons, both five-man and twenty-man ones, and you have to run them with guild members. It gives a lot of experience points and some really good rewards, but the main thing everyone cares about is that they drop crafting materials, so we now have a second way to obtain them."

Jing Huan was precisely in dire need of crafting materials. He was happy to hear this, but then quickly deflated—he wasn't part of a guild.

Moreover, with Sweet Little Jing's persona, never mind joining a guild, it'd be great if she wasn't being hunted down.

He was trying to think of a solution when his phone suddenly chimed. It was a message from the three-person group chat.

Little Road Never Gets Lost: @Little Jing~, when will Jingjing come back today?

Little Jing~: Ah, soon, I'll come back after I eat~

Little Jing~: What's the rush? Eager to run a dungeon?

Little Road Never Gets Lost: No, just asking. No rush, I'm still reading the official guide for the guild dungeons. Take your time eating.

Little Jing~: [Noding obediently]

Little Jing~: Do these new dungeons have any specific guild requirements? I also want to find a small guild to clear them. [Wiping away tears]

 Chapter 05

Little Road Never Gets Lost: What are you saying, you're with us.

Little Jing~: Ah?

Little Jing~: I'm too noob, I'll just drag you guys down…Would Xiang-gege be willing to carry me?

Little Road Never Gets Lost: Your Xiang-gege:

Little Road Never Gets Lost: [Picture]

Jing Huan clicked on the picture.

【[Megaphone] Yearning For: Looking for a guild to run guild dungeons. No requirements other than being a max-leveled guild. Three people will join: Qiya Mountain, Warlock, and Spirit Fox Den. This is a three-person party, no splitting. DM if you have space.】

Guide on How to Fail at Online Dating

Jing Huan didn't expect Yearning For would actually bring him along.

Although Yearning For's reputation had been severely tarnished, he was still nonetheless strong. Just because the top guilds weren't actively recruiting him, it didn't mean they weren't coveting him. He had a sneaking suspicion that Yearning For's in-game DMs were about to explode.

Jing Huan snapped back to reality and opened up his stickers, intending to act cute but gave up after seeing all the funny stickers of NBA stars that he had saved.

He nudged Lu Wenhao with his elbow, calling out, "Hao'er."

Lu Wenhao turned his head. "What?"

"Send me some of those cute stickers you use on WeChat."

Lu Wenhao gave him a strange look. "What do you want those for?"

Before Jing Huan could explain, Lu Wenhao raised his voice as he said, "Oh, Huanhuan! Are you picking up girls now?!"

Jing Huan stared expressionlessly at him.

He hadn't been quiet, and most of the people in the restaurant

looked over. It had also shocked Gao Zixiang who immediately put down his phone to ask, "What's this? Who's picking up girls? Which girl?"

"You've been stealing my photos and posting plushie pictures. Tell me, are you trying to pick up an anime girl fan who loves pink?" Lu Wenhao asked.

Gao Zixiang asked, "Really? That's your type?"

With this reason delivered right into his lap, all of Jing Huan's previous worries about how to fool these two people had all but vanished.

"Yup," Jing Huan said seriously. "But that girl isn't into me yet, so I have to find a way, right? All right, no more bullshit, send me the stickers already. How can I fucking woo anyone when I'm replying this slow?"

"Oh, okay, okay, okay." Lu Wenhao quickly opened up WeChat to give him all his resources.

Jing Huan saved all the pictures, then selected one of two little kittens snuggling and sent it to the group chat.

Little Jing~: [Image] @Xiang

Xiang Huaizhi currently didn't have time to look at this carefully curated sticker.

As soon he sent out that megaphone, his game interface was instantly flooded with friend requests. In less than half a minute, he received over forty DMs.

Mirage had been live for several years, and the server was teeming with max-level guilds. The only difference between guilds was member strength and the number of potion material farms.

Meanwhile, the World Channel was in an uproar.

[World] Always Whaling: God Xiang is actually looking for a guild? [Panic]

[World] Awaiting the Wind: No duh. With guild dungeons coming out, the great god definitely needs to farm them too.

[World] Xiaoluo Lags: How is he a great god? Did you forget what he did recently? And you're still kissing his ass?

[World] Little Hottie: Being a cheater won't stop him from being amazing. Besides, Fae Bae is clearly no saint either.

[World] Puddingggg: Hold up...Shouldn't the focus be on the Spirit Fox Den? It can't be *that* Spirit Fox Den, right...

[World] Awaiting the Wind: I also think it's that Spirit Fox Den!

[World] Is Gege Big: Is there any doubt?

The players surreptitiously started playing a guessing game.

"These people are hilarious." Lu Hang watched with great interest. "How impressive is Little Jingjing? She's only bought the character recently, and now the entire server knows her. Wow. Amazing."

Xiang Huaizhi ignored both him and the World Channel. He opened his DMs, carefully read through each one, and then replied to them.

Since everyone who DMed him came from max-level guilds, he naturally wanted to see the perks each guild offered.

[Private] Wishing You Happiness: God Xiang, you there? Consider joining our South Side of the Painting Pavilion. You can harvest from any of our three potion material farms, and the alchemy room will always have its doors open to you.

[Private] Meteor-ge: God Xiang, join our Shatter the Sky guild. Whatever perks South Side of the Painting Pavilion offers you, we'll give you 10% more.

Chapter 06

[Private] Wishing You Happiness: God Xiang, is that imbecilic Shatter the Sky also DMing you? Let me tell you something: their potion material farm production is very slow, they have internal conflicts every day, and they've caused trouble on the forums several times. You definitely shouldn't join them!

[Private] Meteor-ge: By the way, God Xiang, let me warn you, the South Side of the Painting Pavilion isn't reliable. They use dirty tactics in guild fights and are the number one public enemy of the guilds on this server. It'd be best if you didn't join them.

Xiang Huaizhi knew these two guilds; they would mutually set each other as enemies on a daily basis and fought frequently. He'd rather not get involved.

He continued looking through his DMs and finally found a decent guild called "The World's #1." It was considered a large guild, and although they didn't offer as many perks as the first two, it was peaceful and they didn't like to cause trouble.

Love&peace.

Remembering what Sweet Little Jing said that day, his lips curled up slightly. Just as he was getting ready to discuss terms with that guild leader, a message appeared.

[Private] Bishop Wood: Are you there?

[Private] Yearning For: No thanks.

[Private] Bishop Wood: Would you consider joining Idle Pavilion?

Their messages were sent out almost simultaneously.

[Private] Bishop Wood: ...[Ha ha] Bro, at least let me finish my message before you reject me.

[Private] Yearning For: Mm.

[Private] Bishop Wood: Three potion material farms, the alchemy room open daily, and an officer position.

[Private] Yearning For: Not interested.

[Private] Bishop Wood: Can I ask why?

[Private] Yearning For: Your perks aren't the best.

[Private] Bishop Wood: We can still negotiate.

[Private] Yearning For: Your guild has a history with my party's Spirit Fox Den.

Bishop Wood had already figured that was the real reason. He had also discussed the matter with Echoes of Spring prior to his decision to DM Yearning For.

[Private] Bishop Wood: Everything before was a misunderstanding. I've explained it all to my guild members, and I promise it won't happen ever again.

[Private] Yearning For: Still, let's forget it.

[Private] Bishop Wood: Don't be like that. Okay, I'll be frank: we're looking for you to help us get the first clear of this dungeon.

When *Nine Heroes* officially announced the guild dungeons, they also released the corresponding rewards for clearing it. Guild dungeons would be released in phases and the guild to achieve the first clear in the server will receive fifty reputation points, five community maintenance points, and a twenty percent increase in potion material farm expansion speed for three months. Additionally, the first party to clear the dungeon would be guaranteed high-tier material rewards.

With these guild attribute rewards and the already established gap, Idle Pavilion could remain at the top of the guild rankings even if they didn't complete guild quests for an entire year.

[Private] Bishop Wood: If you join another guild, those high-tier

 Chapter 06

material drops will definitely be handed over to the guild. Our guild doesn't enforce that; we all roll dice, and if you win, it's yours. Your party's Warlock is preparing to craft a divine artifact, right? They must be in need of high-tier materials.

[Private] Bishop Wood: Don't worry too much, Sweet Little Jing is so cute, she surely wouldn't hold a grudge.

Probably not. But she must be resentful after being hunted for so long.

Xiang Huaizhi initially wanted to refuse, but when he saw Bishop Wood mention that they'd roll dice for the high-tier materials, he stopped typing.

He wasn't lacking in high-tier materials; he could always farm more by completing quests, but he couldn't be sure that his party members wouldn't want them.

He opened up WeChat, perfunctorily skimmed through the previous chat messages, and then sent a screenshot of his conversation with Bishop Wood.

Jing Huan was on his way home when he saw the screenshot and stopped in his tracks.

Lu Wenhao urged him, "What, Huanhuan! Hurry up, I still need to get back to do laundry!"

"Oh..." he said faintly. "Coming."

He opened up his phone keyboard, his fingers hovering over it for a long time, but couldn't type a single line.

He really wanted to travel back in time and beat up his past self. Just great, why did he have to create a persona of not holding grudges?

Making him join Idle Pavilion was like forcing a little lamb to jump into a wolf pack by itself, right?! Idle Pavilion might say they won't kill him now, but what about later? What if Regardless of Lovesickness went loopy one day and accused him of seducing her girlfriend? Wouldn't she just pin him down in the guild zone and gang up on him?

Little Jing~: [Trembling]

Little Jing~: ...Will they really not kill me? I'm still very scared, *sobssss*. QAQ

Yearning For would understand after witnessing such a pitiful display, right?

Little Road Never Gets Lost: Don't be afraid! Road-gege will protect you! With the two of us here, they definitely wouldn't dare to kill you.

Little Road Never Gets Lost: Or do you just dislike Echoes of Spring and the others, and that's why you don't want to be in the same guild?

Little Jing~: ...How could I dislike them?

Little Jing~: I don't hold grudges, I'm just a bit scared.

Little Jing~: [Wronged][Wronged][Wronged]

Xiang: Got it.

Got it? Got what?

Jing Huan wanted to ask more, but Lu Wenhao rushed him again from up ahead. He hesitated for a moment and put his phone back in his pocket. He had to figure out how to reject the invite when he got home.

Once home, he turned on the computer and quickly opened the game.

As soon as he entered the game, a guild invitation popped up.

Chapter 06

【Your friend Yearning For invites you to join the guild: Idle Pavilion. Accept, Refuse.】

Feeling utterly defeated, Jing Huan pressed "Accept."

【Guild Announcement: Welcome Sweet Little Jing to the Idle Pavilion Guild!】

Today, Idle Pavilion's guild chat was dead as hell. Since Yearning For and Long Road Ahead joined, barely anyone talked. The few sentences that appeared were all from the player merchants spamming the chat to trade. Then when Sweet Little Jing joined, even those merchants stopped talking.

Jing Huan DMed Yearning For, but he didn't reply. His coordinates remained in the same place, so he was probably busy and actually AFK.

Jing Huan had finished his dailies before going out today, so he just flew over to Yearning For's AFK location, twirling around him out of boredom.

Just as he was about to find a movie to watch, a new message finally popped up in the guild chat.

[Guild] BrbOrNot: Omg, my friend sent me a screenshot tonight that Yearning For actually fired off a megaphone looking to join a guild! Did you guys see that?

[Guild] Peach Cheese Stan: ...BON, did you just log in?

[Guild] BrbOrNot: Yes, I just got home. Peach, did you see the megaphone?

[Guild] BrbOrNot: Wait, let me continue! Yearning For insisted on bringing a Spirit Fox Den with him to the potential guild! And they can't be split up! I bet that Spirit Fox Den is Sweet Little Jing.

[Guild] BrbOrNot: There's definitely something between them, right?!

[Guild] Peach Cheese Stan: ...

[Guild] The Wind is Freer Than Me: ...

[Guild] Sweet Little Jing: ...

[Guild] BrbOrNot: ?

[Guild] BrbOrNot: What's up with you guys? Why's the guild so quiet today, where is everyone?

[Guild] BrbOrNot: By the way, which guild did Yearning For ultimately join?

[Guild] Sweet Little Jing: Who knows, it depends on which guild offered the best perks~ [Cute]

[Guild] BrbOrNot: He he, to be honest, I secretly added Yearning For as a friend. I'll go check which guild he's in now.

Two minutes passed and BrbOrNot still had not returned.

[Guild] Sweet Little Jing: @BrbOrNot did you check? Which guild did Yearning For join?

Xiang Huaizhi had just come back from a call when he saw this message. He couldn't be bothered to scroll through the guild chat, so he replied offhandedly.

[Guild] Yearning For: I'm here.

[Guild] BrbOrNot: ...

[Guild] BrbOrNot: I [Kneeling and kowtowing] ...I'm sorry, I must've been blind just now.

[Guild] Peach Cheese Stan: [Thumbs up] Dope.

[Guild] Cure for Your Sickness: BON, you're really something.

[Guild] Listen to the Rain: I laughed so hard that the auntie next door came knocking on my door and warned me not to raise chickens in the apartment building.

The guild chat instantly grew lively, and Jing Huan also chuckled

Chapter 06

for a while. Just as he was about to continue typing, he was interrupted by a megaphone abruptly popping up in the bottom left corner.

【[Megaphone] Regardless of Lovesickness: Sorry to interrupt everyone, but I need to clarify something. There were some misunderstandings between Idle Pavilion and Sweet Little Jing, which led to some unpleasantness between the two parties. After verification, the character Sweet Little Jing, previously Don't Frown, has indeed switched owners. What I said before about "seeing the character and not the person" was just said in anger; I'm not really that unreasonable.

I sincerely apologize for the trouble caused to Sweet Little Jing during this time and am willing to compensate for the losses incurred due to deaths. I also sincerely welcome Sweet Little Jing, Yearning For, and Long Road Ahead as members of Idle Pavilion. I hope we can all work together to build a wonderful guild.】

Jing Huan was completely flabbergasted after reading all this.

What is going on?

He had a vague idea in his mind and immediately opened Yearning For's friend chat. He didn't even bother acting cute and sent several question marks over.

[Friend] Yearning For: Did you see the megaphone?

[Friend] Sweet Little Jing: ...Mm, but why?

[Friend] Yearning For: Those were the conditions for us joining the guild.

[Friend] Yearning For: Do you still feel wronged?

Jing Huan was confused. When did he say he felt wronged?

He opened WeChat and realized that he had sent three "wronged" stickers in their group chat without much thought.

Guide on How to Fail at Online Dating

[Friend] Sweet Little Jing: ...Not feeling wronged anymore.

[Friend] Yearning For: Good.

Jing Huan rested his fingers on the keyboard, ogling at the word "good." It took him an immeasurable amount of time to snap out of it.

He quickly leaned back, his palm pressed against his chest, feeling his slightly accelerated heartbeat while his brain sounded the alarm.

Here it comes!

This scumbag! Starting to unleash his charm!

Jing Huan took a big gulp of water, washing away those strange feelings, and flew to the guild teleportation portal, preparing to go inside the guild to take a look.

As soon as he was sent inside the guild, he saw a lady resembling the White Snake Spirit[1] reclining languidly on a brown wood chair, lightly waving the fan in her hand. Her white snake tail hung leisurely on the ground; she was the most expensive guild carriage driver.

The guild zone was designed beautifully, with large decorations like waterfalls, rainbows, and ancient-style pavilions dotted around. They weren't any less elegant and heavenly than the game's couple sanctuaries, and only meticulous girls had the eye to create something so lovely.

He suddenly remembered his guild back in his old server. The guild leader had been an uncouth guy, and their guild zone was

---

1 　白 素 贞 - Bái Sùzhēn - A prominent figure from the Chinese folklore "The Legend of the White Snake." A one-thousand-year-old white snake spirit who transforms into a woman.

merely a barren field with nothing around save for the potion material farm.

Having the chance to see such a rare and pretty setting, Jing Huan forgoed the carriage driver and explored on foot. He took just two steps before another person appeared next to him. He had red hair, was dressed in black, and grasped a shining black sword in his hand.

The little spirit fox's steps immediately stopped.

[Current] Sweet Little Jing: Gege~ [Excited]

At the exact same time this message was being sent out, Yearning For disappeared with a swoosh. The carriage driver had probably teleported him away, leaving Jing Huan standing there foolishly. His friendly greeting was still hanging over his head, looking stupid as hell.

Shitty man, so rude.

Jing Huan couldn't help but send out two stickers to the chat.

[Current] Sweet Little Jing: [Contempt][Spitting]

As the two stickers were sent out, the man in black returned, reappearing beside the carriage driver's side.

Xiang Huaizhi had come into the guild zone to make potions. He was chatting with Lu Hang just now, so he hadn't really paid close attention to the game. His hands were also too fast, so by the time he had realized she was there, he had already gone into the alchemy room.

Recalling the figure he saw earlier, he hesitated for a moment and then teleported back.

He squinted slightly, watching the two "rude" stickers linger above Sweet Little Jing's head for seven seconds, gradually growing transparent, and finally disappearing.

[Current] Yearning For: ?

Sweet Little Jing was quiet for about ten seconds.

[Current] Sweet Little Jing: [Contempt] I am holding myself in contempt. Gege, why did you come back~!

[Current] Yearning For: Why are you holding yourself in contempt?

[Current] Sweet Little Jing: [Spitting] It must be because my character looks too plain and my outfit is too ugly, so gege didn't notice me and flew away.

[Current] Yearning For: ...

[Current] Sweet Little Jing: I'm really useless! [Slap]

Jing Huan berated himself apathetically.

[Current] Yearning For: ...I flew away too fast. What are you doing here?

[Current] Sweet Little Jing: This guild's zone is so beautiful, so I plan to take a stroll around. [Cute]

Xiang Huaizhi replied with an "mm" and was about to fly off.

【Sweet Little Jing invites you to join her party: Yes, No.】

[Current] Sweet Little Jing: Gege, let's take a look together?

In all these years of playing *Nine Heroes*, Xiang Huaizhi had rarely explored the in-game zones. In fact, *Nine Heroes* was originally famous for its high-end graphics and beautiful ancient Chinese-style design. Two years ago, the game company had even released an animation that went viral. But he had no interest in that; he still preferred *Nine Heroes'* PK system.

Lu Hang was chatting with others in the guild chat. Thanks to his outgoing personality, he could strike up a conversation anywhere. Mid-talk, he suddenly remembered something and looked

Chapter 06

up to ask only to see that at some point, Xiang Huaizhi had already taken his laptop to bed.

Xiang Huaizhi sat cross-legged, his back propped up against the wall as he stared at his laptop in his lap, headphones on, and his gaze indifferent.

"Xiangxiang.

"Old Xiang.

"Xiang Huaizhi!"

Lu Hang had to shout three times before Xiang Huaizhi looked up. "What are you screeching for?"

"Well, you kept ignoring me...Anyway, don't we have four days off during the last two weeks of next month? How about we go out and have fun for two of those days?"

Xiang Huaizhi said, "We'll see."

"Well, hurry up and make your decision soon. We won't be able to book flights if you agree too late," Lu Hang said. "Where are you? Come help me with this quest; this damn quest requires two people to trigger the fight."

Xiang Huaizhi looked at the little spirit fox bouncing around him. "I'm busy. Just get a random player to do it with you."

Stunned, Lu Hang asked, "What are you busy with?"

"Making potions."

Lu Hang let out an "oh" and said, "All right then."

Jing Huan strolled everywhere with Yearning For, exploring all around, until they arrived at a small stream where he stopped.

"Wow, gege, look at this stream." The little spirit fox crouched down. "There are so many fish!"

[Party] Yearning For: Mm, I see them.

Jing Huan sincerely said, "Wow, it's amazing. How much does it cost to decorate such a large zone?"

[Party] Yearning For: Thousands of yuan.

Jing Huan sighed. "The guild leader is really rich. No wonder they were willing to spend so much to hunt me down before."

Xiang Huaizhi couldn't tell whether she was praising them or complaining.

He hesitated for a moment and typed.

[Party] Yearning For: Sorry.

Jing Huan flinched. "What's going on? Why are you suddenly apologizing?"

[Party] Yearning For: I mistakenly thought you were a scammer before.

"It's okaaay. If it were me, I also wouldn't have believed it at the time." Jing Huan paused. "Gege, you can't speak right now?"

[Party] Yearning For: Mm, roommate is here.

"Oh."

Jing Huan sat there, bored. Yes, he was here to enjoy the guild's scenery, but he had intended to only take a look around, not to explore every corner of it.

After thinking for a moment, he suddenly spoke up. "Gege, can I ask you something?"

[Party] Yearning For: What?

"It's just you and Fae Bae..." Jing Huan licked his lips. "What was your relationship with her? Why did she suddenly hunt me down?"

[Party] Yearning For: There isn't one.

Jing Huan waited quietly for a while, but no second part of an explanation arrived.

 Chapter 06

That's it?

Through clenched teeth, he asked, "I heard from others that there was someone else named Ranxin too...What's that all about, hmmm?"

[Party] Yearning For: I don't know her.

You bastard!

%$...%#$!!

You little shit! You're lucky that we're in-game right now! If you were beside me, if I didn't immediately beat you to the ground, then I'd marry you!

Jing Huan had no place to release his anger and restrained himself with difficulty. Out of the blue, he had his character stand up and, using the "throw oneself into [selected player's] arms" action, did exactly that at Yearning For.

The little spirit fox dropped her whip and pounced on the man. Because he had chosen his angle well, he landed perfectly in Yearning For's arms.

Jing Huan used this action repeatedly, silently chanting in his heart—*Running you over! Kicking your crotch! Stomping on your foot! Bashing your head in! Yanking out your hair!*

Xiang Huaizhi didn't expect her to be so bold. For a moment, he forgot to dodge the action, and so the two stood face-to-face, repeating this intimate action over and over again.

Until a scholar dressed in white robes appeared in the lower-right corner of their screen.

[Current] Bishop Wood: ...

[Current] Bishop Wood: [Shut up]

[Current] Yearning For: ...

[Current] Sweet Little Jing: [Surprised]

[Current] Bishop Wood: Uh, I was just passing by. Are you two actually...

The two people replied at the same time.

[Current] Yearning For: No.

[Current] Sweet Little Jing: Enhancing our relationship. *^0^*

[Current] Bishop Wood: I'm jealous. I'm leaving, I won't disturb you guys.

The little spirit fox finally stopped the "throw oneself into [selected player's] arms" action and waved goodbye to Bishop Wood.

Watching this familiar character flirting with someone else, Bishop Wood couldn't quite understand how he felt at the moment. He looked away, took a screenshot, and posted the picture in the guild's WeChat group chat.

Bishop Wood: [Image] From now on, anyone going on dates in the guild zone will be charged an entrance fee! Twenty gold each time! The money will be used to buy dog food for our single dog[2] guildmates!

Peach Cheese Stan: I wholeheartedly agree!

A Grand Illusion: I also agree!!

Regardless of Lovesickness: ?

Bishop Wood: It goes without saying that the guild leader and vice guild leader are exempt. Speaking of which, how come those two haven't joined the group chat yet?

Echoes of Spring: Yearning For says he'll join later.

---

2 单身狗 – dān shēn gǒu is a colloquial term used to describe individuals who are single, and the 'dog' in this context conveys a sense of pity or self-mockery towards their feelings of being single.

Bishop Wood: Okay.

Why did those two people so tightly pressed against each other in the picture look so familiar?

"The fuck…? Old Xiang?" Lu Hang turned his monitor around to better interrogate Xiang Huaizhi on his bed with. "This is what you call 'making potions'?"

Lifting his head, Xiang Huaizhi gazed placidly at him. "I finished making potions, and I'm just taking a casual stroll. Is there a problem with that?"

"None at all," Lu Hang replied. "Are you guys done strolling around? Hugged enough yet? It's almost time to clear dungeons."

"Mm. I'll ask her."

[Party] Yearning For: Have you seen enough of the scenery?

[Party] Sweet Little Jing: [Bunny nods]

[Party] Yearning For: Pass the party lead to me, we're going to clear dungeons.

[Party] Sweet Little Jing: Okay.

Previously, Yearning For did his quests with a fixed party, but the party leader was the scamming booster he hired. After that scammer ran away, the party naturally disbanded.

The three of them gathered in the main city. Lu Hang had also called over Love is Sharing Noms, however they were still one person short.

[Guild] Long Road Ahead: Anyone up for the Havoc in Heaven dungeon? Q1[3]!

[Guild] Bishop Wood: I'll come, where are you?

---

3   Indicates they're looking for one more player for their dungeon party.

248

[Guild] Long Road Ahead: The main city.

Bishop Wood quickly joined the party, and after exchanging some brief greetings, they entered the dungeon.

Jing Huan's mood had dropped significantly after his conversation with Yearning For. He didn't feel like acting cute or obedient anymore and hadn't spoken since they entered the dungeon. But Lu Hang had no intention of letting them brush it off.

[Party] Long Road Ahead: Little Jingjing, are you there?

[Party] Sweet Little Jing: Yesss.

[Party] Long Road Ahead: Did you just go sightseeing with Xiangxiang?

[Party] Sweet Little Jing: 0.0 Mm! How did you know?

[Party] Long Road Ahead: It was posted in the guild's WeChat group chat.

[Party] Sweet Little Jing: Oh oh.

[Party] Long Road Ahead: Something wrong? Not in high spirits tonight? Normally, you'd be using all those shy stickers by now, right?

[Party] Sweet Little Jing: No, I'm just watching a show.

[Party] Long Road Ahead: All right, well, this dungeon isn't hard. You can keep watching, just set your actions to auto and AFK.

Jing Huan was about to play another game to pass the time when a message popped up in the party chat.

[Party] Bishop Wood: When will you two get married?

[Party] Yearning For: ?

[Party] Long Road Ahead: ?

[Party] Sweet Little Jing: [Surprised] Who?

[Party] Bishop Wood: You and Yearning For.

[Party] Sweet Little Jing: We're not getting married...

[Party] Bishop Wood: [Doubtful] Then, what was that just now?

[Party] Sweet Little Jing: [Shut up] We were just walking around, why would gege marry me?

Jing Huan typed: Although I really want to~, gege doesn't seem to have feelings for me yet—

[Party] Bishop Wood: Oh [Ha ha], then does that mean I still have a chance?

[Party] Yearning For: ?

[Party] Sweet Little Jing: ??

[Party] Long Road Ahead: No way, buddy, what do you mean? What chance? [Surprised]

[Party] Bishop Wood: The chance to pursue Little Jing.

The party chat immediately quieted down.

Xiang Huaizhi was about to send a question mark, but thought for a second and then deleted it.

He looked at the little spirit fox beside him. She hadn't moved in a long time, cleary startled.

[Party] Bishop Wood: Ha ha, why is everyone silent?

[Party] Sweet Little Jing: I don't seem to know you...

[Party] Bishop Wood: Your words wound me, we've obviously chatted several times. [Wronged]

[Party] Sweet Little Jing: ?? Those chats didn't seem particularly pleasant, though.

[Party] Bishop Wood: Not at all, I think you're especially cute.

[Party] Sweet Little Jing: ...You didn't get PTSD from my character?

[Party] Bishop Wood: She is her, and you are you. Plus, we just met and we're in the same guild, so there will be plenty of time to get to know each other in the future.

Jing Huan took a deep breath.

Bishop Wood gazed at the little spirit fox's back, finding it captivating even from behind. He laughed and was about to tease her again.

[Party] Sweet Little Jing: You're a good person which is why we're not a match. Hope you get a great next catch.

Lu Hang laughed so hard that the bed quivered.

"Fuck, Little Jingjing is really talented. I have to hand it to her, I'm impressed. 'Bishop Wood's a good person so they don't match.' " Lu Hang then proceeded to deliberately stir the pot. "So what does she mean by pursuing you? Xiangxiang, don't you feel like you're being subtly insulted?"

He looked up to check on Xiang Huaizhi's reaction.

He wasn't annoyed at all. Gaze lowered, his eyelashes fanned over his cheeks as a corner of his mouth quirked up. "A bit."

At the other end, Bishop Wood did a slight double take and then chuckled heartily.

What was meant to be a bit of joking around with Sweet Little Jing had turned into genuine interest.

[Party] Bishop Wood: I can act out any persona you choose, add me as a friend and you won't lose.

Speechless, Jing Huan thought, *Damn it, I've met my match!*

[Party] Sweet Little Jing: I can only add you as a friend, don't try to make me yours in the end.

With that said, Jing Huan moved his fingers and added Bishop Wood as a friend.

 Chapter 06

"These two are just throwing out rhyme after rhyme." When the two suddenly went quiet, Lu Hang asked, "Why aren't they talking anymore? It can't be that they added each other as friends and are now just DMing?"

Bishop Wood did DM Jing Huan a sticker, but Jing Huan didn't reply because he was busy answering messages in his class group chat.

When his friend message icon flashed, he thought it was Bishop Wood again, so he casually clicked it.

[Friend] Yearning For: Should I add you to the guild group chat?

[Friend] Sweet Little Jing: Are you in it?

[Friend] Yearning For: Yes.

[Friend] Sweet Little Jing: ^^ Then I want to join!

WeChat buzzed once and a new group chat popped up.

【Xiang has invited Little Jing~ to the group chat.】

There were 169 people in the group chat. Jing Huan changed his group chat alias and switched back to the chat. The screen was already filled with messages, all welcoming him and Yearning For.

Yearning For didn't say anything, but after thinking for a bit, Jing Huan decided to greet everyone.

Sweet Little Jing: Hello everyone [Extending out paws]~

Peach Cheese Stan: Hullo.

Bishop Wood: @Sweet Little Jing, why didn't you reply to my DM. [Wronged]

Jing Huan thought to himself, *Why else? Of course, it's because I didn't want to reply to you.*

He was already exhausted from having to pretend to be a girl every day, where would he find the energy to deal with a suitor?

I am a catfisher, I have no emotions.

He held his cellphone, pondering how to tactfully make this person stay away from him.

The guild members in the group chat couldn't make heads or tails of it at first—hadn't Sweet Little Jing publicly confessed her love to Yearning For? Why was their guild officer making such ambiguous comments?

Only BrbOrNot, who was more carefree, decided to pop out and send a teasing remark.

BrbOrNot: Officer, you're being unfair, heh.

Bishop Wood: How am I being unfair? [Smacks head]

BrbOrNot: Sweet Little Jing joined the guild with God Xiang~ [Cute]

Peach Cheese Stan: ...BON, you really have no fear.

Bishop Wood: Ha ha, it's okay. There might not be anything between me and Little Jingjing for now, but I'm compelled to point out that Little Jingjing is single.

BrbOrNot: [Thumbs up]

Awaiting the Wind: Bishop Wood, you're wild.

More people started popping up in the group chat, and Jing Huan thought to himself, *No wonder this dude was scammed out of so much money.*

He finished reading the group chat and then closed the chat window, wanting to pretend that he hadn't seen it. Unexpectedly, as he minimized the interface, he heard another WeChat notification.

Yearning For: @Sweet Little Jing

With Yearning For's sudden appearance in the chat, the lively crowd from before immediately fell silent.

Chapter 06

Jing Huan was taken aback and quickly typed.

Sweet Little Jing: Here, gege~

Sweet Little Jing: [Kitty rubbing paws together] Gege, what's up?

Yearning For: Heal me.

Sweet Little Jing: Coming, coming!! [Umaru drinking Cola[4]]

Lu Hang had been lurking in the group chat and chortled when he saw this. "Come on, Xiangxiang, you have at least seventy percent of your health bar. The dungeon is almost over, so why are you making her come back to heal you?"

Xiang Huaizhi remained expressionless. "I want to kill it faster since I'm in a hurry to complete my dailies. What, is that not okay?"

To help players clear dungeons faster, each sect had a corresponding monster-killing bonus. Xiang Huaizhi's sect bonus was that the higher his health, the higher his DPS against quest monsters.

Lu Hang watched Sweet Little Jing bouncing around and healing Xiang Huaizhi. He nodded sagely. "Okay, sir, whatever you say, sir."

After completing the dungeon, Lu Hang disbanded the party on the spot. Jing Huan was about to fly away when a message popped up on his screen.

【Yearning For invites you to join his party: Yes, No.】

Jing Huan immediately jumped into his party. "What's up, gege?"

Without saying a word, Yearning For flew the party directly to the storage NPC.

【Yearning For gives you Rejuvenation Gem x1.】

4　　This is the main character from *Himouto! Umaru-chan!* who is a closet otaku. She loves drinking cola, eating junk food, and gaming at home, but acts as a perfect, "normal" girl at school.

Jing Huan looked and saw that it was a level eight gem meant to be socketed into a ring.

[Party] Yearning For: Just noticed this was in my storage.

This level eight gem was worth nearly four figures. Jing Huan said, "Thank you gege. How much is it? I'll pay you back."

[Party] Yearning For: No need, it's useless for me to hold onto it.

"No way, you already gave me the ring. It's not fair for you to also give me the gem for upgrades," Jing Huan refused.

He wasn't trying to be polite; his end goal wasn't just a mere few thousand yuan. If he accepted it, it would seem like he was just after Yearning For's money.

Xiang Huaizhi, on the other hand, didn't think much of it. He saw the gem for sale at a stall when he was wandering around the city. It was priced several tens of gold cheaper than its market price, so he bought it without batting an eye.

[Party] Yearning For: If you don't want it, throw it to Long Road Ahead.

"Absolutely not! I'll never give away things that gege gave to me to anyone else!" Jing Huan paused. "But gege, why do you keep giving me things?"

Without waiting for Yearning For to answer, Jing Huan's imagination began to run wild. "Could it be that you've fallen for me?! That's why you want to spend money on me? And you even gave me a ring?"

Epiphany hitting him, Jing Huan cried out, "Oh my god, you gave me a ring because of that?!"

Xiang Huaizhi's confused silence was deafening.

Jing Huan said, "Wait a moment! Gege! No need to say anything

Chapter 06

because I accept! I accept your proposal! Let's go to Yue Lao and get married right away! I'll cover the wedding costs! I'll pay for the bridal sedan chair! I'll organize the wedding banquet! All you need to do is ride the horse in front of my bridal sedan chair!"

Hearing her get more and more outrageous as she spoke, Xiang Huaizhi had to step in and stop her imagination from going more rampant. "I'll sell it to you for 300 gold. You can transfer me the money at whatever time work for you."

"Oh," Jing Huan mumbled as he threw Yearning For the money. "You really won't consider it, gege? We can always marry first and fall in love later."

Jing Huan heard a short light laugh.

Yearning For was laughing. It sounded low and deep.

"No, I won't," he said. "I don't do in-game marriages, and I don't like...marrying first and falling in love later."

It took Jing Huan a moment to shake off his surprise. "You've never been married before?"

"No."

Jing Huan thought that made sense.

Scumbags like to flirt with people, but they wouldn't take responsibility in the end. They weren't even willing to buy a girl her bridal sedan chair ride. Unacceptable!

After the two of them finished their trade, Yearning For disbanded the party and Jing Huan went to the smithy to socket the gem into the ring. He was about to do his dailies when his friend message icon lit up.

[Friend] Love is Sharing Noms: Do you have time to chat?

[Friend] Sweet Little Jing: Yes, what's up~

[Friend] Love is Sharing Noms: Not much, I just wanted to apologize on behalf of Faefae.

[Friend] Sweet Little Jing: ...No need~ She probably wouldn't want someone apologizing for her either.

[Friend] Love is Sharing Noms: ...True. Sigh, she wasn't like this before, but ever since she got together with Yearning For, she's changed a bit.

Jing Huan expressed his understanding; before this had all occurred, he also would've never believed that his jie would become so weak because of a man.

He nonchalantly checked Love is Sharing Noms's profile and noticed that the guild section under her profile picture was empty.

[Friend] Sweet Little Jing: Huh, what happened to your guild?

[Friend] Love is Sharing Noms: Oh, nothing happened, I just left.

[Friend] Sweet Little Jing: [Surprised] Why~? Wasn't your guild pretty strong?

[Friend] Love is Sharing Noms: Didn't want to stay anymore.

Recently, Ji Xiaonian had been spreading rumors in the guild that she had "defected" to Sweet Little Jing's side and blamed her for Fae Bae's rage quitting. Along with a few others, Ji Xiaonian ganged up on her in the guild chat, spewing sarcastic and mocking comments; none of them had anything nice to say to her. Love is Sharing Noms herself wasn't a good-tempered person either, so in a fit of anger, she just left the guild.

[Friend] Sweet Little Jing: But the guild dungeons are going to be released soon, are you not going to grind them?

[Friend] Love is Sharing Noms: I'll just find another guild, I guess.

Jing Huan thought of an idea and started typing.

[Friend] Sweet Little Jing: Wait a bit; don't join another guild yet. I'll go ask a guild officer! I just checked the member count, and Idle Pavilion still has several open slots.

[Friend] Love is Sharing Noms: Ah, no need to trouble yourself, it's fine if I don't clear the dungeons.

[Friend] Sweet Little Jing: It's no trouble~ Wait for me for a bit. [Blows a kiss]

[Friend] Love is Sharing Noms: ...Okay.

Of course, Jing Huan didn't go looking for a guild officer. He wasn't close with the Idle Pavilion members, not to mention, there were still grudges between them. If he could avoid dealing with them then he would. Instead, he tracked down Long Road Ahead, who was tight with the guild members.

[Friend] Long Road Ahead: Nomnom? She left her guild? Why, I remember she was in the same guild as her besties?

[Friend] Sweet Little Jing: [Shut up] Matters between girls are very complicated, don't ask~ Can we add her?

[Friend] Long Road Ahead: Of course we can, and now we can run do guild dungeons together. She plays healer pretty well.

[Friend] Sweet Little Jing: [Bunny nodding] Then I'll tell her to apply to join the guild!

[Friend] Long Road Ahead: Ah, hold on, I'll ask Xiangxiang to talk to Echoes of Spring. Idle Pavilion isn't small, and I just joined a day ago, so I definitely can't just randomly invite people.

[Friend] Sweet Little Jing: ...But gege also just joined the guild. 0.0

[Friend] Long Road Ahead: He's special. If your gege asked Echoes of Spring for a guild officer position, she'd give it to him.

[Friend] Sweet Little Jing: Gege is so cool! [Scattering flowers]

Lu Hang laughed and told Xiang Huaizhi, who was in the opposite bed, what was going on. After receiving his accordance, Lu Hang opened his chat with Sweet Little Jing again.

[Friend] Long Road Ahead: It's done.

[Friend] Sweet Little Jing: …They agreed so quickly?

[Friend] Long Road Ahead: Mhm, there's nothing your ge can't do in this server. Inviting a buddy to a guild is a small matter.

[Friend] Sweet Little Jing: Road-ge, can I ask you something? 0.0

[Friend] Long Road Ahead: Go ahead.

[Friend] Sweet Little Jing: Did you and gege start playing *Nine Heroes* together? How long have you guys been playing~?

[Friend] Long Road Ahead: He played first, and then I started about half a year after him. It's been more than eight years now.

[Friend] Sweet Little Jing: [Surprised] Wow, that long. But why do I feel like…gege doesn't seem to have many friends around?

Jing Huan had always wondered. You could tell from a glance that Yearning For was a veteran player of *Nine Heroes*, but during their time together, apart from Long Road Ahead, he had never seen any of his other friends.

It was a while before he received a reply.

[Friend] Long Road Ahead: Um, how should I put this.

[Friend] Long Road Ahead: Your ge actually used to have quite a few friends and even led a guild. But something happened, and he didn't like making friends in the game anymore.

Jing Huan was taken aback and wanted to continue this line of

 Chapter 06

questioning, but when he asked for more details, Long Road Ahead clammed up.

This half-revealed information aroused Jing Huan's curiosity—what kind of thing would make someone not even want to make friends in the game?

While his mouth responded with "mhm, yup, after all, it's my gege's private matters," his deft hands were already opening the gossip hub—the *Nine Heroes* forum.

The *Nine Heroes* forum was a magical place with astonishing daily traffic that even pulled in numerous non-gamers to explore.

The reason was simple: the place was just full of juicy gossip, with a major exposé every few days. You couldn't even imagine the kind of stuff that got revealed here, and the content was so exciting and scandalous that it was often more interesting than entertainment industry news.

Back when Jing Huan played *Nine Heroes*, he didn't visit this place often. However, after the recent incident with his jie, he had been so infuriated that he spent hours browsing the forum every day. In just a few days, he had mastered all of the forum's features.

He secretly inquired before and found that Yearning For had been playing since Mirage server had launched. He had always been very famous, so if anything happened to his character, the forum would definitely contain traces of it.

Jing Huan logged into the forum with his account, found the search function, and entered the words "Yearning For."

A few seconds later, the search results popped out.

A total of twenty-eight whole pages, and several viral posts. The sheer number of posts startled Jing Huan; he knew that Yearning

For was famous, but he didn't expect there to be such a horrific number of posts about him.

He ignored the posts about Yearning For and Fae Bae, and went straight to the last page, intending to browse through chronologically.

【The new top player on Mirage Server Mastery Rankings: Yearning For, Qiya Mountain.】

【How is Yearning For so good on Qiya Mountain? During the all-server PK, he completely curb-stomped the top Spirit Fox Den player.】

【News—Yearning For has finished the grind for a divine artifact! The attributes are unknown. Could this be the best physical DPS gear in *Nine Heroes*?!】

【Why does Yearning For look so hot wearing such a simple outfit?】

After reading several pages of excessive praise, Jing Huan felt a bit confused.

Yearning For was the only person he'd ever seen who was able to have so many posts praising and flattering him in this kind of forum where vicious call-out posts spread like wildfire.

A simple search of a few of the top players' character IDs from his old server had pulled up posts of trolls, callouts, exposés about their love lives, and scandals. But Yearning For, prior to the current situation, was unexpectedly completely devoid of blemishes, pristinely clean and admired by all.

He snapped out of it and clicked to the previous page. Still a full page of praise.

He quickly combed through it, his finger poised to switch pages when he saw a post at the very bottom of the page.

 Chapter 06

【Heard that Yearning For disbanded his guild?】

Jing Huan's eyes lit up. *Here we go.*

This post had over 300 replies, all of which were dated six years ago, which meant it had already gone viral back then.

Jing Huan spun the scroll wheel of his mouse.

【Original Post: Can someone explain why? I'm very curious!】

1L: As someone from the same server, I don't know. I applied to join the guild many times but never got accepted, even though it wasn't full...Maybe the requirements of a great god are too strict. [Wiping away tears]

13L: No, no, I've seen several of the guild members, and they're not that strong. Many of them are just questing characters, so maybe the guild only accepts people they know?

45L: Guild member here, I'm a noob, and I didn't know any of the great gods in the guild. I just applied randomly and got accepted. This morning, I received the disband notification, but I don't know the details.

57L: Yes...I also woke up to find the guild had disbanded T^T, no more chance to admire the great gods up close!

99L: How come none of the guild members posting know why the guild disbanded? Then isn't Yearning For just too irresponsible? What about everyone's guild contributions?

111L: Replying to 99L, you're wrong, the great god is very responsible. Although he didn't inform us beforehand, he compensated everyone with gold based on their contributions. Reportedly, everyone got their due and then some.

172L: So, after all these replies, what's the reason for the guild's disbandment?!

Jing Huan also raised the same question.

How come even this kind of post is full of pointless flattery?!

He scrolled to the last page and finally found some clues in the final reply of the thread from 377L.

377L: Actually, it wasn't anything major. It seems that the great god's inner member tricked him out of a lot of money. That, and being busy with school, he didn't have time to manage the guild, so he disbanded it.

There were no more replies after this because the forum administrator had locked the post.

After reading it, Jing Huan suddenly lost interest in the subject and propped up his chin to close the webpage.

In *Nine Heroes*, an inner member was the equivalent to a sworn brother.

But he was only interested in Yearning For's romantic affairs; he had no desire to learn about fights between bros.

There was going to be an update in *Nine Heroes* next week with guild dungeons releasing on all servers at noon on Tuesday.

The university cafeteria was bustling with people, the aroma of food billowing everywhere.

"Huanhuan." Gao Zixiang draped his arm around Jing Huan's shoulder with a big grin. "Are you free tomorrow at noon? I need urgent help!"

Jing Huan looked at the extra lion's head meatball that had appeared in his lunch box and bent down to smile at the lunch lady, saying, "Thank you, Auntie." Then he straightened up and said, "No."

"Don't be like that, at least ask me what's so important first."

Chapter 06

Do I really need to?

Jing Huan picked a spot to sit down and opened his lunch box. "Go ahead."

"Tomorrow at noon, the guild dungeons go live, and my party is short a person," Gao Zixiang said. "Can you help us clear the dungeon?"

Jing Huan laughed and said, "I don't have a character, how can I help you with the dungeon?"

"You can use my wife's character! She's getting her nails done tomorrow and doesn't have time, plus her gameplay isn't reliable." Gao Zixiang paused. "Wait, on second thought, you can use my character. You're great at DPS, and my wife's character is a healer, so you probably can't play that."

Jing Huan raised an eyebrow. "Who said I can't play a healer?"

"Ah? Oh, I mean, it's fine if you want to play a healer."

"Don't wanna, not gonna." Jing Huan took a bite of his meal and said, "I really have something tomorrow though, so I can't come."

Gao Zixiang wilted and asked, "What's going on? Can't you postpone it?"

"No, it's just as urgent as your thing." Jing Huan wiped his mouth with a napkin and looked at the milk tea shop in the cafeteria. "Do you want milk tea? I'll go buy some."

Gao Zixiang said, "Sure, get one for Hao'er too. He's been practicing hard as a Spirit Fox Den for tomorrow's dungeon run. Don't you think he's insane? I told him to play his previous sect, but he refused and insisted on mastering the Spirit Fox Den...What are you doing?"

Jing Huan held out his hand toward him. "I'm helping you line up. Since Hao'er is training hard to help you clear the dungeon, it's not too much for you to buy us milk tea, right?"

Gao Zixiang silently handed him his cafeteria card.

The milk tea shop had a long line. If it weren't for Jing Huan's strong craving, he wouldn't have bothered. He stood at the end of the line, studying the menu and wondering whether he should buy milk tea or coffee.

The girl in front of him was wearing a tank top and long pants. It was hard to tell what season it was from looking at her outfit, but she had coordinated her clothes well. She had long hair that grazed her waist, her exposed shoulders were smooth and fair, and a faint fragrance lingered around her.

Jing Huan didn't want to stand too close, so he kept a one-person distance from her at all times. He took out his phone to ask Lu Wenhao what he wanted to drink.

The girl was chatting and giggling with her friend. Who knew what girls talked about, but they started poking each other's bellies. The girl couldn't stand the ticklish sensation and laughed as she stumbled several paces back.

Jing Huan first noticed the fragrance becoming stronger, and when he looked up and saw that long black hair, he realized it was actually the scent of shampoo.

Afraid of touching something he shouldn't, he instinctively stepped back, only to collide with the person behind him on the second step. His left foot also viciously stepped on the person's shoe.

The person behind him hissed, drawing in a cold breath.

Chapter 06

Jing Huan flinched and quickly drew back his foot, whipping around to apologize. "Sorry...Senior?"

"Mm." Xiang Huaizhi lowered his head, staring at his shoe. Jing Huan had stepped pretty hard on it, and the top of the shoe was now deformed.

Having bumped into him twice, Jing Huan felt quite embarrassed and said, "I'm so sorry, I didn't notice that someone was behind me."

Following Xiang Huaizhi's gaze, Jing Huan felt even guiltier when he saw the tip of the white shoe was stained with dust. "I'll go get a napkin..."

As he spoke, he was about to leave the line when Xiang Huaizhi reached out and grabbed his arm. "No need to wipe it, it's okay."

"No way, your sneakers are so expensive."

"It's really not necessary." To divert his attention, Xiang Huaizhi looked ahead. "If you don't keep moving forward, you'll be cut in line."

Jing Huan instinctively exclaimed "oh" and took two steps forward.

He had already confirmed last time on the basketball court that it hadn't been some cockroach-fear-induced delusion; Xiang Huaizhi's voice was indeed very similar to that of Yearning For.

...Come to think of it, even the names are similar.

"Senior," Jing Huan turned his head and asked randomly, "are you also here to buy milk tea?"

Xiang Huaizhi lowered his eyes and said, "Coffee."

Jing Huan suddenly realized that Xiang Huaizhi was much taller than him. He was at least 185 cm, and he also had a much larger

frame than him; with Xiang Huaizhi standing in front of him, he basically couldn't see any of the people behind him.

"What coffee do you drink? I'll treat you," Jing Huan said, "as an apology."

Xiang Huaizhi, not accustomed to letting others treat him, shook his head. "No need, I'll buy it myself."

"Americano?" Jing Huan asked. "Or a mocha?"

"Americano," Xiang Huaizhi eventually said.

"Okay." Jing Huan shifted to the side to make some space for him. "You can stand next to me, Senior. It'll be easier to pick up the orders later."

After hesitating for a moment, Xiang Huaizhi took a step forward.

Taking the coffee that Jing Huan had paid for, Xiang Huaizhi said, "Thank you."

"No problem, I should be the one thanking you. You saved my life on the stairs last time," Jing Huan said with a smile.

When he smiled, his eyes curved slightly, turning into crescent moons. His teeth were also neat and white, making for a very pleasing sight.

Xiang Huaizhi had never seen a guy with a more attractive smile.

Jing Huan suddenly remembered something and took out his phone. "By the way, Senior, can we add each other on WeChat? We can play basketball together in the future...and other stuff like that."

Xiang Huaizhi snapped out of his thoughts and nodded. "Sure."

Jing Huan opened up his QR code and was about to pass it to Xiang Huaizhi when he saw Xiang Huaizhi holding his phone, a slight frown on his face as he pressed the unlock button twice.

Chapter 06

"Sorry." Xiang Huaizhi put away his phone. "My phone's battery just ran out."

Jing Huan didn't mind. Guys generally didn't remember WeChat IDs, so he closed his QR code and said, "Then, rain check. We can add each other when we meet again."

Jing Huan returned to the cafeteria table, and Gao Zixiang immediately leaned over and said, "Huanhuan, were you chatting with Xiang Huaizhi just now?"

"Yeah." Jing Huan gave him a milk tea. "This is yours."

Gao Zixiang pierced the plastic cover with a straw. "When did you get so close with him?"

Jing Huan shook his head and said, "We're not."

"Oh," Gao Zixiang said. "I thought you two knew each other from before."

Jing Huan yawned. He had been up all night to game and had to get up at 8 a.m. for class today. He had been drowsy this entire time. "How can we when we don't even run into each other that often?"

It was easier to do so in high school, where classes were scheduled at the same time every day. But in university, the class times and locations were all different; they even used different basketball courts. He had studied at the university for more than a year, and he only saw Xiang Huaizhi for the first time in the stairwell that day.

"Could've met while gaming, I guess." Gao Zixiang swallowed some tapioca pearls. "Senior Xiang also plays *Nine Heroes*."

Jing Huan was a bit surprised and said, "Really?"

"Really. I know his roommate and he also plays *Nine Heroes*. I

think he's even a top player; I saw him at an in-person player meetup before," Gao Zixiang said.

Jing Huan asked, "Which server are they in?"

"Think it was…Glittering Galaxy? I can't remember."

Jing Huan nodded, murmuring, "Couldn't tell at all."

"Couldn't tell what?"

"That Xiang Huaizhi also games."

Gao Zixiang laughed and said, "Do you think *you* look like a terminally online youth?"

Chuckling, Jing Huan lowered his head to scarf down the remaining braised lion's head meatball.

Xiang Huaizhi returned to the dormitory and swiped the cloth beside the washbasin to wipe his shoe, but the cloth was dry and couldn't clean his shoe properly. He gave up soon after; he'll send them for cleaning when he had some time.

"What happened to your shoe?" Lu Hang came out of the bathroom, rubbing his hair with a towel and looking over. "Wow, those marks are as clear as day. Got stepped on? Who stepped on you so fiercely?"

Xiang Huaizhi said, "An underclassman."

"An underclassman? Which underclassman? You actually know an underclassman?"

It struck Xiang Huaizhi then that he didn't know this underclassman's name; all he could recall was his friends calling him "Huanhuan."

"Why are you asking so many questions?" he asked. "Did you gather all the materials yet?"

"No." Lu Hang deflated at the mention. "I've been megaphoning all morning, but not a single person DMed me. Tell me, why is it so hard for me to get a divine weapon?"

Xiang Huaizhi scoffed. "I spent half a year gathering materials back then."

Lu Hang, who had gathered most of his materials in just a month, instantly felt satisfied.

Xiang Huaizhi sat in front of the computer. Before leaving, he had left his character AFK in a corner of Penglai, and at this moment, there was a little spirit fox sitting in front of his character. Penglai was humongous, so the fact that she could find him was certainly impressive.

Xiang Huaizhi plugged in his phone to charge it, and as soon as it turned on, he heard a gentle ding from WeChat.

Little Jing~: [Fist pump][Cheer][Encouraging]

Little Jing~: First day of challenge: Not Liking Gege!

A brief pause. He tapped out a question mark, but before he could send it, his phone vibrated again.

Little Jing~: Challenge failed!

Xiang Huaizhi couldn't help but smile.

Little Jing~: What is gege doing? Is the weather good over where gege is? Can gege take me to clear dungeons later?

The message with three consecutive "gege's" was followed by numerous hearts.

Xiang Huaizhi was used to it now, and he deleted the question mark.

Xiang: Yes.

Xiang: When will you be on?

Little Jing~: I'm AFKing in Penglai. I'll be back in my dorm right after I finish lunch.

Little Jing~: [Photo]

Little Jing~: I'm drinking milk tea. [Cute]

Xiang Huaizhi gave Sweet Little Jing's photo a cursory glance, but a few seconds later, his gaze drifted back to it.

The photo was focused on a half-drunk cup of milk tea, placed on an orange table. This milk tea shop was a nationwide chain brand, and it had many locations, including their school cafeteria.

But there was an orange table and a window in the corner that he seemed to have passed by a mere twenty minutes ago; he even remembered the small ad for a tutor posted on the window.

Xiang Huaizhi raised his eyebrows in surprise.

Sweet Little Jing goes to the same school as me?

"What photo has you so engrossed?" Lu Hang glanced at him as he passed by. "A selfie?"

Xiang Huaizhi closed the picture. "No."

Lu Hang didn't mind him and said, "Oh, I have classes this afternoon and my character is AFKing in Penglai. If it disconnects, help me log back in."

"Mm."

Xiang Huaizhi made his character fly away from Penglai and distractedly started to do his dailies.

If it was just the milk tea and the table, it would be nothing, but that little ad...He had paid particular attention to it today, so he shouldn't be wrong, and Sweet Little Jing did mention she was a university student before.

Coincidence, or part of a wider plot?

Chapter 06

A few seconds later, he ruled out the latter. Sweet Little Jing was already so clingy to him in-game; if she knew they went to the same school, there was no way that she wouldn't make a move in real life.

Xiang Huaizhi only considered the situation for half a minute before coming to a decision.

If they really went to the same school, he couldn't let Sweet Little Jing find out. It was one thing for her to follow him around in-game, but if she clung to him in real life, he really wouldn't know how to deal with someone like that.

If he wanted to keep this a secret from Sweet Little Jing, then Lu Hang also couldn't know.

"I'm going to buy some food on my way back. What do you want to eat?" Lu Hang asked, completely unaware that his roommate had marked him as untrustworthy.

When he didn't receive a response after some time, he called out again, "Xiangxiang?"

Xiang Huaizhi looked up. "Hm? Just bring me the same as whatever you're having."

After Lu Hang left, Xiang Huaizhi picked up his coffee and took a sip. Having just put down the cup, he saw in-game that his friend message icon started flashing.

[Friend] Bishop Wood: God Xiang, the party for tomorrow's first kill has been assigned. Check the guild interface for details.

[Friend] Yearning For: Mm.

Xiang Huaizhi opened the guild interface where the parties assigned by the guild leader would be assigned, and saw that the five-man party included him, Long Road Ahead, Love is Sharing Noms, and two guild members he didn't know. Despite not knowing the

latter two, he did recognize their IDs: they were both on the Mastery rankings.

The twenty-man party pretty much consisted of all of Idle Pavilion's top players. The setup was perfectly put together, completely flawless.

Xiang Huaizhi glanced through it, then closed the entire interface. He didn't even bother looking too carefully at these people's sects.

[Friend] Yearning For: Before joining the guild, I said that Long Road Ahead, Love is Sharing Noms, and Sweet Little Jing would all be in my party, not to be split up.

[Friend] Bishop Wood: I know, but we discussed it afterward. Putuo Mountains are more stable than Spirit Fox Dens…Besides, this is just the lineup for tomorrow's first kill. After we get the first kill, I'll switch her back.

[Friend] Bishop Wood: Don't worry, Little Jing is in my party, and I'll protect her [Hug]. It's not like our party is weak, we might even beat you to the first kill.

[Friend] Yearning For: Non-negotiable.

[Friend] Bishop Wood: Don't be like that. I'm also looking at the big picture here, and don't you always find Little Jingjing so noisy?

[Friend] Yearning For: When did I ever find her noisy?

[Friend] Yearning For: Either switch her back, or the four of us leave the guild.

[Friend] Bishop Wood: …Okay, I'll have her switched when Echoes of Spring comes online. You know that only the guild leader or vice guild leader has that authority.

Bishop Wood took a screenshot of the chat logs and sent it to Echoes of Springs through WeChat, and she replied very quickly.

 Chapter 06

Echoes of Spring: Got it. I told you before that Yearning For would never agree to let Sweet Little Jing join another party.

Bishop Wood: Sigh, I feel like he normally doesn't pay much attention to Sweet Little Jing.

Echoes of Spring: He doesn't interact with her much, but he does give her stuff. Have you forgotten about that ring? Anyway, I'll switch her party now. Stop teasing Sweet Little Jing, or are you really obsessed with that character?

Bishop Wood: Of course not. With the name change and the new appearance, it's not the same character to me at all. I just really find Sweet Little Jing interesting.

Echoes of Spring: What's so interesting about her?

Bishop Wood: How do I put it...Exchanging a few words here and there or running a few simple dungeons together feels more fun than playing with others. Games are meant to be fun after all.

Echoes of Spring: ...Okay then, good luck. I hope you don't end up clashing with Yearning For; we're all in the same guild, and this would put me and Lovesickness in a tough spot.

Bishop Wood: Ha ha ha, if Yearning For is truly interested in Sweet Little Jing, we'll compete for her, fair and square. We won't fight, don't worry.

Xiang Huaizhi didn't want to compete fair and square with Bishop Wood.

He just felt that he should be the one to take care of the people he brought into the guild. Moreover, if Bishop Wood's party had Regardless of Lovesickness, he was even more determined not to let Sweet Little Jing join them.

As soon as they finished discussing this matter, Sweet Little

Jing sent him a cute sticker, telling him that she was back.

He didn't reply and just flew directly to her side and invited her to his party.

"Good afternoon, gege," Jing Huan greeted cutely.

"Mm," Xiang Huaizhi acknowledged. "Share your dungeon list with me."

[Party] Sweet Little Jing: [Player Sweet Little Jing's dungeon list]

Xiang Huaizhi opened it and glanced at it. The highlighted dungeons were all the ones that he had run with her, while the rest were gray, indicating that the player hadn't done them this week.

Could it be that without him, this person wouldn't do the dungeons herself?

Jing Huan listened carefully and found that although Yearning For and Xiang Huaizhi's voices were similar, Yearning For's was a bit deeper. However alike their voices were, one was a kind-hearted senior, and the other was a peerless scumbag.

He sighed.

"Long Road Ahead is AFK, and that healer isn't here either." Xiang Huaizhi thought for a moment. "I'll take you to do some other quests?"

"Whatever gege wants."

Jing Huan originally thought it'd be a trivial, low-experience reward quest since there were a limited number of quests for a two-person party. He never imagined that Yearning For would take him all the way to the God of War quest NPC.

"Gege..." he quickly spoke up, "isn't this quest too expensive?"

The God of War quest had no player limit and offered high experience rewards, but taking the quest cost one gold. Since the cost

Chapter 06

was high, and there were many other ways to gain experience, almost no one did it. Even Jing Huan didn't choose the God of War quest back then even though he lacked experience points.

"I need the experience myself," Xiang Huaizhi said.

Jing Huan had no choice but to shut up and quietly tag along.

Perhaps it was because it cost gold that the quests were particularly simple; sometimes the quest didn't even require combat.

After grinding for two hours, Jing Huan downed the last sip of milk tea and asked, "How much longer are we going to keep farming, gege?"

"It's up to you," Xiang Huaizhi said. "Did you have something to do?"

"Yes," Jing Huan said truthfully. "I want to play in the arena today, so I want to go early to find a teammate."

Most players who fought in the arena brought their own buddies. Unfortunately, he didn't have many options; Love is Sharing Noms was also a healer, so the two of them would only lose if they went together. Thus, he had to find a random to party up with.

Xiang Huaizhi paused and asked, "Why do you suddenly want to play in the arena?"

When you reached 2,000 points in the arena, the system rewarded you with a random piece of bound equipment, ranging from blue to orange quality.

"Aren't we running the guild dungeons tomorrow? I want to see if I can get some usable gear to get by..." he said softly. "I can't drag you guys down too much."

Jing Huan was originally going to buy equipment directly from the marketplace, but because he had sold himself as a runaway girl

who worked part-time, he didn't dare to recklessly spend money on the game. He also had to pretend to be out working several nights.

He couldn't even spend the money he was rolling in. How utterly miserable.

Xiang Huaizhi said, "If you just get a random party, you'll only be giving away points."

"But I still have to try."

Xiang Huaizhi said brusquely, "There's no point in trying. Anyone who parties up with a Spirit Fox Den in the arena can't be very smart."

Jing Huan's mouth twitched.

As harsh as it sounded, Jing Huan had to admit that he was right.

There were too few skilled Spirit Fox Den players; even a random healer would be more reliable than playing with a Spirit Fox Den.

Jing Huan forced himself to smile and said, "Then I'll have to think of another way."

Xiang Huaizhi remained silent for a moment before asking, "Do you really want to go fight?"

Jing Huan nonchalantly threw out an "mm."

"Then I'll take you."

"Ah?" He hadn't expected that from Xiang Huaizhi. "What about Road-ge?"

"He has plenty of teammates, don't worry about him."

When Lu Hang returned and heard that his meal ticket was going to help someone else rank up, he immediately felt as though he was being abandoned by his dad.

However, after hearing that it was Sweet Little Jing his dad was

 Chapter 06

abandoning him for, he didn't mind it that much. "What? She hasn't gotten the 2,000 points equipment reward yet? Then hurry up and help her get it tonight."

At 7:20 p.m., Jing Huan appeared in the arena on time and joined Yearning For's party. Long Road Ahead and his friend were standing next to them.

[Current] Long Road Ahead: Little Jingjing! [Fist pump]

[Current] Sweet Little Jing: Here! [Fist pump]

[Current] Long Road Ahead: If you run into me later, remember to go easy on me, or I'll drop from the top ranks!! [Angry]

Jing Huan laughed at this. Long Road Ahead really had no shame, even saying such things in the Current Channel.

[Current] Sweet Little Jing: No way! Gege and I will never admit defeat!! [Cute]

Lu Hang was making no headway here, so he decided to take another approach. He poked his head out and said to his dear roommate sitting at the opposite desk, "Xiangxiang, if we get matched up later, just put on a performance. Sweet Little Jing won't be able to tell anyway."

The corners of his dear roommate's mouth drew up into a ruthless smile. "If we do get matched up, just focus on running away."

"Huh?"

"To avoid wasting your weapon's durability."

Who knew if Lu Hang's prayers had an effect, but their parties never got matched up the entire night.

Jing Huan had a fantastic time playing tonight. With his new ring, his healing efficacy skyrocketed. In numerous matches, Yearning For's health bar was full until the end.

Xiang Huaizhi also noticed that. He didn't know if it was because she had been diligently practicing all this time, but Sweet Little Jing's skills had improved rapidly, especially her sealing accuracy, which was so precise it was uncanny. Her control and game sense were all exceptional.

He even felt that she wasn't much worse than Lu Hang, and additionally, she had a healing skill that Warlocks didn't have. He didn't have to worry about his health or the opponent's seals at all; he just had to focus on dealing damage to win.

After another match ended and while Xiang Huaizhi was using a potion, he suddenly asked, "Which game did you play before?"

Jing Huan was flabbergasted for a moment and mentioned the name of a game similar in style to *Nine Heroes*. "Why?"

"Nothing." Xiang Huaizhi glanced at the time. "Get your potions ready, we still have time for one last match."

Jing Huan agreed and quickly refilled his inventory's potions.

Half a minute later, they entered the day's final PK match.

[Current] Bishop Wood: [Surprised]

[Current] Bishop Wood: Little Jingjing. [Shy]

Standing opposite them was Bishop Wood, and standing beside him as his teammate was one of the top ten DPS in the server.

Bishop Wood was still typing, wanting to chat with Sweet Little Jing some more when he saw the person across from him swiftly draw his sword and charge straight at them.

Bishop Wood moved his fingers to seal Yearning For.

【You have been sealed and cannot use spells.】

Bewildered, it took Bishop Wood a moment to finally notice his predicament.

Chapter 06

Four little spiders circled his feet; he had been sealed by Sweet Little Jing.

When had she sealed him? He had just typed a few words.

Bishop Wood stopped joking around and sat up straight, wanting to PK seriously.

Unfortunately, getting CCed right at the start had dealt him too much damage. After breaking free from the seal, the only thing left he could do was CC Yearning For to preserve his own DPS. However, Yearning For was so well-positioned that even after three attempts, none of his spells hit him. So, he switched gears and tried to seal Sweet Little Jing.

Then he realized that he would've been better off focusing on sealing Yearning For.

Had the Spirit Fox Den's movement speed always been this terrifying in PK?

Ten minutes later, he had used up almost all his potions, but his health bar still couldn't recover. It was now only a matter of time.

"Shit, the Spirit Fox Den sect is too disgusting. If they aren't sealing my spells or physical attacks, they're immobilizing me," his party's DPS unmuted himself to complain. Immobilized in place, he was like a punching bag for Yearning For.

Bishop Wood was also suffering. He turned on his microphone to the Current Channel and half-jokingly said, "Little Jingjing… you're usually so cute, why are you so ruthless while PKing? Can't you go easy on me?"

Jing Huan jumped and immediately clarified his position in the Party Channel, "Gege, I don't know this person very well."

Yearning For let out an "mm" and added, "I know."

He switched from his dagger back to his sword and easily took out the opposing DPS's remaining health.

Bishop Wood gave up struggling and didn't revive his teammate. "Little Jingjing, you really don't mind tormenting me like this?"

A few seconds later, he finally received a reply.

The voice in his headset was cool and pleasant, not as sweet as Don't Frown's voice, but still soothing. "Haven't you heard the saying before?"

Bishop Wood was a little stunned. "What saying?"

Sweet Little Jing's next words were ice-cold. "All beautiful roses have thorns."

Bishop Wood's jaw dropped open.

Then can you also prick Yearning For with your thorns?

As Bishop Wood flew out of the battle zone, a line of yellow text popped up on Jing Huan's screen.

【Congratulations on reaching 2,000 points in the arena! We heard that Wu Erlang[5] has a gift for you, go take a look!】

"Gege," Jing Huan immediately started sucking up to him, "I'm at 2,000 points now. We won so many points tonight! Gege is so strong!"

At exactly 9:30 p.m., the arena closed, forcibly teleporting the players to the arena entrance.

Only the party leader could click NPCs, so Xiang Huaizhi gave Sweet Little Jing the party lead. "Go get your reward."

---

5   武松 – Wǔ Sōng also known as "Second Brother Wu" 武二郎 - Wǔ Èrláng is a legendary hero from the classic Chinese novel *Water Margin*, famous for killing a tiger with his bare hands.

Chapter 06

"Okay." Jing Huan walked over to the NPC and silently prayed in his heart.

Not asking for orange gear or a high-tier item. I'm just asking for an item with healing and movement speed attributes; I'll accept blue gear too!

【Are you sure you want to claim the points reward? Bound reward: each character can only receive it once.】

Jing Huan closed his eyes and clicked "Yes," before prying them slightly open—

【Congratulations on obtaining the "Sujin Celestial Robes."】

Blue gear…the lowest tier of rewards he could get.

Jing Huan comforted himself that at least half of his wish was granted; as long as this robe had his desired attributes, all would be well.

He slowly moved his mouse over the robes.

On the other end, Xiang Huaizhi took a sip of water and listened to Lu Hang blabber away. The latter was so angry that he had lost a match to Bishop Wood that he had been ranting about it for half an hour.

It had been ten or so seconds without seeing any messages in the party chat. Xiang Huaizhi was about to ask for an update when—

[Current] Sweet Little Jing: [Wailing][Collapsing]

[Current] Sweet Little Jing: GMs, I…[Strangle neck][Cleaver]

[Current] Yearning For: Hm?

[Current] Sweet Little Jing: [Compendium - Sujin Celestial Robes]

Xiang Huaizhi clicked on the compendium link to take a look. It was just an ordinary piece of blue equipment and had no added attributes—a junk item.

Jing Huan was so infuriated that he could only express his rage in stickers.

The arena's point milestone rewards rarely gave top-tier items, but the chances of getting trash were also low. The system usually provided a decent item that matched the player's sect.

How come, when it came to his turn, he got this piece of shit?!

[Current] Sweet Little Jing: QAQ *Waaaaaah—*

[Current] Yearning For: ...

[Current] Yearning For: It's okay, there's another reward at 3,000 points.

[Current] Sweet Little Jing: I feel like I'll never get a piece of good equipment in my life, gege. [About to cry]

[Current] Yearning For: That's not true, you'll get it next time.

[Current] Sweet Little Jing: Really? [About to cry]

[Current] Yearning For: ...Mm.

[Current] Sweet Little Jing: But how can I get 3,000 points!! QAQ *Waaaaah—*

[Current] Yearning For: I'm here, so you can get them.

[Current] Long Road Ahead: ?

[Current] Sweet Little Jing: T.T Will gege take me to the arena in the future? I'm already miserable. Don't lie to me right now.

[Current] Yearning For: I'm not lying. Let's go, it's time for dungeons.

[Current] Sweet Little Jing: Okay. [Wiping away tears][Hug]

Everyone who had just finished fighting in the arena watched this bizarre conversation in shock.

"What..." Lu Hang was also stupefied. "Xiang Huaizhi, you're abandoning your son just to flirt with a girl?"

Chapter 06

"I've already carried you to the top of the rankings, isn't that enough?" Xiang Huaizhi didn't even turn his head. "Everyone has to grow up sometime."

"Shit." Lu Hang didn't insist that Xiang Huaizhi carry him; he was just curious. "Are you and Sweet Little Jing really together now?"

Xiang Huaizhi said, "No."

"So, you guys were just flirting at the arena entrance?"

And they were speaking like that in the Current Channel, so who knew what base they had reached in their voice chat!

Xiang Huaizhi frowned, pondering his phrasing. "I was just consoling her."

Lu Hang let out an "oh" and said, "Then comfort me too."

"Okay," Xiang Huaizhi said. "When you reach 4,000 points and the system rewards you with a piece of trash gear, I'll comfort you too."

Lu Hang considered then said, "That would be too tragic. To be honest, it's the first time I've seen such a garbage arena reward... Forget it, let's go and clear dungeons."

They did two dungeons together and then decided to call it a night early to prepare for tomorrow's guild dungeon.

"Xiangxiang and I have a class tomorrow morning and will probably be back around 10 a.m.," Lu Hang said. "In that case, let's meet back here at 10:10 a.m. to discuss the dungeon, okay?"

[Party] Love is Sharing Noms: Okay.

[Party] Sweet Little Jing: No problem with that either~

After disbanding, Jing Huan lay on his bed and sent Yearning For a good night sticker. Then he leisurely started checking today's

group chat. His notifications in his three-person dorm group chat had been exploding all night. Since he was busy playing in the arena at the time, he couldn't reply.

Little Jing~: What?

Gao Zixiang: Where have you been? We've already finished discussing everything, and now you show up.

Little Jing~: Was busy, what were we discussing?

Lu Wenhao: [Link Share: A paradise on top of the mountain—Shanxi Resort welcomes you.]

Jing Huan opened the link that Lu Wenhao shared. It was a promotional page for a mountain resort located about an hour's drive away in their city.

Lu Wenhao: Natural swimming pool and hot springs! Half price on all rooms! We have a five-day vacation next month, why don't we all go together?

Little Jing~: Not interested.

Lu Wenhao didn't bother typing him a long screed. Instead, he did a WeChat voice call and used pathos and logos. First, he reminded them that their university lives would only last four years, and if they didn't go out and have fun together a few times, there wouldn't be any chances after graduation. He also mentioned that Gao Zixiang's parents were on a business trip, and he would be home alone during the break which was really pitiful, insisting that Jing Huan had to join them.

Jing Huan's head pounded listening to this. He had thought that, since it was just a few days off, it wouldn't matter if he didn't go home. Releasing a breath, he relented, "All right, how many days are we going?"

"Okay!" Worried that he would back out, Lu Wenhao immediately went to the hotel website to book a room. "Let's go for three days. We'll just book a double room and squeeze the three of us in?"

Jing Huan refused. "I want my own room. Please book me a king bed, okay?"

He didn't like sharing a bed with others, and besides, he needed to bring his laptop. It wouldn't be convenient to have someone around while he was gaming.

The matter was settled, and shortly after hanging up the phone, Lu Wenhao sent over the hotel booking confirmation in a text message.

It was just a spur-of-the-moment trip. Jing Huan glanced at the message, turned off his phone, and went to sleep.

Guide on How to Fail at Online Dating

Chapter 07

Jing Huan didn't have any classes the next day, so he casually whipped up a bowl of noodles for breakfast. After he finished eating, he sat in front of the computer.

As soon as he logged into the game, he received a friend message.

[Friend] Bishop Wood: Come to the guild's YY, 8372xxxx.

Although *Nine Heroes* had a built-in voice chat system, players still preferred using an external voice chat software called YY. Players could change their voice, create rooms, and play background music, making every aspect of it more convenient compared to the in-game voice chat.

Jing Huan downloaded YY in a few minutes and entered the number to join the channel where there were, unexpectedly, 122 people already online.

Jing Huan was stunned. A large guild truly lived up to its reputation; there were so many active people even in the early morning.

"Bishop Wood, swap to your stamina gear today. The combat areas in this dungeon aren't very big, so movement speed isn't going to be as useful." A user named Echo was talking. The female voice

sounded indifferent, and she seemed to be discussing dungeons, "Babe, are you online?"

The user named Lovesickness, with a purple vest badge that denoted her as the channel owner, unmuted herself and said, "I'm on, I'm so sleepy...Who is this ID21934 in the YY? A new level 0 account?"

Jing Huan recognized these two people's IDs. They really were girls.

After confirming that his voice changer was also working on YY, he cautiously unmuted himself and spoke, "Can you hear me?"

"Yes, we can," Bishop Wood said. "Little Jing?"

"It's me." Jing Huan changed his nickname to Sweet Little Jing.

Without hesitation, Regardless of Lovesickness bestowed a yellow channel moderator vest badge upon him. "Good morning, have your party members arrived?"

This was the first time that Jing Huan had spoken calmly with Regardless of Lovesickness, and he felt a bit weirded out. "Nomnom is here, I'll call her over. Everyone else should be here soon."

Echoes of Spring made an agreeable noise and said, "The parties have been assigned, and the dungeon opens in two hours. If you have any questions, ask them now."

Jing Huan had no intention of joining the chat. He opened the marketplace to see if there was any decent but cheap equipment that he could snag.

During the guild members' aimless chatter in YY, somehow the topic of singing came up.

"Lovesickness is a really good singer, along with Peachy. And there's also Faefae...Hey, hasn't it been a long time since our guild held an event?"

"Yeah, I remember over ten thousand people joined our YY during our last singing event!"

"Well duh. Our guild's pretty famous, and the songs were really nice."

"Speaking of which…" Bishop Wood paused for a moment. "Some new girls recently joined our guild. Should we do a little talent show? Little Jing?"

Jing Huan was startled by the prompt. "What?"

"Since the dungeon hasn't opened yet, why don't you sing us a song?" Bishop Wood said. "You have such a nice voice so your singing must also be just as great."

Jing Huan stammered, "I-I can't sing."

"How could that be? I'm sure you can, don't be shy." Bishop Wood laughed. "I also have many YY gifts here. Sing a few lines, and they're all yours."

Jing Huan wasn't interested in gifts; he bought the voice changer to seduce Yearning For, not to sing and go viral.

He was about to refuse when Bishop Wood activated the karaoke mode and put him in the mic queue.

【Bishop Wood sent Sweet Little Jing Flowers x99.】

【Regardless of Lovesickness sent Sweet Little Jing Flowers x3.】

【Peach Cheese Stan sent Sweet Little Jing Flowers x11.】

Flowers instantly filled the screen.

Jing Huan was dumbfounded and trapped.

Thinking she was shy, Bishop Wood chuckled. "It's okay, just sing whatever. No one would dare say you sound bad."

"What are you doing?" A voice that was neither cold nor light interrupted Bishop Wood.

 Chapter 07

Everyone then noticed a white vest badge user at the bottom of the room's member list, named ID21935.

Jing Huan immediately recognized Yearning For's voice, and as if meeting his savior, quickly greeted him, "Good morning, gege!"

Xiang Huaizhi changed his username to Yearning For and asked, "Are you logged in?"

"Yes, I'm AFKing next to you."

"Join the party."

"Coming!"

Bishop Wood was speechless for a moment.

Why did Sweet Little Jing's voice sound so much sweeter when speaking to Yearning For compared to him...

Regardless of Lovesickness didn't care and gave Xiang Huaizhi a yellow vest badge.

"Each party's room is open, just below this channel," Echoes of Spring said. "The room names are the party leaders' names. Remember to enter your room for discussions when the dungeon is about to open, so you don't disturb the other parties."

As soon as she finished speaking, they heard Yearning For say lightly, "Come down." No sooner had he said that, Yearning For jumped into the room with his name.

Before anyone could react, they saw Sweet Little Jing quickly leave the mic queue and jump into Yearning For's room without looking back. It took less than three seconds for both of them to leave.

Looking at the two adjacent vest badges, Echoes of Spring placidly said, "I think it's time you give up, Bishop Wood."

Peach Cheese Stan commented, "I agree."

Youth Chasing the Wind added, "Me too."

Just Be Happy happily threw in their two cents, "And me."

The conversation stopped at this point, and no fourth person joined in. This was because, while they were talking, a white vest badge user named Fae Bae had entered the channel.

The moment she appeared, everyone quieted down, and almost immediately afterward, the guild chat exploded.

[Guild] Peach Cheese Stan: ???

[Guild] Flowing Years: I feel a bit awkward.

[Guild] Love is Sharing Noms: ...

[Guild] Bishop Wood: I'm going to faint.

"How lively." Fae Bae's gaze latched onto the two people in the small room, and her tone was chilling.

"You're the one who left the guild," Regardless of Lovesickness said. "Naturally, only guild members can have the mod vest in the guild YY."

"So you're saying that because I left the guild, we can't even be friends anymore, huh?"

"We stopped being friends the moment you threatened to leave the guild if we didn't keep hunting Sweet Little Jing," Echoes of Spring said bluntly and mercilessly. After all, when Fae Bae spammed those megaphones, she never considered Idle Pavilion at all. "Do you need something?"

Fae Bae sneered. "So I can't come unless I need something? Half the activity in this YY channel comes from my fans. It should be fine for me to hang around here, right?"

Echoes of Spring replied, "Suit yourself."

Fae Bae didn't speak anymore, but remained in the channel.

Chapter 07

The tension from the battlefield frightened the other guild members into fleeing within two minutes, all retreating to their respective YY rooms.

Of course, Jing Huan also saw Fae Bae. He couldn't help feeling relieved that this YY room was locked and that white vest badge users couldn't enter without a password. Otherwise, judging from Fae Bae's attitude, she would've definitely come in and ripped him apart.

The thought of arguing with a girl over voice chat made his scalp feel numb.

Just then, he saw Fae Bae suddenly jump into the room above theirs.

The spectacle of their three usernames resembled a wife catching an adulterous couple in the act.

Before Jing Huan could react, Fae Bae's username changed: *Is it fun being a mistress?*

Jing Huan thought numbly, *There are so many happy people in the world, why can't I be one of them?*

The other guild members were eagerly watching the drama unfold, popcorn in hand, and chatting up a storm in their own rooms.

Peach Cheese Stan said, "This is my first time being so close to a scandal! It's so thrilling!"

Youth Chasing the Wind asked, "Will they start arguing?"

"I don't think so," Red Apricot said. "Yearning For's room is locked, so Fae Bae can't enter."

【YY Announcement: Is it fun being a mistress? has been kicked out of the YY channel by moderator Sweet Little Jing.】

Peach Cheese Stan whistled. "Savage."

Youth Chasing the Wind commented, "That's awesome."

"She really had the nerve to kick her out..." Red Apricot said.

A few seconds later, Is it fun being a mistress? entered the channel again.

【YY Announcement: Is it fun being a mistress? has been kicked out of the YY channel by moderator Yearning For and this ID is banned from entering the channel for 7 days.】

Peach Cheese Stan hollered, "Holy fuck?"

Youth Chasing the Wind exclaimed, "Holy fuck!"

Red Apricot breathed, "Holy fuck..."

Lu Hang scarfed down his breakfast and logged in. The two of them had both woken up late this morning and had rushed to class after just taking a few bites of food. He had been starving for over an hour now.

He logged into YY, asked Regardless of Lovesickness for the yellow vest badge, and then entered their party's room.

"Why are there only you two?" he asked. "Where's everyone else?"

Xiang Huaizhi said, "I don't know."

Lu Hang only then realized that their other two party members were in someone else's room.

"I'll go ask." He jumped into the other room. Since the dungeon hadn't started yet, many people had gathered in this room, and it seemed quite boisterous.

"Nomnom and BON, you two are in our party, why did you run over to someone else's room?" Lu Hang interjected.

The voice chat was silent for a beat. Love is Sharing Noms finally whispered, "I didn't dare go in."

Chapter 07

Lu Hang was stunned and said, "Huh? Why?"

Love is Sharing Noms said honestly, "I was afraid of hearing things I shouldn't hear."

And then I'll get kicked out by Yearning For, along with a seven-day ban bonus gift.

Lu Hang was at a loss for words.

This announcement actually surprised both the popcorn-eating onlookers and Jing Huan.

He didn't really know how to use YY. Although he had used it before when playing *Nine Heroes*, he only knew to push the F2 key to talk and wasn't familiar with how to kick people out. He was thinking about kicking Fae Bae out a second time when an announcement popped up in the system, saying, "This user is no longer in the channel."

Yearning For had been one step ahead of him; not only did he kick her out, he even banned her ID.

In that moment, Jing Huan felt particularly conflicted.

His first thought was that this damn scumbag was trying to seduce him again.

Then he sighed. A scumbag through and through; he had at least "loved" Fae Bae before, but now he could kick her out in front of hundreds of people with little to no regard for her feelings.

"Gege," he called out.

Xiang Huaizhi's tone remained unchanged. "Mm."

"Did she change her nickname to insult me?" Jing Huan deliberately lowered his voice. "She threatened me before, so I kicked her out without thinking. Will she hunt me again? I'm kind of scared..."

Scared?

After some consideration, Xiang Huaizhi came to the conclusion that he had never seen "fear" in Sweet Little Jing's demeanor.

"She won't," he said. "She can't kill you."

Jing Huan wanted to delve deeper into this topic when he saw three people appear in the room; Lu Hang had called over the rest of their party members.

His lips parted slightly, but in the end, he didn't continue.

They first ran the five-man dungeon; the twenty-man dungeon would be released at 3 p.m.

The five members of the party were him, Yearning For, Long Road Ahead, Love is Sharing Noms, and BrbOrNot. The four of them often cleared dungeons together with BrbOrNot being the temporary assignee.

In the eyes of the other guild members, BrbOrNot looked the pitiful little figure, being squeezed in among the party of four; you could almost feel his helplessness through the screen.

That was indeed the case for BrbOrNot. Setting aside the mess that had happened when Yearning For and the others had just joined Idle Pavilion, the most awkward thing was that he had previously hunted Sweet Little Jing.

Yes, he was the Mage in the fixed hunting party.

Sweet Little Jing had even tried to negotiate with him once at the city gate, asking him if he could let her out so she could do dailies.

What had he said at that time?

Oh, he had sent a cleaver sticker.

There was truly nothing left for BrbOrNot to live for.

Yearning For's microphone icon lit up. "Mage, post your stats to the public chat."

 Chapter 07

BrbOrNot didn't dare tarry and immediately posted them.

"Wooow, a 2k magic attack! That's really impressive," Sweet Little Jing chirped. "No wonder it hurt so much when you hit me before. With this kind of magic attack, you must be on the Mastery rankings, right?"

BrbOrNot could hardly breathe.

"If I remember correctly, BON is one of the top five mages, right? What, did you guys meet in the arena?" Lu Hang asked.

"Nooo," Jing Huan replied nonchalantly. "He's just hunted me before."

Xiang Huaizhi stiffened.

"*Pfft—*" Lu Hang couldn't help but burst out laughing. "So it's like that..."

"Is it too late for me to apologize now?" BrbOrNot asked.

"Hmm? It's okay, just a misunderstanding," Jing Huan said while beaming. "He only camped me for seventy-one hours and thirteen minutes, but I don't hold any grudges."

BrbOrNot swallowed hard.

Xiang Huaizhi chuckled and dragged the party to the main city NPC. "Let's meet up first. There's still over an hour left, so let's run another dungeon. Everyone come to the main city storage."

A moment later, BrbOrNot joined their party.

[Party] Sweet Little Jing: Welcome! [Cleaver]

[Party] BrbOrNot: ...

[Party] Sweet Little Jing: Oh! I sent the wrong sticker. Welcome~ [Cute]

A few seconds later, BrbOrNot faced the little spirit fox in the party and used the kneeling and worshipping character action.

It satisfied Jing Huan who controlled the little spirit fox to nod at him.

With an extra DPS, their dungeon clearing speed increased significantly, clearing two dungeons in just over an hour.

At 11:40 a.m., Regardless of Lovesickness sent out a guild announcement, asking everyone to get ready at the dungeon NPC.

Xiang Huaizhi calmly led the party over to the NPC. The guild dungeon NPC was a new character, specifically a clam spirit who was a little girl lying in a shell and blowing bubbles.

The area near the NPC was packed with people, with all 200 guild members present.

[Current] Youth Chasing the Wind: Who stepped on my foot! [Angry]

[Current] Peach Cheese Stan: [Rolling eyes] Can you stop being so tacky.

[Current] Sweet Little Jing: Taking advantage of the chaos to touch gege's hand. *\^0^/*~~

[Current] Peach Cheese Stan: ...

[Current] Echoes of Spring: ...

[Current] Regardless of Lovesickness: ...

Everyone was standing together, so it was impossible to tell who was saying what.

But Sweet Little Jing wasn't like that. Despite being in a crowd, her voice would always be the most recognizable.

[Current] Long Road Ahead: Taking advantage of the chaos to hit Yearning For's head. *\^0^/*

[Current] Long Road Ahead: ...

Chapter 07

[Current] Long Road Ahead: Daddy, I was wrong. Let me back in the party. QAQ

Tranquility written all over his face, Xiang Huaizhi invited Lu Hang back into the party and said, "Check if you have all the correct gear equipped, we're going in."

"It's almost release time, but *Nine Heroes* still hasn't posted the dungeon guide. Guess it must be really hard." Lu Hang sat up straight, glancing at the little spirit fox beside him. "Little Jingjing, don't be nervous, just play well."

Jing Huan crossed his legs as he chewed gum. Adopting a scared voice, he said, "Okay, I'll try my best, my hands are shaking, *waaaaah*."

Like hell he was scared.

In his old server, he was always at the forefront of clearing new content. His game ID still appeared on the list of players who achieved first clears, earning him the title of "First Clear Prince" in the community.

A few minutes later, the dungeon officially opened. But for some reason, all the parties present were still standing there, and after ten seconds, not a single party had entered the dungeon zone.

Lu Hang asked, "Daddy, what's going on? The dungeon has opened!"

Xiang Huaizhi looked at the dialogue box in front of him and frowned. "Can't get in."

The NPC dialogue box read, "Okay, this princess has received your application."

The others obviously couldn't get in either, and many players grew impatient.

[Current] Regardless of Lovesickness: Why can't we enter?

[Current]: Peach Cheese Stan: Could it be a bug? Is it only our server? I was hoping our guild could get the server's first clear...

[Current] Cat Network: Damn, what a crappy server?! If it's not working, just shut them down, okay?

[Current] Love is Sharing Noms: We can't get in either...

"Oh well, it's over." Lu Hang sighed.

Jing Huan said, "Not necessarily."

"What do you mean 'not necessarily'?" Lu Hang said. "We can't even enter the dungeon right now. Who knows how long the fix will take."

"Perhaps the dungeon has already started?" Jing Huan glanced at the NPC. "Didn't you notice the NPC has changed?"

Xiang Huaizhi had. At some point, the little girl in the shell had changed her pose and was now holding a precious pearl in her hand that she was carefully admiring.

Lu Hang glanced over and realized it was true. With so many players obstructing his view, it was difficult to notice earlier.

He was about to continue asking questions when the NPC inside the shell suddenly yawned.

[Current] Clam Spirit Princess (NPC): Hmm~ Who should I eat today?

[Current] Clam Spirit Princess (NPC): How about players Echoes of Spring, Sweet Little Jing, and Peach Cheese Stan...

Jing Huan was given no time to react to seeing his name when the sight before him suddenly transformed, and he was pulled into an unknown zone in the middle of the sea.

There was nothingness as far as the eye could see. Even his hot bar had vanished, leaving him with only his chat interface set to the

 Chapter 07

dungeon channel. He sat all alone in the open sea as if he were trapped in the game bug.

【[Dungeon Announcement] Clam Spirit Princess (NPC): Wrap Sweet Little Jing up in fish roe sauce before mixing in fish eyes, fry in oil until golden and crispy, and then bon appétit. My royal father and I both love eating this, and the dragon king next door is salivating! Unfortunately, she has a foul human scent. Let's marinate her in seawater for nine days first! [Disgust]】

Jing Huan wasn't sure how to react.

Don't eat me if you're so disgusted then!!! You stinky clam!!!

At the same time, a new quest appeared in the upper right corner of Xiang Huaizhi's screen.

【Dungeon quest: Overcome numerous obstacles to rescue your party member Sweet Little Jing! Quest time remaining: 540 minutes】

Five hundred and forty minutes; nine hours. It seemed that one day was one hour in this dungeon.

"Gege…" The voice coming from his headset sounded scared and helpless. "I'm trapped at sea."

"Mm. I know."

Lu Hang comforted her and said, "It's okay, it's nice that you can just lie there and clear the dungeon that way."

But this dungeon was obviously not that simple. Xiang Huaizhi tried clicking on the NPC, but couldn't initiate the battle at all.

【Shrimp Soldier: You can't bully us through sheer numbers! (Challenge, solo quest)】

It took the four of them to try it for them to finally figure out the dungeon's mechanic—one player from the party of five was randomly selected to enter the sea prison, while the other four players completed challenge stages. Interestingly, this challenge wasn't party-based but was a series of solo quests. If one player failed, another one would take their place until all nine stages were completed.

"So this means that if a player passes all nine levels in a row, the dungeon ends just like that?" Lu Hang was befuddled. "Then what's the point of a party dungeon? Might as well just open solo dungeons, wouldn't that be enough?"

Xiang Huaizhi pursed his lips and said, "It's not that simple."

As soon as he said that, Bishop Wood entered their YY room.

"Are you there?" Bishop Wood said. "You need to choose your players carefully for the challenges. Our DPS just entered the first stage and was killed by the boss in three rounds."

"What the?!" Lu Hang shouted. "Three rounds? Isn't your party's DPS pretty strong?!"

"Yup, but the first challenge stage's boss in this dungeon is immune to physical damage," Bishop Wood said expressionlessly.

Everyone in the YY room fell silent.

Without an official guide, no one knew the exact mechanics of these nine challenge stages' boss battles, so they had to grit their teeth and go in blind.

Jing Huan broke the silence. "It's okaaay. If we fail the challenges, we can just exit the dungeon and regroup. At most, this shitty dungeon can trap me for nine hours. I'll watch a few movies, and it'll be over." Taking the first kill wasn't really important to him.

"Don't be so negative," Lu Hang said, cracking his knuckles. "Let's give it a go. What if we make it? The first stage's boss is immune to physical damage, right? No problem, BrbOrNot, you go in first."

BrbOrNot didn't waste any words. "Okay."

Chapter 07

"All right," Bishop Wood said. "We'll continue with the challenges on our side and we'll send you the boss's attributes once we get them. If you guys get to the second stage first, let us know."

Jing Huan sat in the sea, listening to them chattering away like an outsider.

Very quickly, the system announcement popped up: BrbOrNot had passed the first stage.

No one even got a chance to celebrate as ten minutes later, BrbOrNot failed the second stage.

Love is Sharing Noms went in next but also failed the second challenge. This dungeon was really unfriendly to healers.

Love is Sharing Noms was apologetic. "Sorry, almost had it."

"No problem." Lu Hang was practically oozing confidence. "This great lord will break the deadlock."

Although he wasn't a DPS sect, Lu Hang was very skilled as the top warlock. He managed to reach the fourth stage before being killed by the boss immune to sealing.

Yearning For was the only one left who hadn't done any of the challenges.

Seeing the gloomy atmosphere in YY, Jing Huan pondered for a moment on how to comfort them before unmuting. "It's okay, clearing a dungeon blind isn't something you can do in one shot. We'll definitely get it next time."

"There will be no next time," Xiang Huaizhi said.

This dungeon was too much trouble for its worth. Once he had that first kill in the bag, he wasn't going to do it a second time.

A little thrown off, Jing Huan said, "Huh?"

"Go watch a movie." Xiang Huaizhi switched his sword to a sabre

and then controlled his character to chop off the giant crab's claw in one swipe. "By the time you're done, you'll be free."

Nonplussed, Jing Huan thought, *He's at it again, huh?*

He looked at his little spirit fox stranded at sea and heaved a sigh. "Okay, gege, I'll AFK for a bit then?"

Xiang Huaizhi replied, "Mm."

Those in the room who heard their conversation felt that there was a slightly ambiguous air between the two.

Lu Hang chewed on those two sentences and then said, "Old Xiang, are you flirting with the little lady here?"

Xiang Huaizhi didn't even look back. "Stop putting me in your scumbag shoes."

Lu Hang bit his tongue.

Jing Huan tried using all his hotkeys and even contacted customer service. After confirming that he couldn't watch Yearning For's battle in the zone, he resignedly minimized the game window.

He logged into WeChat on his computer and clicked on the dormitory group chat.

Little Jing~: How's your first clear going?

Gao Zixiang: Don't even talk about it, this game is getting freaking insane. What kind of trash dungeon is this? Was it specifically designed to make first clears harder? I had been preparing for so long, but as soon as I enter the dungeon, I get locked up? [Image]

Jing Huan opened the image and saw Gao Zixiang's character sitting in the sea, lost in a daze.

He smiled; it seemed that he wasn't the only one who pulled the short straw.

Chapter 07

Lu Wenhao: Come on, aren't you happy that all you have to do is lie down and wait while others are clearing the dungeon? If you want the full gaming experience so much, then come play my character.

Gao Zixiang: Fuck off, you stinky Spirit Fox Den.

Jing Huan felt attacked right now.

Little Jing~: That's low, bro. It's 2019 and you're still engaging in sect discrimination. You deserve to be locked up.

Lu Wenhao: Yupyup!

Gao Zixiang: ???

Gao Zixiang: Honestly, who in this game doesn't discriminate against Spirit Fox Dens?

Yearning For doesn't.

This thought flashed through Jing Huan's mind for a moment, but he quickly brushed it aside.

He had to hand it to them: these two people were clearly in the same room and still found it in them to argue in the group chat.

Jing Huan stirred up trouble between them, added fuel to the fire with a few words, then closed the group chat and left, not wanting any credit for his achievements and contributions there.

He opened a video app and played the most popular newly released movie, but found it boring after a few minutes so he turned it off.

No one had spoken in YY for a long time. When he opened it, he saw that only he and Yearning For were left in the room; everyone else had gone to other rooms to play.

Pinned to the top of YY was a karaoke hall, with over seventy people already there. Players who failed the dungeon challenge couldn't start a new dungeon for two hours, so those who failed their first blind clear were now all hanging out there.

After taking a second glance, Jing Huan closed it. He knew he wouldn't play this character for long since he had plans to sell it sometime in the future, and he didn't want to get too attached by making friends.

Out of sheer boredom, he opened the official *Nine Heroes* forum to see if anyone had gotten the first kill already and had posted a strategy guide. But instead of a strategy guide, the entire homepage was filled with people cursing the developers.

Jing Huan was about to close the website when he caught a glimpse of a prominent red headline as the top post.

【The 7th *Nine Heroes* Singing Competition is live~ Click here for details. NEW~】

Despite being posted two minutes ago, it had already amassed over a hundred comments, showing how popular this thread was.

This event had been around since Jing Huan played on his old character. It was very festive every year since the rewards were good and many people watched it.

Jing Huan reflexively clicked on the post and read through the participation process. The competition format was the same as the previous years. Anyone could register, and other players could listen to the songs and vote directly in the game's event interface.

He skimmed through the content and jumped right to the rewards.

【First place: A prize of 30,000 yuan, an all-server limited edition mount Purple Phoenix, and the opportunity to sing the new theme song for Nine Heroes.

 Chapter 07

Second place: A prize of 20,000 yuan and an all-server limited edition mount Purple Phoenix.

Third place: A prize of 10,000 yuan and an all-server limited edition mount Purple Phoenix.

Participation reward: All participants whose audio submissions pass the initial screening will receive one of the latest limited edition outfits Bubble Koi.】

Jing Huan now understood why this post was so popular.

The rarer something was, the more value it held, and putting a "limited edition" label in front of anything was bound to raise consumers' interest. It was the same for games; limited edition outfits, mounts, and pets were also super popular. Moreover, this time, the game was offering a participation reward, clearly aimed to encourage players to sign up and actively participate.

Jing Huan felt his head pound as he looked at the event interface—the reason behind the character's extravagant price was because it owned all the limited edition outfits since *Nine Heroes'* launch.

This also meant that he had to obtain the upcoming limited edition outfits, or else his character would significantly drop in value.

But...participating in a singing competition or whatever was never part of his plans. Even when he played on his old character, he never participated in such entertainment events.

"Are you there?" Yearning For's voice came through the headset, pulling Jing Huan back to reality.

Jing Huan raised his hand to close the webpage and said, "I'm here, gege. What's up?"

"Get ready to come out."

Jing Huan was flabbergasted for a moment and immediately

unminimized his game, just in time to see several system announcements pop up.

【Dungeon Announcement: Congratulations to player Yearning For for successfully clearing the ninth stage and completing this dungeon quest!】

He'd only been killing time for not even a half hour, and Yearning For had already finished it?

Jing Huan was still surrounded by the sea, and when he tried clicking around, he still couldn't move.

He was about to ask when he saw a black-robed man carrying a large dimly glowing saber, walk into the zone toward him.

【Yearning For has invited you to join his party. Yes, No.】

Jing Huan clicked "Yes," and the little spirit fox leaped up and landed behind Yearning For.

【System: Congratulations to Idle Pavilion's Yearning For, Long Road Ahead, Love is Sharing Noms, and BrbOrNot. They have cleared all nine stages in a row and rescued Sweet Little Jing from the clutches of the Clam Spirit Princess! They have achieved the first kill of the Clam Spirit Rebellion dungeon on Mirage server!】

Just a few seconds after the system announcements popped up, their YY room immediately filled with many people, all here for the show.

Lu Hang had been busy listening to people sing and hadn't watched how Yearning For cleared the dungeon. "What the fuck? You cleared it in just twenty minutes? And it's the first kill of all servers…Xiangxiang is awesome!"

Jing Huan returned to his senses and followed up with, "Gege is awesome!!"

"How did you clear it?" Bishop Wood was also shocked. "Didn't the eighth stage boss have dual resistances? How did you get through it?"

The damage from both physical and magic attacks didn't deal much damage on a dual resistance boss, and if you sealed it, it would flee within three turns.

Xiang Huaizhi said, "Its resistance wasn't that high, I could still damage it."

Bishop Wood couldn't find any words for a while.

Their party had already wiped at the eighth stage. Their second physical DPS had gone in, and he had complained in YY that he only dealt 300 damage per hit with his sword on the boss.

"Hurry up, hurry up," Lu Hang urged. "Click the NPC and get the reward."

The first kill was guaranteed to drop high-tier rewards, but quantity and who it would go to was a mystery.

Jing Huan had no interest in the reward-collecting process. He was about to make a cup of coffee to refresh himself when several lines of system notifications popped up on the screen—

【You have gained 7,718,372 experience points.】

【You have obtained 433 copper.】

【You have obtained Amethyst x1.】

Shocked, Jing Huan barely had time to react before the system automatically sent their party back to the main city's gate since the dungeon ended.

After a few seconds of silence in the room, he heard Love is Sharing Noms holler, "Little Jing! AHHHH!! SPLIT THE LOOT!!!"

"Damn, an amethyst..." Lu Hang was envious. "Little Jingjing, what is with your luck?"

Amethysts were a higher-tier material for enhancing equipment. It improved equipment attributes and was something rarely seen in the marketplace.

It felt like Jing Huan had been hit with a ton of bricks. He opened his inventory and confirmed it several times before murmuring, "Gege...I got a high-tier material drop."

"Mm, I saw," Xiang Huaizhi said.

"Goddamn...your luck is out of this world," Lu Hang said. "I suppose the steamed buns you got from killing the Spirit King before and the trash that dropped yesterday were all leading up to today's good luck."

Xiang Huaizhi disbanded the party and got ready to replenish his supplies for the twenty-man dungeon.

【Sweet Little Jing gave you Amethyst x1.】

[Private] Sweet Little Jing: Today, I also want to give my love and luck to gege! \\^0^//

Xiang Huaizhi wanted to toss it back to her but discovered the other person had enabled the "refuse items" function.

[Private] Yearning For: ?

[Private] Yearning For: Don't just casually give your luck away to others.

[Private] Sweet Little Jing: Nah.

[Private] Sweet Little Jing: Gege, if you use it on your divine artifact, it'll improve so many attributes! My equipment is all trash, so it's useless on me.

[Private] Sweet Little Jing: Don't give me money, I don't want it.

Chapter 07

[Private] Sweet Little Jing: However...if gege really feels bad about it, you can give me something else. [Shy]

[Private] Yearning For: What do you want?

[Private] Sweet Little Jing: I want to have a couple title with you, gege. [Shy][Blushing][Tapping fingers together]

[Private] Yearning For: Choose something else, or take the amethyst back.

[Private] Sweet Little Jing: QAQ *Waaaah—*

[Private] Sweet Little Jing: Then, I'll get a rain check for now. If something comes to me later on, I'll let you know, okay, gege? T.T

[Private] Yearning For: Mm.

In YY, Lu Hang was still nagging her, "Little Jingjing, hurry up and split the loot, I need some of your luck for the twenty-man dungeon later!"

Jing Huan said, "Okay, wait a moment. I'll go get some money from the bank..."

"Huh?" BrbOrNot paused. "Why did God Xiang suddenly give me money?"

Love is Sharing Noms said, "God Xiang also gave me some..."

"Splitting the loot," replied Xiang Huaizhi.

Lu Hang asked, "Don't you have it wrong, though? Little Jingjing was the one that got the high-tier material drop."

"It's on her behalf." Xiang Huaizhi glanced at the time. "All right, everyone go refill your supplies. Meet at the guild gate at 2:50 p.m."

The room fell silent instantly.

Compared to the five-man dungeon, the new twenty-man dungeon was a walk in the park. It was the simplest type of dungeon:

clearing the small mobs until you get to kill the boss, without any obstacles in the way.

The twenty-man party had plenty of DPS, and the first kill was exceptionally easy to obtain. The first kill reward fell into Echoes of Spring's hands and while it was also a high-tier material, it was far inferior to an amethyst.

Everyone in the party was exhausted by the time they finished the dungeon, and after discussing it, they decided not to run anymore that night.

Jing Huan packed a few servings of spicy hot pot and returned to the dormitory.

Gao Zixiang's guild hadn't gotten the first kill, and he looked distressed. "We were only two seconds behind the others, just two seconds!"

"Stop dwelling on it and just concentrate on eating." Jing Huan broke his chopsticks apart and looked over at Lu Wenhao who was in front of the computer. "Hao'er?"

The person who was usually the gourmand didn't even respond. "I'll be right there, just let me finish watching this video."

Jing Huan asked, "What's he watching?"

"What else? Yearning For's first kill video," Gao Zixiang said.

Jing Huan stilled. "What's so interesting about that? It's just a normal dungeon."

"The dungeon, sure, but clearing five stages solo isn't. You haven't seen how he fought that dual-resistance boss, there's only one way to describe it." Gao Zixiang looked up. "Next fucking level."

Jing Huan couldn't help but glance over at Lu Wenhao's computer screen.

In the video, Yearning For's character had just finished the battle and was going all the way down to the bottom of the sea, stopping beside the little spirit fox.

Lu Wenhao turned off the video and sat down next to them, saying, "Fuck, Yearning For is too cool. He must be the number one DPS player across all the servers, right?"

Gao Zixiang said, "He has been for a while."

"Especially after he killed the boss and went to pick up that female party member while holding his saber…" Lu Wenhao shook his head and *tsked*. "Honestly, if I were that girl, I'd want to marry him in that very second, offer myself to him, you know?"

Gao Zixiang said, "Nope."

"You're not romantic at all. I feel bad for your girlfriend; she's been with you so many years, but she hasn't received a single bouquet of roses." Lu Wenhao turned his head and said, "Right, Huanhuan?"

Jing Huan swallowed the fish tofu without changing his expression and nodded. "Mm, if I were that female player, I would use the amethyst as a ring and propose to him on the spot."

"Yeah exactly, just propose on the spot!" Lu Wenhao's lips stung from the spiciness. He took a sip of water and suddenly realized something was off. "Wait…Amethyst? What amethyst?"

Ever so casually, Jing Huan said, "The first kill reward."

"They actually got an amethyst for their first kill reward?!" Gao Zixiang's eyes widened, and he was so envious that he was about to turn green. "Damn it, if we were two seconds faster, we could've gotten the amethyst too…Wait, how did you know that Yearning For's party got an amethyst?"

Lu Wenhao parroted, "Yeah, how did you know?"

The two of them looked in confusion at the guy who had quit playing *Nine Heroes* two years ago.

I'm fucked.

Forget about the shitty ring and the marriage proposal. Why couldn't you control your big mouth, little Jing Huan.

Jing Huan finished mentally lambasting himself and looked up from his food. "I...heard about it."

"Who did you hear it from?" Lu Wenhao asked. "Do you know anyone who plays *Nine Heroes* besides us?"

"An old friend who I used to game with. We just talked a bit on WeChat today, and he sent me a screenshot of the system announcement to complain." Jing Huan calmly fabricated an excuse in a few seconds.

Fortunately, the two of them didn't think much about it and started feeling envious again after hearing this.

After eating and drinking their fill, Jing Huan was about to ask them if they wanted to go play basketball when Lu Wenhao pulled him over to the computer.

Hands clasped together, Lu Wenhao said beseechingly, "Huanhuan, the society of *Nine Heroes* needs your help!"

Jing Huan had a bad feeling about this. "Help with what?"

As he opened the webpage, he said, "I want to participate in this..."

Jing Huan raised his eyebrows and looked over to see *"The 7th Annual Nine Heroes Singing Competition has begun~"*

Jing Huan looked away and said, bemused, "If you want to participate, then just do it."

Chapter 07

"But as you know," Lu Wenhao said, "my voice sounds like a broken gong, so I can only sing A-Do[1]."

Jing Huan said, "You think you're too good for A-Do?"

"No way, I just have a voice similar to his, but I don't sing as well as him. I definitely wouldn't win a prize."

Jing Huan laughed and said, "You even want to win a prize. Oh, you can probably get the participation reward."

"I want to get the limited edition mount," Lu Wenhao cut straight to the point. "I won't win anything, Huanhuan, but you can! You sing so well, getting into the top three would be a breeze for you."

"Wait, hold on," Jing Huan interrupted him with a complicated expression. "You're not asking me to participate for you, right?"

Lu Wenhao looked at him, emotion welling in his eyes. "You know how I am, Huanhuan." He spoke quickly before Jing Huan could refuse, "The prize money is all yours no matter what place you get, I just want the mount! If you really get into the top three, I'll pay for all your takeout this semester! I'll also save a seat for you every day! I'll go into the class and get your attendance mark even if it's not my class!"

These terms were quite tempting, especially the last one.

Jing Huan only considered it for two seconds before decisively saying, "No."

Lu Wenhao crumpled. "Why not?"

Jing Huan pointed to a certain condition in the competition schedule and said, "You have to sing live in the official voice channel, and if you get into the top three, you have to go to an in-person player meet-up to receive the reward. I don't have the time for that."

---

1   Du Chengyi, stage name A-Do, is a Singaporean singer.

Gao Zixiang nodded and said, "Also Hao'er, you're deceiving the audience and the judges here. Tell me, what's the difference between you and your catfishing ex-girlfriend right now?"

"Shit! It's not that serious!" Instantly, Lu Wenhao got worked up at the very mention of this. "I just want a mount, I'm not deceiving anyone emotionally or financially! It's completely different from those male scammers pretending to be and playing girl characters to catfish men, okay?!"

Jing Huan felt somewhat offended, but he quickly convinced himself that Lu Wenhao's "ex-girlfriend" was indeed a bastard for scamming people out of money.

He wasn't scamming; this was helping to rid the world of evil and acting in the name of justice.

Unfortunately, there were simply too many scumbags, and he could only rid the world of one for the poor girls.

"Forget it, it was just a sudden idea I had." Lu Wenhao realized this plan was indeed a bit troublesome. "I'll just try for the participation reward then."

Many players had already uploaded their entries, and as Lu Wenhao spoke, he seemed to have thought of something. He smoothly opened the competition interface and inputted some filter criteria.

Gender: female; server: Match Made in Heaven.

Jing Huan's lips curled. "You're being too superficial right now."

Lu Wenhao retorted, "I call it having a well-defined goal." That being said, he clicked on a competition entry, and the girl's voice that floated out sounded melodious and emotional.

Lu Wenhao nodded twice like a judge, and then quickly sent a friend request to the female player.

Chapter 07

"Of course you would," said Jing Huan.

"Indeed." Lu Wenhao stepped out to continue listening to other songs.

Seeing him skip several entries in a row, Jing Huan raised an eyebrow and asked, "Why aren't you listening to those?"

"Ugh, look at these songs," Lu Wenhao said. " 'Invisible Wings,' 'Rice Field,' 'Braveness[2].' Not only are these songs overplayed, they're also all inspirational and there to boost morale; no one's interested in listening to them."

Jing Huan froze as an idea popped into his head. He murmured, "Really..."

After listening to some songs with Lu Wenhao, Jing Huan finally remembered his purpose of returning to the dorms. "Want to go play some night ball?"

Gao Zixiang refused, "I'm not going. My wife is going to call me in a bit."

Lu Wenhao was busy replying to the singing girl's message from before and didn't respond to him at all.

Jing Huan gave up and got up to leave, saying, "Then I'm heading back."

"Don't go, Huanhuan," Lu Wenhao called out. "Just stay over tonight, squeeze in with me and we can talk about our trip next month."

"Leaving my big bed to squeeze in with you, are you crazy or am I?" Jing Huan waved his hand and said without turning his

---

2   "Invisible Wings" - 隐形的翅膀 - a 2006 classic by Taiwanese singer Angela Zhang; "Rice Field" - 稻 香 - a 2008 song by Jay Chou; "Braveness" - 勇敢 - a 2015 song by Taiwanese band Mayday.

head, "You guys discuss the trip, I'm fine with anything. I'm going."

On the way back, Jing Huan took out his phone and sent a message to Yearning For.

Little Jing~: What's gege up to?

Xiang: I'm outside.

Little Jing~: What's gege up to outside?

Xiang: ...Watching a basketball game at a court.

Little Jing~: I want to see what gege looks like playing basketball >.<!!

Xiang: Not playing, just watching from the side.

Jing Huan thought, *Go ahead and watch. The best thing that could happen would be if a player slipped and dunked the ball on your head.*

Little Jing~: 0.0 Oh, it's like that. Then be careful, gege, and don't get hit by a ball~

After sending this, Jing Huan imagined Yearning For's character getting hit by a basketball, and inexplicably, his mood improved quite a bit.

Due to this brief exchange, Jing Huan subconsciously glanced at the basketball court as he passed by.

The floodlights in the courts gave Jing Huan a clear and bright view of what was happening inside. Lots of people in their school played night basketball and despite the late hour, the court was crammed with students. This basketball court was near the junior and senior dormitories, so nearly all of the players were upperclassmen. Jing Huan scanned their faces but didn't recognize anyone.

Just as he was about to leave, his gaze was drawn over to the referee's chair at the side of the court.

 Chapter 07

All the guys on the court were wearing jerseys, except for the person sitting in the referee's seat. Whoever it was was wearing a thin white long-sleeved shirt and shorts, his long legs stretched out casually as he looked at the phone in his hand.

A beam of light shone directly on him, highlighting the guy's high and straight nose, his soft eyes and brows, and his side profile which looked more handsome than those male celebrities featured in magazines.

Jing Huan couldn't resist peeking at him a few more times when he saw a player from the adjacent court make a mistake while passing. The basketball drew a beautiful arc in the air as it flew out of the court and toward the bench.

Startled, he blurted out, "Watch out—"

That person quickly raised his head and easily caught the basketball with one hand, then stood up and effortlessly threw it back.

A perfect off-court three-pointer.

The player was momentarily stunned, then clasped his hands together as if apologizing.

Xiang Huaizhi shook his head at the other player, expressing that he was fine while thinking that Sweet Little Jing's mouth must be cursed.

Cursed in a way that nothing good she said would come true, but everything bad would.

Jing Huan was stunned. How did that shot go in?

His reaction speed was also amazing, and…Xiang Huaizhi's palm looked really big.

He was still standing there in a daze when Xiang Huaizhi suddenly turned his head, and their eyes met.

 Chapter 07

Xiang Huaizhi had heard that "watch out." Seeing Jing Huan, he raised his eyebrows in surprise, but before he could react, he saw the boy standing outside the court's chain link fence wave at him.

Xiang Huaizhi hesitated for two seconds, then raised his hand and waved back.

Then the underclassman smiled, turned around, and walked away while seemingly chatting with someone on his phone.

A few seconds later, his phone vibrated.

Little Jing~: Does gege usually play basketball? Can you shoot three-pointers? Can you catch the ball with one hand?

Normally, Xiang Huaizhi wouldn't answer these slightly fan-girl-ish questions. He sat back on the bench and typed.

Xiang: Mm.

Little Jing~: AAAH! I really want to see! Gege must look so hot when playing basketball T.T.

Xiang: Not really.

Little Jing~: I don't care~ In my heart, gege is the hottest!

Little Jing~: o(///v///)o

"Xiangxiang, who were you waving to just now? Were you checking out the underclassmen girls outside?" Lu Hang asked him. He was dripping with sweat after coming off the court. "Oh, were you chatting with Sweet Little Jing?"

Lu Hang hadn't been peeking at his phone; Sweet Little Jing's profile picture was too eye-searingly pink, it was too easy to recognize.

Xiang Huaizhi locked his phone and asked, "Done now?"

"Mhm, we won." Lu Hang looked at his leg. "When exactly can you play basketball again?"

Guide on How to Fail at Online Dating

"The follow-up appointment is tomorrow."

Every night, the sidewalk outside the school was packed with street food stalls, complete with barbecue, hot-and-sour noodles, crayfish, and more. Lu Hang was enticed by the smell, and having just finished exercising, he was famished and dragged Xiang Huaizhi out to find food.

At the barbecue stall, Lu Hang finished a lamb skewer in one go and said, "By the way, Xiangxiang, your headset's microphone is pretty good. Let me borrow it when we get back to the dorm."

Xiang Huaizhi asked, "For what?"

"To participate in the *Nine Heroes'* singing competition."

Xiang Huaizhi stopped chewing and shot him a peculiar look.

"Don't look at me like that. There's a participation reward this time—a limited edition outfit. It's basically free so I might as well grab it," Lu Hang said. "You gonna participate?"

"Not interested."

Outfits were something that could be bought with a click; singing for one was out of the question.

Back at the dormitory, Lu Hang wasted no time in borrowing Xiang Huaizhi's headset and started making ungodly sounds, causing Xiang Huaizhi's temples to throb.

Half an hour later, Lu Hang held his breath as he finished listening to his recording.

"Sounds amazing. If I don't win first place, it would truly be a travesty."

Xiang Huaizhi snorted as he picked up his phone to make an appointment for tomorrow's follow-up consultation. He really didn't know where his confidence came from.

Chapter 07

"Wow, a lot of people from our server are participating in this event. Regardless of Lovesickness, Nomnom, Bishop Wood, Echoes of Spring…they've all registered." Lu Hang clicked on Bishop Wood's recording. "Shit, Bishop Wood sings pretty well. Fine, he barely counts as my rival. You can easily tell that Regardless of Lovesickness sang for Echoes of Spring. Nomnom sings really well, I'll vote for her…"

Halfway through his musings, Lu Hang remembered something and turned around to ask, "Xiangxiang, will Sweet Little Jing participate in this event?"

Xiang Huaizhi asked, "How would I know?"

"Tsk, why don't you care about your party members?" Lu Hang grumbled. "She should participate, right? I remember that the character she bought has all the limited edition outfits, so if she doesn't get this one, its value will drop."

Xiang Huaizhi let him ramble without responding.

He couldn't quite imagine what Sweet Little Jing's singing voice sounded like.

Sweet Little Jing usually liked to act cute in front of him, but her voice wasn't exactly sweet per se. He even thought her voice was somewhat strange; even though it sounded pleasant, it was unnatural.

But how well she sang had nothing to do with him. Lu Hang just kept wailing in his ear for half an hour, so even if it was Jacky Cheung Hok-yau, Hong Kong's "God of Songs" himself, singing in front of him right now, he wouldn't be interested.

After receiving confirmation that he had successfully booked his appointment, Xiang Huaizhi turned off his phone and lights to sleep.

The next day, after his follow-up check-up was complete, the doctor told Xiang Huaizhi that he had recovered well and could start exercising in moderation.

Having gone a few months without playing basketball, Xiang Huaizhi's hands were itching for a match. As soon as he left the hospital, he took out his phone, intending to ask Lu Hang to bring the basketball out. Before he could dial the number, Lu Hang called first.

Xiang Huaizhi answered, "Did you sense Daddy's call?"

"Holy fuck, Daddy, I'm going crazy and laughing so hard." Lu Hang cackled. "Sweet Little Jing is incredible, she really participated in the singing competition!"

"Okay, so she joined. So what?" Xiang Huaizhi paused. "Did she sing badly?"

Even if she didn't sing well, it's not like you have the right to laugh at others.

"No, that's not the problem…" Lu Hang was laughing so hard he could barely breathe. "Do you know what song she sang?"

Xiang Huaizhi asked, "What song?"

"Teacher Tu Honggang's work—" Lu Hang's words echoed loud and clear. " 'Loyalty to the Country[3].' "

Xiang Huaizhi was at a loss for words.

Jing Huan got up at 8 a.m. the next day since he had a morning class. He went down to the breakfast shop, his head sleepily bobbing up and down like he was fishing.

He spent a lengthy amount of time fiddling around last night, trying to learn how to play background music, how to record, how to upload the clip…It took him two hours to figure it all out.

---

3   Chinese patriotic song honoring Han Dynasty general Yue Fei.

 Chapter 07

"Huanhuan, were you out stealing stuff last night?" Gao Zixiang carried over a tray with breakfast for the three of them. "Didn't you leave pretty early yesterday?"

Jing Huan rubbed his eyes and said, "Didn't sleep well."

"Why is your voice so scratchy?" Gao Zixiang sat down. "Did you catch a cold?"

"No."

I just had to record myself several times before I was satisfied, so now my voice is hoarse from singing so much.

A good song is difficult to sing. Jing Huan sighed.

He drank two gulps of soy milk, and the sticky sweetness spread out to the tip of his tongue, waking him up a bit.

"*Pfft—*" Next to him, Lu Wenhao was wearing earbuds and wasn't in a hurry to eat either. This entire time, his eyes were glued to his cellphone, and he couldn't stop howling with laughter.

Jing Huan frowned. "What's wrong with him?"

"He'll laugh at anything. He's been laughing since he got up until now." Gao Zixiang pointed to his ears. "He hasn't taken those off; he even wore them while brushing his teeth."

Jing Huan said, "Oh." Not minding his friend, he lowered his head and took a bite of the soup dumpling. There was just enough filling in there that a lot of soup came out of a small bite.

Lu Wenhao vaguely heard their conversation and took out one of his earbuds. "Hey, Xiangxiang, you didn't check the guild group chat this morning, did you?"

Gao Zixiang shook his head. "The guild group chat is active this early in the morning?"

"Yeah, there are over ninety-nine messages! Someone in the group

chat shared a participant's song from another server in the *Nine Heroes* singing competition." Lu Wenhao started laughing as soon as he thought about it. "It was only posted last night, but it went viral, got tens of thousands of likes, and topped the competition's likes ranking. Isn't that something?"

"So, you've been wearing earbuds all morning just listening to someone sing?" Gao Zixiang asked, "It must be a woman, right?"

"Yeah, but that's not the main point."

Jing Huan leaned over toward Lu Wenhao and said, "Let me hear it. I want to see what kind of singing voice has you obsessing over it all morning."

Lu Wenhao obligingly inserted his earbud gently into Jing Huan's ear.

A familiar song came to his ears. "*The horses gallop toward the south, but the people look toward the north. Looking toward the north, the grass is dry and yellow, with dust flying high!*"

"*Pfft—cough, cough…cough…*" Jing Huan had the shock of his lifetime. Choking on what he was swallowing, his cheeks burned scarlet. He panicked and lifted his hand to swat out the earbud.

Lu Wenhao was taken aback. "Wh-what's wrong?"

Jing Huan shook his head, still coughing badly, unable to say a word for a long time.

Gao Zixiang quickly handed him a bottle of water. Jing Huan took a few big gulps before finally recovering.

"I'm fine…" he mumbled. "I just choked."

"You scared me, your face even turned red from all that coughing," Lu Wenhao said. "Tsk, and you threw my earbud on the ground too. So, how was it? Pretty good, right?"

Chapter 07

There was not a single spot on Jing Huan's face that wasn't crimson. He turned his head, looking completely bewildered. "What you said just now...What's going on with this song?"

Lu Wenhao was equally confused. "Did this song sound nice?"

"Not that." Jing Huan took a deep breath. "You were saying something about the likes ranking..."

"Ohhh, this song reached the top of the likes ranking, with over 100,000 views in a night. This proves that *Nine Heroes* isn't dead; all that talk about player loss was just bullshit." Lu Wenhao laughed.

Still muddled, Jing Huan blurted out, "How did this song rank first in likes?"

Nonplussed, Lu Wenhao asked, "What do you mean? Isn't it sung really well?"

Jing Huan slowly came to his senses, not a shadow of drowsiness left in him. "I meant...didn't you say last night that no one listens to this kind of old, inspirational song?"

After returning home last night, he had spent a long time deliberating before finally landing on "Loyalty to the Country." It wasn't just inspiring, it also instilled positive energy. He sang this song during his high school boot camp and was even the lead singer at the time.

Because he was a bit of a perfectionist, he'd feel horrible listening to the recording if just one part wasn't sung well. Therefore, he recorded it a bunch of times before uploading the entry.

According to his plan, his uploaded entry would soon be buried among many other entries. He could get the participation award without trying to compete with the others.

"This song isn't just inspirational anymore," Lu Wenhao remarked. "Isn't this more of a novelty?"

Jing Huan restrained himself from saying anything, but it didn't stop him from thinking, *Calling the cops now.*

Gao Zixiang curiously picked up the earbud and listened for a few verses.

Honestly, although the song choice would render people speechless, this girl sang it so passionately that she sounded quite imposing. The more he listened, the more he was hooked.

"It really is good." Gao Zixiang suddenly thought of something. "But Huanhuan is better. Huanhuan was the lead singer when our class sang this song during our high school boot camp. Pretty awesome, right?"

"That is awesome," said Lu Wenhao. "Queue it up during karaoke next time!"

Jing Huan was no longer in the mood to listen to what they were saying.

This matter left him in a daze all morning. As soon as class ended, he rushed home without even stopping to eat. He opened the game, and the moment *Nine Heroes* loaded, his computer lagged slightly.

【Is Gege Big has sent you a friend request.】

【Let's Date, Adorable Miss? has sent you a friend request.】

【Fallen Autumn Leaves has sent you a friend request.】

It seemed to be never-ending. The right side of his screen was filled with friend requests, without a single gap in sight. Jing Huan had played this game for years and had never seen this kind of explosion before.

He wasn't sure what to do when a megaphone suddenly popped up on the left side.

【[Megaphone] Mud Bloomed Flowers: Sweet! Little! Jing! Is! Online! Now! Coordinates are the Outskirts (81, 22)】

Chapter 07

Jing Huan scarcely had any time to be surprised before he saw an endless number of characters pour in from outside the zone, and in an instant, he was surrounded by players.

【Let's date, little jiejie has invited you to join his party. Yes, No.】

【Awaiting Dawn has invited you to join his party. Yes, No.】

【Twilight Breeze has invited you to join his party. Yes, No.】

Countless system prompts inundated him, giving no time for Jing Huan to even click "Refuse." His game character was completely blocked out by the pop-ups that he couldn't move. He managed to find a gap and quickly zoomed away, escaping back to his in-game home.

Nine Heroes had a housing system with many gameplay features, but Jing Huan had no interest in tinkering with it. His home was the lowest-tier house in the game.

[Friend] OFF!: Are you there, goddess? [Starry-eyed]

Geez, now they're even addressing me differently.

[Friend] Sweet Little Jing: ...Your goddess isn't here, but I am. What's going on today?

How could something as simple as a song blow up like this?

[Friend] OFF!: You got exposed on the forums.

[Friend] Sweet Little Jing: ???

Jing Huan's first thought was: *At last, the day I appear on the gossip forums has finally come.*

It was okay; he was willing to sacrifice himself for public entertainment.

[Friend] OFF!: Now you have become a goddess in the hearts of all male *Nine Heroes* players.

[Friend] Sweet Little Jing: ...

Guide on How to Fail at Online Dating

[Friend] Sweet Little Jing: *Nine Heroes* has finally driven its players crazy.

OFF! really wasn't making stuff up. A post had appeared on the *Nine Heroes* forum today, detailing everything that had transpired since the ID "Sweet Little Jing" had been born.

First, she had bad luck; the ignorant girl bought a notorious female scammer's character and was hunted and insulted for several days until she finally proved her innocence. Then, without holding any grudges, she joined Idle Pavilion and obtained the first clear of the guild dungeon for them.

What a strong and magnanimous girl!

Next, she was dedicated; since buying the character, she had eyes only for Yearning For. She was also fearless in the face of threats and Yearning For's ex's hunts. Not only that, she boldly confessed her love in a live stream and refused to give up even after being rejected X number of times by her beloved.

What a brave and steadfast girl!

Finally, there was her singing voice; she sounded nice, and in song choice, she was both meticulous and positive. One glance and you could tell that she was a good girl with a patriotic heart, completely different from those women who sang "Meow, Meow, Meow[4]" or "Shape Up[5]."

What an honest and cultured girl!!!

Jing Huan felt like flipping a table as he read this.

---

4   Literally "Learn to Meow" - 学猫叫 - Xué Māo Jiào, a 2018 song by Xiao Panpan. Popular for its catchy melody and playful lyrics, it became viral with lots of singing covers and dance challenges.

5   Literally "Small Waist," 小蛮腰 - Xiǎo Mán Yāo - by Momo Wu, a 2015 song with playful lyrics about staying active.

Chapter 07

He never created this many personas!!

Jing Huan closed the forum and enabled the "reject messages from strangers" feature. Finally, the screen cleared up a lot.

He teleported to the main city to do dailies, but before he could even get any quests, his screen was flooded with party invites.

Nine Heroes didn't allow you to disable party invites. Jing Huan stood dumbstruck in the main city for a while, unable to move a step, and could only dejectedly return to his in-game house again.

Fame is so annoying.

He stood in his humble abode, at an utter loss as to what he could do until he opened his friend list and saw that a certain friend's name was lit up.

[Friend] Sweet Little Jing: Gege! T.T

[Friend] Yearning For: ?

[Friend] Sweet Little Jing: So many people are blocking my way. I'm trapped in my house right now and can't leave at all. QAQ

[Friend] Sweet Little Jing: Can you help me? [Wiping away tears] I haven't done any of my dailies today.

When he was alone, other players could invite him to join their party at any time. But if he was already in a party, he could no longer be invited, and players applying to join his party wouldn't trigger any pop-ups; he could just accept or reject them from the party menu without it hindering him.

Unfortunately, a solo party didn't count as an actual party in *Nine Heroes*. Even if he created a party with just himself, the system would still consider him a solo player and enable the setting for him to accept party invites.

So now he only had three possible solutions: one, wait for the enthusiasm of the players outside to dissipate; second, log off; or third, find someone to form a party with to do dailies together.

Jing Huan didn't actually have high hopes that Yearning For would help him. He could've called over some other friends on his friend list but he decided to DM Yearning For first.

His one and only reason was to make his presence known after logging in.

He opened his friend list, mulled over it for a while, and then clicked on Love is Sharing Noms's chat.

"Nomnom, are you there? Can you help me make a party—"

In the seconds between him finishing his message and him about to hit send, he received Yearning For's reply.

[Friend] Yearning For: Where are you.

[Friend] Sweet Little Jing: (*·Δ·*)!!

[Friend] Sweet Little Jing: Gege, come to my house! The house number is 1219!

About ten seconds later, a black-robed man appeared in the zone.

Xiang Huaizhi glanced at the somewhat simple and crude small house, created a party, and then invited Sweet Little Jing into it.

"Which quest first?" he asked.

A few seconds later, Sweet Little Jing unmuted her microphone. He heard her cough before saying, "Let's start with the sect master ones, gege."

"Got it."

The male players camping the sedan carriers to the housing zone seized the moment when Sweet Little Jing appeared to send her party invites—

 Chapter 07

【Sweet Little Jing is already in Yearning For's party, invitation failed!】

The male players were befuddled. Wasn't Yearning For supposed to have still rejected her despite being moved by Sweet Little Jing's stalking?

Jing Huan relaxed in the party, comfortably completing his quests while thinking about what to do next.

He was a catfisher, so naturally, he should hide as much as possible. Those *Nine Heroes* forum users were sharp; what if someone actually saw through him?

But he still wanted to get that participation reward, so it wasn't like he could just withdraw from the competition. In the midst of his annoyance, a yellow line popped up in-game.

【Fae Bae has set you as a private chat recipient, please check your private chat channel.】

Fuck, what does this girl want again?! Is she just a ghost that is determined to haunt me or what?!

[Private] Fae Bae: Wow, men, prizes, you want it all. You are really something.

[Private] Fae Bae: Just wait for the semifinals. I refuse to believe you can win with the same cheap trick twice.

Jing Huan was a little surprised. He opened the event's competition interface and discovered that his ID was at the top of the likes ranking, with Fae Bae right underneath him.

He clicked Fae Bae's entry and listened to it.

It actually sounds really nice. It's a pity I can't say the same about her brains.

Jing Huan was about to mock her but stopped before sending

his message as an idea came to him. Eyebrows raised, he suddenly burst out laughing.

Sis, you served yourself on a platter, so don't blame me for this.

Xiang Huaizhi didn't know why he agreed to help Sweet Little Jing with her dailies when he still had his own to finish. He led the party to the Spirit Fox Den's sect master and helped her finish her quest. Suddenly, a familiar name appeared on the left side of his screen—

【[Megaphone] Sweet Little Jing: Fae Bae, I believe I've been very tolerant of you, but you keep pushing my buttons, so I refuse to be polite anymore. Here's my answer: You can have the singing competition, the top spot for the likes ranking, but MY GEGE! IS! NOT! UP! FOR! GRABS! No matter how many times you threaten me or hunt me down, MY LOVE FOR XIANG-gege! WILL NEVER CHANGE!!!】

This megaphone lingered in the game for a long time, eventually vanishing when it reached the time limit.

Fae Bae was completely shocked and even forgot to put out her own megaphone to override Sweet Little Jing's.

Never, in a million years, did she expect Sweet Little Jing to make a move like this. Eyes nearly popping out of her head, it took her a long time to react.

[Private] Fae Bae: ???

[Private] Fae Bae: We were clearly chatting in DMs, why did you have to go and blast a megaphone? And acting like a little green tea bitch with what you said, huh?

[Private] Sweet Little Jing: Aren't you the one who loves spamming megaphones? I thought you would prefer to communicate with people this way~

 Chapter 07

[Private] Sweet Little Jing: Besides, how am I acting like a green tea bitch? [Question] Wasn't everything I said the truth?

Fae Bae was about to type out a reply—

【[Megaphone] Sweet Little Jing: Don't worry, Fae Bae; I never wanted to compete with you for first place in the singing competition. I only joined to get the participation reward so I hope you won't bother me anymore. As for everything else...Unless gege gets back together with you or gets a new girlfriend, I won't give up. If you want to kill me, go ahead, but just remember to hire a better assassin next time, heh.】

Fae Bae was so enraged that smoke was about to erupt from every single one of her orifices.

What was with her "if you want to kill me, go ahead?" She absolutely wanted to kill Sweet Little Jing, but who was the one who had two pieces of equipment destroyed?!

【[Megaphone] Masked Beauty: Honestly, Fae Bae, you're going too far. If you want revenge, then go kill Yearning For...What does it have to do with Sweet Little Jing?】

【[Megaphone] Small Gentleness: The sis from the previous megaphone led people to hunt down Sweet Little Jing before. This kind of behavior has really dumbfounded me.】

Fae Bae knew full well that she was being unreasonable for hiring people to hunt down Sweet Little Jing and cursing her out in YY.

But so what?

This was just the online world. Once she turned off the computer, she went back to reality either way. Her real life wasn't going the way she wanted, but she shouldn't be unhappy while gaming. And...

If she couldn't have him, then no one else could.

She hesitated, then opened a certain besties' group chat and pasted the megaphone message into it.

Faefae: Great, now I'm the bad guy. ^^

Before long, her "besties" helped her out.

【[Megaphone] Ji Xiaonian: How very interesting. What evidence is there to prove that Sweet Little Jing isn't the same female scammer as before? Her voice might be different because of a voice changer, and a hired player would explain her improved gameplay. Besides, everyone in the server knows that Yearning For and Fae Bae haven't truly broken up yet, so why is she trying to interfere? What's she plotting?】

Jing Huan did not reply to Ji Xiaonian; he had no inclination of getting into a megaphone-spamming catfight.

He had just wanted to find an excuse for his passive participation in the singing competition while pissing off Fae Bae a bit. Also…

Jing Huan glanced at Yearning For, who was currently leading him through a quest.

Despite the countless hints he had sent to Yearning For, both publicly and privately, their relationship remained as mere party members. If this continued to drag on, wouldn't his wonderful university years be completely wasted on this scumbag!!

He decided to be a straight shooter; he was going to launch a direct attack on Yearning For!

Jing Huan swallowed the golden throat lozenge in his mouth and sweetly called out, "Gege…"

【[Megaphone] Yearning For: We never got together, so there's no need to break up.】

This megaphone put a stopper on any further words from Jing Huan.

Chapter 07

Outside of gathering materials, Yearning For rarely used megaphones. And with this technically being the first time he addressed the relationship between him and Fae Bae, it caused an uproar in the World Channel.

[World] Little Garfield: What does he mean they never got together?!

[World] According to Keikaku[6]: ...What can I say? Once a scumbag, always a scumbag.

[World] With You: Can Sweet Little Jing get her eyes checked? If she doesn't cut her losses, she'll be the next Fae Bae.

[World] Ephemeral: One is willing to pitch, while the other is willing to catch. A scumbag and a slut—it's a perfect match!

Xiang Huaizhi muted the World Channel and unmuted himself. "Talk."

Carefully, Jing Huan asked, "You aren't angry, are you?" Before Xiang Huaizhi could speak, he added softly, "I just...like you so much. I didn't mean to drag you into this."

This was the first time in Jing Huan's life that he said he "liked" someone other than his family. Because he felt guilty, his voice was extremely frail when he said "like."

But these small details were perfectly conveyed to the other person through the sound card and wires, conveying a girl's nervousness and shyness.

Xiang Huaizhi was used to her enthusiasm, but in this moment,

---

6   The fan translation of Episode 24 of the anime *Death Note* translated - 計画通り - keikaku dōri - as "Just according to keikaku" with a translator note saying Keikaku means plan. This is just a meme of keeping some untranslated terms when there was an English equivalent.

he felt a little dazed. He managed to come back to his senses a few beats later.

"No," Xiang Huaizhi said. His voice sounded normal. "But I suggest you move on to someone else as soon as possible."

"...Why?"

"I don't do online relationships," Xiang Huaizhi deadpanned, "and I won't fall for you either."

If he said that to any other girl, she would probably be heartbroken by now.

Tucking his chin in his hand, Jing Huan said pitifully, "I know…I never thought I could really be with gege. I'm already happy enough raiding dungeons and fighting in the arena with gege."

On the other end, Lu Hang's DMs were about to explode. All the popcorn-eating gossipers from the guild were DMing him, trying to get some insider information about Xiang Huaizhi and Sweet Little Jing.

Lu Hang typed "I don't know" to each message, looked up, and said, "Xiangxiang, you'd be blind to not see how infatuated Little Jingjing is with you. I think you should give it a try."

"Do you think this is like trying food samples?" Xiang Huaizhi asked.

"It's not like you're dating for real, you're just getting married in-game. It only costs a hundred gold, it's no big deal," Lu Hang said. "Little Jingjing seems pretty cute to me. Don't become ships that pass in the night."

"Why don't you go after her yourself if you think she's so cute?"

Lu Hang muttered, "I don't have the balls to steal your girl…"

Xiang Huaizhi was about to retort when he saw the little spirit fox in the party suddenly change into a black miniskirt, with her tail

 Chapter 07

dyed gray-white. When the two characters stood together, they didn't clash at all.

[Party] Sweet Little Jing: Couple outfit. \^0^/

He stared at the little spirit fox's tail for a while, then his fingers pulled her to the quest NPC without saying anything.

Jing Huan kept his word and started to slack off after entering the semifinals of the singing competition. He stopped singing popular songs, switching to children's songs, and he sang them terribly. He went off-key thrice with one verse.

At first, there were some players who voted for her, deeming her interesting, but as it happened more often, everyone lost interest. The number of likes gradually decreased, and Jing Huan was finally able to relax and focus on his real purpose here.

Several of them had gathered together today to raid a dungeon.

[Party] Sweet Little Jing: Gege~ Are we still playing the arena tonight? ^^

[Party] Yearning For: Sure.

[Party] Sweet Little Jing: [Hugging thigh][Cheerleading team]

[Party] Long Road Ahead: By the way, Old Xiang and I will be going out next week. Our online time might be sporadic those days so we might not have time to run dungeons. You guys can find a temporary party to do quests with.

[Party] Sweet Little Jing: 0.0 Next week? Which days?

[Party] Long Road Ahead: Wednesday to Saturday.

[Party] Sweet Little Jing: What a coincidence~ I'm also going out with my classmates those days. Are you guys traveling?

[Party] Long Road Ahead: Hiking! [Cheer] And you?

[Party] Sweet Little Jing: Wow~ That's amazing. The weather is a bit chilly, so I'm going to the hot springs with my classmates. [Cozy]

Xiang Huaizhi read through their conversation, and his gaze grew a bit heavy.

Their school was clearing out the classrooms for exam-taking next week; this was why they had a break, and not because of any special holidays.

This couldn't be a coincidence; Sweet Little Jing really did go to the same school as them.

Right about then, Love is Sharing Noms suddenly turned her microphone on, and her voice sounded very weak. "Sorry...I think I might have to get off after this dungeon. I really can't hold on. I don't even have the strength to type."

[Party] Sweet Little Jing: What's wrong? Don't feel well?

"Yes," Love is Sharing Noms said. "My stomach hurts...you know."

Jing Huan was flabbergasted for a moment. What was he supposed to know?

[Party] Sweet Little Jing: Ate something bad?

Love is Sharing Noms paused. "It's just that time of the month."

[Party] Sweet Little Jing: [Question] Hmm?

[Party] Long Road Ahead: Aunt Flo visiting?

"Yeah, I don't know why, but my stomach feels especially bad this time. I've never had this before." Love is Sharing Noms asked, "Little Jing, do you usually get cramps?"

Jing Huan's mind went blank.

Wait, do girls really talk about this kind of stuff?!

He thought for a moment and typed.

 Chapter 07

[Party] Sweet Little Jing: No pain. 0.0

Love is Sharing Noms was surprised. "No pain at all? Really? All the girls around me usually feel awful."

Jing Huan immediately changed his tone and said, "Well, occasionally, but it's not that bad…"

"Right, no need to be embarrassed, pain is normal." Love is Sharing Noms asked, "Is your Aunt Flo regular? What day does it usually come? You always seem so lively."

Jing Huan bullshitted away. "At the beginning of the month…If you're not feeling well, just go AFK and rest. I can solo-heal this."

Love is Sharing Noms asked, "Ah, you're fine on your own?"

"No problem, I'm amazing!" Jing Huan said. "Hurry. Go, go."

Love is Sharing Noms went AFK. Just as Jing Huan breathed a sigh of relief, he heard his phone vibrate.

Nomnom: xxxx brand cotton tampon, copy this description and go to Taobao…

Little Jing~: ??!!

Nomnom: Buy it! Doesn't your Aunt Flo come at the beginning of the month! That's next week, so remember to bring it along when you go soak in the hot springs!!

Nomnom: Don't worry, it's very easy to use and doesn't feel weird! Nothing will leak! It won't hurt either!

Jing Huan swallowed. He sent out his thanks and immediately closed WeChat. He was too embarrassed to take another look at that link.

In the evening, he and Yearning For went to fight in the arena together.

After a PK match, Xiang Huaizhi suddenly asked, "So, you're going to soak in the hot springs next week?"

Surprised, Jing Huan said, "Hm? Yes, I'm going with my classmates. What about it, gege?"

"There don't seem to be any holidays next week."

"Our school has to keep our classrooms empty for people to take their exams, so we have several days off," Jing Huan said docilely and without much thought. "What about you, gege? Do you guys have a break next week too?"

Xiang Huaizhi said, "No, we're skipping class."

Jing Huan let out an "oh" and put on a coquettish tone. "Can I send WeChat messages to gege on those days?"

"I can't stop you."

Ever since Jing Huan confessed to him via megaphone, Yearning For rarely replied to his WeChat messages. Every once in a while he would reply to one, but it would be brief.

Jing Huan pouted. "Will gege reply to me?"

After a moment of silence, Xiang Huaizhi said, "If I have time."

Glossary

Guide on How to Fail at Online Dating

Xiang Huaizhi

Jing Huan

Guide on How to Fail at Online Dating

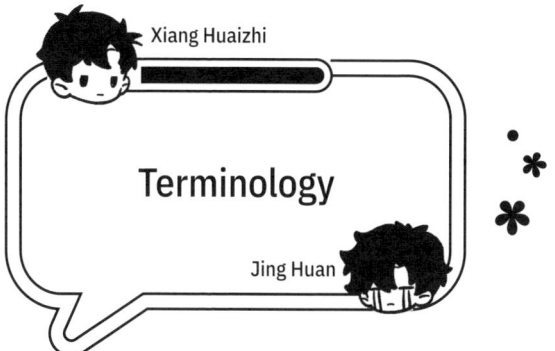

AFK: An acronym for "Away from Keyboard," typically used in online settings and gaming. It can mean that someone is physically away from their computer, or it can also indicate that the game is minimized and they are "away from the game."

AFK Grinding: This can mean that the game has an "auto-battle" feature, where you can have your character automatically fight for a certain amount of turns while you are free to do anything else. This could also mean actively grinding but it requires low effort, such that you can do something else like browsing the internet while playing.

Alt: Short for "Alternate account," it is a secondary character created by a player for purposes of farming or to pretend to be a different person.

AoE: An acronym for "Area of Effect." It refers to any ability, spell, or action that affects multiple targets within a specific range, instead of just a single target.

Attributes: Specific stats, bonuses, or effects that enhance an item's performance or grant additional abilities to the user. These are things that influence a character's effectiveness in combat by modifying their damage, skills, healing output, etc.

Blind: This refers to attempting a dungeon, boss battle, quest, or any in-game activity for the first time without prior knowledge, preparation, or external guides (i.e. videos or tutorials). Players typically like to do this for newly released content.

Booster: A booster is typically a hired individual who plays your account for you to either farm, grind, increase your rank, level you up, or do anything that you specify. It's generally a paid service people use to maintain or increase their character rank/status.

Buff: A temporary effect that enhances a character's stats or abilities, such as increased health, damage, speed, healing, etc.

Camping: The act of staying in a specific location, often for a long period of time, to achieve a goal such as gathering resources, waiting for enemy spawns, or targeting other players to PK them.

Carry: Refers to a scenario where a skilled or powerful player (or party) helps a less experienced, under-leveled, or weaker player to complete content (a quest, a dungeon, etc). This term can also describe a player who performs exceptionally well in a party, so they "carry" the party to victory.

CC: An acronym for "Crowd Control," and is someone whose role in a party is focused on controlling their enemy by preventing them from moving, casting spells, etc.

Cooldown: The waiting period after using an ability, item, or skill before it can be used again.

Crafting: The process of creating items such as weapons, armor, potions, tools, or other in-game items using materials gathered in dungeons, wilderness maps, or other methods.

Dailies: This refers to daily quests, dungeons, or any task that reset every 24 hours, allowing players repeated opportunities to earn rewards. This encourages players to regularly log in to do them every day. If something resets every week, it is called "weeklies."

Debuff: A temporary or permanent negative effect applied to a character or enemy that weakens their stats or abilities.

Direct Message (DM): This is a private communication channel between players, anything that is considered a one-on-one conversation is a DM. This includes things like in-game private chats, whispers, or when you message a single person.

DPS: An acronym for "Damage Per Second," which in gaming means, someone whose role in a party is focused on dealing damage to their enemy.

Glossary

Dungeon: A party-based instance where players face challenges, enemies, and bosses, often for rewards like gear and experience.

Equipment: This refers to the items a character wears to enhance their abilities, stats, and performance. This includes weapons, armor, accessories, and tools and is important to a player's gameplay.

Experience Points: A numerical measure of a character's progress toward leveling up, earned through completing quests, defeating enemies, or other in-game activities.

Farming: The intentional and repetitive collection of specific resources, items, or materials. It is used interchangeably with "grinding" except typically for loot.

Gear: This is a more casual way to refer to a player's worn equipment.

Grinding: Repetitive actions like killing enemies, doing quests, or crafting to gain experience, resources, or items.

Health Points: The numerical representation of a character's life. When health points reach zero, the character dies and needs to respawn.

Inventory: A character's personal storage space for holding items such as gear, weapons, crafting materials, quest items, potions,

etc. There is often a limited amount of inventory slots, and excess needs to be stored in a storage box.

Loot: Items, gear, or currency that is dropped by enemies or obtained from completing quests, challenges, or dungeons.

Level: A level in *Nine Heroes* represents a measure of the character's progression, strength, and overall experience points in the game. Levels are gained by earning experience points.

Leveling: The process of advancing a character's level by reaching the required experience points through activities like completing quests, defeating enemies, or participating in events. Leveling a character increases a character's stats, unlocks new abilities, and can unlock new maps or zones.

Main: Short for "Main Account," which is the primary character that a player focuses on, and usually plays on a game.

Mana Points: A resource used to cast spells or activate abilities. Mana is consumed when using abilities and can regenerate over time, or with the help of items or skills.

Marketplace: An official buying and selling platform in *Nine Heroes* that allows players to spend real-life money for in-game items.

Merchant Union: In *Nine Heroes*, this is where players sell their in-game items to other players for in-game currency.

 Glossary

Mob: A mob, short for mobile or mobile object, is a computer-controlled non-player character (NPC), or an enemy that players fight.

Mounts: Rideable creatures or vehicles that allow players to move faster (compared to walking) across the game zones. They are often used for aesthetic purposes.

NPC: An acronym for "Non-playable character." These are characters programmed by the game developers to have specific roles, actions, and dialogue. A player can normally interact with them, they can be quest givers, merchants, etc.

Party: A small group of players who team up to complete objectives, often sharing experience points and loot. In *Nine Heroes*, a party is typically considered 2-5 people.

Potions: Consumable items that provide temporary benefits or restore health points or mana points. Once it is used, the resource is gone.

Pickup Group (PUG): A group of players assembled randomly, where people normally don't know each other. It typically occurs through an in-game matching system or by opening up a party recruitment.

PvP: Player vs. Player gameplay where players compete directly against each other in combat or objectives. In *Nine Heroes* this is called "Player-Killing (PKing)."

Rarity: Equipment in *Nine Heroes* is categorized into tiers, often denoted by color codes or labels. These include Common (White), Uncommon (Green), Rare (Blue), Epic (Purple), and Legendary (Orange). There are also low-tier and high-tier consumable items, like potions.

Respawn: A a character, enemy, or resource reappears in the game after being defeated, used, or gathered.

Sect: A sect in *Nine Heroes* is a specific character archetype or role that determines the abilities, skills, and playstyle of a player's character (similar to that of a typical gaming character class). Players choose a sect as part of their character identity.

Skills: Special abilities or actions that a character can perform, often tied to their sect or role. These are used in combat, crafting, or other gameplay, and can be unlocked as the character levels up.

Stats: Short for statistics, stats are numerical values that represent a character's performance and capabilities in specific areas such as attack power, defense, speed, healing effectiveness, critical hit chance, health points, mana points, etc.

Storage Box: A game feature that allows players to store excess items, gear, or resources they do not want to carry in their character's inventory. It is an extended storage space, often found in specific locations, and must be accessed at that location to store or withdraw items to and from the inventory.

Support: It is a role that is focused on supporting the party rather than dealing damage to an enemy as their main purpose, for example, by buffing the party or debuffing the enemy, healing their party, or CCing their enemy. Of course, they can also deal damage.

Teleporting: This is an ability to instantly transport a character or party from one location to another within the game. It's faster than walking, riding, or other forms of travel.

Wilderness/Town/Arena Map: This represents the game's specific zones that a player can traverse. For example, The Riverside of Bianliang is a wilderness map, it's an open-world area zone where players can go to kill monsters. Another example is the Main City, as a Town Map, which is a safe zone where players rest.

Wipe: When an entire party is defeated in combat during a dungeon. This typically resets the dungeon and the party can try again from the beginning, or a save point.